Sweet Madness

A VEILED SEDUCTION NOVEL

HEATHER SNOW

D0191675

A SIGNET ECLIPSE BOOK

SIGNET ECLIPSE
Published by the Penguin Group
Penguin Group (USA) Inc., 375 Hudson Street,
New York, New York 10014, USA

USA | Canada | UK | Ireland | Australia
New Zealand | India | South Africa | China

Penguin Books Ltd., Registered Offices: 80 Strand, London WC2R 0RL, England
For more information about the Penguin Group visit penguin.com.

First published by Signet Eclipse, an imprint of New American Library,
a division of Penguin Group (USA) Inc.

First Printing, April 2013

SIGNET ECLIPSE and logo are trademarks of Penguin Group (USA) Inc.

ISBN 978-0-451-23967-9

Printed in the United States of America
10   9   8   7   6   5   4   3   2   1

ALWAYS LEARNING   **PEARSON**

"*Sweet Enemy* combines romance, history, and intrigue into one excellent read. Readers won't be able to put it down. A fast-paced plot and captivating characters make [this] a must read for all historical romance fans."
—Romance Reviews Today

"Liliana was a wonderful heroine and was so vastly different than the other historic heroines that I have read before. . . . This was a fantastic book and I still can't stop thinking about it. . . . Heather Snow is definitely an author to watch." —Night Owl Reviews

"*Sweet Enemy* has it all—inventive plot, two wonderful characters, and a suspense thread that serves a real purpose and is integral to the story. Combined with solid writing and a romance that soars, this is one of the best books of the year so far." —The Romance Reader

"Amusing, delightful, and charming. . . . The characters are well developed and the writing is highly engaging. I was vested in the characters and their goals from the start." —Manic Readers

"A breath of fresh air with its clever and distinctive heroine." —Fallen Angel Reviews

"Sure to gain Ms. Snow many, many fans."
—Romance Junkies

"An entertaining historical starring a wonderful independent female amateur sleuth and the target of her suspicions." —Genre Go Round Reviews

"Heather Snow has done a phenomenal job of writing characters a reader can connect with. *Sweet Enemy* is a must read for any historical romance fan!"
—Fresh Fiction

This book is dedicated to My Boys and My Girls. . . .

To Jason and our *amazing* sons: I couldn't have done any of this without your unflagging support and sacrifice. Thank you for encouraging me to chase my dreams. I love each of you so very, very much.

To Karen, Keri, and Leigh, my fearless critique partners and, more important, my dearest friends: Thank you for pushing me to believe in myself and helping me to tell the story that needed to be told. You know I couldn't have done it without you. Now the world (or at least the part of it that reads my books!) knows it, too.

Acknowledgments

Writing is certainly not a solitary journey, and I had some wonderful people along with me during the creation of this book:

Special thanks to Christie Novak and Tatiana Henley, who were subjected to the roughest draft I've ever written, but who loved it anyway and helped me to see that there was a good book in there!

Thanks to the ladies of #gasleak12: Erin Knightley, Erica O'Rourke, Eliza Evans, and Hanna Martine, for your amazing, super story mojo (and for having the good sense to leave that condo before we blew up!).

Thanks to my parents, Tom and Sarah Fry, for all that you do.

Thanks to Gabrielle Wingert, for helping keep my little darlings entertained while I was writing.

Thanks to Georgina Green and Carolyn Deane Reece, who gave me not only encouragement along the way, but also the occasional (and completely loving) kick in the pants when I needed it.

Thank you to my editor, Danielle Perez, who once again showed amazing faith in me—a sentiment that is priceless.

And finally, thank you to all of the readers who reached out to tell me how much they were anticipating Penelope and Gabriel's story—it is with you in mind that I write each and every word.

Prologue

Yellow suited her. Gabriel Devereaux's gaze followed the young woman's lithe form as she floated around the dance floor in her partner's arms. Her flowing skirts of lemon, shot with some sort of white embroidered flowers he couldn't name, barely brushed the ground as she twirled in the moves of the waltz.

He'd never liked blondes who wore yellow. They faded into their ensemble, like a monochrome painting that failed to draw the eye. Not so Lady Penelope. No, she seemed to glow, brightening everything and everyone around her like a ray of early-summer sunshine. Having known her but a few days, Gabriel had a feeling Lady Penelope was the type who refused to fade into anything.

He was glad of it, for her sake. Michael had a tendency to overshadow most ordinary people.

"Lusting after our cousin's new bride, are you?"

Gabriel's jaw clenched with indignation as his gaze snapped to the man who'd sidled up to him. He bit his tongue against a stinging retort, however. The most scathingly witty rejoinder would be lost on Edward, anyway, even were his brother sober enough to comprehend it.

"Don't be ridiculous," Gabriel drawled lazily. Of course he wasn't lusting after Lady Penelope, even if his skin tingled with inconvenient awareness as the happy couple twirled by. He fought the strange need to follow them with his eyes and instead turned toward his youngest sibling.

Edward's bulbous nose shone bright with the redness of drink. Gabriel frowned. When had the man become such a sot? The night was much too young to be so far gone. But even foxed as Edward was, his eyes glinted with a knowing look.

Hell. Edward might have become a drunkard in the years Gabriel had been away, but his brother also knew him better than perhaps anyone. Edward must have seen something in his expression to speak as he had, and Gabriel feared he knew what it was.

Jealousy.

His gaze strayed back to the dancers as he lost the battle not to look. This time, however, he forced himself to focus on his cousin Michael, 3rd Baron Manton, whose teeth were bared in a beatific smile. And why wouldn't he be in raptures? Michael, it seemed, had found love.

And *that* was what Gabriel envied. Not the lady in specific, but the *idea* of her. Could finding the right wife bring back *his* smile?

Not that I deserve that.

Gabriel forced his gaze away.

"Well, it's too late now"—Edward sniffed, taking a healthy swig of what must have been some rather potent punch—"for both of us."

Gabriel glanced sharply at Edward, drawn by the hollow anger in the man's voice. Surely he wasn't saying . . . But Edward wasn't looking anywhere near the dance floor or the newlyweds. Instead he stared toward the west corner of the ballroom.

Gabriel followed his line of sight, wincing as he recognized his brother's wife, Amelia, flirting shamelessly with a well-known rake.

Edward tossed back the remains of his punch with a low growl, then wiped his mouth against the inside of his cuff. "Excuse me, brother," he said curtly before stalking off.

Hell and hell again. Gabriel made to follow. He was head of the family now, much as he didn't relish the role. It was his duty to head off any potential scene that might spoil his cousin's wedding ball.

Gabriel slowed as Edward made an abrupt turn, in the opposite direction from his wife, and pushed out of a set of French doors into the night instead.

He watched his brother's departure with frustrated sadness. How things had changed, for all of them.

"Lord Bromwich?"

Gabriel jerked as a gloved hand slid over his forearm and gripped him lightly. He fisted his own hands before he even realized what he was doing.

"Oh—I—" A nervous laugh bubbled from Lady Penelope's lips, making her seem younger than her twenty years. Her pale green eyes widened at whatever she saw upon his face, and her hand fell away from his arm.

Wariness swept over her expression, darkening her eyes much as a quick-moving storm cloud shaded spring grass into a deeper hue.

And that made him feel much older than his own seven and twenty.

He forced a smile, even as he forced muscles tensed to strike into relaxation. "Lady Penelope, forgive me. I—" What could he say? *I'm sorry that I nearly just planted you a facer?* Since the wars, he didn't do well with the unexpected. "I was deep in thought and . . . didn't hear your approach."

"Of course," she murmured, but she didn't show offense. No, rather she looked at him in a thoughtful way that nearly made him squirm. "And I startled you," she continued, nodding slowly, as if in understanding. "How insensitive of me. Forgive *me*, my lord. I shall endeavor not to take you by surprise again."

Gabriel felt his brow knitting over the bridge of his nose. He didn't know Lady Penelope well. Was she mocking him? Or was she simply being polite? Because she couldn't possibly understand how the long years spent fighting on the battlefields of Europe had changed him, could she? He'd never spoken of it.

"Now, however," she said brightly, and to Gabriel's

surprise, she placed her hand on his arm once again. Her bow-shaped lips spread in a smile that seemed to burst through any cloud that still lingered over them. "I do believe you are meant to stand up with me for this dance."

Gabriel blinked rapidly at her sudden change in countenance. He couldn't help but draw in a sharp, deep breath, quite dazzled by it. How could a simple smile dispel the remaining tension in his limbs? But it had, and more than that, it filled his chest with something . . . warm. Something pleasant. Something he was afraid to name.

He was saved from trying as Lady Penelope tugged at him. "The dancers are already lined up." Her blond head, with ringlets adorned by yellow violas, tipped toward the top of the room as she looked up at him expectantly.

Of course. As head of his family, he was to partner his cousin's bride as she led the next dance. *That* was why she'd approached him. Gabriel shook off the strange sense of connection he'd felt with her and hastened his step to follow.

Unease curdled in his stomach as they reached the head of the line. Since the wars, he didn't do well in ballrooms, either. In fact, he hadn't even attempted to approach one since he'd returned from the Continent. It was all too . . . close. Too many people jostling about for space. Too much noise. His chest tightened painfully.

But he hadn't been able to refuse his place at a family wedding. As they took their place perpendicular to the split line of dancers, Lady Penelope slipped her hand in his and raised their joined arms. A fine sheen of sweat chilled the back of his neck.

Time to gird your loins, old man. All he had to do was make it through this one dance, and then he could retire for the evening.

He waited for the dizziness, prepared to fight off the vertigo that usually assailed him when he stepped onto a dance floor. But strangely, it stayed away.

The strains of violins filled the air first, joined almost immediately by the notes of a pianoforte in a lively tune he didn't recognize. Gabriel did his best not to grimace, waiting to see what dance his partner would choose. He hadn't danced in years and knew nothing of the current steps. He hoped she picked something simple that he could easily emulate without making an arse of himself.

A flute piped up in merry accompaniment, signaling the start of the dancing.

Lady Penelope squeezed his hand. "Never fear, my lord," she whispered. " 'Twill be over in a trice."

Before Gabriel could reply, she flashed her smile at him once more and bent her torso away from him. Then she turned in a vaguely familiar step. When she grasped both of his hands and pulled him into the move, his body went easily, willingly, as if his muscles remembered the dance from long ago.

Only a few steps in and he realized that was because they did. Lady Penelope had chosen a simple country dance, popular in years past, and one that blessedly he knew. Relief washed over him, his cold sweat breaking into a warm one as she pulled him into the energetic skips and turns that left him unable to think of anything but the dance.

Like a battalion of soldiers following their commander, the next set of dancers fell in behind them as they made their way down the line in the progressive dance, one pair after another, until all were stepping lively.

All in all, the dance took nearly half an hour to complete. Gabriel would wager he smiled more in that thirty-minute span than he had in the previous month. But even more unusual—he hadn't experienced the crushing fear he'd come to associate with ballrooms ever since that night on the Peninsula. Instead, blood coursed through his veins, exhilarating in a way he'd forgotten he could feel.

He glanced over at Lady Penelope as they stood across from each other, their part of the dance now finished. She grinned and clapped in time with the music, watching the other dancers finish their sets. But Gabriel couldn't take his eyes from her.

Was it the dancing that made him feel so alive? Or the dancing partner?

Lady Penelope's face was flushed from exertion, her green eyes bright with merriment. Tiny ringlets of her blond hair had dampened with perspiration and now clung to her temples and nape. She was the quintessential picture of an English rose—all slight and pale and graceful, with delicate ankles and wrists, a patrician nose and dewy skin. Everything a young Englishwoman should be.

Everything he'd fought to preserve.

Why shouldn't I seek my happiness? he thought. There was more than one Lady Penelope in the world. Perhaps it was time he ventured out from his self-imposed exile and found a wife of his own.

He'd need a lady a bit older than Michael's bride, of course—and one more worldly. He'd make a terrible husband for an innocent young debutante. He'd seen more death and destruction in his years than anyone should be burdened with, and it had changed him. He'd also need to look for a woman who was not quite so . . . sunny. All that brightness might be a shock to his system, accustomed to living in darkness as he was. But the point remained.

A spot of applause broke out as the last of the dancers came to a breathless stop. Gabriel broke his gaze away from his cousin's wife and joined in.

Michael bounded over from his place in the line as the clapping died down. "Gad. Haven't danced that one in an age."

Damn, but Michael seemed like such a young pup. It was hard to remember he was only two years Gabriel's junior. Gabriel had often envied the seemingly inexhaustible energy Michael exuded. His cousin never tired. With his typical exuberance, he threw an arm around his bride and brushed a kiss on her temple. "Were you feeling nostalgic, dearling?"

Lady Penelope returned her husband's squeeze with a fond smile. "Indeed I was," she answered lightly, but her eyes met Gabriel's.

And in that moment, Gabriel knew she'd chosen the

dance specifically with him in mind. She'd sensed his distress, even though he'd fought to suppress it. She'd also interpreted at least part of it for what it was and picked a dance he was likely to know. He marveled at her intuitiveness. And at her consideration.

Just as he realized that she hadn't been mocking him before. Somehow, she *had* understood. How, he couldn't fathom. Perhaps someone else she knew suffered as he did. Her cousin had recently married the Earl of Stratford, a man who'd been grievously injured in the same battle Gabriel had been. Maybe Stratford experienced the same gnawing restlessness, the overvigilance, the insomnia . . . the nightmares. Reliving battles won and lost, night after night after night . . .

"Well, no more of that, my love," Michael declared. "From this moment on, we only look forward." He swiped a glass of champagne from the tray of a passing footman. The servant stopped, and thirsty dancers swarmed him for the rest of the libations as the poor man's eyes widened comically.

Michael snagged a flute for his bride and another for Gabriel before raising his own in an impromptu toast. "To our future!" He touched his glass to Penelope's, the crystal kiss ringing with a high-pitched *ting*.

"To your future," Gabriel agreed. His gaze strayed once again to Lady Penelope. "I wish you every happiness."

Michael gave him a hearty slap on the shoulder that tipped champagne over the rim of Gabe's glass, splashing his hand and wrist with the frigidly sticky stuff. His cousin followed that up with a half squeeze that constituted affection amongst the males of the species, sloshing yet more liquor onto Gabriel's shoes.

Lady Penelope simply murmured, "Thank you, Lord Bromwich."

"Gabriel," he insisted, kicking droplets of champagne from his feet. At the dip of her brow, he explained, "We're family now."

"Then thank you, Gabriel."

"Yes, thank you, Gabriel," Michael parroted before plucking the still full champagne flute from Lady Penelope's fingers. "Now come, wife," he said with an exaggerated waggle of his blond brows, as if he relished the word. Then his voice dropped to a low tone, infused with an intimacy that made Gabriel turn his head. "Let us away."

"Let's do," Lady Penelope answered eagerly, and the happy couple hurried off together.

As he watched them depart, Gabriel was finally able to name that elusive feeling that had filled his chest when Lady Penelope had first smiled at him.

Hope.

Hope for *his* future.

Gabriel swallowed what little champagne remained in his glass, raising it in his own toast. "May it be as blissful as theirs."

Chapter One

The West Midlands, February 1820
Two and one half years later, shortly after the death
of Mad King George III

Lady Penelope Bridgeman, Baroness Manton, alighted from the carriage, her sturdy black kid boots crunching gravel beneath them as she stepped onto the drive of Vickering Place.

At first glance, the seventeenth-century mansion looked like any other palatial spread. No fewer than a dozen chimney blocks jutted from the slate roof, each spouting puffs of smoke that spoke of toasty fires within, keeping the residents of the brown brick home warm in defiance of the chilly February winter.

Ivy strangled the west wing of the structure, as well as the walls leading up to the entrance of the main house. The vines were brownish green and barren now, but Penelope imagined they would be beautiful to behold come springtime. So would the large ornamental fountain that fronted the house when it was once again filled with water, as well as the acres upon acres of parkland that surrounded it when they were greened up and in bloom.

However, Penelope fervently hoped she would have no occasion to visit Vickering Place in the spring. Indeed, she wished she weren't here now.

The carved oak door was opened for her before she even gained the top step of the stoop.

"Lady Manton." A thin man, clad in a serviceable black suit, greeted her by her name, though they had never met. She supposed she shouldn't be surprised. Visitors were likely regulated here and expected well in advance.

"Mr. Allen, I presume?" she inquired, pulling her dark wool cloak tighter around her as a frigid wind nipped across her nape. She stamped her feet in an effort to warm them, her eyes shifting involuntarily over the man's shoulder to the roaring fire she could see blazing from a hearth within.

"I am he," Mr. Allen confirmed stiffly, but he did not step aside to allow her inside. Penelope rubbed her gloved hands together and looked pointedly at him. Finally, the man relented. "Please do come in," he said, but his tone was clear. He did not want her here.

She slid sideways past him before he could change his mind, grateful for the blast of warmth as she crossed the threshold into a well-lit foyer. Her eyes were immediately drawn to the painted ceiling that arced high above, depicting fluffy clouds in a blue summer sky that faded into the throes of a brilliant sunset around the edges.

She hadn't expected such a cheerful scene.

A woman's desolate wail sliced through the hall, raising the hair on Penelope's arms, even covered as they were with layers of wool and bombazine. The high-pitched cry was cut off abruptly, leaving only an eerie echo ricocheting off of the marble walls of the foyer.

Penelope shivered. *That* was more in line with her expectation of Vickering Place. The illusion that the manor was still a country mansion fell completely away. Certainly the flocked wallpaper of gold damask and the plaster molding and expensive artwork that lined the walls spoke of its aristocratic history, but Vickering Place had been sold by its owner and converted to a private sanatorium for lunatics. A place where the wealthy sent their sons and daughters, their mothers and fathers, their wives and their husbands— for treatment, or simply to hide them away from society.

As Michael's family had done to poor Gabriel.

Mr. Allen, she noted, seemed unruffled by the noise, almost as if he hadn't even noticed. One grew used to it, she supposed. Allen extended an arm to usher her into what appeared to be his office, and as Penelope took a seat in a plush armchair across from his stark, imposing desk, she strove for a similar sangfroid even as her stomach churned with nerves.

"I'm afraid your journey may have been in vain, my lady," Mr. Allen began, lowering himself stiffly into his own seat. "It seems his lordship has descended into a fit of mania this morning. When he gets like this, he can be very . . . dangerous. I cannot, in good conscience, allow you near him. For your safety's sake."

Penelope winged a brow high at the subtle condescension in the director's nasally tone. She pursed her lips.

Mr. Allen, apparently misinterpreting the reason for her irritation, said defensively, "I *did* send a messenger to the inn where you are staying, but he must have just missed you. I am sorry you had to come all this way."

Penelope barely resisted the urge to snort. The only thing *he* was sorry about was that she'd come at all.

She waved a dismissive hand. "Your man delivered the message in plenty of time. However—" However, what? She'd been a fool not to anticipate this sort of resistance. She'd gotten spoiled, working with her cousin Liliana, the Countess of Stratford, over the past year and a half, treating ex-soldiers and their families. No one ever questioned Liliana because she was a woman. Her cousin had a brilliant mind that commanded the respect of her peers, male and female.

Penelope, however, had neither Liliana's intelligence nor presence. She chewed her lip, trying to imagine how her cousin would handle Mr. Allen. She took a deep breath and stiffened her spine. Well, she didn't know exactly what Liliana would do, but she knew how her own formidable mother would handle the man if this were a domestic situation.

She adopted her best "lady of the house" tone, all clipped and commanding. "*However*, it is my understanding that Vickering Place is a *private* sanatorium. Your guests are here voluntarily, at the behest of their families, are they not?" She raised both brows now, staring Mr. Allen down. "At their very *expensive* behest."

At his stiff nod, Penelope could almost taste her victory. She reached into her cloak, efficiently pulling out a packet of letters from Gabriel's family, detailing their wishes. Her hand trembled a bit as she leaned forward and handed them across the desk. "Then I expect to see his lordship immediately. In whatever condition he may be in."

It was Mr. Allen's turn to purse his lips, which thinned to the point of almost disappearing as he skimmed the letters. Disapproval lined his features, but all he said was, "Very well."

Penelope gave the director a curt nod and rose to her feet. She exited the office on her own, not waiting to see if he followed. He did, of course, and quite quickly. He seemed the type who would detest having her roaming around his domain on her own.

"This way, my lady." Mr. Allen rattled a heavy set of keys, plucking the head of one between his fingers as the others settled with a jangling clank on the ring.

As they made their way down a wide hallway, another howl rent the air. A man's this time, Penelope thought. The cry was accompanied by a harsh, rhythmic clanking, as if the poor soul banged something against metal . . . bars perhaps?

An ache pierced her chest. She couldn't imagine

Gabriel in a place such as this. The moment she'd met him, she'd sensed he was cut from similar cloth as Liliana's husband, Geoffrey. Both ex-soldiers, both honorable and courageous. Gabriel had a commanding air, an independent and self-reliant streak that must chafe against confinement. It had to be driving him mad to be locked up so.

No, madness is what brought him here.

Penelope shivered. She'd have never believed such a thing about Gabriel two and a half years ago, but he *was* blood related to Michael, and if Penelope knew anything, she knew now that Michael had been mad.

The affliction had driven her husband to take his own life barely six months after they'd been married.

Penelope's steps faltered. Oh Lord. What made her think she could be of any help to Gabriel Devereaux? She'd been worthless to Michael when he'd needed her. Worthless.

Mr. Allen halted, as if noticing his footfalls were now the only ones ringing on the marble floors. He turned to look over his shoulder. "Have you changed your mind, then, Lady Manton?"

Yes.

Penelope's chest tightened, her breaths coming with great difficulty as the horror of another frosty winter day invaded her mind.

He's not breathing! Michael!

Penelope shook her head, as much to dislodge the memories as to reply to the director. "No. No, of course not." Yet her voice was much more assured than her feet. She had to force them to get moving again.

Mr. Allen fixed her with a doubtful look before turning back to lead the way once more.

She was not that naïve young society wife anymore, Penelope reminded herself. For the past two years, with Liliana's encouragement, she'd thrown herself into studying the inner workings and maladies of the mind. At first, it had been a way to distract herself from her grief, but then she'd realized she had a gift.

People of all classes had often told her she was easy to talk to, so when Liliana had suggested she spend time just talking to the ex-soldiers served by the private clinic that she and her husband, Geoffrey, had built, it had been easy to say yes. And that one yes had turned into a calling, one that had met with some success.

Which was why Lady Bromwich, Gabriel's mother, had visited Penelope in London and begged her to visit him. Well, that, and the marchioness knew she would keep news of Gabriel's condition private. She'd been married into their family, after all, and they counted on that loyalty for her silence.

Mr. Allen stopped before a massive wooden door, its brass knob polished to a high shine. He pulled the door open easily, revealing the heavy iron bars that had been installed to barricade the entrance of the suite of rooms that had recently become Gabriel's home.

The director slid the key into the lock, twisting it with an efficient click. The bars swung open noiselessly, too new yet to creak with rust.

Penelope schooled her features, trying to prepare herself for anything. She smoothed a nervous hand over her widow's weeds, her mood now as somber and dark as the colors she always wore.

What kind of Gabriel would she encounter beyond that threshold? If his affliction was similar to Michael's, he could be flying high, gregarious and grandiose, awake for days with no end in sight. Or he could be a man in the depths of despair, wallowing in a dark place where no one could reach him, least of all her.

Was she ready to be faced with the stuff of her nightmares?

Penelope swallowed hard. Yes. Because Gabriel was still alive, still able to be saved. Whatever she must do, she would do it, if only as penance for what she *hadn't* been able to do for Michael.

Penelope stepped into the room, at least as far as she could before shock stilled her feet. "Oh . . . my . . . God," she whispered, amazed she could push even those three short words through the sudden tightness of her throat. "Gabriel?"

For a brief second, Penelope wondered if *she* were the mad one. Because what she was seeing couldn't possibly be real.

Gabriel—a very *naked* Gabriel, she couldn't help but note with widening eyes—was cornered in the far side of the room, nearly trapped by two attendants who steadily approached him. With a strength and quickness that didn't seem human, Gabriel lashed out to his left and snagged the corner of a heavily carved rococo chaise longue with one hand, pulling it toward him as if it weighed nothing. A high-pitched screech grated as the wooden legs dragged in screaming protest across the floor. He angled it on the diagonal in front of him, effectively creating a barricade from the grasping attendants.

"Curse you, you devils," Gabriel rasped in a scratchy voice that pricked at Penelope's heart.

The stark fear in his eyes turned that prick into a full-fledged pierce. Poor Gabriel was looking at the men as if he truly saw them as the demons he called them.

"I am burning alive already. Does that not satisfy your thirst for revenge?" he cried, muscles and tendons straining against the skin of his neck.

Penelope could only watch in horror as Gabriel snatched a pitcher of water from a nearby sideboard and tipped it back. He gulped noisily, not seeming to notice that most of the water missed his mouth, running down his unclothed skin in dripping rivulets that pooled on the floor at his bared feet. Penelope's gaze followed the trail of liquid as it traversed lean muscle, over his chest, where tiny droplets clung to the dark hair there, down his stomach to . . .

Dear God, he truly was completely nude—

A blur of black linen blocked Penelope's view as Mr. Allen stepped in front of her. "My lady, I must insist you leave this instant—"

An explosion of glass shattered against marble, jerking both of their attention back to the drama unfolding in the corner. Gabriel had smashed the empty pitcher against the floor, and shards of crystal skittered in all directions.

Well, she'd be hanged before she allowed Mr. Allen

to toss her out of the room. She took advantage of the distraction to dart farther into the parlor so that the director would have to choose between bodily removing her or helping his staff members to contain Gabriel.

Allen shot her a dark look over his shoulder but moved towards the fracas. She thought to offer her assistance, but there was little she could do with Gabriel when he was in the grips of full-blown mania.

"Ah, Christ," Gabriel groaned. "Am I to have no relief?" Water glistened on his skin as he glared accusingly at the men who were slowly skirting either side of his barricade, crystal grinding beneath their boots. "If *your* thirst cannot be quenched, then neither shall mine be? Is that the way of it?"

"My lord," Allen said soothingly, raising his hands as he advanced on the chaise longue from the center. "You know we never deny you sustenance."

"Trickery!" Gabriel accused. "Water that does nothing to wet the throat. Clothing that burns." He scratched at his arms, and Penelope winced at the white lines that appeared on otherwise swarthy skin. Was that why Gabriel had shed his clothes? Because they'd irritated his skin?

What madness *was* this? She'd never seen anything like it.

Penelope held her breath as the attendants and Mr. Allen closed in on her cousin-by-marriage, a man on either side with the director standing near the center of the chaise. Her heart sped, thumping against her throat as if she were the one trapped. She prayed they did not hurt Gabriel in their bid to subdue him.

One of the men lunged for him then, attempting to catch him about the waist. She gasped as Gabriel leapt vertically, pulling his knees high as his feet landed upon the chaise in a move most reminiscent of a large cat. The attendant missed, falling to the ground with a surprised grunt.

"My lord!" Mr. Allen shouted, then raised his hands in what Penelope assumed he meant as a soothing gesture. "My lord," the man said again, more calmly as Gabriel straightened. "Please, there is nowhere for you to go."

Penelope's gaze darted to the other attendant, who was creeping behind the chaise while Mr. Allen had Gabriel's attention.

"We mean you no harm," the director said, his voice a soft lull.

But she could see that Gabriel was beyond words. The skin on his face was pulled taut in a terrified grimace. He wasn't even looking at the director at all, she realized, but rather at the floor. He looked as if he longed to run for it, but was afraid to step down. His eyes darted to and fro, clearly seeing something that wasn't there. Something that frightened him terribly.

"No," he groaned. "No! Stop tormenting me so. There was nothing more I could have done!"

The intensity of his fear raised gooseflesh on Penelope's skin as tears pricked hot against the backs of her eyelids. What on earth did Gabriel think he saw?

Just then, the second attendant clipped his boot against the leg of the chaise, alerting Gabriel to his presence behind him. He tensed, crouching low on the chaise again. Mr. Allen chose that moment to make his move.

And so did Gabriel.

He flew. Leapt, really, but with an energy that seemed inhuman. With the added advantage of the chaise's height, he easily cleared the top of Mr. Allen's head, who had bent to try to capture him. But how did Gabriel think he was going to—

The tinkling of thousands of crystal teardrops rang in the air as Gabriel's outstretched hands found purchase in the lowest tier of the massive chandelier above them. His momentum turned the chandelier into a pendulum, swinging him away from his captors.

Penelope watched in awe as the fast-moving glass caught the weak winter sunlight from the mullioned windows and cast shards of colored light dancing upon the walls. Dozens of snuffed candles lost their mooring, raining down like wax-covered twigs in a particularly vicious windstorm. Light and shadow played against Gabriel's naked skin, muscles flexing as he held fast.

Lord, he'd be beautiful to paint.

Penelope blinked. Goodness, where had that inappropriate thought come from?

So shaken was she that she didn't even register that Gabriel was swinging right toward her until far too late. She threw up her hands to protect her face at the last moment, but nothing could protect her from the force of fourteen stone slamming her to the hard marble floor.

"Oh!" Pain exploded in more places than she could feel at once. Everything hurt. Her backside, mostly, which had taken the brunt of the impact. But her left shoulder had come down hard next, and the back of her head smarted terribly, as, curiously, did her chest.

She blinked to clear her vision, glancing down to find the top of Gabriel's head, his face buried directly in a rather delicate position. So *that* is what had caused that sharp jolt of agony. His forehead must have collided into her breastbone when he landed atop her. She winced. That was going to leave a bruise for certain.

As other sensations returned to her stunned system, she realized she lay quite pinned beneath Gabriel's larger frame. His naked, still dripping wet frame. Even the layers of her widow's weeds couldn't shield her from feeling him against her or from the moist heat that seeped through to her skin.

"Mmph," she groaned. She bent her elbows and planted her palms on either side of herself in an attempt to wriggle free.

Gabriel's head jerked up then. His eyes fixed on her, and Penelope couldn't contain a gasp. She'd never seen pupils so dilated. They reminded her of an eclipse—only one where the new moon passes between the earth and the sun, not quite blacking out the larger star entirely. Instead, the warm gold-flecked iris that remained made a fiery ring around the enlarged black pupil. The effect was startling. And unsettling.

They both went entirely still. Indeed, it seemed if the very world did. Even the scuffling of the other men in the room seemed to slow and fade away. Her heart beat wildly in her chest, as wild as the man lying atop her.

"Penelope?" he rasped, sending a jolt of sympathy

rushing through her. He blinked several times, either trying to focus or in disbelief that she was actually here. Probably both. For all that they'd been friends once, they hadn't seen each other since Michael's funeral.

"Yes. Yes, I—"

Gabriel tightened his arms around her in a sudden grip that forced any remaining breath from her lungs, as if she were the lone buoy in a turbulent sea.

He held her tight to him for a brief moment. But at the clumping of three pairs of boots rushing toward them, Gabriel released her and whipped his head around to glance behind him.

He jerked his gaze back to her. "Penelope," he said again, his voice urgent and harsh. "Help me."

"I will," she vowed, just as urgently, even though she had no idea if she even could. What she'd just witnessed was much worse than she'd been led to expect.

Gabriel tensed, shifting his weight so he could scramble away from his pursuers. She tensed, too. If he kept running, kept fighting, she wouldn't be able to help him. No one could in his current state.

"I will," Penelope whispered once more, knowing there was only one thing she could do.

She wrapped her arms and legs around him, locking them as best she could around his larger, thrashing form, and held on for dear life. She had to keep him here long enough for Mr. Allen and his men to reach them.

When Gabriel realized her intent, he let out a howl of angry betrayal that sent a shiver coursing through her. Belatedly, Penelope wondered at her foolishness. Gabriel could snap her in two if he so wished. The man she'd known would never have done such a thing, but he was *clearly* not in his rational mind. Even Michael, who had loved her, had hurt her in his mania. She cringed, but tightened her grip on Gabriel all the same.

Penelope panted with effort. *Dear God.* She wasn't certain she could hold on to him much longer. The muscles of her arms and thighs trembled with strain and ached like the very dickens.

"Shhh," she crooned. She tried to turn her death grip into more of an embrace, meant to soothe. " 'Twill be all right, I promise," she whispered, even though her voice trembled with what very well might be a lie.

Gabriel struggled for a few more seconds but then relaxed with a groan of defeat.

Had her vow to help him been a lie, too? After what she'd just witnessed, she was very much afraid Gabriel was beyond help.

As he was pulled from her arms, Penelope prayed she was wrong about that.

Chapter Two

A harsh groan pulled Gabriel from a dreamless sleep. Odd. He very rarely *didn't* dream . . . not unless—

The groan came again, close this time. Too close. Had that pitiful sound come from him? Gabriel fought to open his eyes, but the struggle hardly seemed worth the effort. It was as if his lids were sealed together with wax.

A light touch brushed his forehead. Just a cool arc of sensation, like delicate fingertips caressing his skin. The phantom stroke brought a whiff of mandarin and vanilla, but it faded quickly. He'd probably imagined it, as he did so many things these days.

Still, he tried to reach out and capture the—

He couldn't move his arms! Alarm clenched his gut as Gabriel strained harder, panic clawing its way up his throat and forcing his eyes to unstick.

"Ah!" He sucked in a pained breath and slammed them shut again as blinding light seared them.

"Dim the lamps," he heard a woman's voice command. "I believe his eyes are sensitive to the light."

Gabriel desperately wished to see who was speaking, but he didn't risk the agony. He tried again to move to no avail. His heart hammered faster as he fought against whatever held him down.

God! Christ, not again!

Harsh, rapid breaths echoed loud in his ears. His own, he knew. He could feel the hot puffs of air against his upper lip.

Calm yourself, man.

Gabriel forced himself to think. She'd said "dim the lamps." There were no lamps on the battlefield to be dimmed. Nor did he smell the stench of blood and death or the horrid aftermath of decomposition. He was not in Belgium. *He was not.* That was . . . years ago. He was sure of it.

He flinched as a hand touched his face.

"Shhh, Gabriel. 'Tis all right."

Again, the scent of mandarins and vanilla teased his nose.

"Cease your struggles," the woman crooned in the darkness.

Gabriel relaxed, turning his face into a soft palm.

"That's right," she said. "Sleep."

He drifted in and out of consciousness, his stomach churning in rolling waves. He had no idea how long he floated in that turbulent sea, but his first thought as true awareness crept in was *Devil's balls.* He hurt everywhere. It was as if he'd been tossed violently onto a beach by an angry Poseidon and now lay naked and bruised in the surf. His skin felt stretched and dry, as though he were covered with a coat of rough sand that had been baked on by the sun.

He moved to stretch his knotted muscles, but his arms wouldn't budge. His eyes flew open and he squinted into near total darkness. But he could see enough. He'd been strapped into a bloody straight-waistcoat. Again.

Hell. He'd had another episode.

Gabriel grimaced, and even that hurt. He searched his mind, but gave up after a few moments. There was a great void where his memory should be, and his head felt swollen and thick. The last thing he remembered, he'd been . . . reading. Yes, reading crop reports Edward had sent up from the estate. Benign business matters. Nothing that should have sent him into such a state that he now found himself trussed up like a madman.

Like *a madman*? *Gabriel, you* are *a madman.*

A sharp ache twisted in his middle as everything in him screamed denial. But how could he continue to think otherwise? It was getting worse. How long would it be until the madness overtook him completely?

"You're awake."

Gabriel started as a woman's voice reached him in the darkness.

The heavy velvet drapes that hung around his bed parted, and a silhouette appeared in the void. Females were not allowed to attend to male guests at Vickering

Place. Yet here one stood. Her lithe shape was unmistakable. Not curvaceous but most assuredly feminine.

He must still be in the throes of the episode, then. People who'd witnessed his madness told him he often talked to people who weren't there while he was in the grips of his delusions.

"Your body seems to have cooled," the figment of his imagination murmured, nodding as if that made her happy. "Dare we risk a little more light?" she asked him.

He had no idea what he dared, but he nodded anyway. Something about this apparition made him feel safe, and truthfully, he wished to see what pretty face his mind had conjured up to soothe him, even if he wouldn't remember her later. He never did.

She reached up and tugged the drapery to one side. The fabric scraped roughly along the wooden canopy. Daylight slowly crept in, revealing the shape of a nose, the curve of a lip, the tilt of a chin—

Oh no. No, no, no, no, no. Every scintilla of good feeling flew from Gabriel in a rush.

Penelope? "Do you know where you are, Gabriel?" she asked him.

He must have looked as horrified as he felt, because she raised one hand out before her in a calming gesture. "'Tis all right if you don't," she assured him.

"Of course I know where I am," he snapped defensively, as mortification fast forced out his confusion, replacing it with shame.

Of all the people to see him thus.

And yet . . . what the hell would Penelope be doing

here? He'd not seen her in two years. In fact, she wouldn't even know he was in Vickering Place, would she? She couldn't be real.

He tried to blink away the remaining blurriness in his dry, burning eyes as he looked more closely at her. She was dressed entirely in black, as he'd seen her last at Michael's funeral. That made no sense. A woman was required to wear mourning clothes for only half a year after the death of her husband. Penelope should have long moved out of her blacks and into the happier colors of her youth. Wouldn't the *real* Penelope be wearing something sunnier by now?

That meant he'd invented her, didn't it?

Well, he'd just put her to the test. Ask her a question only he and she knew the answer to.

A grim snort of amusement escaped him. Idiot. If *he* knew the answer, so would a phantom Penelope, given she would have sprung from *his* mind. That would be no sort of proof.

There was nothing for it but to swallow what was left of his pride and ask the question.

"Are you real?" he croaked, feeling desperate. Pathetic. But maybe, if he conversed with her long enough, he would get his answer one way or another. If she weren't real, eventually she'd say something that made no sense.

Penelope's blond brows knit as her head tilted slightly left. "You . . . you cannot tell?"

He gave a slight shake of his head, but even that small movement threatened to send his world spinning again. He fixed his eyes on her to steady himself, looking for any clue that might tip the scales one way or the other. "Usually I can. But you must admit, your being here is *not* usual."

Her features pursed in an expression he'd not seen on her before. An interesting mix of perplexity and . . . guilt? "Your mother did not tell you she asked me to come, then?"

Gabriel's stomach clenched. Mother *had* mentioned she'd arranged for someone to see him. Someone who might help him kick this horrid affliction. He'd agreed to see this new doctor, of course. He'd do anything to regain control of himself.

But Penelope wasn't a doctor *and therefore wasn't real*. His mind had just mixed his fantasy with an actual conversation he'd had with his mother.

Gabriel released a pent-up breath as relief infused him, overwhelming him so much that he *almost* forgot he was restrained like an animal.

Phantom Penelope's lips quirked. "What has put that smile on your face?" she asked, her voice tinged with amused curiosity.

Gabriel smiled wider. He couldn't help it. "I just deduced that *you* are not really here." Belatedly, he feared that by voicing his realization, he might make her disappear. While he'd never wish the real Penelope to witness his disgrace, he was strangely comforted by the imagined one. He didn't wish her to go—not yet.

"Ah," she answered. Her brows dipped further, but she didn't try to convince him otherwise. "And this makes you happy?"

"Indeed." What could it hurt to speak the truth? She

was only in his head, after all. "I could not live with myself if you ever truly saw me like this. However, since we've established that this isn't real, let us talk of other things."

"Mmmm." She nodded slowly. "Such as?"

"Such as . . ." Gabriel felt one side of his mouth rise in a half smile of chagrin. What did one talk about with one's fantasy woman? He had no idea.

But he did know what he would say to the real Penelope—*if* he were a whole man again. Words that had burned in his soul for months, years even.

He was grateful that he'd never had the courage to voice them. It would have been a horrible mistake, unfair to both of them, especially given everything that had happened to him since Michael's death.

But he could say them to *this* Penelope. Maybe that would be enough to finally purge her and the damnable hope she'd wrought in him from his heart. Yes, maybe *that's* why his mind had called forth her image, so he could once and for all let the hope of her go. Because the bleaker his future became, the more that impossible hope hurt.

Gabriel took a deep breath, amazed at how hard his heart hammered in his chest even though none of this was truly happening. "Such as how I feel for you. How I've always felt for you."

"Gabriel—"

"I've wanted you for so very long."

Penelope's mouth hung open, much as he imagined it really might have done had he been fool enough to utter those words to her after Michael's death.

But saying the words aloud did seem to lighten his heart, so he pressed on. "There is something about you that *awakened* me, Penelope. From the moment we met, you made me yearn for things I had long put away. I never would have told you then, of course. You were my cousin's wife. But after Michael died, it was torture for me not to—"

"Please!" Her voice rose on the imperative even as her palm clamped down over his mouth.

Funny, he knew the mind to be a powerful thing— after all, his had tricked him considerably in the past months—but her "touch" jarred him more than he would have expected. The heat from her hand, the warm, sweet citrus smell of her skin, the pressure of it—it all felt so very real.

"Please," she repeated more softly. "Say nothing more you will regret."

A man's muffled voice came from somewhere behind her. "Mr. Carter informs me our patient is awake and speaking."

Allen?

Penelope's hand disappeared from his lips as the draperies were pulled wide.

Gabriel blinked against the brightening light. As his vision adjusted, he saw the director and one of his regular attendants standing there.

But Penelope was still there as well. Not as he remembered her, but as she *would* be, were he seeing her today—two years past when he had seen her last. Older. Sadder about the eyes and, yes, oddly still dressed in black. But still heartbreakingly beautiful.

"Yes, he is," she said, looking at Allen rather than at him. And worse, the director was looking at *her*.

Gabriel stopped breathing, the horrible reality quickly sinking in, even if he couldn't quite get his mind around it. If *Allen* was talking to Penelope—

"He also appears to be calm and lucid," she went on. "Surely you can remove his restraints now."

Oh Christ. She *was* real. What was she doing *here*?

"I'm surprised you are so willing to trust, Lady Manton," Mr. Allen replied, "given his lordship nearly crushed you to death only yesterday."

Gabriel's gaze flew to her. "What?" He struggled against the straight-waistcoat.

"You are upsetting Lord Bromwich," Penelope scolded in an authoritative tone he'd never heard her utter before. "You are also making too much of the incident."

"What the hell happened?" Gabriel demanded. Curse his memory! And curse these damned restraints!

Penelope placed her hand on his shoulder to still him. "It's nothing to worry about, Gabriel." But when she looked at him, he knew. Knew that whatever it was, she'd witnessed him at his worst. He could see the concerned pity hovering in pale green eyes that had once looked upon him with laughter. Even if he couldn't remember his actions, were they anything akin to things he'd been told he'd done during past episodes . . . Gabriel squeezed his eyes shut against the truth.

This was worse than a nightmare.

He opened them again as he sucked in a breath. And then he'd gone and told her how he—

"Now that Lord Bromwich has recovered, I insist he

be released from these bonds. I am sure a bath and a change of clothing would also be in order."

No, what would be in order would be for a great gaping hole to open beneath him and suck him down to the very depths.

Beside his bed, Allen and Penelope stared each other down like opposing generals trying to take the same territory. The director stood stiff and imposing. "You cannot expect to stay while we—"

"Of course not," Penelope answered. "I shall, however, remove myself *only* to Lord Bromwich's parlor. No farther."

Allen's lips pressed together in an unhappy line while Penelope's eyes narrowed with determined stubbornness as a silent battle waged between them. Dark smudges marred the pale skin beneath her eyes, however. Allen had said she'd been here since yesterday. She must have watched over him all night. Why would she do such a thing?

Well, he might not know why she was here, but he damned sure wasn't going to allow the director to treat her inhospitably while he figured it out.

"Have a supper tray brought up to Lady Manton in the parlor immediately," he commanded.

Both Allen and Penelope snapped their gazes to him. Penelope relaxed visibly and offered him a slight smile while Allen's lips thinned further.

"Thank you, Gabriel, but I shall wait to take my refreshment with you. We shall talk when you are ready to join me," she added gently before turning to depart the bedroom.

He watched her go. Shame, anger, confusion and despair roiled inside him. When he was ready? That would never be. How could he face Penelope now that she had seen what he had become?

Penelope paced the floor alongside the bay window in the parlor, watching the sun make its early-winter dive for the horizon. Servants bustled about stoking the fire and lighting lamps, wall sconces and the dozens of chandelier candles before nightfall closed in.

Others laid out a light evening repast, setting the table much as would be expected in a nobleman's country home—with linens, fine china, crystal and silver. It gave the whole moment a very surreal quality.

She cut her eyes once again to the closed doors of the bedchamber. It had been more than an hour since she'd left Gabriel in the care of Vickering Place's staff. She'd heard nothing from the room. No raised voices, no thumps. Nothing to indicate aught was amiss. But as the time dragged on, it was becoming more difficult to resist the urge to see what kept him.

She suspected pride might have something to do with why Gabriel hadn't presented himself. She winced as she recalled how his face had blanched white when he'd realized the truth of her presence and what he had revealed to her.

I've wanted you for so very long.

Penelope smoothed an open palm over her fluttering stomach. She couldn't even think about *that* shocking admission right now. She was sure it meant nothing.

Just words whispered in the dark to someone he thought wasn't there.

No, words whispered to you, *whether he thought you were real or not.* She frowned, unsettled.

Well, whatever it meant, it was likely adding to his embarrassment—an emotion that would do neither of them any good if she were to be of any use to him. And she was determined to be. Though she very much feared she might be in well over her head, from the moment he'd begged for her help last night, her heart was committed to the task. She could never desert him now.

She looked at the door once more. She'd give him five more minutes, and if he didn't show, she'd march right back into his bedchamber and—

The door cracked open, swinging outward with a barely audible creak.

Gabriel stepped across the threshold, looking very much the man about town. Penelope caught her breath. Not that she'd expected him to be in the altogether, as she'd last seen him in this room. But neither had she anticipated him looking quite so dashing, considering the circumstances.

I'd like to paint him like this as well.

She frowned, pushing the errant thought away.

His buff pants were topped with an ivory-and-wine-striped waistcoat covered by a burgundy jacket. The cut was quite handsome, as was the contrasting chocolate velvet trim that so complemented his dark brown hair. A snowy-white cravat completed the image, as if he were just a man popping by for a friendly call while going about his business.

Penelope experienced an odd sense of being transported back in time. How many times had Gabriel done just that during the early days of her and Michael's marriage? Too many to count. In fact, he'd come around so often Michael had once joked that if anything ever happened to him, she wouldn't have to look far for a replacement husband. She'd laughed then, thinking nothing of it. But now . . .

After Michael died, it was torture for me not to—

She forced Gabriel's words out of her mind.

"You look well, Gabriel." The compliment was automatic but sincere. It also reminded her of what a veritable fright she must look after these past many hours spent by his bedside. She tried to smooth her riotous curls. They bounced right back into disarray as she removed her hands. Her hair was hopeless even on the best of days, much less when she'd been up all night. "I hope you didn't go to all that trouble for me," she added self-consciously.

Only after she heard the words aloud did she realize how they might be taken. She felt her eyes widen even as a shutter came over his deep golden brown ones. "N-not that you would dress to please me—" Oh, dash it all. The last thing she wanted was for there to be any more awkwardness between them than the situation already merited. She and Gabriel had always been easy in each other's company, and there was no reason to let the last few hours change that. She shook her head and huffed a self-deprecating laugh. "What I mean to say is simply what I said. You look well, Gabriel."

Gabriel's stance relaxed, but only a little. He didn't

smile with her, however. "You look tired, Lady Manton."

She ignored both the insult and the "Lady Manton," easily recognizing his attempt to throw up protective barriers between them. His well-tailored appearance was likely more of the same.

"You also looked famished," he added with a frown. "Allen tells me that you refused to leave, not even to take meals."

She answered his charge with a smile, trying to lighten the mood. "I was afraid if I left your rooms, he would bar them against my return." She shrugged. "I'm afraid our Mr. Allen doesn't much like my being here."

"Yes, well, neither do I."

Penelope drew back at his unexpected rudeness, her smile fading. "I'm sorry?"

"I don't know what my mother was thinking, Penelope, but you shouldn't be around me." A muscle ticced in his jaw, the only indication that Gabriel was not as coldly calm as he seemed. "Allen informs me that I hurt you yesterday, quite badly."

Ah, that explained it. "Well, Mr. Allen needs to learn not to overexaggerate," she retorted, grateful that her clothing hid the ugly bruising from Gabriel's sight. "As well as not to interfere," she grumbled.

"Do you mean to say," he demanded, his voicing rising with his agitation, "that I did *not* swing from that chandelier like an uncivilized ape and hit you full force?" He pointed up at the fixture without looking at it, as if she could mistake which chandelier he meant.

"That I did *not* knock you to the ground and pin you beneath me?"

Gabriel stepped toward her and she reflexively took a step back. The movement caused her hip to twinge. She sucked a swift breath between her teeth.

His lips firmed and his eyes narrowed.

Dash it all again. Either she'd confirmed for him that she was in pain, or he thought she feared him. Likely both, and neither good. She took a deliberate step forward. "I would hardly call you an ape," she countered. "Nor uncivilized. Did Mr. Allen say those horrible things?" She gritted her teeth. "I am going to give that man a piece of my—"

"No, I did." Gabriel exhaled a deep breath and tunneled the fingers of one hand through his hair as he turned away from her. She could tell by his posture he was castigating himself.

She followed, placing her palm against his shoulder. He stiffened beneath her touch. That wouldn't do. She wouldn't be able to help him if he buried himself in guilt or self-flagellation. "Gabriel, despite what was happening inside your mind yesterday, you never tried to hurt *anyone*. Goodness knows you could have, but you were only trying to get away from whatever it was you saw."

He breathed shallowly and he tensed against her palm, as if he were containing some great emotion. But he didn't pull away from her. That was progress. She decided to push it a little further.

"What *did* you see?"

His hands fisted at his sides. "I . . . don't know."

"Do you mean you can't describe it? Perhaps if you tell me what you can—"

"No." He did shake her hand off then and stalked a few feet away. "I mean, I can't remember it. Not *any* of it. Not what happened. Not you. The only reason I know what I do is because Allen filled in the details."

"But that makes no sense," she murmured, more to herself than to him. She'd known yesterday while observing Gabriel that his symptoms were unlike any she'd seen before. However, in every case of lunacy she'd studied, either in person or in books, the person had *some* recollection of the episodes. They might be confused memories, disjointed ones or flashes out of sequence, but to have no memory at all?

What exactly was she dealing with? Helping Gabriel was proving to be much more challenging than even she'd prepared herself for. And yet the idea of walking away curdled in her stomach.

"Nothing in my life makes sense anymore," he said bleakly, finally turning around. He walked purposefully back toward her, stopping when they were nearly toe-to-toe. The torment in his eyes solidified her conviction to stay with him and see this through.

"Especially not your being here," he said. "While I thank you for your charity, I wish you to leave."

Penelope blinked up at him, unable to believe what he'd said. "What?"

"I wish you to leave," he repeated firmly. "Go home, Lady Manton."

Chapter Three

"Go home?" Penelope repeated. She crossed her arms over her chest, and her brows dipped into a belligerent vee. "I'll do no such thing. How can you think I would consider leaving?"

Her resistance confused him. Why did she care? They had not seen each other in two years. And if he were honest, he mustn't have meant that much to her in the first place, else why would she have stopped allowing him to call after Michael's funeral? He'd been turned away from her town house more times than he cared to remember with no more explanation than her butler's pat "Lady Manton is not at home to visitors, my lord." The impersonal rejection had stung terribly, made all the worse because he'd thought they'd been friends.

"I am not giving you a choice," he insisted. Allen

had shown him the letter of introduction Penelope had presented upon her arrival, giving her complete access to him per his mother's wishes. "It is unfortunate that Mother dragged you into this, but she had no right. My family may have locked me away in this place, but *I* direct my own care."

Penelope's eyes narrowed and her chin tilted mutinously. The gesture took him aback. She'd always been such a sweet sort. "I see. And that's going swimmingly for you, is it?"

Anger heated his cheeks. "Now, see here—"

"No, *you* see here. Your mother tells me that your episodes have been getting worse and coming more frequently." Penelope's expression softened to one of concern, perhaps even worry.

His ire faded at the sight. Regardless of why she'd rejected him before, it was clear from her face that she had a care for him.

"All I meant was that perhaps the care you've been getting isn't the kind you need," she suggested.

His gaze held hers. "And you know what it is I need, then?" He moved closer to her, not thinking, simply drawn to something in her pale green eyes. Damn her, but that wretched hope that she seemed to engender in him flared bright in his chest. "Nothing that a multitude of doctors has tried has worked, but *you* have some magic cure to offer?" he murmured. His voice sounded suitably doubtful, but as he stared into her steady gaze, he found himself half believing she might.

She wet her lips nervously and took a tiny step back from him. The small move broke the spell just as surely as a dousing of frigid water would, leaving him cold inside. He made her uneasy. She probably thought he might attack at any moment. Given all that Allen said had happened yesterday, he couldn't blame her. But it still pained him.

"Of course not," she answered, as if his nearness hadn't disturbed her. "But I *have* had some experience helping people through difficult times. Particularly men who have served in the wars."

"You do?" He'd wondered why his mother had enlisted her aid. He wasn't sure what reason he'd expected, but it certainly wasn't *that*. Gabriel studied Penelope for a moment, trying to picture the darling young society wife he'd known ministering to hardened ex-soldiers. "I don't understand."

She nodded, as if expecting that response. She took a deep breath and Gabriel had the feeling she was fortifying herself.

"After Michael died, I was . . ." She looked off for a moment, as if searching for the right word. "Devastated," she finally chose.

The way she uttered the word sent a shiver through Gabriel. The inflection in her tone and the desolation that flashed briefly in her eyes rumbled through his heart like thunder after a streak of lightning.

It wasn't that the sentiment was wrong. In fact, it was precisely the word he would expect a young widow to use. And yet she said it in a way that made him think the loss had been deeper than that of her husband. A loss of her innocence, perhaps?

That he understood. He'd lost his own on the battlefields and had witnessed too many others do the same—earnest young men facing the unimaginable horrors of war. They'd looked much like Penelope did right now. What could possibly have put that haunted look in her eyes?

"Somehow, I made it through the funeral and the transfer of estate to Michael's brother. I even got settled in my own small townhome. But after the shock wore off, I . . . Well, let's just say I hid in my rooms for weeks. I refused to come out, much less receive anyone."

"Not just me, then," he murmured, unthinking. Her startled gaze flew to his, and his cheeks heated as her brow dipped thoughtfully. Damn it. He'd never meant her to know that she'd wounded him so long ago.

"No, everyone," she confirmed. "Even my family. Until one day, my cousin Liliana bullied her way past my staff and dragged me off to stay with her and her husband." A wry smile twisted her lips. "I don't know if you remember her from the wedding, but she is rather headstrong."

He did remember the tall brunette on the Earl of Stratford's arm. He also remembered the fondness he'd witnessed between the cousins. "She must have been quite worried about you."

"She was. But even with all of her concerned prodding, I remained mired in my own despair."

"That is understandable," he said, though the idea of the sunny girl he'd known wallowing alone in her grief shook him. He'd never imagined her so. "You loved Michael very much," he murmured.

"I did." Her eyes slid away from his, and her lips

thinned into something that should have been a smile but wasn't quite. "Of course."

Gabriel frowned, sensing something deeper in her words. Had her and Michael's marriage been troubled before his death? But before he could press her on the matter, she rushed on.

"Liliana decided that what I needed was a distraction from my grief. She insisted I accompany her every day to the clinic that she and her husband established to care for ex-soldiers and their families. After some time, I started working with men who suffered from battle fatigue." She tilted her head and pinned him with a curious gaze. "Have you considered that your affliction could stem from traumas you experienced during battle?"

He regarded her. "I'd be a fool not to have," he answered. He still had the dreams of death and battle and even the waking nightmares occasionally. "In fact, I have often wondered if that is where this lunacy got its start."

The dreams had brought on terror and confusion, but he'd take that every day of the year over the bouts of madness that had marked his past months. "But even were that the case, it has gone far beyond anything I suffered from the wars. And therefore beyond both your experience and your best intentions, I'm afraid."

"I will admit I've never seen a situation *quite* like yours," she said tactfully. "But don't underestimate me. I daresay my methods will be better than what you've endured thus far. Mr. Allen told me of the purges, the cold baths, the leeching." An involuntary shiver shook her shoulders. "He said you even asked to be blistered?"

This time the shiver was his. He'd never forget the agony of hot plasters being placed on his skin, raising blisters that were then lanced and drained.

"That's barbaric, Gabriel. Why would you let them do such a thing?"

"Why do you think?" he shot back in clipped tones. This time it was he backing away from her, ashamed. Did she know everything of his time in this madhouse? "Because some bloody doctor told me it could heal me. Some blather about the overstimulation of my nerves and restoring my natural balance, and hence my sanity."

The worst part of it was that he'd thought it had worked. For a few hopeful weeks, he'd been episode free and begun to dream about returning home and picking up his life. But then he'd had another episode, one worse than any before it. "I'd have done anything to be the man I once was," he finished in a low voice.

Penelope surprised him by not allowing his retreat. She followed, placing herself so close he could detect her subtle scent. She tilted her head up slightly. She wasn't a short woman, but neither was she tall. Rather, she was the perfect height to capture his gaze and his attention.

"Then don't send me away," she said. "I may have started down this path unintentionally, but I have helped many men in the last two years—men who suffered terribly. I can help you, too."

He turned his head in slow denial. The very idea of laying himself bare to Penelope horrified him. However unbarbaric she might think her methods were, they would be sheer torture to him, just by virtue of who administered them. Even if he thought she could help, he couldn't bear it. "No."

Her lips firmed into a stubborn line. "I gave my word."

"I don't hold you to any promises you made my family."

"My promise wasn't to them, Gabriel. It was to you."

"*I* never asked for your help," he stated gruffly.

"Oh, yes, you did." A pink flush tinted her cheeks. As close as they were, he could see the rapid beat of her pulse in her throat. "Yesterday. When you—when we were on the floor, just there." She tipped her head to the left.

Ah, yes. When he'd apparently knocked her to her arse and then mauled her. All whilst he was wet and *naked*, if Allen were to be believed. And given Penelope's flaming cheeks, he probably could be.

"You may not remember, Gabriel, but I do. You recognized me. Even in the midst of your mania, you called my name. You hugged me to you and begged me for help. I won't turn my back on that."

Ah, Christ. Gabriel scrubbed his hands over his face, wishing he could hide behind his palms forever. Or at least until she gave up and went home.

But he couldn't. He dropped his hands and strove for a calming breath. But it quickly turned into a snort of grim amusement. After years of imagining it, he'd finally had Penelope in his arms—with one of them in the buff, no less—and he couldn't even remember it. *That* might be the cruelest part of all of this.

The irreverent thought brought huffs of laughter. Not the joyful kind, but the near silent kind that takes over when one is faced with a situation where one must either laugh or cry.

"Gabriel?"

Penelope looked so startled that the laughter came in earnest then. It probably made him appear crazier to her, but he couldn't help it. Damn, but it felt good to laugh.

A tremulous smile tilted her lips, and for a moment it was as if they were back in the parlor of the Mantons' London townhome, sharing a joke or a funny bit of gossip as they'd done many times during her marriage to his cousin. It made him feel like his old self, something he'd almost forgotten how to be.

And he knew then that he couldn't force her to leave tonight. Tomorrow, most likely, but not tonight. After all, it was a little late to close the stable door. The damage had already been done.

"Truce, Pen." He held his hands up in surrender. "Truce. We can sort it later." He walked over to the table and pulled out a chair for her. "For now, I wish only to dine with you, as we did when we were friends."

Penelope looked to the chair Gabriel held out to her and debated but a second. Then she quickly stepped to it and settled herself before he could change his mind.

She'd been certain there for a moment that he was going to have her tossed out. She doubted she could have stopped him, either, as she suspected Mr. Allen would be only too happy to comply with Gabriel's wishes.

She might then have had to ask Gabriel's family to pressure him to see her, but she knew that coercing him would likely make him more resistant. The only way she could see being able to help him was if he welcomed it.

That was crucial to her form of treatment. In her quest to understand mental maladies, she'd learned many conflicting theories of how to best treat the sufferer. Some suggested illnesses of the mind were an imbalance of body humors to be treated like a disease, while others insisted it was a defect of the soul. There were myriad theories in between.

Penelope didn't consider herself particularly learned, nor as intelligent or experienced as others in the field. She'd simply taken from the different disciplines the bits that made sense to her and applied them when she felt they'd be helpful.

But in order for her to discern what would be most helpful, she'd need Gabriel to be a willing participant, and for that she'd need his trust.

She smiled at him as he took his place across from her at the table. He smiled back, but the gesture was forced and tight. They apparently had a long way to go on that front.

Penelope squared her shoulders and kept her smile in place. Every journey started with a first step, didn't it?

But where to step first?

She was granted a reprieve as servants placed platters of roasted meats, buttered potatoes and what looked and smelled to be a savory pudding made from pastry, vegetables and meat drippings. Her stomach let out a loud growl. Her eyes flew wide, and she clapped her hands over her middle in embarrassment.

Thankfully, Gabriel let the moment pass without comment, other than to say, "Tuck in," as the servants withdrew.

She did. As she chewed a bite of perfectly spiced venison, she discarded topic after topic as a conversation starter. Given his earlier confession, even the most innocuous salvo had the potential to be taken wrong. The last thing she wished was to cause Gabriel more discomfort.

Penelope swallowed her food around a tight throat. Why was this so hard? People talked every day. And yet, when she next opened her mouth, all she seemed capable of doing was to pop a perfectly buttered potato into it.

Before the next bite, she commented, "Dinner is quite excellent." There. It might have been lame, but food was always a safe topic.

"Yes. My family insisted on sending a chef to Vickering Place with me," he answered dryly. "Apparently it is quite all right to lock your relative away, so long as you ensure he eats well."

Penelope stopped chewing. So much for that. An awkward silence stretched out between them as she tried to think of something else to say.

"'Twas an impossible hope, I see." Gabriel took a sip from his water goblet.

She looked expectantly at him, her fork poised to spear another potato.

"Thinking we could spend an evening as friends," he murmured so softly she had to strain to hear him. He set his goblet down with a loud click. "In this place."

An ache tugged at her chest, and she realized why this was so much harder than it had been with others she'd helped. With strangers, she had nothing more invested than simple human kindness. With Gabriel . . . they had been friends.

Coconspirators, even. He'd been in the market for a wife then, and many a female acquaintance had pestered her for an introduction to her handsome new cousin. She'd had great fun playing Cupid.

She'd had great fun with him in general, truthfully. She had also been grateful for Gabriel's company. Not long into her marriage, it had become clear that Michael had too much energy even for her. Her husband's exuberance was charming, but it also exhausted her. Some evenings, she found herself content to let Michael go gadding about the ballrooms, and he was just as content to leave her in the escort of his cousin.

But all that had ended with Michael's death. In her grief, she'd cut everyone—including Gabriel—from her life and turned inward. She had not considered that she might have hurt him. She'd been unable to consider anything but her own pain.

She should have been a better friend.

Well, she couldn't change the past, but she would do her best to be the friend he needed now. Penelope reached across the table and covered his hand with hers. "Nothing I've seen or heard has made me think any less of you, Gabriel."

His lips twisted in a wry smile, even as he pulled his hand from beneath hers. "Then you must have had a very low opinion of me, indeed."

Her heart twinged. Nothing could be further from the truth. But she doubted Gabriel would believe her if she said as much. No, the best way to convince him would be to rebuild the easy relationship they once had.

She cocked a brow at him. "Only in your whist playing skills," she said archly. "You were a deplorable partner, you know. Cost me more pin money than I care to remember."

His eyes widened. Then he barked a laugh, precisely as she'd hoped. She smiled back and felt the tension ease a bit between them.

"I *was* awful," he admitted with a shake of his head. But a smile played at his lips. "I always wondered why you continued to partner me."

"Someone had to," she said, laughing. "Michael flatly refused, and I couldn't very well let you sit across from any of the eligible ladies. If you'd have lost *their* pin money, they would have been quite vexed with you. Not the wisest wooing strategy, I'm afraid."

He snorted. "Ah. Well, thank you for sacrificing for the cause."

"You're welcome," she said pertly. "By the way, you owe me five hundred seventy-eight pounds and nine shilling. Interest, you know."

And with that, conversation came more easily between them. As they ate, they talked of everything and yet nothing at all. She was careful not to mention much of the past two years, and so was he. It was like a conversation out of time, but such a pleasant one. They laughed quite a bit. And Gabriel visibly relaxed, which lightened her heart.

By the time they'd polished off a delectable walnut cake stuffed with raisins and almonds, Penelope's cheeks ached from smiling, and her hopes were high that they'd made significant progress. Tomorrow would be even better.

But it was becoming difficult to keep her eyes open, thanks to the combination of her satiated appetite and the sleepless night before.

"Thank you for the superb company," she said, rising from the table. "However, it is a good half-hour ride back to my rooms at the White Horse, so I must be going. But I shall return promptly in the morning. Shall we say right after breakfast?"

Gabriel rose as well, but his smile faded, to be replaced by the guarded expression of earlier in the evening. Penelope's good humor seeped away as he came around to stand before her.

He reached out and took her hand. His skin was warm against hers and his grip tight. He brought it to his lips, closing his eyes as he pressed a firm kiss just above her knuckles. A long kiss. A kiss that rang of finality.

Her breath caught.

"Thank you, Pen, for your graciousness," he said

fiercely as he released her. "You've given me more to-night than you can know. But I meant what I said. I don't want you to come back."

She watched in stunned silence as he turned on his heel and retreated toward his bedchamber.

"Gabriel, wait!" she cried. "Please," she implored more loudly when he did not slow. "There is something else you should know."

He stopped and turned back. She hated how tightly he held himself, as if it pained him to look at her. She hated more that she was about to add to his distress, but he had to know what was at stake.

She licked her lips, trying to think how to soften the news. In the end, all she could do was say it outright. "Your family is preparing to swear an affidavit to the Lord Chancellor to have you declared *non compos*."

The blood drained from his face, but other than that, he gave no sign that he even heard her. Did he know precisely what that meant?

"Once an affidavit is sworn, a petition will be made and a public commission appointed to determine your sanity. On the testimony of the staff of Vickering Place alone—"

"They will most assuredly find me a lunatic," he finished, no emotion in his voice. "They will judge me incapable of conducting my own affairs and strip me of the responsibilities of my title and estates."

She nodded, trying very diligently not to let her own emotions show on her face.

His fists clenched at his sides, which was the only warning she had before he exploded. "Even of my own *person*. Christ! And they sent *you* with this news?" He raked a hand through his closely shorn locks. "My own damned family, and they couldn't tell me this themselves?" He began to pace in an agitated swath.

"I convinced them to stay the affidavit."

He stopped midstride and turned to pin her with his gaze. "You did what?"

"At least until after I'd had the chance to see you," she hurried to explain as she crossed to where he stood. "I told them that if your lunacy is related to your time in the wars, there was a good chance you could be cured."

Gabriel huffed, even as he pinched the bridge of his nose. After a long moment, he dropped his hand to his side. "And after what you've seen, Penelope? Do you *really* think I can be cured?"

"I don't know," she was forced to admit.

He lowered his head. "And if I do not cooperate?"

"Then they intend to visit the Master extraordinary next week," she had to tell him.

The air between them crackled with frustration. His. Hers. He refused to look at her. She knew he hated this—maybe even hated her for bringing such ill tidings. She knew his pride was in tatters.

She also knew she was his last hope.

She studied him in the silence. He was leaner than he had been two years ago, and there were strands of gray near his temples that had not been there before. His brown eyes had always been shuttered, but they were stonier now. Still, he was the same man. Troubled, certainly, but the same.

Penelope reached out and curved her fingers under his chin, lifting his face to hers. "I want you to listen to me," she said, and her pulse shot up as his eyes locked with hers. She released him now that she had his full attention. "From the day we first met, I'd always thought you to be an exemplary man. In fact, I would not have believed my opinion of you could rise any higher."

He broke eye contact, clearly disbelieving her. She was losing him.

So she reached down and snatched his hands, squeezing them. "But I would have been wrong, Gabriel," she insisted.

His gaze snapped back to hers.

"I cannot imagine anything more terrifying than what you are living through. And yet you haven't given up. You are a fighter. I can see it in your eyes."

And she could. Anger lurked in their golden brown depths, as did fear and sorrow. But so did determination. It lit them from within.

"I cannot know what it is like to suffer as you do. I cannot know if we'll meet success. But I do know that as long as you are still fighting, I won't give up either. I swear it," she vowed.

They stood there, holding hands, locked in a silent communication that she doubted either of them consciously understood. But she sensed his resistance crumbling.

"It's not polite for ladies to swear," he said softly.

"Dash politeness."

One corner of his mouth turned up. "Indeed." He

extracted his hands from her grip. "And dash my family and the Lord Chancellor, as well, I suppose."

"Double dash them," she agreed.

He nodded. "All right, Pen. You win."

Not an overly optimistic agreement, but she would take it. Because for some absurd reason, enough hope soared in her chest for the both of them.

She only prayed those hopes weren't what ended up dashed.

Chapter Four

The click of a key echoed loudly in the room, followed by the metallic churning of tumblers giving way and the muffled clang of bars swinging open just outside his door. Gabriel came to his feet as his eyes fixed on the rectangle of paneled wood, the last barrier that separated his "parlor" from the rest of Vickering Place.

His heart kicked in his chest in what could only be anticipation. He'd spent half the night alternately praying for Penelope to come to her senses and not show this morning and the other half willing her to keep her vow. Now he would find out which contrary wish had been granted.

She sailed through the opening door and Gabriel's shoulders relaxed as he released a breath. She'd come. Foolish chit. And yet Penelope smiled so widely that even he couldn't help but feel optimistic in the glow of it.

"Good morning, Gabriel." She stopped a scant two feet in front of him, the hem of her dark cloak swirling slightly around her legs. The crisp scent of a winter morning reached his nose, carried in on her fur-collared manteau. He breathed in automatically, as if his senses craved the sharp contrast from the stuffy staleness of his rooms.

She peered around his shoulder to the table where he'd been sitting. "Oh, good. I see you've breakfasted."

He blinked at her, and the stirrings of a smile tickled his mouth. "Ah, yes." Then a thought arrested the grin before it could form. "Why? Are you planning some horrid treatment for which I'll need fortification?"

The corners of her eyes turned down, and her nose scrunched up in a sympathetic wince. "I'm afraid so."

"In that case, I wish I hadn't eaten that second helping of sausages," he grumbled as said extra serving turned over in his stomach.

"Never fear, my lord," she murmured softly. " 'Twill be over in a trice."

Gabriel's breath caught. Did Penelope know those were the very same words she said to settle him before their first dance so long ago?

Or was her phrasing simply meant to mollify, as she would a child before requiring him to down a particularly revolting remedy?

Either way, he had to trust that she would treat him with as much concern and sensitivity down this path as she had that wedding dance.

"If it is any consolation, what I have in mind does come with certain benefits," she promised.

A wholly inappropriate thrill charged through him. He tamped it down. She hadn't meant anything close to what his body heard. Still, he couldn't resist asking, "Such as?"

"Freedom." Pen flashed him a grin that turned a bit wry at the edges as she tipped her head back and to her left to indicate an unhappy-looking Carter. "Or at least the illusion thereof. Mr. Allen insists I bring *him* along." Pen made a moue of distaste. "I explained that it would not be necessary, but he refused to allow us out of doors otherwise."

The attendant stood in the corner, bundled up in a greatcoat and scarf and sporting a fierce scowl—clearly not relishing his role as outdoor watchdog any more than Penelope did.

"Go on." She flicked her fingers toward Gabriel in a backward wave. "Don warm boots and a coat. It's chilly today."

Enthusiasm buzzed through him at the very idea of a day spent outside. And yet it was February. He glanced toward the window. The day loomed gray, and forbidding clouds blotted out the sky, threatening to wring sheets of rain down upon them.

He looked back at Penelope. Her cheeks appeared chafed and the tip of her nose had a pink tint to it. While it rarely got overly cold in this part of the country, the wind and moist air could quite chill one to the bone. "Perhaps we should wait for a sunnier day. I wouldn't risk your health."

Penelope waved a dismissive hand. "Pish. You knew me only as a London society wife, but I was raised on a country estate. My only playmate was my cousin Liliana, and she abhorred being cooped up indoors where my mother might hound her into some feminine pursuit. If I didn't wish to be lonely, I had to keep up with her."

Gabriel frowned, unconvinced.

"Did I mention her favorite places to play were muddy swamps and bogs?" Pen wrinkled her nose. "Believe me, I am far from fragile."

Hard to imagine her, who he'd once heard a group of ladies grousing always looked as if she'd stepped off of a fashion plate, traipsing around after her cousin through the marshes, her clothes covered in mire.

Still . . . "I've seen many an able-bodied soldier fall prey to the elements," he argued. "One doesn't have to be fragile to catch one's death."

"No, I suppose one doesn't. However, I must insist." She cocked a challenging brow. "Unless *you* are not feeling up to it, of course."

Gabriel hastened to fetch his winter garments.

Minutes later, he stepped past a frowning Allen into the outside air for the first time in weeks. Penelope stayed close to his side, while Carter followed behind after grumbling something indiscernible to the director.

As they reached the bottom stair, Gabriel paused and simply breathed it all in. Damned if he didn't have to force himself not to throw out his arms, turn his face up to the dreary sky and turn in circles as he would have in his nursery days.

He caught Penelope's knowing smile out of the corner of his eye just before she pulled the hood of her cloak over her head.

She turned to him, looking very much like Red Riding Hood would have were the girl dressed in black rather than crimson. "Mr. Allen tells me there is a path through the gardens that leads into the wood. Shall we venture there?"

She might look like Red Riding Hood, but she sounded very like the Big Bad Wolf . . . a little too innocent to be safe. He had a feeling this was where whatever horrid treatment she had in mind began. Still, he nodded. "Lead on."

Penelope set a brisk pace. They walked in silence for some time, the only sound being their boots crushing leaves and dead grass beneath them, echoed by Carter's heavier footfalls from behind.

Blood hummed in Gabriel's veins. It could simply be dread over what she might have planned for him today. Or it could be that Penelope was by his side. But either way, he couldn't remember the last time he'd felt this invigorated.

Or this much his old self.

With every breath of fresh air that pumped through his lungs, that feeling grew.

"Did you know that emotion can be directly tied to motion?" Penelope asked after a time. Her voice had a breathy quality to it from the exertion. "If you observe someone who is lost in their melancholy, for example, you notice that often their shoulders are slumped and their movements are sluggish. Their breathing is shallow and slow. Have you ever noticed that?"

He glanced sideways at her. "Not particularly, no. While I've experienced some melancholy since the wars, *my* madness is more of the raving sort, wouldn't you say?" he returned dryly.

His big bad she-wolf gave him a decidedly sheepish look. Still, she persisted. "Define 'some melancholy' for me. Do you mean occasional sadness? Or do you ever experience periods of extended despair?"

He heaved a sigh. "So, you brought me outside to interrogate me."

"Yes."

He stuffed his gloved hands into the pockets of his coat. "Takes some of the joy out of the morning, I'd say."

"I *am* sorry."

He let her apology linger in the air for a few steps. "Wouldn't it have been simpler to talk in my rooms? Warmer, at least." He glanced back at the sullen attendant, shuffling along some paces back. "Carter would have thanked you for it."

"I imagine he would," she agreed. "However, I care naught for Carter."

Implying she did care for *him*? Suddenly Gabriel no longer felt quite so surly about the whole thing.

"As to bringing you out here, my reasons are many. First, the emotion-to-motion connection I mentioned earlier seems to work both ways. On one hand, the melancholic's despair depresses their body systems, hence the sluggishness and shallow breathing. However, if that person were to *consciously* choose to stand straighter, take deep breaths or engage in some vigorous activity, oftentimes their mood is improved just by those simple physical motions. I'm not certain why it works, but that has been my observation."

"Hmmm," he said, just to let her know he didn't disagree. He did feel quite the thing after only a quarter hour's walk.

"Second, the soldiers I know are men of action and they are most comfortable on the move. I thought you might feel more yourself out here."

As he had from the moment they met, Gabriel marveled at Penelope's gentle intuitiveness. "You were right," he confirmed, breathing the crisp air through his nose.

"Most soldiers I've treated spent the majority of their time out in the elements. Days and nights, for months—sometimes years—at a stretch. Assuming your military experience was anything like theirs, it is only natural that you would be most at home outside."

It seemed Penelope's natural instincts were now borne out by her experiences helping other soldiers. He was still getting his mind around that.

His eyes scanned the rugged winter landscape that comprised Vickering Place's grounds, but in his mind's eye he saw the colorful autumn foliage of his home as it had been when he'd last been there. "My servants complained that they couldn't catch me indoors," he admitted. "Sometimes I had legitimate reasons to remain out. Surveying the fields, visiting tenants. But other times, I just couldn't bring myself to stay inside." Those days had been when he'd felt his best. Even before his current madness, being outside and active had done more to keep his wartime nightmares away than anything else had.

Yet, since these more frightening bouts of mania had taken hold, he'd imprisoned himself indoors . . . hidden himself away long before his family decided to finish the job and send him to Vickering Place. Had he compounded his illness by his choice? It made sense. His attitude and perspective had deteriorated every day—which, at the very least, hadn't made him feel any better. He'd been a fool not to have realized it.

But Penelope had, and because of her insight, he felt more alive in the past hours than he had during months of hellish treatments on the advice of more educated, esteemed doctors. If she had been in his life at the time the mania started, would he have gone this far afield?

He cut his eyes to her. Penelope had said she'd helped other ex-soldiers. She had no reason to be untruthful about that. She wouldn't be here if she didn't think she could do the same for him.

Perhaps he should open up to her, just a bit, and see where it led.

He glanced back over his shoulder to see how closely Carter followed. The attendant had fallen back several yards and was sullenly kicking his feet at the occasional rock that littered the path. Good. He might have to show weakness to Penelope, but he'd be damned if he'd do so in the hearing of the other man.

Satisfied that their conversation would be private, he said, "For the first several months, I had to force myself to sleep in my rooms. I felt so"—Gabriel searched for the word—"confined. I'd spent so many nights out under the stars that lying beneath a ceiling, surrounded by walls, seemed more like a tomb than a bedchamber."

"Hmmm," was all she said. She fell quiet, leaving him with an odd urge to fill the silence.

He reached a hand behind his neck to massage away a sudden tension instead. Just confessing this one innocuous thought made his muscles tighten just as badly as being cooped up indoors at night once had.

"But a marquess can't just pitch a tent on the heath without setting the gossips to wagging," he said lightly, hoping to end the exchange. "So . . ." He tossed in a shrug to make it seem as if the whole matter were of no consequence.

"So you suffered night after night at the expense of your own comfort."

He huffed. He should have known she wouldn't let the matter drop. "My comfort should be of no consequence to you."

"But it is," she insisted. Then she added carefully, "To a point."

He glanced askew at her.

"Gabriel, you must know that in order for me to help you, we are going to have to discuss some very *un*comfortable things."

He'd known she was going to say that. He turned his face away, focusing on the stripped trees they passed, every craggy bend and every knotty blemish on the wood bared to the eye by winter's harshness. Is that how he would look to Penelope if he let her in? Scarred and ugly inside?

"But we needn't start there. We can ease into our conversation with more pleasant things," she suggested.

A single fat drop of rain chose that moment to splatter against his cheekbone. "That leaves out the weather as a topic, then," he drawled, wiping the moisture from his cheek. "Speaking of, it is looking ominous." He glanced up at the colorless sky. All right, so perhaps that was stretching the truth a bit. No more drops were forthcoming. But the clouds were clearly fat with it. That should be enough to win him a reprieve from her questioning. "We should return."

Penelope glanced up as well before shooting him a look better suited on a governess—one who was well accustomed to her charges trying to get out of their lessons.

"I'll hardly melt," she intoned, "and neither will you."

"Carter might," he grumbled.

She let that pass without comment and continued trekking ahead.

Damn. He could turn on his heel and walk back himself. Carter, he knew, would follow gladly. But he also knew Penelope would just pester him there. The only way to avoid her questions would be to demand that Allen bar her from Vickering Place.

But without her help, he'd end up in a local tavern, put on display by the commission for lunacy in a public trial that would be gossiped about for years to come. His chest clenched at the mere thought.

"To hell with pleasantness, then," he growled, his

voice sounding uncharitable even to his own ears. But he cared not. She would have to take what she could get. "Ask me what you need to know to cure me."

She stopped and turned toward him. He stopped as well, standing very still as Penelope eyed him. "You understand that there is a real chance that no matter what we do, you won't wholly recover."

He kept his gaze locked with hers. "There's a larger chance of that should we do nothing."

She nodded. "All right," she said, and resumed walking down the footpath, leaving him to follow.

He did, though he had to pick his way carefully. The path she'd chosen had likely been well kept when Vickering Place had been a country manor, but now it was overgrown in places and bare in others, with the occasional knotted root protruding through the earth.

When he caught up to her, she said, "These episodes you've been having, have they always been like the one I witnessed?"

She'd certainly taken him at his word and dove right in, hadn't she?

He cleared his throat. "As I have no memory of what exactly you witnessed, I couldn't say," he answered, his voice tight. Perhaps this had not been such a good idea. "But given what witnesses have said of my behavior whilst I am blacked out, my guess would be no." Christ, he sounded like a formal arse. Rather like his butler at home. But it felt somehow safer to remove his own personality from the conversation. "I am told each one is worse than the one before."

She seemed to think about that for a moment. "Did

you experience anything similar before you gained your commission and went off to war?"

He gave her a curt shake of the head.

A look of relief flashed on her face. At least he thought it was relief. It was hard to tell with the hood of her cloak obscuring part of her profile.

"All right, can you remember when the first episode occurred?"

As if he could forget such a thing. It was, up until that time, the second-most terrifying thing that had ever happened to him. "Nine months ago."

Penelope snapped her head around, coming to a halt on the path. She pushed the hood of her cloak off, he supposed to get a clearer look at him, and her eyes were wide in her face. "But that would be nearly four years after the war ended."

"Yes."

"That is . . ." Her face shifted from disbelief to guarded. "Unusual," she finished.

He raised a brow. "I take it from your tone you do not mean 'unusual' in a good way."

She winced. "It's only that, if your illness sprang from battle fatigue, I would have expected it to start shortly after you returned home. Perhaps even before." She crossed her arms and brought a fisted hand up to her mouth, tapping her gloved thumb against her lips in what seemed to be a nervous habit he'd never noticed she had before.

He wished *he* had a nervous habit to employ, as her obvious dismay was draining his confidence in their success. "Meaning you now suspect that my madness comes from somewhere inside me rather than as a result of my war experiences," he concluded.

"Well, I have never heard of a case where someone had no symptoms for four years and then develops bouts of mania overnight."

He considered that depressing thought for a moment. "I do have *other* problems that started during or just after the war," he offered.

"Oh, good!"

She said it so enthusiastically, he couldn't resist a dry snort. "I'm glad my misery brings you such joy."

Her cheeks turned a becoming rose. "That did seem rather unfeeling of me," she admitted.

"Coldhearted," he agreed, but he lifted his lips to let her know he was in jest.

She smiled back. "Tell me about them."

That was enough to wipe the smile off of his face, but Pen simply nodded encouragingly.

Gabriel tried to remember back to those earlier days, when sudden overwhelming vertigo and unexplained panic were the worst of his problems.

"The first time I became aware that something had changed inside me, I was at a ball on the Peninsula. It wasn't long after Wellington's victory at Vitoria. Spirits were high and everyone felt like celebrating."

He kept his eyes straight ahead, determined to pretend that he was simply telling her a story, as if none of it had happened to him. "Even though the Peninsular War would go on for another ten months, those of us who were there knew that we'd broken Napoleon's stranglehold in Spain."

Penelope didn't say a word, just let him talk, which he appreciated. It made it easier, somehow.

"I, along with most of the officers, attended a ball held at the home of a wealthy landowner. There was nothing unusual—just the typical throngs of people dressed in their best, gaiety, dancing, noise—nothing I hadn't experienced a hundred times during the Season at home. Nothing that should have bothered me . . ." He couldn't go on past the tightness closing his throat.

"But it did," Penelope said quietly when several heartbeats had passed.

"Yes," he croaked, no longer able to hold the memories at a distance. The crush of people. The air, heavy and close. "I couldn't breathe." The feelings came back to him now, though not as intensely as they once had. This was far from the horrid squeezing in his lungs he used to feel, where air could barely scrape in and out.

"You felt trapped," she said, understanding somehow.

He nodded jerkily. "I pushed on, but when I came to the dance floor—" Images assailed him. Whirling dancers, colors swirling about. He closed his eyes and pressed a hand to his forehead, just above his temple.

"Were you dizzy?" Pen asked. "Light-headed and sick to your stomach?"

He nodded, opening his eyes. "All that." He took a deep breath, then another. "I had to fight my way out of the room," he admitted, ashamed of his weakness.

"What happened when you made it outside?" she asked quietly.

His heart had hammered so hard and fast in his

chest, he'd feared it would explode like the new fragmenting shells his troops had begun using in battle. "Eventually I returned to feeling normal," was all that he said. "Shaky, but normal."

"Did you try to go back inside?"

He shook his head. "No. I went back to the mess for a stiff drink."

"And did that help?"

He raised an eyebrow. "I drank myself into oblivion," he recalled, "so yes."

"Hmmm." He heard Pen's breathing beside him as they continued to walk. But whereas before, being outdoors had made him feel free enough to fight off the bad memories, now they were closing in. With each step, he stretched his limbs as far as they could reach, trying to regain that sense of being unconfined. But it wasn't working.

"Did you experience such things again?" she asked.

He wanted to demand that she stop asking so many questions. Every bloody word out of his mouth could only damn him as pathetic and weak in her eyes. He glanced over at her, expecting to see the same pity he'd seen so often on the faces of his family, but instead she looked at him with steady encouragement. As if she *expected* his answers.

Perhaps she did. Maybe the other men she'd treated had had similar experiences. Maybe she looked at him that way because she knew she really could help him.

That flicker of hope inside his chest sparked higher once more. If there was a chance she was right, he'd answer her damned questions as long as he could.

"No. Everything was fine until I attended another ball," he forced himself to say. "There weren't many opportunities for such entertainments, so it wasn't until Paris in 1814, when Wellington was installed as ambassador to France."

"I see. Would you say it was better or worse?"

"I wasn't as taken by surprise by it, so in *that* sense, it was better. But really, it was the same. I avoided ballrooms after that," he said, "even when I was all but ordered to accompany Wellington to various events." He shoved his hands into the pockets of his greatcoat to hide his clenched fists. "In fact, I didn't step foot inside a ballroom again until your wedding ball."

Penelope turned her face to him. Twin lines formed between her brows as her mind worked. Her eyes cast up and off to the side as if she were searching her memory. "I knew you were uncomfortable," she said, "but I had no idea it was as bad as all this."

It hadn't been. Not that night. But he couldn't tell her that it had been *her* who had somehow kept the panic away. It would reveal too much.

"But," she went on, her voice laced with confusion, "you attended several balls after our wedding, both in Town and in the country. Did the dread just fade with time?" she asked, her delicate features rearranging themselves into lines of puzzlement as she studied him.

No. It had been hell. He'd hated every single one of them. But he'd forced himself to attend, knowing that would be the best place for him to find a wife of his own.

And after a while he'd given up that pretense and admitted to himself that he'd gone only so that he could be with *her*.

But he could never say anything like that, either. Could never tell her that truth. A hot, raw vulnerability scraped through him. "I can't do this anymore, Pen," he rasped.

"You *can*." Her voice was forceful and sympathetic at the same time. Her expression shifted to match. "Whenever a topic becomes too difficult, we can just move to another and come back when it isn't so painful."

He shook his head, causing her to rush on. "Let us leave the war behind for a while and talk about your life before you bought your commission," she suggested. "Perhaps we can find some clues as to why this mania is afflicting you by looking into what you were like before the wars."

But he didn't want to talk anymore. He sped his steps, pulling ahead of her by several feet.

She followed, of course. He should have known she wouldn't let him escape her.

As she came alongside him, she said, "You never answered me earlier, when I asked you to define your bouts of melancholy. Would you say they were severe? Did they last for more than a day or two?"

He let out a harsh breath. "No. No, I have moments of darkness, but I wouldn't say they are extreme. Or prolonged."

"But did you have them before you went to war?"

Gabriel thought about her question, wondering

where she was leading. He was fast learning that Penelope's softly spoken queries tended to lead somewhere. "Yes. Some. Not as often as after, though."

The crunch of their boots filled the silence between them for several steps. Gabriel glanced up at the sky as they walked without speaking. The clouds had darkened—not quite ominously, but rain was certainly not far off. He might win his reprieve after all.

He turned his head to Penelope, about to suggest they turn around and head back toward Vickering Place, when she asked, "What about the opposite?"

He blinked, lost for a moment in the conversation as his mind had been on the impending storm. "What do you mean?"

"Well, rather than feeling low, have you ever experienced rushes of exhilaration instead? States of excitement where you were so filled with energy that you thought you could do anything? Perhaps even gone without sleep because of it?"

He huffed. "Why? Is that common with battle fatigue?"

"No."

"Then why have you brought it up?" he asked, hearing the slight bafflement in his voice.

"No reason," she demurred.

But he didn't believe her. What had she said before she started this line of questioning? That she was looking for clues to explain his mania in his life before the wars. "Are extreme high feelings an indication of madness?" he asked, curious.

Pen didn't look at him. "They can be," she said vaguely.

"Well, no worries on that count. I have never been anything like that. If fact, the only person I've known who could be described as such was"—a sick feeling flooded him, leaving a sour taste on the back of his tongue—"Michael."

He stopped walking.

She did not.

"Penelope."

She stuttered to a halt at his command, but she didn't turn back to face him for a long moment. When she did, her normally peach complexion had washed white, making the redness on the tip of her nose stand out like a cherry.

His sick feeling worsened.

"Are you saying my cousin was mad?"

Chapter Five

"Mad?" Penelope echoed, unable to say anything else as her mind whirled.

Gabriel's eyes flashed bright as he narrowed them on her face. There was an intensity in his gaze that reminded her so much of Michael that it hurt to look upon him.

"Of course not." But her voice sounded unconvincing even to her own ears.

How had their conversation turned so fast? She'd been cautiously thrilled by the progress they'd been making. But then he'd figured out exactly where her questions were leading and turned them on her with knifelike precision. She hadn't even known she'd been cut until her heart started bleeding.

She wouldn't discuss Michael with anyone. She would not.

"I believe we've accomplished enough for this morning," she said, relieved when her voice didn't tremble. "I suggest we go back to the manor and warm ourselves. You can get some rest, and we can start again this afternoon."

She tugged the hood of her cloak back up, shielding her face from him as she turned to retreat. Now that her heart was sliced open, every painful memory she'd worked so hard to put behind her seethed in her chest, stinging just enough to let her know they were still there. Waiting for her to uncage them. She needed to be alone when they broke free.

"No."

His voice rang with such command that Penelope immediately stilled. Gabriel closed the distance between them, coming up behind her. She didn't have to see him to know. She *felt* him, the way a blind woman sensed things she could not see. She heard the scrape of leather and cloth, smelled subtle hints of sandalwood and sage on the breeze, and her body tingled with the realization that he was close by.

"You will answer my question. Was my cousin mad?"

She whirled. Even though she'd known he would be there, his nearness startled her, sending a shimmer of alarm through her. No . . . not alarm, she thought. Awareness. Of him. As a man.

Oh, no. Her head shook of its own accord. No, no. That was completely unacceptable.

Gabriel's eyes narrowed further upon her. He thought she was denying his demand, she realized.

Better that than the truth.

She backed away from him. "That isn't relevant," she said as she turned back toward Vickering Place and started off at a fast clip.

"The hell it isn't!" he called after her. "Michael and I share the same blood. If he was crazed, then my madness could be inherited."

Penelope kept walking. It wasn't long before she spotted Carter. The attendant must have given up on following them, as he was sitting on the stump of a felled tree, waiting for them to return. He leapt to his feet as she neared, his face twisting first with an "about time" expression and then with confusion as his eyes darted from her to Gabriel—who she assumed was still some distance behind her.

Let Carter make himself useful and see that Gabriel made it back to the manor safely.

"Penelope, wait!" Gabriel's voice and footsteps were muffled by her cloak's hood, but it sounded as though he were coming up fast. A second set of footfalls echoed those, letting her know Carter was close behind. Good. Gabriel wouldn't wish to air his private family business in front of the attendant.

Still, she sped up her pace just the same, blinking against tears that blurred her vision.

She was well aware of what she was doing— avoiding. Avoiding Gabriel, avoiding his questions about Michael, and avoiding the sudden recognition of an unholy attraction to a man who was not only her cousin-by-marriage, but for all intents and purposes, under her care. *And quite likely mad on top of that.*

But it was the best she could do in the moment. She needed time to think. She dashed a tear away from her eye. She needed time to—

"Oh!" Penelope's toe caught on something and she stumbled. A wrenching pain shot up her leg as her foot tried to stay put while her momentum sent her pitching forward. She cried out as she landed hard, first on her knees and then on her stomach and chest, the side of her face coming to rest on the overgrown footpath.

"Pen!" She heard Gabriel's worried shout, felt the rumble as he and Carter came running.

Lord, her calf was afire. And something pricked at her cheek. She lifted her head, blinking as she got her bearings. Dried yew needles stuck to her skin. They covered the path, dropped from the ancient fragmented trees that lined it, their branches stretching and entwining into snarls of barren foliage. Had she tripped over a root? She'd been so caught up in trying to get away that she hadn't been watching her footing. Fool.

She wiped the dead needles from her face, groaning as she pushed herself up from the ground. Strong hands caught her beneath her arms from behind and turned her as she eased into a sitting position on the path.

Gabriel knelt beside her. He smoothed her cloak's hood off of her head. But his palms remained, warm against her skin, cradling either side of her face as he tilted it gently. The intensity in his eyes had gone, replaced by concern. "Pen, are you hurt?"

She shook her head, as it seemed her lips refused to utter the lie. Goodness. Her knees smarted, for one, and her right calf burned. Thankfully she'd landed on her front rather than her still sore backside. Between his landing upon her person not quite two days ago and her own just now, muscles she'd never even felt before twinged in protest. "I'll be fine," she insisted. "If you could just help me to my feet?"

"Of course." Gabriel gained his own feet in a graceful movement. He slipped an arm behind her, beneath her shoulder blades, curving his hand around her rib cage, where he could get a decent grip. The heat of his touch, even through her cloak, sent warmth flowing through her chest. He placed his other hand upon her hip to guide her as he pulled her to her feet.

Penelope tried to steady herself. The sooner she did, the sooner there would be no reason for Gabriel to touch her. No reason for her to feel sparks where his strong hands gripped her. But as she straightened, she sucked in a pained hiss. Agony flared in her calf as her right leg collapsed beneath her.

She sagged against Gabriel, shifting her weight to her left.

"You *are* hurt," Gabriel accused, a fierce frown pulling at his features.

"No, it's only—" She cried out again as her calf bunched in an unrelenting squeeze. "Oh! Ow!" She hopped on her left leg as if trying to get away from the pain. But the spasms wouldn't let up. Her muscles rolled and bunched again.

"Is it your calf? Is it cramping?"

She bit her lip against the pain, nodding jerkily.

Gabriel lowered her to the ground. When he released her, she braced herself by placing her palms slightly behind either side of her hips as he came around to kneel at her feet. Without asking permission, he reached his hands beneath her skirts and squeezed them around her calf tightly.

Penelope gasped as her muscles fought against his grip.

"Just breathe, Pen," he encouraged, his gaze catching hers. "Through your mouth, like this." Gabriel panted in quick, harsh breaths.

She kept her eyes on his and did as he asked.

"That's right," he crooned. "Just focus on your breathing."

"I'm"—*pant, pant*—"trying!" *Pant, pant.* But the squeezing was merciless.

Then his fingers started moving, massaging.

"Oh!" she cried, throwing her head back. For a moment, the flare of agony was so much worse, she didn't know if she could bear it, but then . . . it loosened. Just a little. Gabriel kept up his ministrations, molding, squeezing, rolling her knotting muscle until the tide started to turn. Deftly, he kneaded with strokes of alternating length until the clenching subsided.

Penelope was finally able to take in a deep breath, then another as her body slowly relaxed. But now that the pain was no longer overpowering her nerves, she began to feel other things. Things strangely familiar and yet not. Pleasurable things.

She tugged her calf from Gabriel's grasp. " 'Tis better now," she murmured as she smoothed her skirts back down to her ankles. She glanced over at Carter, embarrassed that the man had likely seen too much, but the attendant had thankfully turned his back.

Gabriel gained his feet and extended both hands to her. "Let me help you up."

She stared at his long, capable fingers, encased in gloves of the softest leather. Hands that had touched her with gentle healing, that had rescued her. Her stomach fluttered. It would be a mistake to let him touch her again. Yet she wasn't certain she could rise on her own.

She took his hands.

It *was* a mistake. Even through both of their gloves, she felt it—a frisson of connection she couldn't deny. It was as if now that her mind had noticed the attraction, it pulled her inexorably.

Gabriel lifted her to her feet as if she weighed nothing. She balanced her weight on her left side and gingerly placed her right toe on the ground to test her injured leg. She winced and pulled her foot up again.

"What does it feel like?" he asked.

"My calf quivers like a strung bow," she answered. She feared it would start that horrid clenching again. But it did not. "There is a deep ache—one that threatens to cramp again with little provocation."

He nodded. "You may have torn your muscle. Strained it, at the least. We shall need to keep you off of your feet." His hand, which was still at her back for support, slid down to her thighs as he made to scoop her up.

Penelope's breath caught. In a panic, she pivoted on her good leg, evading his grasp. She nearly toppled as she overbalanced, but with a few little hops, she managed to stay upright and put a bit of distance between them. "What are you doing?"

His lips flattened. "Carrying you back to the manor, of course."

Oh, no. She wouldn't be able to bear that. Her senses, which had been asleep for so very long, had most assuredly awakened—and it felt as if they intended to make up for lost time.

"Nonsense," she said, wobbling a bit. She glanced down the lane. They were a good quarter mile from Vickering Place, she'd bet. Drat. This was going to hurt like the dickens. Still . . . "I can make it back on my own."

Gabriel didn't speak, but raised a sardonic brow at her that spoke volumes.

"Oh, all right," she conceded. Perhaps she would need his help, but she had to keep the touching at a minimum. "But there's no need to carry me." She glanced over at Carter. "If the two of you would just get on either side of me—sort of like crutches. It will take some time, but I am certain I can make it—"

The clouds chose that moment to open up, as the storm that had been threatening all morning finally made good.

Lines of annoyance bracketed Gabriel's mouth as rain pelted them. Droplets of water found those tiny furrows and traveled them before dripping off of his chin. He started toward her.

"Gabriel," she implored, putting her hands palm out before her. "If anyone should carry me, it should be Carter." She glanced at the attendant, who frowned uncharitably at her. Blaming her for the fact that he was stuck out in the rain when he could be inside, dry and warm, no doubt. Still, better to be carried to the manor by an irritable stranger than to be pressed close to Gabriel all that way. "He's—he's burlier."

Gabriel rolled his eyes. Without even slowing his stride, he bent, slid an arm behind her knees and the other around her shoulders and scooped her up into his arms. Before she could utter another protest, he cradled her close to his chest as he turned them toward Vickering Place.

"This is ridiculous," she grumbled. Gabriel, however, just kept silently trudging ahead. Rain dripped down the stark lines of his face, but it didn't seem to bother him. She imagined that as a soldier, he'd grown quite accustomed to marching through inclement weather without voicing complaint.

She had the feeling she could rail at him to put her down the entire way, and he would just ignore her as completely as he did the storm.

Well, she may have to accept her fate, but being cradled like a child made her feel as if she'd given up all control. She slid one arm over his shoulder and tugged herself up, shifting the balance a bit. Gabriel allowed it, adjusting to her adjustments without comment.

Her gloved palm now rested against his chest, where his heart beat vigorously with its extra burden—so strong, so steady.

While she'd become a bundle of nerves. The side of her that was pressed up against Gabriel burned hot. With each step, his muscled frame moved against her, leaving her tingling and breathless. Her other side, the one exposed to the chill and rain, felt strangely numb in comparison. The dichotomy of cold and heat sent her poor body into shivers.

Gabriel tightened his arms around her, and despite everything, she felt the strangest sense of security. "We're almost there, Pen."

She glanced toward the manor, the imposing house barely visible behind the haze of fog that was being chased away by the rain. They had quite a ways to go yet, in truth. In the meantime, foreign-yet-familiar stirrings swelled in her middle. Dear Lord, what was wrong with her? Was she destined to desire broken men? First Michael and now Gabriel. And not a one in between.

Penelope took a deep breath. She had to get ahold herself. All right. If she were advising someone who came to her with unwelcome feelings they wished to banish, what would she tell them to do?

Penelope chewed on that thought a moment. Well, she would suggest they face their emotions straight on. Often just looking at things for what they actually were dispelled fears and other such unhealthy thoughts.

She was going to have to face this attraction to Gabriel and pick it apart. She studied him in profile. His face was more angular than it had once been. He was leaner than he had been two years ago, as well, though the change simply made his shoulders appear broader, she noted. His brown hair, while it had never been overly long, was now closely shorn. Austere, she'd describe him.

Yet he was still a strikingly handsome man. Maybe even more handsome than she remembered.

Penelope mentally shook herself. She wasn't supposed to be looking for things that made Gabriel *more* attractive, dash it all.

Besides, his form wasn't the type she'd ever fancied. Physically, he was as different from Michael as . . . well, as night was from day. Michael's blond beauty and romantic features that had so captured her youthful heart contrasted in every way against Gabriel's dark appeal.

Perhaps that's why *you're drawn to him,* a voice whispered in her head. *Because he is nothing like the man who broke your heart.*

A tear slipped from Penelope's eye, only to be caught up in the rivulet of raindrops and washed away, hopefully unseen. That was unfair. Michael couldn't help that he'd hurt her. He had been a sick man.

As is Gabriel.

Something inside her went cold. Penelope wiped at her face, taking in another deep breath. Right. That was precisely what she needed to kill her wayward longings—a healthy dose of reality.

'Twas a cruel irony that the first physical stirrings she'd felt since Michael's death were for a man she could never be with. She would *never* again live with the kind of instability that had marked her first marriage. Her traitorous body had best get on the same plane with her mind on this. She was frankly amazed the two were so far apart.

But wait . . . What if they weren't? She knew better

than most that the body oftentimes echoed the mind. Whatever malady plagued Gabriel ignited her curiosity; she could not deny it. She might simply be mistaking excitement from the challenge of his case with physical attraction.

Her body relaxed against him with relief. Yes. Yes, that must be it.

At least that's what she told herself all the way back to the manor.

The door to Vickering Place opened shortly after Gabriel stepped onto the main path. A servant rushed out with a large black umbrella, followed closely by Dunnings, one of the sanatorium's more gorilla-like attendants. Allen, Gabriel noted, stayed dry and warm, watching from just inside the doorway.

As the two parties met a few yards from the stairs, Gabriel pulled Penelope tighter to him. It had been an exquisite torture to carry her so close to him. The endless walk had felt as if he were in the second circle of Dante's hell, the one reserved for those souls who were overcome by lust, with his punishment being to carry the object of his desires for eternity without being able to have her.

Yet he'd be damned if he'd relinquish her to Dunnings.

His worry was for naught, however. "Need help with him?" Dunnings grunted to Carter with a narrow-eyed gaze at Gabriel. Carter shook his head in a quick negative.

Hell, had Dunnings assumed *he* was responsible for

what had befallen Penelope and was therefore a danger?

Gabriel let out a harsh breath and continued his trek up the stairs, slowing only enough so that the other servant was able to keep his umbrella over Penelope's head.

"Lady Manton tripped upon a root," he said as he gained the top step, just as Allen opened his mouth presumably to ask.

"I can speak for myself," Penelope scolded, for his ears only.

Gabriel shrugged, drawing a surprised "Oh!" from her as she rose and dropped with the movement, coming to settle more closely against his chest.

"I warned you that this excursion was ill advised," Allen said in his pinched nasally voice, giving them an equally disapproving look that lingered on the puddles they were dripping on the marble floor.

"Nonsense," Pen answered in a tone that quite impressed Gabriel. Not every lady could put a man in his place while in the ignoble position of being carried like a child by another man. "His lordship made excellent progress this morning. Had it not been for my unfortunate tumble, I would claim it a complete success."

Gabriel huffed. Oh, they'd made progress, all right. But not nearly as much as they were going to. If she thought he would let her continue to dodge his questions about Michael, she was crazier than he.

But first he had to get her dry and take a look at her calf.

"Lady Manton has injured her leg. I expect she will be unable to properly walk on it for a few days."

Penelope started in his arms. "Surely it's not all that bad."

"She will require a room here until she recovers."

This time, it was Allen who started. "That is *quite* impossible, my lord." He sniffed. "Vickering Place is not an inn."

Gabriel raised an imperious brow. "I am well aware of what Vickering Place is and is not. However, I am also aware funds are quite dear. I will, of course, cover the expense of her stay plus additional coin for the trouble." He was still Bromwich, after all. His family couldn't wrest control of the finances from him until the hearing, at least. "Have the best room made up for Lady Manton immediately."

"I hardly think—" Pen began.

"Now, see here—" Allen spouted at the same time.

Gabriel ignored them both, turning on his heel with Penelope still in his arms. "*Until* then," he said loudly enough to overpower their arguments as he strode for his rooms, "she shall wait in my parlor. Allen, go ahead of me and unlock the doors."

God, it felt good to be decisive again. Better than it had felt to be outside. He'd been so intent these past months on staving off his descent into madness that he'd lost a part of himself. Forfeited it to fear. He vowed not to let that happen again. No matter what the future brought, he would not forget who he was. Not while he had presence enough to remember.

Gabriel moved to the right of the hallway to let Allen

know he expected him to pass and do his bidding. After only a moment's hesitation, the man did, but not without continuing his protest.

"All of the rooms that might be suitable are occupied by other inmates," the director said as he fumbled with a large metal key, fitting it into the lock. He turned his wrist with a quick flick and the bars opened. "The best we could do would be to find Lady Manton a bed in the attics. *Hardly* befitting a lady of her station," he intoned.

Gabriel frowned as he carried Penelope over the threshold. That wouldn't do. He couldn't have Pen treated little better than a servant. "Unacceptable. She shall have to take my rooms, then."

"Your rooms?" Allen's black brows winged high. "And where would you sleep?"

"The attics, of course."

Allen's lips turned down into a disapproving frown. "I am sorry, my lord, but the attics are not properly secured for a man of your . . . condition."

Humiliation burned in his gut. "I have never had an episode right on top of another," he growled. "A few days in the attic should not be an issue."

Allen's face settled into an expression that was supposed to be sympathetic but fell short. "Nevertheless, I cannot allow it."

He said it in a placating tone—one used on children who demanded privileges they were not yet mature enough to handle. The smarmy prig. Allen clasped his hands in front of him in a show of subservience, but Gabriel knew the man enjoyed lording what authority he had over him.

Well, not anymore. He would no longer allow it. "Very well," he said tersely. "Have a cot brought into my parlor and I shall sleep there."

Allen opened his mouth, but Gabriel cut him off. "Have Carter stay here with me, if you must. But this discussion is at an end."

Allen had good sense enough to retreat. Having a marquess as a patient was quite a boon when trying to convince other well-paying peers to place *their* loved ones at Vickering Place. He wouldn't want to risk making Gabriel angry enough to demand his family move him to a different sanatorium, would he? The loss of income, not to mention prestige, would be a blow.

Gabriel dismissed the director with a command to bring tea and hot water, and to send for Penelope's things.

Pen held her tongue until Allen departed.

"I cannot stay here, Gabriel."

He looked down at her then. It was bad enough he'd had to argue with Allen over the matter. He was not about to fight it with her, too.

He lowered her gently to a standing position, his arms staying loosely around her for support, choosing not to address her statement. "Rest your weight on your good leg while we get you out of this cloak."

He shrugged off his own coat as she pursed her lips. But she complied. His blood was still boiling over his spat with Allen, but he fought not to let it show. He needed to be gentle with Penelope as he helped get her settled, as she must be quite tender after her fall.

Gabriel carefully removed her sodden cloak, circling

her as he tugged so she didn't have to move any more than necessary. His knuckles brushed against her shoulder, her forearm, her wrist. They skimmed along her back, every incidental touch soothing his anger and yet transforming his frustration into a different sort entirely.

He guided Penelope to a nearby chaise and helped her to sit, then moved a few paces away to put some distance between them. He shook her cloak, flinging the droplets of water that clung to the fur collar every which way. He imagined it was himself he was shaking, willing himself to let his impossible desire go.

"It's fortunate that you have an eye for quality," he remarked, trying to get his mind on anything but how the inside of the garment was still warm from her heat. How it smelled of her. "As soaked as your cloak is, your dress seems mostly dry. I feared we might have to raid a maid's closet until your bags arrive from the inn."

Penelope sighed, repeating her earlier declaration. "I cannot stay here."

Damn. It seemed he would have to fight her, after all. "You can, and you will," he commanded. "I'd wager you tore your muscle." He laid her cloak over the arm of a chair before dragging an ottoman over in front of her. "It will not heal properly if you go about walking on it. I've seen too many soldiers develop a permanent limp because they didn't have the luxury of staying off of their feet."

Pen looked down at her lap. Hell. His intention hadn't been to shame her into acceptance. Penelope, he was beginning to understand, had a keen appreciation for what soldiers had sacrificed to keep England safe and must hate even the implication that she was being ungrateful. Still, he was glad his words had worked.

He settled himself upon the tufted fabric of the ottoman, facing her, and scooted it back until there was just enough room between them that he would be able reach down and pull her calf into his lap to examine it.

When he looked up to tell her what he intended to do, the sight of her sitting so close arrested him. The moment held such intimacy . . . Christ, it was as if they were not Penelope and Gabriel. Not a widow and a lunatic. But instead, a simple husband and his wife, at home in their own parlor, settling in for a quiet afternoon in front of a toasty fire.

A swift ache of longing stole his breath.

He uttered a low curse. He'd thought he'd put aside dreams of her long ago. When he'd realized he was fit for no one, least of all someone as precious as Pen.

Her eyes widened, almost as if she could read his mind. But then her gaze darted away. She shifted in her seat, inching back as far on the chaise as she could get from him. "J-just the same. I cannot stay here. Not with you."

Her apparent fear was like a swift kick to his gut.

"Of course," he bit out, understanding dawning. "Even you are afraid of being locked in with the madman."

Chapter Six

"Your pretty words of progress were for Allen's benefit, weren't they?" Gabriel accused, his face tightening. Penelope had never seen an expression that was both so angry and desolate at the same time.

"*No*, of course not," she insisted. But why wouldn't he think that when she was acting like a scared child? Still, she couldn't tell him it was her own jumbled feelings she feared and not him.

Gabriel pushed away from the chaise. The wooden legs of the ottoman he'd been seated on screeched as he rose and turned his back on her. Several strides away, he came to a halt. He slid a hand through his closely shorn hair in an agitated swipe before fisting his fingers at the back of his neck, as if struggling to contain some fierce emotion.

Penelope wished she could see his face, so she'd know what he was thinking.

After a few heartbeats, he turned back to her, one corner of his mouth lifted in a self-deprecatory smile. "It's all right, Pen. I wouldn't wish to be locked in with me, either."

"Gabriel . . ." What a horrid person she was. A low, awful wretch. She was allowing him to heap coals upon his own head to save her pride. Perhaps that yew root had been a sign—and her tripping over it some sort of divine justice. After all, she'd been running away from him for her own self-preservation, completely ignoring what *he* needed. Which was more important?

Penelope chewed at her lower lip. If she insisted upon returning to the inn, Gabriel would forever believe that it was because she was afraid of him—no matter what she said to the contrary. Even if she returned at first light, damage would surely be done. She'd put all the progress they'd made at risk to save her own heart. She couldn't do that.

"Thank you."

His brow furrowed.

"For your rescue," she said simply, answering his unasked question. "For your kindness. For your chivalry."

A spot of color blotched his cheekbones, and his mouth pressed into a tight line.

"But you needn't forgo your own comfort for mine," she went on, her decision made. "I can certainly make do on the cot."

Gabriel relaxed when he realized she meant to stay. But an appalled expression quickly twisted his features. "You will do no such thing. You shall sleep in *my* bed."

His words sent heat licking traitorously through her middle. A vision of the two of them intertwined in tangling sheets scorched her imagination. And although Penelope knew he hadn't meant it *that* way, her whole body flushed just the same.

"O-only until I am well," she agreed. Opposing him was likely to do more harm than good. His back was already up over Allen's attempts to thwart him, and she didn't want Gabriel associating her with that man. No, she needed to be seen as an ally—or better yet, a trusted friend—if she were to help him find his way back to himself.

Which she intended to get back to doing immediately. She took in a deep breath and lifted her lips into a smile. "Well, now that we have that settled, do you feel up to discussing more about your time in the war?"

Wariness crept over Gabriel's face, his eyes clouding with it. Then he narrowed his gaze on her speculatively. "That depends," he said, "on whether *you* feel up to discussing my cousin."

Her smile died on her face.

Gabriel crossed the room in an instant, dragging the ottoman close to the chaise again. He dropped onto it and leaned toward her, his large hands gripping his knees. His fingers made puckering depressions in the wool of his breeches, and his knuckles whitened.

Sitting lame on the chaise, Penelope was well and

truly trapped. Gabriel was not going to relent—not until he got answers, she knew. Answers she wasn't prepared to give.

"Michael was my first cousin, Pen. Hell, our mothers were *twins*. Our blood may as well be that of brothers. If Michael *was* mad—" His voice cracked on the word. His throat worked, swallowing. "I have a right to know if this lunacy runs in my veins."

Her chest tightened and her breaths shortened as swirling emotions took the place of the air in her lungs. Grief. Shame. Anguish at the unfairness of it all. She could continue her refusal to discuss her husband. That was *her* right. But it would be wrong of her. Selfish. Gabriel *did* deserve to know what he might be up against.

She felt her chin tremble as she said, "Michael *was* ill, yes."

Gabriel rocked back ever so slightly, as if her confirmation of his fear had been a blow . . . one he'd expected maybe, but a blow still. "Then there is no hope for me," he said with a bleakness that chilled her.

"I don't believe that," she said fiercely. She didn't believe any person was hopeless. Even Michael could have been helped, could have been saved. If she would have been different, smarter, a better wife.

But she was not that same silly girl. And she *had* helped soldiers like Gabriel. It wasn't the same. "Everything you've described to me today, all of your symptoms, sound very much like what so many other soldiers have gone through. And recovered from, I might add."

His gaze pierced her. "And what you saw two days past?"

Penelope winced before she could check the gesture. Gabriel's episode had been awful. Nor could she explain it. Yet . . . "Your affliction is nothing like Michael's," she assured him. "What you are suffering may very well be rooted in your wartime experience—"

"Or it could be *madness*," he countered hotly, "exacerbated by battle fatigue. Christ, Pen. If the lunacy is in my blood—"

"We can't know that. Not until we treat the symptoms we can see. And what *I* see is a man scarred by the trauma of his past."

"Oh?" he scoffed, the word tinged with despair. "And what did you see when you looked at Michael?"

Penelope stopped breathing altogether, the swift slicing pain stealing even the will to draw air. The moment drew out until she had to inhale. But nothing eased the ache in her chest, as memories she'd fought so hard to cage flew free, battering her heart with angry wings.

She scrubbed her hands over her face and buried it in her palms.

Strong fingers encircled her wrists, firm but not forceful. His skin burned against hers as he tugged her trembling hands down to her lap.

"You have to tell me, Pen," he said, his eyes boring into hers. "You know that."

"Yes," she murmured. She did. Had to tell him all. She pulled her hands from his and tucked them into her middle. He let her go and straightened back onto the ottoman to give her some space.

Penelope closed her eyes for a moment, marshaling both her strength and her memories.

"I saw what everyone saw," she finally said, looking at Gabriel once more. "Charismatic, fun-loving Michael. So full of life and vitality. You remember what he was like." Bitterness crept over her. Not at her husband, but at her own naïveté. She'd seen only what she wanted to see, caught up in her own schoolgirl desires. She'd never looked beyond his handsome face and the excitement he'd roused in her. "I was struck blind by him."

Gabriel didn't say anything to that, just dipped his head slightly, inviting her to go on.

"Michael was everything I thought I wanted. Not only did he have the wealth and title that my family required I marry, but he was young and dashing and we even shared our love of painting—" She broke off. None of that mattered now. "I set my cap for him and married him before anyone knew what had happened. I thought I'd made the match of a lifetime." She huffed. "But I was a fool."

And that foolishness had cost them both terribly.

She shifted restlessly on the chaise. Curse her strained calf. She wanted to bound to her feet, to get away from Gabriel's regard. But she couldn't. She squeezed her hands together so tightly they burned.

"Only a few weeks into the marriage, I realized something was very wrong. Michael had always been an early riser and seemed to go to sleep only after . . . I did." Heat stained her cheeks, and she glanced away. The one place her marriage had never lacked was the bedroom. Michael had approached lovemaking with the same vigorous exuberance he had everything else in his life, leaving her breathless and exhausted more nights than not. He often had to have her twice or even three times before he would finally sleep.

"But then I noticed a flurry of new paintings in his studio and I realized he could only be working on them at night, when he should have been sleeping. He wasn't napping during the day to compensate, but neither did he seem lacking in energy. In fact, he was not acting much different from normal. Except I noticed an increase in his intensity. Minute at first, but it built quickly, and within days he would be practically vibrating with it."

Gabriel was frowning. "I remember something like that," he said. "Of course, I only saw it when we were young men about town, carousing our way through most nights. He could put our entire set to shame, go on for days. I used to envy him his stamina."

"Be glad you didn't have it," she said solemnly. "The price Michael paid was steep."

Gabriel tilted his head. "What do you mean?"

"Well, after weeks of subsisting on that inhuman energy, he inevitably crashed. And from the heights at which he flew . . ." She raised her shoulders in a slight shrug. "The devastation was awful," she whispered.

Gabriel's jaw flexed. "And is that when his madness would strike?" he asked. "Would he have episodes then, too?"

She knew he was trying to measure himself against Michael, looking for commonalities that would paint him with the same madness. She shook her head quickly. "No, no episodes—at least not like yours." She pressed her lips together, thinking how best to explain. "But yes, that was when his madness would strike. Well, part of it anyway."

Gabriel's brows furrowed.

She knew she wasn't making sense. She tried again. "You see, Michael's illness was one of extreme, intense exhilaration followed by horrid periods of despair. He—he exhibited different forms of mania at both ends of that pendulum.

"I didn't understand that, though. Not then. I only began to see how much of a problem we had when one day I awoke and he was just *gone.* He'd disappeared without so much as a note to me. I finally learned from the servants that he'd fled to Leeds just before sunrise, taking only his paints and his valet. At least, they assumed he'd gone to Leeds because that's where he'd always gone when he vanished without word."

"He left you in the night?"

"Yes." She remembered the shock. And then the anger at what she considered his utter disrespect toward her. She hadn't realized then that he'd been sick. Hadn't realized many things. "As I would come to learn, his behaviors had almost a cyclical pattern, repeating themselves—sometimes not as intense as the time before, sometimes much worse."

Gabriel's face lost a touch of color. "My episodes do the same."

"Repeat themselves, you mean?"

He nodded distractedly, his eyes darkening. "And vary in intensity."

She shook her head. "But you told me yourself that you'd never experienced high feelings like Michael's. I do not think you can compare the two."

He grunted, not sounding as though he believed her logic.

"And your episodes are over in a matter of hours," she pointed out. "Michael's, however, would last for days, sometimes weeks at a time."

That seemed to surprise him. "Weeks?"

"Yes. Both the highs *and* the lows. But I get ahead of myself," she said, feeling unusually tired. "At the time, I didn't know what to think of his behavior. I just knew I was not going to stand for it. So I followed him, posthaste. He was thrilled to see me when I arrived. In fact, he acted as if nothing were amiss, proclaiming me the most beautiful sight he'd ever beheld, even travel worn and spitting mad as I was."

She remembered her utter confusion, how at a loss she'd felt. How was one supposed to manage a husband whose actions seemed unreasonable? Particularly when he did not see the situation the same?

"He apologized profusely. Said he must not be accustomed to this husband business yet. He told me he was used to running off to the country when his creativity peaked because he painted better there. Then he begged me to forgive him. He promised not to do it again, and I believed him. I loved him so." She'd been so innocent then.

"But what I didn't know was that he was in the middle of one of his high cycles. I told myself he'd simply exhausted himself with his art, and that a nice rest in the country had been precisely what he needed." She sighed. "But deep down, I think I knew something was wrong. I started paying closer attention. Michael still wasn't sleeping much, though now he took pains to hide it from me. And his personality shifted."

"Shifted?" Gabriel watched her closely. "How?"

"It's hard to explain. Michael was always confident and charismatic, but all of a sudden it was like he was . . . more. More gregarious. More energetic. It was like his mind suddenly overflowed with ideas. He started new canvases only to throw them out half finished because he'd thought of something better. He talked too fast, drank too much, but he was so *happy*. Until he wasn't."

She hated remembering this part. The day that had shattered her dreams of her marriage. "One afternoon, Michael hadn't come down for luncheon or tea, so I decided to bring him some refreshment. I thought perhaps he'd gotten lost in his art and had forgotten the time.

"I went upstairs to the nursery, which he'd made over as his studio while we were in London. He was pacing in front of the bank of windows. The sun streamed in, bright and golden—which was why he'd chosen that room for his painting, of course. Michael's profile was limned in the shimmering light. He was so beautiful, I caught my breath, and for a moment I remember thinking he looked very like the archangel he was named after."

She closed her eyes, remembering. "But then I noticed that his hair was disheveled, as if he'd been tugging at it. Also, his easel lay toppled on the floor and paint had been flung all about.

"I'd barely spoken his name when he turned such a fierce glare upon me that I froze still. I just stood there, like a statue." She huffed. "*Englishwoman Bearing Tray*, carved from granite and marble."

She opened her eyes and sought Gabriel's. His were fixed on her with rapt attention. She latched on to the strength in his gaze, and oddly enough, it seemed to help her get the rest of the story out.

"But then he flung a paintbrush at me. I still remember the shock, standing there looking dumbly at the garish splotch of red paint soaking into my favorite lavender morning gown. It sort of melted into the fabric, bleeding into a red violet . . . I might have stood like that for hours had another brush not come whizzing past my head. When the third brush came, I dropped the tray and threw my hands up to protect my face."

Her voice didn't sound like her own as she spoke. She was distancing her emotions from the conversation, she knew. And Gabriel, bless him, was just listening. Letting her speak at her own pace, even though she could see he was bursting with questions.

"Everything shattered," she said. "Broken china littered the floor about my feet as hot tea soaked into my slippers. Michael was shouting at me. Angry words, mostly. Nonsense. He demanded to know who I thought I was to disturb him. Accused me of thwarting his work, of distracting him, of trying to make him weak. He kept screaming that I could never understand his genius."

Her voice rose in agitation with every remembered indictment, despite her best intentions. Her arms ached with how tightly she held herself. "All the while, he hurled supplies at me. I—I tried to defend myself with words, but he would hear nothing I said. So I fled. I threw a cloak over my stained clothes, pulled the hood up to hide my face and ran from the house."

She could still feel the cold bite of winter wind, even after all of this time. "But there was really nowhere I could go. I didn't wish my family to know how Michael was. Certainly not our friends. So I just walked. For hours. Until I was too exhausted to go on."

Gabriel listened, jaw clenched tight.

She took a few shaky breaths, fighting to stave off the emotions roiling through her at the memories. When she spoke again, she was grateful her voice did not betray the tumult within.

"The house was quiet when I arrived home. Only our butler greeted me at the top step. Michael had locked himself in our chamber shortly after I'd left and had barred anyone from entering aside from his valet. I didn't know what to do. I may have been Michael's wife, but I'd been in the household for only a matter of weeks. And I was still reeling, so I chose the cowardly way out and went to a guest chamber for the night."

Gabriel finally broke his silence. "You weren't a coward, Pen. You were all of twenty."

She shook her head, discounting his sympathy. Perhaps she'd have deserved it at the time, but certainly not by the end of her marriage. Certainly not now.

"I didn't sleep a wink that night. Michael, however,

slept for three days. The next morning, I'd gathered my wits. I demanded to be let into our rooms to confront Michael, but he slept so deeply it was like watching the dead. I imagine his body simply shut down after so many weeks going without enough sleep. His valet and I forced at least water down his throat at regular intervals, but that was all he would rouse for. And when Michael did finally wake, he was a different man."

Gabriel had gone white. "Did he remember afterward?" he asked quietly.

He was thinking of his own episodes, she imagined. She knew he'd been told of his own erratic behavior, of smashing water pitchers and slinging insults. But she'd witnessed one of Gabriel's episodes and had spoken with both Allen and Gabriel's mother about his others. He'd clearly been delusional. Michael had been cruel. Intentionally cruel. So wrapped up in himself that anyone and everyone was beneath him. At least when he was at his highest.

And when he was at his lowest . . .

"Yes," she said. "He remembered everything, and the knowledge tore him apart. He dissolved into tears, apologizing to me and clinging to my skirts. It broke my heart, but it was clear something was horribly wrong with him. For the next several days, Michael refused to come out of our rooms. He was sluggish. His eyes were dull. His spirits had sunken so low . . . He wouldn't eat. Wouldn't paint. Wouldn't even talk to me, not about anything of importance—and there was nothing I could do for him."

She released her hold on herself and returned her hands to her lap then. She still remembered the sense of surreal bemusement at what had happened next. "And then one morning when I went downstairs, he was in the breakfast room, polishing off a plate of kedgeree," she said, turning her palms up in imitation of a helpless shrug. "He *grinned* at me as I stood slack jawed and staring. He rose from the table, crossed to where I was and chucked me under the chin, of all things. Then he gave me the sweetest kiss." She closed her eyes. "And just like that, he was back to his old self. The man I'd met and married."

She blinked several times, no longer able to hold off the tears. "I was so relieved to have him back," she said, shaking her head slightly. "I can't tell you how much. I begged him to see a doctor, but he brushed off my concerns. He said he'd just gotten too immersed in his painting and hadn't taken good enough care of himself, and he promised he would be more vigilant with his health. I vowed to myself to make certain he did, that I would be a good wife, would see to his needs."

She straightened then, her hands balling into fists on her lap. "But I failed. There were a few peaceful weeks, until one night, an awful storm woke me. I immediately noticed Michael was gone from our bed. I found him in his studio, of course. He said the thunder had woken him and he hadn't been able to go back to sleep, and he allowed me to coax him back to our room. He assured me everything was fine. But I became anxious and started watching him more closely. And I saw it—bit by bit, day by day, his personality took on an edge. Subtly, at first, but I knew it was building toward something.

"I developed an edge of my own. A nervousness twisted inside me, screwing another turn every day. Anytime I expressed concern, Michael dismissed it. To our family and friends, he seemed as gregariously Michael as ever."

Gabriel nodded, obviously recalling that time in his mind. "I never noticed anything wrong with him."

"I did. I knew he was off, even though I couldn't seem to make an argument for any one thing that would prove it. He had an explanation for everything I could voice. We fought constantly, me pressing him to seek help, him insisting I'd become an overbearing nag." She huffed a bitter laugh. "And I was. I felt helpless and confused, alternating between hounding him and leaving him to his own devices. But no matter which tactic I employed, the cycle would start again."

She shook her head, the frustration still fresh, even after two years. "It was horrid, living that way, like I *knew* I was perpetually walking along the precipice of a cliff, but I couldn't see the edge. I was just certain it was there and that if I made the tiniest misstep, I would fall to my death. I began to tread lightly in my own house. And it went on this way for months."

She stared at him then, her eyes wide as she implored him to understand what she must tell him next. "And then one morning, after a particularly nasty row, Michael was gone again. I knew it the moment I woke up. It was like waking in an entirely different house. A weight was missing from my shoulders."

She broke off, swallowing hard. "He'd gone to Leeds again. He'd left a note, at least. But I refused to follow him that time. I—" Her voice cracked then, and fresh tears slipped down her cheeks. "I was relieved he was gone," she whispered, confessing one of her great sins.

Gabriel was watching her closely. She knew he must realize she meant Michael's final trip to Leeds. The one he'd never come back from. "But—you were there when Michael had his accident."

She kept her eyes on his as fresh tears spilled hot onto her cheeks. "No. You see, I refused to get caught up in his cycle again, so I lingered in London a few days. A sort of protest. But I didn't want to give up on Michael. I so desperately wanted him to get help. I made a plan to confront him and force his hand, and then I set off for the country once again." She looked down at her lap and forced the words out. "But I was too late."

She heard Gabriel's swift intake of breath, knew he understood the secret she'd been carrying for so long.

"Michael's death was no accident, was it?" he whispered.

She looked up at him. Let him see the truth in her eyes.

"My God," Gabriel said. "My cousin killed himself."

Chapter Seven

*S*uicide.

Gabriel knew he still sat solidly on the ottoman, yet it seemed as if the floor were falling away beneath him. He grabbed on to the sides of the stool for support, the leather cool and slick beneath his sweating palms.

Christ. Why would his cousin purposefully take his own life? Michael had everything: wealth, title, talent, a broad set of friends and acquaintances. Gabriel's eyes strayed to Penelope's tear-streaked face. A perfect wife . . .

Only madness could have driven Michael to such an extreme.

Gabriel's chest squeezed as he accepted the truth. The pain was swift and slicing. He hadn't realized until this moment what Penelope's coming here had given him—a tiny sprout of hope that he wasn't mad, that he could be cured. The idea that she might truly be able to help him recover himself had rooted inside him without his even knowing it. But now that burgeoning sprig of optimism shriveled as if it had been watered with blood—*his* blood, poisoned by the madness within.

He closed his eyes as fear turned his insides cold. Would his madness eventually drive him to such a desperate place that he might do the same as Michael had done?

Everything in Gabriel vehemently shouted no, but his fun-loving cousin was the last person he would expect to do such a thing.

And God knew *his* rational mind absented itself during his episodes, to the point where he had no memory of them even. It took but a moment to take a life, as he well knew. What was to keep him from the same fate?

"We were told Michael's death was an accident," he croaked, part of him still refusing to believe. "Are you certain—"

"He left a note," she said quietly. "But even if he hadn't, by the way I found him—" Pen's eyes closed, squeezed tight against whatever she was seeing in her mind's eye. Gabriel could practically see her force the thoughts away as her face smoothed into a blank mask. When she opened her eyes again, all emotion was gone from them. "There is no doubt."

She'd found her husband dead by his own hand. God. Gabriel shook his head, unable to grasp the horror of it all.

"When I arrived in Leeds, Michael wasn't at the

house. I was told he'd gone out onto the estate alone, early that morning. The staff didn't seem concerned. Apparently he often did that, particularly when he was in one of his creative flurries. So I unpacked my things and sorted a few household issues, but as supper approached and he still hadn't returned, I decided to go looking for him.

"His valet insisted on accompanying me, but I refused, thank God. I'd worked myself up, you see, to confront him about his illness, and I wanted to do that in private.

"By the time I found him at his hunting box, it was near nightfall. I remember my stomach was in knots, both relieved to have found his horse tied outside and anxious about the confrontation to come. I stood on the stoop for what seemed like hours, marshaling my courage, but when I walked inside—" She shook her head stiffly. "Well, it was evident he'd been dead for some time—likely all day."

Gabriel's stomach rolled—not because of the details she'd shared, but because of the knowledge that Pen had come upon such a scene alone. As a soldier, he'd seen death come in many horrifying forms, and he knew firsthand what damage a gunshot could do. It was awful to see under any circumstances. But at least war was some justification for ugly death. How much worse must it have been for Pen to witness, knowing that Michael had chosen to inflict it upon himself when he had everything to live for? And Penelope had been carrying this around with her since that day?

"I don't know how long it took me to come to my

senses," she said, "but I do remember the coldness that slid over me. How my body seemed to move of its own accord. I cleaned things up as best I could. I arranged certain items to make it seem as if he'd had an accident whilst cleaning his hunting rifle. I couldn't"—Pen swallowed then, and he knew she was not as calm as she wanted him to believe she was—"couldn't let Michael's memory, or your family, be shamed. Only after I finished did I return to the house for help."

Gabriel could sit there no longer. He shot to his feet and walked a few feet away, settling into an agitated pace—grateful she couldn't follow. What hell she had been through because of her husband's madness. And she'd covered it up out of loyalty and love.

So many things made sense now. No wonder she'd cut him out of her life after Michael's death. Though he was dark where Michael was fair, the resemblance between them was well noted. And even if his very countenance didn't remind her of her dead husband, her memories would have. Any that had him in them also had Michael, if not present then implied. Gabriel was surprised she'd ever been able to be in the same room with him again.

"What are you thinking?" she asked warily.

Gabriel shook his head, unable—or unwilling—to voice the turmoil within. So many feelings, so many fears, so many questions. Why on earth was she here now? Why was she trying to help *him*? After what had happened with Michael, why would she invite this madness into her life again?

"I know this must upset you—"

He nearly snorted. That was like saying Waterloo had been a skirmish.

"—but I am here to help. Won't you come back over here and sit? We can talk it through."

He stopped pacing and turned back to her. God, she was beautiful. She'd wiped her tears away, but her green eyes shone bright in their aftermath. Strong, resilient Pen—offering to comfort him after all she'd been through.

He would *not* put her through any more of it. The fact that Michael had been mad upped the likelihood that he would eventually descend into madness, too. Penelope had witnessed more than her fair share of that. "No, Pen. I think you've had enough."

She pressed her lips together, but did not press him further. "All right," she said, and he could hear grateful exhaustion in her voice. "Later, then," she acquiesced, misunderstanding his meaning.

"No."

She blinked up at him, her lips turning down into a frown.

"I am humbled that you came here," he said, the scratching in his throat making his voice hoarse. "I realize now what it must have cost you."

She opened her mouth to argue, but he didn't allow it.

"And I believe in you, Pen. Believe in what you are doing. I find it commendable—inspiring even—that you've chosen to treat battle fatigue in *otherwise healthy* soldiers. But I am *not* whole, Pen. And I can't allow you to stay around me any longer."

Her chin firmed, even as hurt flickered over her lovely face. But he could not relent, for her sake.

"Once your leg is healed, I want you to leave Vickering Place for good."

Sleep refused to rescue Gabriel from his thoughts. Not that any person of normal hearing would be able to rest, what with Carter's god-awful snores reverberating through the darkened parlor. Although he'd heard the attendant grumble that he wouldn't be able to sleep a wink while locked in with a madman, Carter now slumped in an armchair situated very near the closed bedroom door, drool dangling from one side of his mouth.

Gabriel looked at the door for the thousandth time since Pen had retired. Pale moonlight now glinted off of the brass knob. Was she sleeping peacefully just beyond? Gabriel thought it highly unlikely. And not simply because he doubted the wood's ability to muffle the buzz of Carter's sawing.

Gabriel shifted uncomfortably on his makeshift bed. Penelope had argued fiercely at his dictate, but he'd held firm, and finally she'd given up. Not given *in*. He recognized the difference. Not once had she agreed to leave. No, she might have been exhausted when she'd bid him good night, her green eyes swimming with frustration, but he had no doubt she was lying in his bed, plotting her argument for tomorrow.

He shut his eyes again, willing his mind to quiet so that he could rest. He'd need his strength to withstand her.

A pained cry brought him bolting upright. His heart pounded in his ears as he blinked, disoriented. He listened for a long moment, but all he heard was Carter's arrhythmic snoring. His body relaxed. He must have nodded off and dreamt the noise. God knew he'd relived the pain and misery of the battlefields many a night.

Gabriel lay back once more, the air chill against his skin. And then the cry came again—definitely from the bedroom. *Pen.*

He was to the door in seconds, his hand turning the knob. He glanced down in alarm as it made an awful squeaking, but Carter didn't stir. Gabriel wasn't surprised. The man slept like the dead or he'd have woken himself up ten times over. Still, he slipped into the bedroom and shut the door quietly behind him. The last thing he wanted was to have to put up with the ill-tempered lout should he rouse.

"Pen?" Gabriel whispered into the dark room.

She cried out again, startling him. He rushed over to the four-poster and jerked the curtain aside, eyes scanning her as well as they could in the blackness. Pen tossed her head back and forth on the pillow, wincing in pain, though she didn't appear to be awake.

Her calf must be spasming. Sometimes healing muscle did that, particularly at night, when it was most relaxed. He dragged one side of the drapes wide, then ran his palms down her leg until he found her calf. His hands dove under the coverlet, his fingers seeking the knotting muscle as he began to rub.

And yet . . . her calf didn't bunch beneath his touch as it had this afternoon. Why had she cried out, then?

A tiny whimper reached his ear, but it wasn't pain he heard in it—it was fear. He knew it. Recognized it from his own experiences. She was having a nightmare.

He let go of her leg and returned to the head of the bed. His vision had adjusted to the darkness just enough to see that she slept still, even as tears leaked from the sides of her closed eyes.

Gabriel wiped his fingers gently across her forehead. Her skin was cool to the touch, clammy even. Empathy filled his heart. He knew the horror of dreams all too well.

"Shhh, Pen." He gently caressed her face, past her cheekbone to her jaw. When he reached her chin, he stopped, moving his hand back to her brow to start the soothing trek again.

She instinctively pressed into his touch in her sleep, as if seeking comfort.

Well, he might no longer be fit for much, but that was the one thing he could offer her—at least for to-night. Gabriel bent and slipped his arms beneath her shoulders and knees. He lifted Pen and cradled her on his lap as he settled himself on the bed. She burrowed into the warmth of his chest, as if seeking shelter— shelter he was only too glad to give, as he was certain her bad dreams could be laid at his feet.

If he hadn't pressed her about Michael, she'd probably be sleeping like a babe.

But he couldn't take today back. Wasn't even certain

he would if he could. Knowledge was power, as they said. He wasn't certain what he would do with the truth that his madness very well could be inherited and therefore possibly not within his control. But what he *could* do, tonight, was stay with Penelope so that she wasn't alone in her nightmares, even if she never knew he was here.

As he held her close, he gave in to the temptation to stroke her hair. He loved the texture of her riotous curls. They weren't exactly soft, but they slid nicely over his skin. And after his fingers threaded through them, they bounced back into place, stubborn and re-silient. Like Pen herself.

God, she felt right in his arms. He couldn't deny that thought any more than he could stanch the longing that welled up in him.

Her chest hitched and she nestled closer, one of her arms slipping up to weave itself around his neck. As her chin tucked into the notch of his collarbone, her warm breath brushed rhythmically against his skin, sending jolts of heat through him.

Gabriel stiffened all over. God, even in her sleep, Pen could make him harder than the walnut headboard at his back.

He shouldn't be here. It was both heaven and hell to have her in his arms. But he couldn't bring himself to leave, either. So he closed his eyes and just held her, as he'd imagined doing so many nights before. The dark-ness surrounding them only opened his senses further. His skin tingled where her sleep-warmed body molded itself into his. Her sugary citrus scent mixed with the fresh smell of rainwater that had dried in her hair, making him wish he could breathe her in for eternity.

Gabriel shifted and opened his eyes. He decided to stare up at the canopy—he couldn't look at Pen or he'd never be able to resist the temptation of dropping his lips to hers and tasting her sweetness.

Rein it in, man, he scolded himself. He was just here to comfort her, to reassure her while she slept. Nothing more. He lay there and tried desperately to think of anything but what it might be like to have her, but it didn't work. His heart beat harder and his breath came faster with each passing moment.

Then he noticed that Pen's breathing matched his own. He had but a moment to ponder that when she cried out, "No!"

She came awake with a sob. It seemed to catch in her throat, becoming a hiccupping breath instead.

He reflexively tightened his arms around her and she shrieked.

"Shh, Pen. It is I."

"Gabriel?" she said, blinking against the darkness—whereas his eyes had long adjusted. Her expression was both stricken and disoriented as she tipped her face up to his.

"Yes," he murmured, stroking her hair once more.

It took a few seconds for his answer to sink in, but then she whispered, "Oh, thank God!"

Gabriel's heart tripped as Pen wriggled in his lap. The arm that had been tucked between them snaked up to join her other around his neck as she pulled herself face-to-face with him. He groaned as her hip brushed against his hardness, but she didn't seem to notice as she moved to her knees between his legs and framed his head between her hands.

His breath caught and he was unable to move, unable to tear his gaze from hers as her eyes roamed over his features—almost . . . hungrily?

"Thank God," she murmured again, and even in the darkness, he would have sworn that her gaze dropped to his mouth.

And he knew he wouldn't be able to take another breath without kissing her. Without knowing once and for all the bliss he'd craved for so long.

He leaned forward at the same moment she did, and a strange heat flared between them, spiraling up thei—

A god-awful snore rent the air, barely muffled by the bedroom door. It was followed by a series of painful-sounding snuffs.

Pen jerked in his arms. Hell, he startled too, crushing her to his chest protectively as his heart pounded a frantic beat.

Penelope stiffened a scant second before she pushed herself away from him. Her eyes wide now, she scrambled off of his lap, sliding to the floor in a fluid move.

"Oh! Ow, ow, ow," she whispered harshly as she landed on her sore calf.

Gabriel slid to the edge of the bed and planted his feet on the floor as Pen hopped away from him on one leg, like a hare that had escaped a hunter's trap with its life but without the use of one of its lucky back feet.

Damn it all. What kind of bounder was he? He had no place—no place at all—even *contemplating* what he'd almost just done. But good Christ, the way she'd looked at him. The way she'd murmured her thanksgiving that he was there, almost as if she were grateful to find him in her bed . . . He'd been unable to think at all.

Pen shot him a wary glance over her shoulder as she reached the vanity. She snatched a robe from atop it and donned it around her serviceable night rail. When she finally turned back to face him with a wobbly, one-footed pivot, she crossed her arms over her chest as if to add another barrier between her person and his inappropriate advances.

"What are you doing here?" she asked, keeping her voice low.

"You cried out," he explained as he raked a hand through his hair, still trying to get the burning need that had yet to leave his blood under control. "More than once," he added defensively. "I came in to make certain you were all right."

She didn't say anything to that. Nor did she question how his checking on her had turned into crawling into her bed and cradling her while she slept—and had almost led to a disastrous mistake, as that near kiss surely would have been for both of them.

Instead she took in a breath and nodded.

He stood slowly, not wishing to make her any more nervous than she was. "You shouldn't be stressing your calf like that," he said as he advanced carefully. "Won't you let me help you back into your bed?"

She shifted on her feet instinctively and winced at the pain.

"Come, Pen. I promise I won't bite," he coaxed as he

reached her. He smiled when she allowed him to slip a supportive arm around her shoulders. "Though apparently I *will* attempt to steal kisses from you while you are sleep drugged and vulnerable," he teased as he helped her cross to the bed once more.

She huffed a laugh and relaxed against him, for which he was immensely grateful.

They didn't speak as he helped her back into the center of the bed and propped pillows behind her back. When she was comfortable, he stepped back and stood there, feeling both awkward and tense.

"Thank you," she said. "Again."

He shook his head. "Was it a nightmare?"

She nodded, and regret swamped him. "You dreamt about Michael, didn't you? About finding him. God, I'm sorry, Pen," he whispered, his voice gone to gravel. He felt as if his gut was full of the pulverized stone as well. "It is my fault. If I hadn't made you dredge up the past—"

"No," she said forcefully. "You had a right to know."

But that didn't make him feel any less of an ogre.

"I—" She swallowed, audible in the quiet darkness. "I *did* dream about that night, but it wasn't Michael's lifeless body I found in that hunting lodge. It was yours."

Gabriel's breath caught.

"It was you lying there. You who'd taken your own life." Her voice cracked, and he wished he could better see her face. "*All because I failed you*," came her desperate whisper.

"Oh, Pen," he murmured. He couldn't stand there

beside her and let her suffer alone, no matter that it would be foolish to take her into his arms again. He moved to the bed and sat half on it, leaving one leg to brace himself on the floor. Then he pulled her into his side, relaxing into her when she did not resist. "You could never fail me."

She didn't respond—only trembled against him, her dream probably still very fresh in her mind's eye. So *that's* why she'd been so glad to see him when she'd woken, why she'd scanned his face as if she'd been afraid she would never see it again. He'd mistaken her look for one of desire, but it had simply been one of immense relief.

Christ. Pen was a nurturing soul, having always taken people under her wing. He'd seen it from the way she'd treated her servants to the way she always made a point to publicly praise those of lesser social stature than herself in the ballrooms of society.

And now she felt responsible for him, so much so that he was haunting her dreams.

"No matter what becomes of me, it would never be your fault, Pen."

She sniffed against his nightshirt but did not agree.

"It wouldn't," he reiterated, not liking the listless way she slumped in his arms. He tried to lighten the moment. "Admittedly, you can drive a man to distraction, but if lunacy runs in my family, then I was mad *long* before you met me."

"That's not funny, Gabriel," she murmured quietly.

Hell. None of this was. "Pen, your being here these past days hasn't done me any harm. You've *helped* me.

You've given me some hope. You've reminded me of who I am."

She lifted her head from his chest, tipping her face to his. "Then why are you trying to force me away?"

For your own good, damn it!

But was it? He'd never seen Pen so fragile as he had today. Forcing her to talk about Michael's death, when it had been clear she didn't wish it—hell, she'd practically maimed herself trying to outrun the conversation—had tilled up her worst memories. And now he'd become part of them, tied in her mind.

If he sent her away now and the worst happened, would she always blame herself?

He thought about the burdens he carried from the war. Guilt crippled him at times, from decisions he *knew* he'd had no choice but to have made. But knowing and *believing* were two completely different animals in the dark, when the dreams came.

He couldn't send her away. Not now. It wasn't as if he'd deteriorate into complete lunacy overnight. He'd let her stay—just until he could convince her that he was not her responsibility.

He closed his eyes, thinking this might possibly be the worst decision he'd ever come to. When he opened them again, he stared down into her face, so close to his own. So very close.

"All right, Pen. You win. But you must promise me that if your methods don't succeed, you will not blame yourself."

Her tongue darted out to wet her lips; then she said,

"I promise." But they both knew one couldn't promise such things. She couldn't even hold his gaze—laying her cheek against his chest again instead.

He dropped his chin and rested it atop her head. Misgivings, uncertainties and worries whirled through his mind—he wouldn't sleep a wink, he knew. Would Penelope? Or would her nightmares plague her through the night?

"You should try to sleep," he murmured. "I will stay with you awhile."

"That wouldn't be proper—"

"I'll leave before sunrise," he said, loath to let her go. "It's just, well, when I first returned to England, I dreamt of the war almost every night. There were times the images were so vivid that I refused to go back to sleep for fear of having to relive it all over again."

She shivered in his arms, and he suspected she knew exactly what he meant.

"I think it would have been easier had I not been alone." He shifted on the bed, adjusting her smoothly as he swung his other leg up and then settled them both, with her cradled beside him. "Let me stay here with you, just until I am sure you are sleeping peacefully. It is the least I can do since I am the one who brought this all back up in your heart. It is my fault you had such horrid dreams."

For a long moment, he thought she'd deny him. But then she nodded and tucked her head into the crook of his arm.

They lay there like that for long, quiet moments. Penelope seemed to relax more and more, sinking into him, as if the contours of their bodies were made for each other . . . filling him with bone-deep contentment.

But as she drifted off to sleep, he heard her murmur, "No, Gabriel. The fault is my own."

Chapter Eight

Penelope woke surrounded by the enticing mixture of sandalwood and sage.

Gabriel.

Memories flooded in like the sunlight that streamed through the windows of the bedchamber. She glanced to her side, but true to his word, Gabriel had gone. The pillow next to hers still bore the imprint of his head, however, and she stared at that spot for long moments.

It had been nearly two years since she'd shared a bed with a man. And never had she spent a night in someone's arms simply for the comfort they offered. Michael's nighttime visits had been for lovemaking—after which he would drop off to sleep with his back to her or slip out to his studio.

An odd sensation swelled in her chest, disconcerting and unnerving. Though nothing untoward had happened between her and Gabriel last night, those few hours in his arms seemed more intimate to her than any she'd ever spent.

She'd told him everything—well, almost everything. She waited for the stomach-clenching regret to come, but strangely, it didn't. It had been painful talking about Michael and his death, but she actually felt lighter in her heart than she had yesterday. Maybe because she hadn't sensed any indictment coming from Gabriel.

Of course, he didn't know the whole truth. No one did—not even Liliana, though her cousin had dragged some of the story out of her.

But there was no reason anyone would ever need to know the rest. She vowed she wouldn't make the same mistakes with Gabriel as she had with Michael. She was much wiser now—at least more learned. She hoped that was enough.

Penelope rose quickly, anxious to pick up where they had left off in Gabriel's treatment before he changed his mind about letting her stay. It had been a close thing, and he'd capitulated only grudgingly. She meant to prove that he'd made the right choice.

After a quick toilette—slowed by only a minimal amount of limping, she was happy to note—Penelope was ready to join Gabriel in the parlor. Anticipation fluttered in her middle at seeing Gabriel in the light of day after spending the night cradled in his arms, innocent though it had been.

Not quite innocent, her mind whispered. All right, so her thoughts *may* have drifted to the carnal a time or two as she'd lain against his muscular contours. And when she'd fallen asleep the last time, Gabriel had once again been the focus of her dreams. But this time he'd been very *much* alive and very much—

Heat stained her cheeks as she pushed open the door that separated the bedchamber from the rest of the suite. The distinctive scent of smoked bacon greeted her nose, as did the yeasty aroma of hot rolls and a glorious whiff of strong English tea. Penelope's stomach rumbled, pushing aside any lingering embarrassment. Besides, she was actually looking forward to spending the morning with Gabriel, she realized. More than she would have expected.

Until she saw who else was sitting at the table.

Both men rose when they saw her, Gabriel—looking well in light pantaloons contrasted with a waistcoat of bottle green paired with a coat the same golden brown as his eyes—and Mr. Allen, somber in serviceable black, like her.

Still, she hoped she never looked as pinched and forbidding as the director of Vickering Place did right now.

Gabriel smiled in greeting—a welcoming smile, if a bit strained. "Good morning, Lady Manton. I trust you slept well."

"I did, thank you," she replied with a sweet smile of her own. He knew she'd slept well, as he had been the reason. When he'd offered to stay with her in case the nightmare returned, she'd been sure she'd never be able to sleep again. But she'd drifted off in the safety of his arms and hadn't woken again until bright sunlight forced the issue.

"And how is your leg this morning?" he inquired politely—and a little stiffly, due to Mr. Allen's presence, no doubt.

"Better than I expected," she answered, carefully making her way toward the table to join them. "Given how much it hurt yesterday. There is little pain this morning, more of an aching heaviness."

"Then you should be able to return to the inn this evening, I expect," Mr. Allen said. The words were polite, but something about his tone set Penelope's teeth on edge. He seemed more than pleased with the prospect of her leaving them.

"Oh, not quite yet," she demurred, and embellished her limp a smidge as she crossed the rest of the distance. "Pain is still pain, and I wouldn't like to risk permanent injury." What she *truly* didn't like was the idea of Mr. Allen trying to get rid of her. She glanced at Gabriel. "That is, if Lord Bromwich is amenable to another night or two on a cot."

"Of course," came Gabriel's staunch reply.

She took the seat held out for her by a servant and smoothed the linen napkin on her lap as the men settled themselves just after her.

Breakfast was an awkward affair, her delight in the well-prepared fare dimmed by the stiff silence of the diners. Gabriel shot speculative looks at Mr. Allen over his plate, whereas the director shot similar glances at her—with a bit of what she suspected was condescension tossed in. Only a few bites in, Penelope lost her appetite altogether.

She couldn't contain a small sigh of relief as the painful meal came to an end. "Well," she said, injecting a brightness she didn't feel into her voice as she stood, "that was lovely. I am certain you have a full day ahead of you, Mr. Allen. Overseeing Vickering Place is quite a task, I'm sure. Lord Bromwich and I have a full day ahead, as well—and I'd like to get started immediately."

"Excellent," Mr. Allen intoned, dabbing at the corner of his mouth before discarding his soiled napkin. "As I intend to spend the day with you, observing your *methods* for myself."

Unease and irritation warred for supremacy in her middle. Mr. Allen sitting in with them? What sort of progress could she expect Gabriel to make if they could not talk alone?

"While I'd be happy to engage in a theoretical discourse regarding my methodology, my style of treatment requires a good amount of deeply personal discussion, of the type I am certain Lord Bromwich would like to remain private."

If possible, Mr. Allen's face grew even more pinched. "Nevertheless, *I* am the director of Vickering Place, and Lord Bromwich is under *my* care. I appreciate that his family has asked for you to see him, but if you wish to continue, you will do so under my conditions."

"Allen," Gabriel growled.

"No," she interjected as she noticed Dunnings, Carter's beefier and more foreboding counterpart, stand more alert at his post in the corner. The stoic attendant added a hint of menace to the gathering that she didn't care for, particularly when she saw him fist one hand at his side.

"If that is what you wish, Mr. Allen, I will be happy to have you join us," she lied. Perhaps he would get bored soon and go back to his responsibilities elsewhere.

When the three of them were seated—she on the chaise, Gabriel and Mr. Allen in opposing wingbacks—Penelope cleared her throat. "Well, as we discussed yesterday, Lord Bromwich," she began, sending a what-else-can-we-do smile at Gabriel, "I believe much—if not all—of your condition may have its roots in battle fatigue—"

Mr. Allen made a scoffing noise in his throat. "*That* is your supposition? Lord Bromwich suffers from mania, Lady Manton. Or have you forgotten how you found him when you first arrived?"

The flush of anger made her cheeks hot. "Of course I haven't forgotten. However, aside from his episode, he has been completely lucid."

"Many lunatics have lucid moments," Mr. Allen countered coolly.

"Moments, yes. But I've never heard of one who is lucid most of the time. There is normally some hint of instability in between bouts, of which I've seen no evidence," she shot back.

"You are hardly the expert."

"*Enough*, Allen," Gabriel warned while Penelope bit down on a sharp reply. She held up a staying hand in his direction. She could handle Mr. Allen on her own.

She pasted a calm smile on her face and trained her gaze on the director. "Perhaps not. However, I have studied maladies of the mind quite extensively, and

I've never seen a case like his. What I have seen, however, is evidence that cruel treatment has been shown to make a patient's condition worse, rather than better. Looking through Lord Bromwich's records, I notice you've advocated several horrifically painful procedures for him. Bleeding, cupping, purging, blistering—"

"All perfectly acceptable forms of treatment for lunatics," Mr. Allen said, his eyes narrowing on her.

"All antiquated and barbaric."

He sniffed in a very what-does-a-lady-like-you-know-about-it way and said, "All treatments good enough for our king."

"Who was never cured and *died* of his madness," she retorted, which earned her an angry glare from Mr. Allen.

Penelope would never believe that many of the treatments inflicted on those who suffered from lunacy were appropriate or helpful. To her, it went against every bit of humanity and common sense she possessed.

But she knew that wasn't why she was angry enough with Mr. Allen to be as rude as she'd just been. Her argument was simply a surrogate for what really burned her—that the director refused to even contemplate that Gabriel was not crazed but rather broken in a different way. A way that might not require him to be locked away in Vickering Place for the rest of his days.

But she shouldn't have antagonized him so. She wasn't certain what had come over her. She was typically sweet and genteel in her dealings with others. She *knew* making Mr. Allen angry would do little to win him over to her way of thinking.

So she took a deep breath and said, "I apologize. I understand that we both wish what is best for Lord Bromwich. We simply have differing ideas about how to accomplish it." Her next words galled her to say, but she did anyway. "I do hope you will forgive that I am very passionate about my own."

Mr. Allen sat stiffly in his chair, his expression not changing in the least. "The equilibrium of the mind can be dislodged by a surplus of passion, Lady Manton. That is a *well*-documented cause of insanity."

Tiny hairs rose on the back of her neck at his response, not caring for either his tone or his sentiments.

"Yes, well, while the effects of battle fatigue are *less* documented, the majority of Lord Bromwich's symptoms fall within them," she said, attempting to steer the conversation to less treacherous territory. Gabriel's jaw had clenched tight when she'd checked his defense of her earlier, and now his fists were balled at his sides. Dunnings had inched closer to their grouping, his eyes darting between the three of them. And Mr. Allen had clasped his hands in front of his chest and was rhythmically stroking the knuckles of one hand with the fingers of his other.

She directed herself at Gabriel now, realizing that Mr. Allen wasn't going to listen to anything she proposed. "I believe we can lessen and perhaps even cure some of those symptoms through uncovering the hidden associations behind them."

"What?" both Gabriel and Mr. Allen said in unison.

Penelope thought about how best to explain. "I think we can all agree that the mind is very powerful and mysterious. Doctors and mental philosophers have argued for years over where defects of the mind originate and how to cure them.

"I happen to fall into the school of associationists. We believe that all people start out as blank slates and that the things we *experience* in our lives connect to our reason. Our reason then forms a conclusion about our experience and associates that experience with corresponding ideas and experiences we've had to drive our future actions."

Both men looked at her with twin expressions of confusion on their faces.

She couldn't blame them. She suspected she had sounded rather like Liliana did when her cousin tried to explain chemical theory to her.

"Think of it as cause and effect," she suggested. "A child touches a hot stove, they experience a burn and then their mind makes the association that stoves can be painful and the child does not touch a stove again. This is a very simplistic example, of course. But our minds do this for everything that we experience in life.

"Sometimes the associations are obvious. But sometimes our minds will connect illogical things *unbeknownst* to us—*particularly* when we experience trauma, like that of wartime service—that can take over our senses and force us to behave in ways we do not understand."

"Ridiculous," Mr. Allen said with a dismissive shake of his head.

But a peculiar, interested look came over Gabriel, as if her words made sense to him. As if he were willing to listen further, perhaps even be willing to let her test her theory.

But they'd never be able to dig deeply enough into his psyche to expose and banish his faulty associations and to effect lasting change in his life with Mr. Allen's negative presence.

Dash her injured leg. If she were healthy, she could take Gabriel outside to walk and talk, where Mr. Allen might be less inclined to follow. Judging from his pasty white skin, he did not seem the outdoor type. But until she healed, that was not an option.

She could only hope Mr. Allen would lose interest now that he'd decided she had nothing to offer, and leave them to it.

Four days later, she was wishing Mr. Allen would lose significantly more than interest. His way to the manor from the gatehouse that she'd learned was his private residence, perhaps. Or maybe his licensing—as Vickering Place served more than one lunatic, the sanatorium had to be visited at least once a year by the Royal College of Physicians under the 1774 Madhouses Act. She was so frustrated with the man, she even caught herself wishing he'd lose his health—not for good, of course. Just for a few days, so that he would have to stay home. Then she could speak to Gabriel alone.

For despite Mr. Allen's outspoken disdain for Penelope's theories and practices, he insisted on being present whenever she was with Gabriel. And if something required the director's presence elsewhere, either Dunnings or Carter were stationed near. She might just be unreasonably suspicious, but it seemed as if the attendants stayed closer than they had before—certainly within earshot at all times. Dunnings was more vigilant than Carter, she'd noticed. But the result was that she and Gabriel had made no progress since their night in his bedchamber.

Her leg, on the other hand, had improved dramatically and she'd been able to return to the inn two nights ago. However, her plans to get Gabriel outside once she was well had been thwarted by Mother Nature. Penelope had never much cared for rainy days—but at the moment, she detested them.

She shook the offending drops from her umbrella as she waited beneath the portico. This morning, just as yesterday, her stomach was knotted and tight. She could not shake the fear that one day—maybe even today—Mr. Allen would simply refuse her at the door.

He'd never seemed particularly happy to welcome her—had done so only at the demand of the Marchioness of Bromwich. But now it seemed as if his dislike of Penelope had outstripped his desire not to anger Gabriel's influential mother. And Penelope wanted to know why. She had to resolve whatever Mr. Allen held against her, for Gabriel's sake.

When the director opened the door, he nodded curtly and stepped aside so that she could enter, and a little of her tightness eased. As a servant took her cloak and umbrella, Penelope turned to Mr. Allen, hoping today might be the day they came to some sort of truce.

"Before we visit Lord Bromwich, I was wondering if we might have a private word," she said.

The director's dark eyes narrowed over his long, bony nose, but he extended a hand toward his office.

When they entered the room, Mr. Allen moved to stand behind his desk. Rather than take a seat, Penelope walked to the desk as well, taking a stand in front of it.

Unfortunate though it was, she was well aware that at the current moment, Mr. Allen held most of the power in this situation. If he was willing to risk the ire of Gabriel's family and the potential loss of income should they decide to move him elsewhere, the director could toss her out this very moment. Therefore, she chose her words carefully.

"I appreciate how accommodating you have been in allowing me access to Lord Bromwich," she said, impressed with herself that she had not choked on the lie. "I also understand that you do not hold the same views as I in regard to his treatment."

Mr. Allen snorted, not even putting a polite polish on his contempt for her since Gabriel was not here to witness his rudeness.

Penelope pursed her lips. What was it with this man? Did he think women had no place in an asylum except as patients? Did he simply believe that her theories were rubbish and that she would do more harm than good?

An ugly thought crept into her mind. Or did he just not wish for Gabriel to recover? After all, as unfortunate as it was true, most people believed lunatics could not be cured but simply contained. Being responsible for housing and caring for a mad marquess would be both prestigious and lucrative for Vickering Place. Mr. Allen would have an easier time convincing other wealthy peers to put their loved ones in the same sanatorium as a marquess's family entrusted him to.

Penelope scolded herself for such a lowering thought. No, Mr. Allen was likely just convinced Penelope did not know the first thing about treating a madman. She might have the opportunity to prove him wrong if he would just consent to work *with* her. And hopefully, eventually, get out of her way.

She kept her voice very polite. "However, I do think we both have much to offer Lord Bromwich. His family has entrusted us *both* with his care," she reminded him. "Could we not find a way to cooperate with each other?"

"His family . . . ," Mr. Allen drawled, lowering his chin and pinning her with an uncomfortably speculative gaze. The director brought his hands together in front of him and twiddled his thumbs in a slow circle. "I wonder if they will still *trust* you when informed of your *questionable* methods."

They were back to this? She held her temper. "The marquess's family came to me *because* of my 'questionable' methods. They, too, wonder if battle fatigue might be behind Lord Bromwich's episodes," she pointed out in case the director thought to make a case to Gabriel's family.

But rather than accepting that argument, Mr. Allen lifted an eyebrow in not-so-subtle challenge. "Indeed." He actually *tsk*ed at her as his index fingers formed a steeple. "Carter reports to me that Lord Bromwich crept from his bedchamber in the early hours of the morning a few days past. The same bedchamber in which *you*, also, spent the night. I am quite certain that is not the sort of care the marquess's family had in mind."

Penelope gasped, unable to contain her shock. Nor could she stop her face from heating—with outrage, naturally, although Mr. Allen would likely interpret it as something else. "I had an unpleasant dream and cried out in my sleep. His lordship was simply making certain I was well."

She winced inwardly. Even to her, the truth sounded rather pathetically unbelievable.

Mr. Allen's steepled fingers tapped against one another. "I see. All night, of course."

Penelope clenched her jaw tight and breathed in deeply. "As we were then both awake, we took the opportunity to talk more about his illness."

The director smirked at her. "If you say so. However, it is my duty to look after the best interests of the inmates within my care. As such, I have written to Lord Bromwich's brother, Lord Devereaux, detailing my concerns."

Penelope felt sick. She'd just bet he had, with relish—no doubt casting everything in the worst possible light. Would it be enough to sway Gabriel's family? The self-assured look on Mr. Allen's face said he seemed to think so.

He confirmed her assessment by adding, "I fully expect that his family will revoke your access to him any day now. And you can be assured, Lady Manton, that the moment I receive their reply to that effect, I shall take pleasure in removing you from the premises myself."

From his oily smile, Penelope knew he would, indeed.

"I shall also happily prevent you from having any further contact with my patient in future."

Dear Lord, this was awful. She didn't *think* Gabriel's family would do such a thing, but it was only Gabriel's *mother* that she'd met with. Mr. Allen had sent his messenger directly to Gabriel's brother, Lord Edward, who was standing in as head of the family. As unfair as it might be, the reality was that the men of the world had the final say in such matters. Was Edward Devereaux the type of man to side with the opinions of another man over a woman's, as so many men were?

If so, she could be shut out of Gabriel's life for good.

Or for as long as he was confined to Vickering Place, which, given her thoughts on the chances of Mr. Allen's treatments actually helping Gabriel to recover, might as well be for good.

Penelope's chest squeezed. Dare she wait until Mr. Allen's messenger returned to discover if that were to be the case? And even if Lord Devereaux decided in her favor, Mr. Allen had made it clear he would thwart her at every turn. Maybe, then, she should convince Gabriel's family to move him. Maybe . . .

She couldn't risk Gabriel's future on maybes. Maybe Gabriel was mad. Maybe Michael's lunacy did run in his blood. But she knew in her heart that battle fatigue played some part in it all. Whether it exacerbated his madness, or whether his episodes simply sprang from it, she *knew* she could help him.

But not here.

If she were going to keep her promise to Gabriel, her promise to *herself* that she would do whatever it took to help him, she would have to get him out of here.

And she'd have to do it before Mr. Allen got his reply.

The only blessing in the rain was that it appeared to have delayed the expected messenger. As fortuitous as that was, Penelope needed a fair day for her hastily devised plan to work. A fair day and a fair amount of luck.

She got the first three days later. The sun crept over the horizon that morning, and when Penelope arrived at Vickering Place just before midday, it still shone king in the sky with nary a cloud in sight.

Penelope swallowed her nerves as she stepped down from her carriage. The lack of rain was appreciated, but several other things had to go well if she were to succeed—the least of which was gaining Gabriel's cooperation with her scheme.

As usual, Mr. Allen met her at the door. The director had lost his gloating smile as the days had crept by without the expected reply from Gabriel's family, but today it was back in all its smarminess—in anticipation of what the sunny day might bring, no doubt. Clearly he'd decided the messenger had been kept away by the rain as well.

"Lovely day outside, is it not, Lady Manton?" he

said all too pleasantly as she stepped past him into the foyer.

"Indeed," she agreed. "I should like to take Lord Bromwich for a walk along the grounds again today."

One of the director's black brows rose. "Not planning another convenient fall, are we?"

Penelope gave him a benign smile, refusing to rise to his bait even though her ears burned. Her plan hinged on getting Gabriel out of the manor house, and Mr. Allen had proven himself to be a spiteful sort. He might refuse just to vex her. She tried to make herself sound chastened, defeated, unthreatening. "Sunshine can be so restorative. I just thought it might do his lordship some good."

Mr. Allen considered her request as they made their way to Gabriel's suite of rooms. "Lord Bromwich has seemed somewhat improved since your last foray. I suppose it cannot hurt," he acceded. "As long as Carter goes with you, of course."

Triumph twinged in Penelope's chest. Just a tiny bit. She'd cleared one hurdle, but there was much that could yet go wrong. Still, having Carter as their minder was ideal. He paid much less attention to them than Dunnings did.

"Besides," the director went on as he inserted his key into the heavy lock leading to Gabriel's parlor, "the outdoors is as good a place as any to make your farewells."

A cool calmness came over Penelope as she slid past Mr. Allen into the room. She *would* be saying farewell today if all went as planned, but to Vickering Place—not to Gabriel.

Carter grumbled, of course, but Penelope did not think the man's heart was in it. All of them had felt the strain of the long, tense days inside Gabriel's rooms. She suspected the attendant was actually looking forward to the change of scenery.

Within half an hour, she, Gabriel and Carter were making their way through the back gardens.

They weren't the only ones taking advantage of the break in the weather, she noted. Along one path, an attendant pushed a rolling chair with a frail-looking elderly man, who seemed to be asleep. On a bench near the drained fountain, a heartbreakingly young woman sat rocking back and forth, muttering to herself, while another attendant stood off to the side.

Penelope glanced to Gabriel, who was walking beside her. His gait was steady and sure, his steps quietly confident. His sharp gaze scanned the landscape, as if appreciating and assessing it for all that it was—much like she imagined he once had battlefields. Alertly. Intelligently. Completely lucid.

He didn't belong locked away in a place like this. Even if he never entirely conquered his episodes, perhaps she could help him manage them enough so that he could live on his own estates. If they weren't entirely successful and his family went ahead with having him declared *non compos*, perhaps Devereaux could be persuaded to settle a lesser property on him and hire a caring staff to attend him. She could teach those around him to help him through mild bouts of mania. If he were to improve enough that the episodes came fewer and farther between, he might even lead a satisfying life—albeit different from the one he'd been born to.

Her conviction that she was doing the right thing—if not necessarily in the best possible way—grew.

"Shall we take the same route as we did last week?" she suggested, turning that way.

But Gabriel resisted, coming to a halt. "It's been raining for days, and that path was treacherous enough before." He frowned. "I shouldn't want to risk you re-injuring your calf. Let's just stick to the garden today, shall we?" He steered her onto a well-tended pea gravel path that circled it.

Dash his considerate nature. This was no time for him to be all protective of her health. She had to get him on that path and away from the house.

But for now, she followed. If she were too adamant, Carter might suspect something. As they reached the halfway point of the circuit, she took a chance and pitched her voice low, speaking out of the side of her mouth toward Gabriel. "If we stay in the garden, we will never be able to distance ourselves enough from Carter to talk."

Gabriel slanted his eyes to her curiously.

"When we come around, take the path we did last week." She gave him a pointed stare that she hoped conveyed "or else."

The corner of his mouth tipped up in a half smile, but he barely dipped his chin to let her know he understood and agreed.

Penelope's heart started racing as they cleared the third turn. She glanced past a female patient and her minder—who were coming toward them—to the entrance of the path she wanted to take. Only a few more yards to go. Once they were headed toward the rear of the property, all she had to do was convince Gabriel to walk a bit farther than they had last time and then—

"Lord Bromwich."

Penelope's gaze snapped back to the path they were on. The two women had stopped in front of them, bundled up in heavy hooded cloaks. Even though the sun was lovely today, it was still February.

"Miss Creevey." Gabriel greeted the speaker warmly, stopping as well. "I didn't know you were scheduled for a visit today."

"M'lady was otherwise engaged this afternoon," the young woman replied, "so she gave me an 'alf day. You know I like to spend any time I can with Ann."

Penelope tugged discreetly at Gabriel's arm. They did not have time for a social visit at the moment.

But he mistook her meaning. "Forgive me," Gabriel said. "I've failed to make introductions. Lady Manton, Miss Creevey and her sister, Mrs. Boyd."

"A pleasure," Penelope murmured with impatience, barely sparing the ladies a glance. She knew she was being rude, but they really needed to move along.

"As you are here, will you join us for tea this afternoon?" Gabriel asked Miss Creevey.

"Perhaps I shouldn't," the woman said, ducking her head, "being as you have a visitor yourself."

"I'm sure Lady Manton wouldn't mind," Gabriel assured the woman.

"Of course not," she agreed quickly. Anything to bring this tête-à-tête to an end.

"All right," Miss Creevey said. "I shall join you later, then." With a nod, the woman led her sister past them in the opposite direction while Penelope tugged Gabriel toward the old pleasure path.

As they turned onto it, she sped her steps. Gabriel followed suit, whereas Carter did not. His crunching footfalls fell increasingly behind them, just as she'd hoped. He kept them in eyesight, but not exactly earshot—much as he had the last time they'd gone this way. With any luck, he'd decide to rest on the same stump he had before as well, expecting they would walk on a bit and then turn around as they had before. She'd hate to have to resort to her alternative strategy.

"Out with it, Pen," Gabriel said, startling her from her thoughts. "What exactly is it you have in mind?"

She blinked at him, wondering if she was that obvious. The shrewd look in Gabriel's eyes suggested she was.

Dash it all. Did Carter suspect? She glanced over her shoulder. The attendant was shuffling along, falling farther behind, so probably not. If he had, perhaps Gabriel's invitation to Miss Creevey for tea this afternoon had put the attendant off any ideas that something was afoot.

Should she tell Gabriel now? No. Something told her she'd have a better time getting his cooperation if she didn't give him much time to think about it.

So she asked a question of her own as diversion.

"How do you know Miss Creevey? I don't expect you invite every patient's family up for tea."

It was Gabriel's turn to blink at her. Then his eyes shuttered. Penelope's curiosity kicked. She'd asked the question as a delaying tactic, but now she found she really wanted to know the answer.

"Miss Creevey visits her sister every week that she's able, as I'm sure you've surmised," he said finally. "Mrs. Boyd lost her husband at Waterloo. He—" He hesitated, closing his mouth. "Lieutenant Boyd served in my company, actually, which is how I came to know both sisters. Miss Creevey is kind enough to visit *me* now, as well, when she comes to see Ann."

"Oh," Penelope said. She had an odd sense that there was more to the story, but she didn't have time to delve into it now. They'd just passed Carter's stump, which meant it wasn't far to where the hired carriage should be waiting.

She started walking faster.

Finally, she saw it—the scarf she'd tied to a tree three days ago to let her know where they would need to cross into the woods. She hurried to it and tugged it free.

"What's this?" Gabriel asked as he gained her side.

Penelope looked behind them, squinting her eyes for any sign of Carter, but the attendant was not in sight. Her heart pounded in her chest. Almost there.

She turned to Gabriel and took his hand. "Do you trust me?"

His brow furrowed as he stared at their joined hands. "Do I—" His golden brown eyes flicked to hers. "Of course."

His immediate affirmation warmed something deep within her that she didn't have time to analyze right now. Instead, she tugged at him and started into the woods. "Good. Then come on."

"Pen—" he said, but he followed. The undergrowth was thick now. She had to trample over knotted vines and wiry branches as brambles tore at her skirts. But she kept moving forward, pulling Gabriel along behind her as quickly as she could. If Carter hadn't sat down upon his stump, he very well may have reached the edge of the woods and realized where they'd gone—could even now be either in pursuit of them or rushing back to Vickering Place to sound the alarm.

She was breathing hard by the time they broke free of the woods and came out onto a narrow country lane. Her chest eased a bit when she saw the waiting carriage, right where she'd expected it to be.

She let go of Gabriel's hand to yank another scarf free from a skinny young tree, which she'd tied there earlier this morning to let the driver know where to meet her.

"What the hell?" Gabriel burst out.

She turned to him then and winced at the gathering storm clouding on his face. Dash it all, they had no time to dither about this.

"You said you trust me," she reminded him. "Now prove it. Into the carriage with you."

Chapter Nine

"**A**re you mad?"

Gabriel glanced incredulously between the normally sensible Penelope—who looked worse for the wear after their flight through the forest, with sticklers dotting her cloak and skirts and a stray twig sticking from her falling coiffure—and an old black carriage waiting at the side of the road. Did she think to kidnap him? That must be what was happening here. "Christ, Pen. One week at Vickering Place and you are crazier than I am."

"Neither one of us is crazy," she said, "but, Gabriel, we *must* leave here now."

He felt three steps behind in the conversation. Indeed, he was still looking back and forth between her and the terribly small conveyance. Its driver was perched on the box with a bored look on his face, as if it was an everyday occurrence to pick up passengers on a back road who'd just burst out of the woods behind a sanatorium.

"Mr. Allen intends to toss me out. Today, if he has his way."

"What?" He fixed his gaze on her solely now.

"He knows we spent the night in your bedchamber together, and he assumed the worst. He made horrible accusations when I confronted him the other day about how he's been thwarting us. I tried to explain, but he's been threatening me ever since."

Shock gave way swiftly to outrage. "The blackguard—"

"The *only* reason he didn't lock me out then was because I have the blessing of your family. But he's written to your brother. I can only imagine the awful things he said, and if your family sides with him against me, I won't be allowed to see you again."

Anger fisted in his sternum. How dare Allen upset Penelope so much that she was willing to do something this foolhardy?

And yet would it be such a bad thing if Allen did banish her from Vickering Place? It would solve the problem he'd been struggling with. Surely Pen wouldn't be able to blame herself for anything that happened to him then, if she didn't have a choice about staying.

He took one look at the fiercely determined set of her chin and realized he was fooling himself if he thought that. She would worry, she would plot—she wouldn't let it go.

Still . . . "Then I will write my brother myself and explain the truth. You'd be allowed back after a few days."

"Maybe, but I'm not willing to take that chance. All it would take would be for Mr. Allen to convince him that I am a danger to you, or even simply incompetent, and it would be easy for your brother to justify the wisdom of staying with the status quo."

A quiver of unease slipped down his spine. He hated to even think it of Edward, but last time Mother had visited, she'd groused that he and particularly his wife, Amelia, had become *very* accustomed to spending the family's money in Gabriel's absence. She'd gone so far as to say that if he didn't get himself well and take back the reins of the family posthaste, they would all end up in the workhouse by year's end.

Money, and the power it provided, could be terribly addictive. It mightn't take much justification for Edward to decide Gabriel should stay at Vickering Place indefinitely.

And he'd become convinced he would never get better here.

He'd been thunderstruck the other day when Penelope was trying to explain her ideas about rogue associations. Her words had rung so true somewhere deep inside of him. Perhaps simply because he wanted to believe so badly that he was not mad, but it didn't *feel* that way.

Months he'd been here, willingly subjecting himself to whatever treatments Allen and the visiting doctors tried. Nothing had worked. If anything, the gray cloud of melancholia hung heavier over his head—not to mention that the mania had gotten worse. But if Penelope was to be believed, if there was true hope for him to reclaim his life . . .

"We must hurry," she said, interrupting his internal debate. She glanced worriedly at the tree line. "Carter is bound to have noticed our absence by now. There is no going back, not for me. So you've got to choose, Gabriel."

Christ. What a choice. He no longer trusted that Allen had his best interests at heart. He didn't know if he could trust that his brother and sister-in-law wouldn't use this opportunity to lock him away for good. And he damned sure didn't trust himself.

But he trusted Penelope. Not that she would be his savior, but that she would try her hardest.

Heaven help her. He was choosing her. "Let us go, then."

Penelope's shoulders slumped with relief. Had she really thought he could deny her anything? He was a fool when it came to her, though not as big a fool as she was, apparently.

She nodded and turned for the carriage. The driver, seeing they were finally ready to embark, hopped down from the box.

Hell. He'd been so caught up in the situation of leaving Vickering Place that he hadn't much considered the method of accomplishing it before agreeing. He stared at the tiny conveyance, his throat tightening up. The damned black box looked like a hearse. No, he decided. A hearse would be bigger. This was a coffin.

He stared at the carriage door through which Penelope had just disappeared. The interior was dark, and with Pen's dress being black as night, it was as if the carriage had swallowed her whole.

As it will me. The irrational thought shook him. He took a deep breath. He had no love of close spaces, hadn't had since Waterloo. But the traveling coach had just enough room for one on the driver's box, and a small man at that. The bench on back barely held another wiry man. If Gabriel was going with Penelope, inside it would be.

Best not to think about it too long. The carriage dipped as Gabriel levered himself up and in. The old coach had certainly seen better days. Though the sun still shone outside, the aged interior of the conveyance was unfashionably dark and boasted no windows. A pair of lamps cast feeble sputters of light over the black walls and worn cushions.

He settled himself across from Penelope, doing his best not to step on her skirts.

He tried desperately not to think of small, dark spaces. His chest tightened anyway. He widened his nostrils and tried to breathe more deeply, but the air was heavy and musty and did little to relieve him.

He looked over at Penelope, hoping his distress was not obvious. Thankfully, she was occupied arranging her skirts. Gabriel's knees brushed against the black wool and she looked up, offering him a smile. He returned a tight one of his own, but shifted uncomfortably in the seat, pressing his shoulders against the thinly padded squab as he surreptitiously tried to stretch out a little. Christ, he could touch either side if he extended his elbows.

Pen's lips twisted into an apologetic line, understanding. "I'm afraid this was the best I could manage on such short notice. I had to leave my personal conveyance prominently displayed at Vickering Place, so as not to raise any suspicions. My man has instructions to return to London after we are discovered missing. If anyone takes it in their mind to follow him, hoping he will lead them to us, he'll be going the opposite of our destination."

The carriage dipped once more as the driver gained his seat and again as the other hopped on back. A small jerk and they were under way.

"Headed north, are we?" Gabriel strove for a light tone, pushing the words through his closing throat. "I suppose it is too much to hope that we are for Gretna Green."

Pen opened her mouth and then snapped it shut, a becoming blush of pink staining her cheeks, just visible in the flickering of the carriage lamp. "I'm afraid so," she replied, pursing her lips on a smile.

"That *is* a shame," he murmured as the carriage picked up speed. He leaned his head back and closed his eyes. "I'd always imagined if I ever made a mad dash north, it would be for happier reasons." As opposed to stark raving mad ones. What was he thinking, escaping Vickering Place with Penelope? And did he really think he would be able to make it, enclosed like this, to wherever it was they were going?

"I believe this *will* end happily, Gabriel," she said, leaning forward to place her gloved hand over his fisted one, which rested upon his knee.

He cracked one eye open, taking in her concerned look. Perhaps he had not done as good of a job hiding his distress as he'd thought. He vowed to do better, opening his other eye and pasting an easy, if not wholly genuine, smile on his face. "Then I will have faith in *your* faith on the matter."

She smiled as well before letting go of his hand. He focused on that smile, ignoring the darkness that threatened at the periphery of his vision, fighting off his growing panic as the carriage rolled farther from Vickering Place.

It helped, looking at Pen. It always did. Her heart-shaped face was as smooth as alabaster. She had a delicate but stubborn chin, with just the hint of a dimple creasing it. What was that old saying . . . *dimple in the chin, the devil within*? Yes, well, Pen had certainly shown a strength of will he'd not known she possessed before. And a recklessness he'd not expected.

"How long have you been planning this mad scheme of yours?" he asked. Perhaps talking would take his mind off of the pressing fear.

She flushed. "Since Mr. Allen threatened me three days ago. I knew then I would have to resort to drastic measures. So when I went back to the inn that night, I made my plans and hired the carriage to wait for us there until we could make our escape."

Gabriel widened his eyes. "These poor men have been sitting out in the elements, waiting for us to show?"

She gave him a wry grin. "Only during the days, while I was with you at Vickering Place. Just in case the weather broke long enough for us to justify a walk. But don't worry. They haven't complained a bit. And they've been well compensated."

They must have been, not only to wait those many idle hours, but to be willing to liberate a lunatic from an asylum and ferry him to parts unknown. He wondered what Penelope had told them about him, what reassurances she must have given. Then another thought occurred. "What would you have done if Carter had followed us?"

Penelope's face pulled into a slight wince. "I must admit, I'd counted on his laziness to aid us. I'd hoped he would wait on that fallen stump again. But had he not . . ." She gave a little shrug. "The coachmen were prepared to subdue him until we made our escape."

Gabriel gaped at her.

"That part would have cost extra, of course," she added.

"Of course," he agreed automatically. He raised a brow at her. "I never would have taken you for the bloodthirsty sort, Pen."

She wrinkled her nose. "I doubt it would have come to *that*. Carter doesn't strike me as the sort to sacrifice himself for principle's sake. I imagine he would have meekly allowed himself to be tied to a tree until someone came looking for us."

He imagined she was right. He also imagined from the determined glint in her eye that if it *hadn't* happened that way, they would still be in this tiny old carriage hurtling north.

He glanced down at Penelope's gloved hands, which were clasped tightly in her lap. She wasn't as calm about this course of action as she was pretending to be.

Damn. Carter might not be one to sacrifice himself, but Penelope was. Had she thought through the possible consequences of their actions? Gabriel shook his head as the reality of what they were doing settled on his shoulders, pressing in on him as much or more than the tightness of the space did. "Pen," he said seriously, "Carter is *probably* still sitting there on that stump, grousing to himself, or more likely, snoring away. Despite what you said, we could go back—"

Her eyes snapped to his, and she huffed. "No, Gabriel, I know what I am doing." But a creak of leather belied her confidence as her gloved hands squeezed more tightly together.

"What *are* we doing?" he pressed. "Or rather, where are we going? I assume you have a plan." They certainly couldn't go to his country estate—it had been taken over by Edward and his brood when Gabriel had been sent to Vickering Place. And as far as he knew, Penelope's only residence was her town house in London.

"To Somerton Park."

Her answer surprised him. "The Earl of Stratford's seat?" Stratford was married to Penelope's cousin, he knew. He also knew the cousins to be close.

"Yes, it is the perfect solution for our needs."

He looked away, focusing on the wall that separated them from the driver. The only good thing about that idea was that Shropshire wasn't so very far away. He'd be cooped up in this carriage a matter of hours, rather than days.

At least Stratford and his wife wouldn't be at their country home. He knew the earl to be heavily involved in politics, and Parliament had convened early this year because of the Peterloo massacre last fall. That must be why Penelope had chosen the place. Still . . . "Stratford doesn't mind us making use of his home whilst they are away?"

"Oh, Geoffrey and Liliana are in residence, though Geoffrey does come and go regularly, what with Parliament in session. But Liliana is due to deliver their second child in a matter of weeks, so they decided against going up to Town this Season."

Gabriel sat up straight, banging the top of his head against the carriage ceiling. Damn it all. He leaned forward and rapped his fist against the wall, brushing Penelope's shoulder in the process. "Stop this carriage at once," he bellowed.

The carriage rocked to a halt, causing both him and Pen to sway into each other.

She grabbed on to him to keep from being pitched to the floor. "Gabriel! What are you—"

"You *are* mad," he accused. "How could you even think of putting your family in danger?"

Her expression of surprise rearranged itself into an offended frown as she released his arm. "You're not dangerous, Gabriel. You've not hurt anyone. Both your mother and Mr. Allen have told me as much."

"Yet," he said darkly. "Bloody hell, Pen." He ran his hand through his hair, knocking his elbow against the wall with the movement. "It's bad enough that you insist on being with me and all my unpredictability, but I refuse to put a gentlewoman and her *children* at risk. Think of somewhere else to go."

She narrowed her eyes on him, her mouth tightening in a stubborn line. "We can take whatever safety measures you want. We'll utilize extra footmen or even hire minders, if that makes you happy. But we are *going* to Somerton Park."

The carriage bounced as the driver hopped down from the box.

"Listen, Gabriel," she said fiercely, her pale eyes flashing green sparks. "I didn't just choose Somerton Park because it is a lovely destination. We *need* Geoffrey's protection. You may still be considered *compos* in the eyes of the law, but that offers very little protection to a man who witnesses would claim suffers from lunacy. You know as well as I do that your family can have you taken back to Vickering Place by force. Who knows what they are thinking after receiving Mr. Allen's report? And once they learn we have left . . . All they would have to do is overtake you physically, and I would not be able to stop them. But Geoffrey *can*," Pen insisted. "They wouldn't dare come onto his property and try such a thing."

He'd been free of Vickering Place for only minutes, but it seemed an eternity in his mind. Just the thought of going back, of being locked away again—no matter how gilded the cage—only intensified the trapped feeling he was already fighting. "How do you know Stratford will offer me sanctuary?"

"Because I already asked it of him and he agreed. They are expecting us any day. Both he and Liliana are well acquainted with the challenges men who've come back from war face," she said. Her voice was probably meant to be reassuring, but in reality, it scraped him raw. "You couldn't ask for more sympathetic hosts."

Shame burned in his chest, mingling with his unreasonable fear. It crept up his neck, making even his ears hot. "I don't want sympathy, Pen," he bit out. "I want—"

The door to the carriage opened with a groan, and the driver poked his head through the opening. "Beg pardon, m'lord, m'lady. Is there summat amiss?"

Gabriel looked at the man, who glanced warily between the two of them. This was his last chance. If he went on with Pen, he would not only be involving her in this mess, but now her cousin and that woman's husband. Did he have that right?

He could demand they turn around. And if that didn't work, he could push past the driver and walk back to Vickering Place. His eyes strayed to the open door. It would be so easy. It was already all he could do to stay inside the coffinlike carriage anyway.

And yet Pen must truly believe he had a chance to be cured if she was willing to call in such favors. Could he turn his back on her and her family's generosity?

It galled him to have to accept the charity of others,

and his nerves burned with the desperate need to escape these close confines. But neither torment was strong enough to quash the damnable hope that Penelope's faith in him gave him.

Gabriel gave a slight shake of his head. "No. My apologies, driver. Carry on."

The coachman sniffed against the cold as he turned around, mumbling something as he shut the door. The carriage rocked as the man resumed his seat, then jerked back into motion.

"It is the best choice," Pen said. "You will see."

He closed his eyes, praying she was right.

As she watched Gabriel's eyes flutter closed, Penelope offered up her thanks that he hadn't balked. She'd seen the panic on his face. Had known he was considering going back, even if he had to leap from the carriage. She would have hated to order the coachmen to tackle and truss him up for the ride to Somerton Park, but she would have done it.

"There *are* other reasons, aside from Geoffrey's protection, you know," she said, determined to set his mind at ease. "First, no matter what else we may be dealing with, I know you agree that at least a part of it is battle fatigue, yes?"

He grunted his assent but did not open his eyes.

"Isolation only makes it worse. You need to be around other people, people who can offer social and intellectual stimulation and appeal to your rational self. Not only will Geoffrey and Liliana be at Somerton Park, but they employ several ex-soldiers on the estate."

But Gabriel wasn't listening to her. His face had gone eerily pale and his chest rose and fell entirely too fast.

Her gaze dropped to his hands, which gripped the seat of the carriage so hard they trembled. Penelope's heart leapt into her throat. "Gabriel, what is the matter?"

His eyes flew open and beads of sweat popped out onto his forehead, glistening in the feeble light of the carriage lamps. He shook his head at her, as if to deny anything was wrong. But then he seemed to think better of it. "Can't"—he sucked in air—"breathe," he said, tugging at his cravat.

His fingers fumbled at the task. Penelope scrambled to help him, her own breath catching in her throat. She had to partially straddle him to reach him. She bent awkwardly over him, bracing herself with one hand on the squab beside his head. She used her other hand to pull at the knot until it gave way. White linen slid over her black gloves as she loosened the neck cloth. "Is that better?"

He nodded, taking in great gulps of air. His body quivered, tense as a bowstring against her. "Not even . . . a half hour away from Vickering Place . . . and I'm already descending into . . . madness."

He tried for a self-deprecating smile, but his breathing was still too rapid for Penelope's comfort, and seemed to be getting faster.

She'd seen this before. Many men suffering from battle fatigue experienced sudden attacks of nerves. Oftentimes it was brought on by a sudden noise, or a flash of memory, or being forced into a situation that reminded them of the trauma they'd experienced, whether they were aware of it or not. She had no idea what might have caused his. It could simply be the stress of the situation. Or the fact that he was leaving the perceived safety of the sanatorium.

Or . . . Gabriel *had* been acting strangely since the moment he stepped into the carriage. She glanced around at the tight, dark interior. Could it be he had a fear of enclosed spaces?

She framed his face with her hands and turned it up to hers. "No, you are not," she assured him. If he truly worried that an episode was imminent, he would never calm down. Already, his heart pounded, his pulse visible in the hollow of his throat. "You have no warning before your episodes, remember? This is simply an attack of nerves, and it will pass. Just keep looking into my eyes."

His gaze latched on to hers, panic glinting in his golden brown eyes. She reached down and found his hand, placing it palm down upon her chest. Then she returned her hand to his cheek. "Try to match your breathing to mine, Gabriel," she said, taking slow, deep breaths through her nose and blowing them from her mouth. "Feel the rise and fall and focus on meeting the rhythm. In through your nose . . ."

He nodded jerkily and gave it his best effort, his nostrils flaring as he inhaled. But he couldn't seem to get enough air and opened his mouth to take in more. His panic was intensifying, she knew.

She had to find a way to calm him, had to jar him out of this before he spiraled out of control.

She could slap him across the face. No. No, she couldn't bring herself to do that.

So she did the next best thing.

She kissed him.

Chapter Ten

It was a desperate measure, to be sure. Certainly an ill-advised one. And as she pressed her lips tightly against his, Penelope wondered if it would even work.

Beneath her, Gabriel's chest still heaved, even as the rest of him went rigid with shock. Bursts of cool air struck her upper lip as he was left to breathe only through his nose now that his mouth was sealed by her own in an awkward kiss.

For a moment, it seemed as if he were calming. But then he lashed out, his fist striking the carriage door beside them. Dash it all. This wasn't helping.

She pulled back from the kiss. "Look at me, Gabriel," she commanded.

Wild golden brown eyes fixed on her. Their gazes held and he ceased struggling. It was an improvement, but his breathing was still too rapid.

She couldn't sustain her half-bent position much longer. She twisted her legs and settled herself across his knees. There, that was better. Now she could caress his jaw with one hand, while her other moved to tug gently at his ear. She rubbed her fingers in opposing directions over lobe and cartilage, as she might soothe an animal.

Bit by bit, he came back to her. She felt it first in the subtle relaxing of his muscles against her. "That's right," she crooned, not stopping her ministrations. His shoulders lowered slightly as some of the tension ebbed from him . . .

And flowed directly into her.

For every bit that his breathing slowed, hers picked up. For every degree he loosened, she tightened. For every touch of wildness that left him, tempestuousness swelled within her. It was as if their bodies strove to share his burden equally. The sense of connection frightened her, but not enough to dampen the thrill of it.

And then Gabriel was there with her, his eyes clear and staring into hers. Their chests moved in the same harsh rhythm. His arms had come around her waist in a fierce grip, and she clung to him as well, as if they were balancing together on the edge of a tipping point. She didn't know how they got here, but she knew one thing. No matter which way they fell, madness awaited them.

She touched her lips to his again.

This time, there was nothing awkward about it. Gabriel moaned deep in his throat, rising up to meet her even as he crushed her to him. There was no tenderness in this kiss. Just a conflagration of desire. His, hers, she wasn't sure which burned hotter.

She decided it didn't matter much as Gabriel's tongue breached her lips. She opened wide for him, inviting him in even as he drove to possess her mouth with his own. Their mutual boldness tore a moan of pleasure from her as she clutched at him, both with hands and with the suction of her mouth as she pulled him deeper into the kiss.

Hunger crashed through her, swirling down her spine and settling in low places.

Gabriel shifted his hold, lifting her slightly as he twisted her, trying to bring her closer. It seemed only natural to shift as well. She brought one of her legs around so that she could straddle his. Her breasts slid deliciously against his chest as she settled atop him. At the same time, he braced his feet upon the carriage floor, bringing them into intimate contact.

She broke from the kiss with a gasp as shards of excitement cut through her. Lord, it had been so long since she'd felt this alive. Even through layers of clothes, she could feel the size and length of him. But it wasn't enough. She needed to feel more.

Penelope braced herself with one hand against the squab again and brought the wrist of her other hand to her mouth. Grasping the leather edge of her glove between her teeth, she pulled it over and off of her hand before letting it drop, forgotten. She did the same on the other side, desperate to touch him with her bare skin.

"Pen," he groaned with a longing that echoed in

her chest. She answered him with one of her own, but as she started to slide her hands down his chest, his fingers dove into her coiffure, stopping her exploration.

What was left of her hairpins after their dash through the forest scattered this way and that, landing on the wooden floor with tiny clicks. Riotous curls sprang from their mooring, falling heavy around her face even as Gabriel levered his upper body off of the seat to fit his mouth once again to hers.

She sucked in a breath through her nose, expecting the onslaught their previous kiss had been. Instead, he rubbed his tongue sinuously against her. It brushed the corners of her mouth, tested the texture of the inside of her cheeks, skimmed over the surface of her teeth, before swirling with hers in an intimate dance, silken yet rough.

Sweet frustration rode Penelope. She'd never been kissed thus, this teasing give-and-take that left her insides quivering. She was no innocent. Even though it had been more than two years since she'd been intimate with a man, her body knew what came next. Knew and wasn't accustomed to waiting for it once she was this far along. She clenched her knees against his hips and undulated against him, as if to spur him into giving her what she craved.

But other than to move his large hands to her hips and pull her more tightly against his hardness, he didn't hasten his seduction. If anything, he slowed his kiss. Stopped even, moving his lips from her mouth to her throat, licking her there, a hard push of his tongue against her pulse that sent it racing ever faster. She moaned as tension corkscrewed inside her.

He *had* to give her some relief. She bucked again, instinctively trying to drive him over the edge, but all it earned her was a hoarse chuckle against her skin that raised gooseflesh. Drat the man! She was bursting with need and here he was, taking his sweet time, in possession of complete mastery over himself . . .

Penelope's breath caught as cold washed over her.

What am I doing? She'd kissed Gabriel in a desperate bid to break him free of his panic and bring him back to his senses. Well, it had worked. Better than she could have imagined, but she'd lost herself in the process, hadn't she?

Embarrassment flushed her skin as she jerked away from his questing mouth.

Gabriel grunted at her sudden movement. He blinked up at her with surprise before his brows dipped in confusion. "Pen?"

"I'm sorry," she blurted, shoving off of his chest. She lifted her knee and twirled off of his lap in a move that would have made even the most demanding dance master proud. She landed gracefully on the seat across from him, plastering her shoulders against the squab to put as much distance between them as she could.

For a moment, only their heavy breathing filled the carriage. Penelope couldn't bring herself to look over at him. She kept her eyes firmly on her boots as she heard the squeaking of his seat cushion—Gabriel straightening, no doubt. Finally, fabric rustled as he adjusted himself.

"Penelope . . ."

She lifted her eyes to him then. Gabriel looked as she felt, as if balanced on the knife's edge of desire and trying to hide it. He sat a little too straight, the hard line of his jaw was a little too sharp, and his eyes were a little too dark, clouded with passion. "What—"

"I—I don't know what came over me," she said, her voice shaky. But that wasn't entirely true, was it? She might not know what had possessed her to initiate that second kiss, but she knew all too well what had come over her once she had. Lust, pure and simple. It had scorched her rational mind to a cinder.

Even now, molten heat churned through her center— the hot ache of longing. It had been years since she'd felt desire like this. During her marriage, she'd enjoyed a rather vigorous intimate life, so it wasn't the need that surprised her. It was how quickly the budding awareness she felt toward Gabriel had turned into lust with a simple touch of her lips to his.

She brought her hand to her lips now, her cool fingers doing little to soothe them. "I'm sorry," she said again, as much to herself as to him. "I shouldn't have kissed you."

Much less all that had come after.

Gabriel didn't say anything for a moment, just continued to watch her with his steady gaze. She was just beginning to think he intended to let the matter drop with her apology when he asked, "Why did you, then?"

"I—" How could she answer him when she didn't know herself? At least not about *that* kiss. So she cleared her throat, straightened her shoulders and gave him her reason for the first. "It was necessary for your treatment."

His eyes widened. Clearly he hadn't been expecting that.

Nor had it come out the way she meant it. "To snap you out of your panic, of course," she clarified. "And it worked, did it not? You are no longer distressed."

He blinked and looked around the interior of the coach, his forehead furrowing thoughtfully. "I'm not," he said, a touch of wonder in his voice. Then he looked back at her with a raised eyebrow. "Though I'm beginning to think Allen was right to accuse you of immoral practices . . ." His voice was teasing, but his eyes were still dark with unspent passion, as she imagined hers were.

She felt her face flush, but she teased back. "I *did* consider slapping your face instead. It might have worked just as well. Do you think he would have approved of that method more?"

Gabriel gave a faux shudder. "Most likely. But *I* wouldn't have enjoyed it nearly as much."

He smiled at her and she smiled back, even as her cheeks flamed hotter. Then he leaned back against the squabs and closed his eyes, resting his clasped hands over his stomach and crossing one ankle of his outstretched legs over the other, presumably to sleep.

Penelope released a pent-up breath. She had no idea what he must be thinking. She was only grateful he seemed inclined to let the matter go. Perhaps they would be able to move past this moment as if it never happened.

She dearly hoped that was the case.

"Pen?" he asked, cracking one eye open to look at her. "Do you treat all of the men you've helped with kisses like that, or is it only me?"

"I— What?" she sputtered. "*No*, of course not."

He let his eye fall shut as he nodded. "Only me, then," he said, and she could have sworn the far side of his mouth curved up in a smile.

And she knew he wasn't going to forget any more than she was.

Gabriel didn't know how much time passed as he reclined in the carriage across from Pen, feigning sleep. All he knew was if he opened his eyes and looked at her, she'd be back in his lap, skirts tossed above her waist and he'd be inside her before she knew it.

Christ, her lips had been sweeter than anything that had ever graced his tongue. He'd never be able to untaste her. Nor would he forget the feel of her against him or the low moans she made that were so different from her normally dulcet voice.

Not that he was complaining, but what the hell had *that* been all about?

He remembered her pulling him back from the brink of darkness, her voice calling to him, her touch soothing him. And then she'd kissed him and fire had licked through his body, burning away everything but her, bursting into an inferno that had gotten out of hand. If she hadn't come to her senses—

They'd both be crying out their pleasure right now.

He stifled a groan and shifted in his seat, twisting his

hips to the side so that his desire wouldn't be quite so obvious if she glanced his way.

"You don't have to pretend sleep for my sake, you know."

He opened his eyes and glanced over at her. She'd repaired her appearance as best she could. He'd felt her gathering her hairpins from the floor earlier and had he been a gentleman, he would have assisted her. But he hadn't trusted himself yet.

Hell, he didn't trust himself now. Even in that dull black gown, with her blond ringlets not quite tamed, Penelope looked divinely kissable.

His eyes fixed on the corner of her mouth, which was turned up in a wry smile. He imagined running his tongue along—

"After all, what is a little kiss amongst friends, eh?"

His eyes snapped to hers. She was still smiling, but it looked a bit forced. She was embarrassed, then.

He uncrossed his legs and straightened in his seat, trying to decide how to respond. He didn't think it would be polite to point out that *that* had been far from a *little kiss*. Particularly when it was apparent from Pen's overly light tone that she was trying very hard to make mince of it.

"I only mean to say," she went on as he was still pondering, "we needn't make more of it than it was."

"Mmm," he murmured noncommittally. He almost stopped at that, but damn it all, that had been the singular most enticing kiss of his life, and he wasn't ready to pretend that it had never happened. He leaned toward her ever so slightly. "And what, exactly, was it?"

Pen swallowed. "Well . . . you know."

He raised one eyebrow to indicate that he very well did not know, and her cheeks flamed. She'd replaced her gloves, he noted as he watched her wring her hands in her lap. Perhaps it was cruel of him, but he enjoyed her nervousness. It meant that their kiss had not been an everyday experience for her, not that he expected it was with Pen. It also meant she'd been as affected as he by their all-too-short interlude.

But unlike him, she seemed determined to forget it. Pen straightened her spine and pursed her lips into a firm line. "A simple case of animal spirits, if you insist upon putting a name on it."

He narrowed his eyes upon her.

"Not that we have anything to feel guilt for," she rushed to assure him, misinterpreting his irritation. "We are both young and unattached, and—*and* we were in the midst of an intense moment. 'Twas only natural."

"Natural," he drawled. It certainly felt natural now. They sat so near each other in the tiny carriage that he could smell her arousal, an undercurrent wrapped in mandarin and vanilla. Sweet yet heady, like the woman herself. It made him want to—

"But it was also a mistake," she insisted. "One that cannot happen again."

Gabriel crossed his arms, leaning back into the squabs as he studied her. Her coloring was high enough that he noticed it even in the dim lamplight. He also found her word choice interesting . . . Was she trying to convince him? Or herself? "Cannot?" he asked silkily. "Or will not?"

Pen inhaled sharply through her nose, taking his meaning. "Either," she insisted. "B-both."

But a slow smile overtook him. He couldn't help it. As much as Pen pretended otherwise, she wanted him. *Him.* He didn't believe that rot about animal spirits, though she probably did. Her way of justifying, he'd guess, but to him it reeked of "the lady doth protest too much."

Gabriel had to stop himself from crowing with satisfaction. For the first time in months, he felt . . . powerful. As he used to. Like a man in his prime *ought* to.

More important, though, was what he didn't feel: Hopeless. Sorry for himself. Or at a disadvantage.

In this, at least, Penelope was vulnerable to him rather than the other way around. Or at least equally vulnerable.

And he quite liked that idea.

"What happened was a onetime occurrence. There is no place for . . ." She trailed off, visibly struggling for words. "Intimacy between us. It won't help at all in your recovery."

"Ah," he murmured, enjoying this. "But I thought your particular method of treatment was all about intimacy. Baring my soul to you and all that."

"Your soul, yes. Other parts, no," she said primly, and he couldn't help but laugh, a booming sound that startled them both as it ricocheted back to them off the carriage walls. Then they both shared a smile.

"I am *serious*, Gabriel," she said, but her words lacked bite in the face of their mutual amusement.

"I know you are, Pen," he acknowledged. But he made her no promises. He hadn't felt this optimistic or

alive in an age. It seemed as if he'd left his old life behind him at Vickering Place, and what waited ahead
was unknown but filled with both fears and possibilities. He wasn't about to close off *any* avenues that
might lead to this sort of happiness becoming his
everyday reality, no matter what Pen said.

But even his small acquiescence seemed to make her
feel better. She visibly relaxed, and spent the rest of the
trip to Somerton Park in a constant stream of chatter. It
wasn't like Pen to talk so much, but he knew she did it
to avoid any more conversation about that kiss or their
feelings about it.

He didn't mind. He'd always loved her voice. He
could listen to her for hours. He enjoyed her easy smile
as she spoke of her family and envied the obvious
fondness she had for them.

He did think it odd that she mentioned more than
once how brilliant Lady Stratford was. Pen seemed to
think that her cousin would be an incredible boon in
their cause, even more so than Pen herself. Silly woman.
Not to take anything from Lady Stratford, but didn't
Penelope realize that the only reason he had any hope
at all was because of *her*?

It wasn't long before the carriage rolled through the
manor's gates. In truth, it had to have been more than
three hours, as dusk now threatened on the horizon.
But to Gabriel, it had seemed only moments.

As he stepped from the musty carriage into the crisp
evening air, he marveled that the earlier pressing dread
had not haunted him once after that kiss. No, after he'd
had Penelope in his arms, it was as if his body had

shifted all of his awareness to her, leaving no room for the fear.

As he watched her now, greeting her cousin with an enthusiastic hug, one thought reverberated through his mind, despite all that he'd vowed to protect Penelope from his madness.

If only I could keep her with me always.

Chapter Eleven

The cold marble railing of the central balustrade slid smoothly beneath her palm as Penelope rushed down the steps of the grand staircase the following morning. Her slippers swished in her haste, echoing and reechoing off of the stone walls and floor.

She'd overslept—or rather, *under*slept, if one were to put a fine point on it. But it hadn't been nightmares that had kept her awake. No, her fitful dreams had been of another sort entirely.

She never should have kissed Gabriel. And not just for the reasons she'd given him last night. No, it was because now that she'd opened that door, the flickering of desire she'd felt for him had swept through and kindled into an inferno. She might not call it raging at this point, but she'd never felt this intensity of longing in her life, not even with Michael. And that terrified her.

That's what she got for following her instincts. Why hadn't she just slapped Gabriel instead?

She checked the breakfast room, but wasn't surprised to find it empty, given how high the sun had already been in the sky when she'd glanced out of her window this morning. Liliana and her husband, Geoffrey, were early risers.

Penelope *wanted* to be an early riser, but too many years as a society darling had trained her body to city hours. Even if she hadn't been tossing and turning with frustrated desire last night, she'd have had a difficult time rising with the sun.

Gabriel, however, had not. The maid who was tidying his room had said he'd gone below shortly after dawn. She chewed at her lower lip as she made for the library. What an awful person she was, leaving Gabriel to his own devices in a strange place. She only hoped he was getting on well with her cousins.

A quick search of the library, drawing room and even the music room turned up nothing. Where was Gabriel? And everyone else, for that matter?

She was searching for a servant to ask when she heard her cousin's muffled voice floating down the hallway. She followed the sound.

Penelope turned the corner to find Liliana and another woman exiting the back staircase that led to the nursery. Liliana was gesturing with her hands while she spoke, and the other woman nodded politely every so often as they came her way.

Penelope stopped and waited.

When Liliana noticed her, she broke into a smile and

waved her over. "Pen," she said warmly. "Meet Miss Eden. Miss Eden, my cousin, Lady Manton."

The young woman bobbed a curtsy.

"Miss Eden is interviewing to be our new nurse once the babe arrives," Liliana explained.

"Ah," Penelope said with a smile. "Well, Miss Eden, I do hope you are the energetic sort. My niece can be quite a handful, and I imagine any sibling of hers will be nothing less."

"Yes, m'lady. Shouldn't be a problem," the young woman said.

"Well, don't let me interrupt," Penelope said to Liliana. "If you could just tell me where to find—"

"We're actually almost finished. Give me one moment?"

Penelope nodded and followed the two women toward the exit. As they walked, she couldn't help listening in on the conversation. Liliana was talking over her daughter's routines, and the nurse was giving suggestions. But the more Penelope listened, she realized that for some reason she did not like Miss Eden.

She couldn't explain it. The nurse was well dressed, clean and polite. She answered Liliana's questions with a quiet confidence. Indeed, she'd not said or done anything to give Penelope such a queer feeling. And yet there it was.

"Thank you for coming, Miss Eden," Liliana was saying as she left the woman with the housekeeper, who would presumably show her out. "I shall be in touch."

Liliana turned to Penelope. "Let us go to the parlor

and sit for a moment. I cannot be on my feet these days as much as I am accustomed to," she said with a wry smile, curving her hands beneath her very rounded belly.

"Actually, I'm looking for Gabriel. Do you know where he's gone?" Penelope asked they turned back down the hallway toward the parlor.

"He rode out with Geoffrey this morning, to inspect the property."

"Ah." She allowed herself to relax for the first time since she'd awoken to find Gabriel gone. "I am glad. I was hoping the two of them might get on well, what with them both being old cavalrymen."

"Yes, I assumed that was part of the reason you brought him here," Liliana returned as they entered the Red Parlor, so named for the bright red damask-covered walls, broken only by white columns and trim that was heavily picked with gilt.

"I've watched you treat enough men to have gleaned some of your tactics," she went on as she lowered herself onto the settee. "I know you try to help them reconnect with others within their sphere, be it friends, family or other soldiers. I have also noticed you prescribe an exercise regimen first off. When I shared that information with Geoffrey, he was only too happy to help on both fronts. Since I am unable to accompany him on our morning rides these days"—she rubbed her palm in circles atop her burgeoning stomach—"I believe he's looking forward to the company."

Penelope, who'd taken a seat in the armchair angled catty-corner, reached over and squeezed her cousin's hand with gratitude. How fortunate she was to have Liliana and Geoffrey in her life. Who else's doorstep could she have shown up on—with a man she'd kidnapped from a lunatic sanatorium, no less—and know they would *both* be welcomed?

"Tactics?" Penelope said teasingly. "Fronts? You are beginning to sound like your husband, you know." Before inheriting the earldom, Geoffrey had been a decorated officer and had come home from the wars a hero. It was also whispered about town that he planned political skirmishes as carefully as he'd once planned battles.

Liliana's face lit with a soft smile. "I suppose I am. It must come from being in each other's company so often."

Penelope smiled as well, but her heart knew a moment of envy. Liliana had married a scant month before Penelope had wed herself. And yet nearly three years later, her cousin was so very obviously happy in love, whereas she was a widow and so desperately alone.

It was more than just that Liliana's husband was alive and hers was not, however. Penelope understood that all too well. Liliana had chosen a man who completed her—who needed what she had to give and was capable of giving what she needed in return. Whereas *she* had unknowingly bound herself to a man who needed much more than she could ever have given him. She and Michael had been doomed to fail from the start. Perhaps if she hadn't been so foolish, focused only on marrying well and living the life of a society wife, she'd have seen the signs before it was too late.

Penelope blinked away a sudden stinging in her eyes. There was nothing to be had from dwelling on what she could not change. The only thing she could promise herself was that she was not that foolish girl any longer. She would choose better next time.

And there would be a next time. As inconvenient and ill timed as this attraction to Gabriel was, it showed her one thing: The part of her that longed for male companionship no longer lay dormant. Perhaps it was time to reenter society, to put her slippered toe back in the water. Perhaps find another husband.

She watched her cousin, who was busy tucking a pillow behind her to make herself more comfortable in the late months of her confinement, and another long-buried desire came back to her with a fierceness. She wanted children of her own.

Which reminded her of Miss Eden.

"Were you simply interviewing Miss Eden, or have you already offered her employment?"

Liliana gave her an odd look but said, "I've as much as offered. It's been a bit difficult to fill the position. Charlotte is not old enough for a proper governess, and yet she is entirely too precocious for our current nurse-maid to handle. I need someone who can manage both the new baby and an uncommonly curious two-year-old, and Miss Eden seems up to the task. Why?"

Penelope hesitated. She didn't wish to cost a person their post, and yet something just didn't sit well with her regarding the nurse. "I don't have a good feeling about her. It's nothing I can explain. She just made me uncomfortable."

Liliana frowned. "She comes with excellent letters of reference."

"It's probably nothing," Penelope demurred. She used to live by her instincts, but since she'd made so many mistakes with Michael, she questioned her feelings as much or more than she listened to them.

But Liliana looked very thoughtful. "No, you've always had good instincts, Pen. You see things in people that I never could. You read them well. It's a gift I've long envied you. If you're worried, then I am. I will have Geoffrey dig deeper into Miss Eden's references before I make a final decision."

Penelope was torn between several thoughts at once. First, she was humbled that her cousin had unwavering faith in her. Second, she was astounded that Liliana had ever envied *her* anything. Penelope's uncle Charles had been a chemist, and Liliana had always been her father's daughter, eschewing the frivolous life Penelope had embraced. If anything, Penelope always envied Liliana her unique intelligence and steady character.

And third, "How can you think I have such great instincts when I married a maniac?"

Liliana tilted her head and eyed Penelope much as she likely did one of the specimens in her laboratory. "I know you think you should have seen signs of Michael's illness, but I disagree."

Penelope shook her head. "If I hadn't been so impulsive, if I'd have approached life more staidly, more *logically*, like you do, maybe—"

Liliana actually laughed. "Don't say that. You are perfect just the way you are. Do you think I would be who I am if you hadn't been in my life? When your mother tried so very hard to change me after my father died, you always accepted me for who I was and what I wanted for my life. You encouraged and loved me when I thought no one else did, seeing only the person I was inside.

"And look at all of the good you've done at the hospital. I've spent the past two years treating people's bodies. You've spent them treating people's *souls*. You take knowledge and apply it organically, changing and molding different theories into what a person needs most. I could never do what you've done. You've made a difference in those men's lives and the lives of the people who love them. That's worth more to the world than logic."

Penelope stared at Liliana, unable to breathe. Did her cousin really see her that way?

"I must say, however, absconding from the sanatorium with Lord Bromwich was a rather extreme thing to do," Liliana went on. "Were you acting on instinct when you decided on that course of action?"

Penelope knew Liliana well enough to know there was no judgment in her questions, only curiosity. "Yes, because I know in my heart he wouldn't recover there."

"Many people don't recover, Pen. It's a sad fact of life."

She frowned. "True, but I *know* Gabriel can."

"Hmmm," Liliana murmured. "That doesn't sound like a very logical reason for doing such a thing. Yet I can see you feel strongly that Lord Bromwich has a chance."

"I've never been so sure about something," she admitted, "yet so afraid of being wrong."

Liliana reached across and took her hand. "And that's what I meant before. A logical person like myself would never have done what you have. Lord Bromwich is getting this chance because *you* are who you are. You follow your instincts, even when you are afraid."

Penelope had to blink back tears.

"Now," Liliana said, blinking suspiciously herself, "tell me why you are so certain."

She took in a deep breath. "Well, aside from his episodes, every other difficulty I have observed or that Gabriel and I have discussed fits easily within the diagnosis of battle fatigue."

Even his panic in the carriage yesterday, which she was attributing to an abnormal fear of enclosed spaces rather than madness, was typical.

Just thinking of that reminded her of how she'd arrested that panic—and every second of the toe-curling kisses that had followed. Penelope flushed warm and hoped Liliana didn't notice how pink her cheeks must have turned.

"Can severe battle fatigue bring out mania?" Liliana asked.

Penelope nodded. "Yes, and of course I'm considering that. But I'd expect to see signs of instability outside of his episodes, which I'm not. I also can't ignore his blood connection to Michael, but again, there were *warnings* before Michael would go into one of his fits." She sighed, frustrated. "Gabriel's episodes are nothing like that. It's the strangest thing, Lily. It's almost as if I'm dealing with two different illnesses altogether."

But that couldn't be right, could it? If anyone would know, it would be Liliana, which was one of the reasons she had been so anxious to bring Gabriel here.

She leaned toward her cousin. "Is there anything you can think of that might explain the incongruities?"

"You are the expert in cases of madness. I'm afraid I can speak only to the physiological, but I'll be happy to try. Could you describe all you witnessed?"

She told Liliana how she'd first encountered Gabriel at Vickering Place, detailing all that she'd observed of his behavior while caught up in his episode. She left out the part about him landing atop her and how he'd recognized her and begged for her help. *That* seemed too personal to share, even with Liliana. She told herself Gabriel would be mortified if she spoke of it, but she suspected she simply wanted to keep that moment for herself.

Liliana listened intently, but now a frown tangled her brow. "Could you go back to the episode now and repeat just the physical symptoms?"

"Of course," Penelope replied, recognizing that look on Liliana's face. Something had caught her cousin's attention and she was puzzling over it, which was precisely what Penelope had hoped. She pictured Gabriel as he'd been that day in her mind's eye, wanting to give Liliana every possible detail she could. "He was overheated and scratching at his skin—"

"How did you know he was overheated?" Liliana interrupted. "Were his clothes soaked through?"

"Um . . . no. He'd, um, stripped off all of his clothing." Penelope's face flushed with the memory of Gabriel's nakedness.

Liliana's violet eyes widened. "*All?*"

Penelope nodded quickly. Now that she was not caught up in the shock of the moment, her mind recalled the hard lines of his body with more vividness than she'd noticed at the time. Every exquisite, explicit detail.

"Yes," she replied, trying to hurry past that revelation before Liliana commented on her blush. "And he was scratching at his skin as if the clothing had irritated him."

"Hmmm," Liliana repeated, watching her a little too closely. But thankfully, she didn't pry. "You said he was not perspiring, though?"

"No. His skin was hot to the touch, but dry. He also seemed desperately parched, but no matter how much water we gave him, it was never enough to quench his thirst." It had been awful, listening to him beg for more to drink. She'd felt so helpless.

"Oh, and his pupils were enlarged," she went on, "so much that his eyes were like black marbles in his face. They were extremely sensitive to the light, too, even hours later."

Liliana was nodding and tapping her index finger against her lower lip. "Have you seen any of these same symptoms since, even to a lesser degree? Either individually or in combination?"

Penelope blew out a frustrated breath. "No."

"Let's say I knew nothing about Lord Bromwich's

mental state and was presented with an otherwise perfectly healthy patient..." Liliana settled further against the back of the settee, still tap-tap-tapping her finger, thinking while Penelope waited anxiously for her cousin's opinion. "If that were the case, I would say that what you have described sounds very much to me like the body's rejection of something. Perhaps something Lord Bromwich may have come into contact with or ingested."

Penelope's breath caught with shock. "What?"

"You said yourself that your instincts are telling you to look elsewhere. If his mania doesn't stem from madness, the next logical place to look is the physiological."

Gooseflesh pimpled her forearms even as Penelope told herself not to get her hopes up. Still, she scooted forward in her seat, leaning toward her cousin with an anticipation she couldn't seem to quash. "Is it possible? Truly?"

"Certainly. The human body is a complex and mysterious thing, much like the mind. I believe we could study either one of them for centuries and never fully understand all there is to know."

Good Lord. If Gabriel's episodes of mania were not madness but something else altogether—

There would be no reason to put a stop to his kisses, some horridly wicked part of her mind whispered.

There will be *no more kisses*, she fired back. To herself. Lord, perhaps she was the mad one. "But what could cause such a reaction?"

Liliana's face scrunched up into a wince. "Well, that I can't answer. I don't actually know of any one substance that would cause the combination of symptoms you mentioned."

Penelope deflated a bit, her shoulders slumping as she eased back in her seat.

"The fact that his pupils were dilated brings to mind a reaction to medication. An opiate like laudanum would affect the eyes. However, an opium eater would have pupils like pinpricks, not marbles. I know of no medicine offhand that causes the reverse."

Drat.

"The severely dry mouth can be attributed to a multitude of things, so we can't really discover anything from that alone." Her finger was tapping her upper lip again. "You said Lord Bromwich was scratching at his skin. Did you see any eruptions? Like hives or boils, perhaps?"

"No," Penelope said, slipping further back into the armchair. "His itch seemed to come from the inside."

"Odd," Liliana answered. "I would expect a reaction to a food to have at least some external manifestation. But that doesn't mean we are not onto something." Now she pulled her lower lip between her teeth and worried it a moment, lost in thought.

Penelope tried to fight her growing disappointment. "Even if we can explain away the other symptoms, can one even ingest something that causes him to see things that aren't there?"

"Now, that I can answer with a definite 'yes.' Ingesting ergot can create delusions in its sufferers, for example. Even mania. As well as the extreme heat and thirst you described."

And just like that, hope flooded the discouragement out of her heart. "That is the fungus that grows in rye, is it not? If Gabriel ate bread made with diseased grain—"

"He would have been retching, as well as convulsing, most likely. As would everyone else who might have shared his meal. No, I doubt Lord Bromwich suffers from ergotism," Liliana said. "Especially not if, as you've said, these episodes have recurred with some regularity. I'm simply stating that there *are* natural substances that can cause mania in an otherwise sane person. I just do not know of any that fit with the other symptoms you mentioned."

And Penelope didn't know any person who knew as much about chemistry and medicinal herbs as Liliana. If she didn't have an idea of what it could be . . . "Well, so much for that," she said, hoping she didn't sound as dejected as she felt.

Liliana laughed, shaking her head. "I don't know everything, Pen. But I'd be happy to do some research." She patted her middle. "It isn't as if I can be out wading in the bogs collecting specimens right now." Her lips twisted. "I cannot even work in my laboratory these days. You wouldn't believe how much glassware I've knocked to the floor and shattered with this stomach of mine. It is sad. And expensive!"

The cousins had a laugh over that, and then Liliana placed her hands low on her hips and pressed her shoulders back into the settee, stretching. "Ah." She sighed, closing her eyes for a moment as she settled back into the cushions.

That moment stretched into two. Then three. Just when Penelope thought perhaps Liliana had nodded off, she said, "Sometimes the mistakes we make in life change us for the better. We learn and grow. You need to start trusting yourself again, Pen."

Penelope swallowed against a suspiciously aching throat. Then she cleared it. "Yes, well, I'll leave you to your nap. Did Geoffrey say when he and Gabriel were expected to return?" If they wouldn't be back for a bit yet, maybe she'd pop up to the nursery and visit her darling niece.

"Mmmm," Liliana murmured, already drifting off. "I expect they will be out most of the afternoon. Geoffrey said something about needing to inspect the new shaft at the mine."

The mine? How would Gabriel be able to do that? He'd barely made the carriage ride yesterday. Being in the dark underground would be impossible. Just attempting it might be enough to throw him into a panic. Surely he wouldn't even try.

And yet she'd worked with soldiers enough to know how men were with other men, loath to reveal any weakness.

The nursery would have to wait.

The thunder of hooves beat the turf as Gabriel pounded along, staying slightly behind Stratford and his mount as they charged up a shallow hill. The brisk late-morning air whipped his cheeks, its clean crispness filling Gabriel's lungs—and lifting his spirits.

Galloping into the eastern horizon, the sun bright in

his eyes and the harsh exhalations of man and beast loud in his ears, he felt nothing but pure exhilaration.

So how could Penelope's suggestion possibly hold water? She'd said that things that reminded him of the war might throw him into episodes of battle fatigue. But if anything would bring to mind his wartime service as a cavalryman in the 10th Prince of Wales Own Hussars, it would be galloping at high speeds over an open field. And yet he felt stronger than he had in months.

Granted, the sights, sounds and smells of the battlefield were far from those of the pastoral scenery of rural Shropshire. But one would think his mind would still make whatever mysterious association Penelope had been trying to explain to him.

Stratford slowed his horse as they crested the summit of the hill, and Gabriel followed suit, reining in beside him.

"Not bad horsemanship, Bromwich," the earl called, leaning forward to pat his charger's neck. When Stratford straightened, he looked over and grinned. "For a Hussar."

Gabriel snorted, but a corner of his mouth turned up in a smile. He found he liked Geoffrey Wentworth. The men hadn't had much occasion to socialize in the past. They'd known *of* each other, of course. But Stratford had been a few years ahead of him in school. There hadn't been much opportunity for fraternization during the wars, either. While they'd both been light cavalry, Stratford had been 12th Light Dragoon.

"Take heart, man," the earl went on, with a laugh.

"At least you lot got to sport those fancy collars and *dashing* mustaches."

Gabriel gave Stratford a good-natured scowl at that. He'd hated those uniforms, with all of the elaborate braiding and colorful layers. They had been Prinny's idea, of course.

No, the man is King George IV now, Gabriel reminded himself. Much had changed in the weeks he'd been locked away at Vickering Place—not the least of which was the death of the mad king.

Well, anyway, that damned uniform had not been very practical in the midst of battle. Nor had those cursed mustaches. They'd itched. Not to mention they'd trapped dust around one's mouth, making everything taste perpetually of dirt.

"I believe you labor under a grievous misassumption, Stratford," Gabriel retorted dryly. "We Hussars didn't ride behind you because you were faster, but because *someone* had to be there to save your arses."

Stratford gave a shout of laughter before turning his horse along the ridgeline.

They rode companionably for a while, each man enjoying the freedom in his own way. Gabriel hadn't known what to expect when Stratford had invited him out to ride this morning. He'd half expected to be grilled thoroughly about his madness. Hell, that's what *he* would have done to a suspected lunatic staying in the same house as *his* wife and family. He'd want to know if the man posed a danger.

But Stratford had been welcoming and gracious, treating him with nothing but quiet respect.

"You know," Stratford said as they ambled along, very near the cliff edge overlooking a wide valley, "I'd heard that you and your men were the ones who met Blücher and the Prussian army. If you hadn't directed them to us . . . if they hadn't drawn off Napoleon's reserves when they did . . ." The earl's eyes narrowed into the distance. "Well, let's just say even the peasants would be speaking French by now."

Gabriel pressed his lips together into some semblance of a smile. Well, it was supposed to be a smile, but more likely it had been a grimace. As always when someone mentioned Waterloo, a queer feeling rose up in his stomach. People told him he'd been a hero that day, but he didn't remember that. All he remembered was that he was the only man in his hand-chosen company who'd come home from that fateful charge alive.

He usually gave a perfunctory nod and then changed the subject when it came up. But Penelope had said that his illness might be helped by facing whatever traumas he'd experienced during the war. He could hardly face this one if he had no memory of it. Perhaps talking with a man who had been on the battlefield that day would help him recall something that might help. "You heard correctly, but I have no memory of any of it."

Stratford turned a startled gaze on him.

"The last thing I can recall is the damned cannonade." The French had lined up on the ridge above La Haye Sante and fired directly into Wellington's center and left flanks. The awful booming and the acrid stench of powder and smoke and burned flesh came back to him like a sense memory.

Beside him, Stratford was nodding, remembering the same moment, though probably from his own place on the battlefield. "Yes. It was the worst barrage I'd ever faced in my dozen years of soldiering," he said solemnly.

Gabriel understood all too well what Stratford meant. He'd been scared witless, but those quiet words were as close as a soldier would ever come to saying as much. "Well, we knew we were in danger of the French cutting us off from the expected reinforcement of the Prussian army. One of my men was tasked with ferrying messages between Blücher and Wellington. The Prussians had been coming up a little behind but parallel to our own forces. But with the French forcing Wellington back, it became clear that the planned rendezvous point would no longer work."

His chest tightened as he remembered the precise moment that realization had hit home. "I knew we'd have to reach the Prussians and get them turned in the right direction. I chose a few of my best men to ride through the French lines."

"Good God, man," Stratford breathed. "That was a suicide mission."

"Yes." Guilt burned in Gabriel's gut. "If I could have been assured that I would have made it to Blücher alive myself, I would have gone alone. But you remember how it was."

Stratford nodded grimly.

"I did my best to select men without families, men without children at least, as most had wives or sweethearts." Or were supporting camp followers. "But some of the family men insisted on coming along."

"Brave souls."

"Indeed. Fourteen of us shed our coats and hats, so as to be less recognizable as British soldiers, and set off in pairs by different routes. And then . . ."

"Then?"

Gabriel's hand fisted tightly over the reins. "Then nothing. That is the last that I remember. I woke up in hospital a week later. I am told that I did reach Blücher—I know this only because the man mentioned my name to Wellington himself afterward. I am also told that I was in on the charge, but as I said, I have no memory of any of it."

"What of the others?" Stratford asked.

"Lost. To a man."

Stratford winced. "I am sorry," he said, genuine regret in his voice. Gabriel nodded. Stratford likely did understand, to a point. As a leader of men, he'd have lost many himself. But Gabriel also knew Stratford's Waterloo experience had been far different from his. The earl was famously known for rescuing several men that day, even taking a bayonet that was meant for another—one that had laid him up in a Belgian hospital for months.

Whereas he had led his men to slaughter.

"Were you taken to Brussels, then?"

Gabriel nodded. "Apparently, I was found three or four days after the battle ended. I never knew where." He could only imagine what horror that must have been. The battlefield had been littered with the decomposing bodies of men and beasts—all made worse by the mud and humidity. "It is likely a blessing I cannot recall anything of that."

"Yes. But once you woke, could no one fill in the gaps for you? What about the person who found you alive?"

"No one knows who found me. I simply arrived at a church near Waterloo in an ambulance cart with a few lucky others, clinging to life. I was transferred on to a hospital in Brussels after they were unable to wake me. Since I'd removed my jacket and hat—and the insignia that would have identified me as a British officer—no one even knew who I was until I was able to tell them. Everything that happened between when I set off on my mission and when I awoke is lost to me."

The men rode side by side, each lost in their own reflection for a time.

Finally, Stratford broke the silence. "I didn't wake properly for weeks. Fever, you see. I was quite delirious for some time. But when I did awaken, I remembered all," he said, his voice low. "Every terrifying, excruciating moment." He turned his gaze to Gabriel, and Gabriel recognized the haunted look in the earl's eyes. "Honestly, I don't know which is better."

Gabriel nodded, and Stratford turned his face back toward the horizon.

Strangely, Gabriel felt lighter after that morose conversation. Perhaps Pen was right. Talking to someone who had experienced some of what he had did make him feel better. Stronger somehow.

Several thoughts struck him with that realization.

When he'd first met Penelope, he remembered wondering if she had understood him so well because her cousin's husband had suffered from the same things he did. It would make sense. After all, Stratford had been campaigning for twelve years, nearly four years longer than Gabriel had. And he'd suffered a grievous injury and painful recovery—if that wasn't traumatic, Gabriel didn't know what was.

Perhaps that was one of the reasons Stratford had funded the hospital for ex-soldiers that he and his wife ran, and where Penelope worked—because he knew firsthand what men back from the wars struggled with. If the earl had suffered from battle fatigue and made it through, maybe there was hope for him.

He should just ask the man. And yet the very idea made his tongue taste of dust, much like those damned mustaches once had. Men didn't talk about such things, particularly not with other men.

Still, Penelope seemed to think the talking was helpful.

He cleared his throat. "Forgive me, but may I ask you a rather personal question?"

Stratford turned his face to him. "Of course."

"I assume—" The damned lump in his throat remained, so he cleared it again. "I assume, what with the hospital and all, you are familiar with battle fatigue."

The earl dipped his head in a nod.

Gabriel held his gaze, but it took effort. Damn. It was harder to ask the bloody question than it had been to take on the French infantry. "Did you ever suffer from it?"

A kind sympathy clouded Stratford's eyes. "No. At least not in the way Penelope has described it to me. My war wounds were strictly physical."

Gabriel looked away from him, his cheeks heating with embarrassment. And anger. What the hell was wrong with him, then? What flaw in his character did he harbor that made him susceptible to this weakness and not Stratford? God damn it.

"Well, *mostly* physical," Stratford amended after a moment's thought. "I will admit that I returned to England a changed man. Things that had once seemed so important were now foolish to me. I had difficulty picking up the reins of my old life. It no longer seemed to fit me."

Gabriel grunted his agreement. Yes—to all of that. But Stratford hadn't gone mad because of it.

"The people in my life no longer fit, either. Had I not met Liliana . . . Well, she's truly the one who healed me. I don't mean physically, though she did help there. She is brilliant that way. But more important, she healed my *soul*. I wouldn't be the man I am today without her," he said quietly.

Gabriel looked over at him. Men didn't talk of these things, either. Stratford gave him a half shrug and a wry smile before turning back to the path ahead.

Stratford hadn't had to make himself vulnerable to him, and Gabriel suspected he'd done so to make him feel at less of a disadvantage. He liked the earl all the more for it.

Only short minutes later, they reached the edge of a wide valley. "Ah, here we are." Stratford tapped his heel and led his horse onto the narrow path that descended into the small village below.

Gabriel followed behind, coming beside Stratford again when they reached the bottom.

"I thought we were visiting your mining operation," Gabriel said, his eyes scanning what looked to be the beginnings of an estate village instead. A tidy row of houses seemed to have sprung up from the ground only very recently, their architecture uniform and attractive, mimicking the Palladian styling of Somerton Park's manor home. The homes had grand mullioned windows that opened onto one side of a small village green, and each of the front doors was painted a muted green that contrasted pleasingly with the red brick.

There was also a larger building that looked a bit older and more temporary in nature, as well as a squat building boasting a sign that declared it a small tavern. A line of what looked to be shops skirted the other side of the green, with a large stone gazebo completing the square at the far end.

"We are," Stratford said, pointing several yards into the distance, where indeed Gabriel could see a stone façade built unobtrusively into the hill on the far side of the valley. "That's the entrance to shaft one."

A squat arch lay in the center of the wall, the black entrance to the tunnel covered with metal bars. Somewhere deep within that hill, miners worked to drag wagons of lead ore back to the surface. Gabriel's throat tightened just thinking about it.

"Two is over there." Stratford pointed to another hill farther on, with a similar entrance cut into it. "And we plan to sink three next year. I'd hoped to have it in operation this year, but splitting my time and funds between this and the soldiers' hospital has slowed things down a bit."

"And this village?" Gabriel asked, intrigued.

"Is where the men who work here live. I opened my land to mining only so that I could employ ex-soldiers, you see. They've come from all over England to settle here, and we put the profits into building housing and such first, and then once we're solvent, we hope to fund more employment projects."

Gabriel raised his eyebrows, looking around at the small village with renewed interest. He'd known that Stratford had fought tirelessly in Parliament the past years to better the plight of the hundreds of thousands of soldiers who'd returned to England without prospects. His admiration for the man grew when he realized that Stratford had put his own personal fortune where his mouth was, as well.

"Most of the men live in the barracks there, as they have no families," he said, pointing to the more temporary barnlike building Gabriel had noticed. "However, as they marry, we are working on building homes suited for wives and children. Already there are several wives, a few infants and even the occasional toddler. I imagine we'll have a right village before we know it."

Stratford exhaled with what seemed to be satisfaction as he surveyed what he had created. Gabriel felt a stab of envy. The earl was doing something of meaning with his life and with his resources. He had *purpose*.

The restlessness that had gnawed at Gabriel these past years bit viciously now, the pain of it—of the utter uselessness he'd been reduced to—streaked through his chest.

Stratford brought his mount to a stop near the barracks and dismounted, tying his horse off. Gabriel slipped off of his own mount, securing the chestnut next to Stratford's.

The earl pulled a timepiece from his breeches pocket by its fob and checked it. "My foreman should be meeting us here any moment." He glanced toward the mine entrance, squinting. "And right on time."

Slipping the watch back into its pocket, he nodded to a stocky man who emerged from the entrance of shaft one. The foreman looked to be no older than they and carried himself with the swift, confident stride of a military man.

The two shook hand like old friends. "Tom," Stratford greeted.

"Major," the man returned with a smile, confirming Gabriel's impression.

Stratford made the introductions, and then the foreman asked, "Are you ready to inspect the new section of tunnel?"

"Indeed," Stratford answered, and followed the foreman toward the gaping black hole in the earth. He glanced over his shoulder. "Coming, Bromwich?"

Like hell. "I prefer to remain aboveground, if it's all

the same," he said as nonchalantly as he could around his tightening throat.

"Suit yourself," Stratford said amiably. "I shouldn't be more than an hour. Feel free to look around. Pop into the tavern, if you like."

Gabriel gave a nod of assent. He turned away, unable even to watch the black hole swallow the two men.

He didn't go straight to the tavern, though the need for a drink was strong after all he'd revealed to Stratford earlier. Instead he wandered around the small village, marveling at what the earl had created here. He walked the line of shops first. Some were empty, waiting for the village to grow to fit them. However, a baker was hard at work, as was a smithy and a combination draper/tailor. As Gabriel walked along, the shopkeepers gave him curious but friendly nods.

On the other side of the green were the cottages. Gabriel stopped at one on the far end and peered inside through a window. It looked to be empty. He decided to try the door and found it unlocked. "Anyone here?" he called into the cottage before opening the door fully.

When no one answered, he walked in. Feeble though the winter sunlight was, it cast enough light through the windows for him to appreciate the fine aspects of the cottage. Though not overly large, the design made good use of the space. It was far nicer than any of the tenant cottages on his own estate in Birminghamshire.

Gabriel imagined the men who lived and worked here counted themselves lucky, and not just because of the fine accommodations. The plight of too many ex-soldiers was perilous indeed, and Stratford had saved them from an uncertain future. It seemed the earl was a hero on and off the battlefield, whereas he was struggling to manage even his own life—his very sanity. What good was *he* to anyone?

After a half hour or so, he found his way to the pub. The pleasant earthy scents of wood smoke, roasting meats and ale greeted him as he pushed into the tavern. Like everything else in the village, the taproom was clean and new with bright, airy windows. It was also empty, save for one barmaid who was wiping down tables. She didn't even glance up when she heard the bell, only said, "You lot are early today. Well, you know the drill. Sit anywhere you like. Luncheon will be ready soon."

Gabriel chose a chair near one of the large windows and stared out over the green, still thinking of the power of purpose in one's life. Stratford had it in spades, and it seemed to bring him great satisfaction. Penelope had spoken of it, as well. About how her work had given her life meaning after Michael's suicide. Had given her a reason to go on.

The gnawing in his chest had settled into a dull ache, but now it flared up again. He had been ambitious once. A leader of men. But his illness had stripped him, laid him bare, and he despaired of ever being that man again. After all, who in their right mind would ever follow a madman?

Who even had need of one?

"Sorry to keep you waiting," the barmaid said. He

turned away from the window to face her. "What can I get for y—"

The girl's eyes widened with recognition, much the same as his must have.

"Major Devereaux?" she said wonderingly. "Is it really you?"

Chapter Twelve

The young woman's eyes went even wider as she slapped a hand over her mouth. "Oh, a pox on it. I mean Lord Bromwich, o'course."

Gabriel couldn't resist a grin at her salty language. You could take the girl off of the battlefield . . . "Mary Finley," he said warmly, coming to his feet to greet her. "Is that really you?"

As she bobbed her head, he marveled at the changes in her. She might still sound like the woman he'd known, but everything else had changed—and for the better. When he'd last seen Mary, she'd been gaunt and sallow skinned, her blue eyes dull and haunted. The woman who stood before him now looked as healthy as a country milkmaid, her cheeks full and rosy, and her eyes twinkled in a way that turned her rather plain features quite lovely.

She flashed him a happy smile. "Hard to believe, in'it?"

It was. Not that he was being uncharitable, but Mary had not lived an easy life as an unofficial camp follower, living, working—and sometimes fighting—alongside the army as they battled their way across the Continent.

She'd been a very young peasant girl who'd followed her beloved to Spain, but he'd fallen at Badajoz. Gabriel didn't like to think of the things she must have done to survive unprotected. It was only several months later that Gabriel had come to know her, when she'd attached herself to his regiment and had become a regular fixture around their campfire. Eventually, she and one of his lieutenants had grown quite close.

"Whatever are you doing *here?*" he asked, still trying to reconcile the Mary of his mind with the girl before him.

Her cheeks flushed, and she twisted her apron between her fingers. "You're not angry with me, are you, m'lord? I know you went out of your way to get me that position at the Silver Swan, and I appreciated it, I did. But I met a nice man there, and then he got on here at the mine and—" She shrugged ruefully.

So that explained how she'd gone from working at the inn in Birmingham where he'd placed her to a pub on the Earl of Stratford's private estate in Shropshire.

"But I would hate it if you thought me ungrateful," she finished, her face scrunched with worry.

"Don't even think it," he assured her. "I only ever

wanted to make certain you had a roof over your head and decent prospects after . . ."

Mary pressed her lips together and nodded, neither of them having to finish the sentence: after Lieutenant Baker had fallen during that fateful mission at Waterloo and left her once again alone.

She breathed in and put a smile back on her face, even if her eyes had saddened with memory. "Well, I got a right fine roof over my head now." She pointed out of the window at the row of cottages. "That third door is me and my husband's. And by summer's end, our baby's, too," she said, settling her hands over her middle.

"That's wonderful, Mary—er, *Mrs.* . . . ?"

Her smile widened then, revealing a dimple in her cheek he'd never noticed before. "It's Mary Landings, now, m'lord," she said proudly.

"Well, my felicitations on both counts, Mrs. Landings." Gabriel heard the distant tinkling of a bell behind him—the door opening, most likely. It seemed as if the lunch crowd was arriving.

Mary reached out and took both of his hands, her eyes bright with suspicious moisture. "I'm only glad I got to see you again so I could thank you proper. I wouldn't be here if it weren't for you." She squeezed his hands to emphasize her point. "And don't think I'll ever be forgetting it. You didn't have to do what you done, not even for the *real* widows you helped—much less a girl like me. You're an *angel*, m'lord—just like your namesake," she finished, her face flushing red.

Then she reached up on her tiptoes and kissed him

on his cheek before dropping his hands and skirting past him to greet the incoming patrons.

Gabriel stood there a long moment, a bemused smile on his face. He'd been called many things in his life, but despite his given name, *angel* had never been one of them. Michael had always been the one who'd drawn that comparison, with his blond good looks, Byron-esque features and charm. Whereas Gabriel had always been considered raw boned and earthy, not to mention brooding—even before the war changed him.

Nor did he think he deserved to be called angelic now. What he'd done for Mary Landings had cost him nothing but some coin, of which he had plenty to spare. Sure, it had taken some time and effort on his part to track her down, but he'd owed her that after sending Baker to his death.

The familiar guilt twinged, but curiously, not as strongly as usual. Seeing Mary happy, healthy and well settled filled him with a deep sense of reward that seemed to push out the guilt—or at least not allow it as much space in his chest. The gratitude that had shone in her eyes had both humbled him and honored him.

He had made a difference in her life. And small though it was, just knowing that made a difference in *his*. He'd forgotten what that felt like.

"The service is quite friendly here, I see."

Gabriel started at Penelope's voice, turning to find her standing a few feet behind him. He blinked and looked again. She was dressed in her customary black, with some sort of small bonnet tied on at a jaunty angle. As always, despite its dour color, her ensemble was quite proper and fashionable. But that wasn't the reason he'd had to look twice.

No, it was that Penelope looked far from proper in it. Her color was high and her hair decidedly mussed. And she was windblown, judging from all that and the slight chafing on her cheeks. She must have ridden here like the devil. Blond ringlets had pulled away from their pins and now clung to her face much as he imagined they would if a lover were to run his fingers through her locks and let them fall where they may.

It was all too reminiscent of how she'd looked last night in the carriage—save that last night, her lips had been red and swollen from his kisses. His blood heated, even as his eyes dropped to her mouth.

Christ, he certainly felt anything but angelic now.

"Pen," he said, his voice gruff with sudden arousal. "What a lovely surprise." He stepped closer, delighted when her flush deepened. Was she, too, remembering their kiss?

But the look she gave him was not one of desire. Instead, curiosity and—could it be jealousy?—narrowed her eyes. "Do you know that barmaid?"

He glanced over to where Mary was laughing with a table of patrons as she served them their ale. Then he returned his gaze to Pen. Oh yes, her eyes had a little more green to them right now, did they? The fact pleased him. Very much. "Yes."

Pen narrowed her eyes on him expectantly, and he took pity on her.

"From the wars. She was the"—he thought how to put it delicately—"*inamorata* of one of my lieutenants."

Understanding lit her face. "I see," she murmured. And she likely did. It was a little-discussed reality of military life—never mentioned in polite circles, of course. But having worked so closely with soldiers, Penelope had to have heard of the camp followers.

While each company allowed four to six wives to travel with their husbands, the army tended to turn a blind eye to the other women who followed along. Many soldiers picked up companions along the way, sometimes from amongst the local populations, sometimes taking on the lover of a fallen comrade.

The women were expected to earn their keep by cooking, washing and, all too often, nursing the wounded—among other duties.

"She seemed to very much appreciate some service you did her," Penelope said, not even trying to disguise her interest.

She'd been listening to their conversation? His humor fled. He'd been prepared to tell her how he knew Mary, but nothing more. "I—"

The tavern door slammed open, cracking against the wall as a boisterous group of miners piled in, their laughter loud and jarring. The small room was filling quickly, and soon it would be rather crowded.

Gabriel took Penelope by the shoulders and gently turned her, placing an arm behind her back to usher her toward the door. "Let us walk outside," he suggested.

Penelope allowed Gabriel to escort her out of the tavern. She'd noticed him startle at the sudden noise, but he'd hidden it well. He'd obviously not gone down into the mine with Geoffrey, either, so she really had nothing to be concerned about.

Except for her own feelings. *They* were certainly cause for alarm. She cared for Gabriel much more than was wise. She'd acknowledged that fact as she'd demanded Geoffrey's dog cart be made ready in the stables. What else could explain the reckless disregard for her own safety as she'd raced the two-wheeled conveyance over dangerously hilly countryside, just to make sure Gabriel was well? To be here in case he'd needed her?

It was ridiculous, really.

What was *more* ridiculous was the burst of jealousy that had torn through her when that barmaid had taken Gabriel's hands and kissed him so familiarly. He had responded warmly to the woman, as well. There was some sort of deep connection between them, and it left Penelope feeling, well, protective.

She snorted. Who was she kidding? She didn't feel protective. She felt possessive.

And that was not good, either.

That didn't stop her from wanting an explanation, though. She slipped her arm through his as he led her down the steps and into a stroll along the green.

"You were saying?" she prodded.

They walked along the green in silence for a few moments, until Penelope began to wonder if he planned to answer her at all.

Then he cleared his throat. "Mary, ah, accompanied my regiment for the better part of two years."

The maid had been a camp follower?

Penelope glanced up at him and saw that a spot of color dotted his cheek. Was he embarrassed? He shouldn't be. She'd known the moment his lips had taken hers yesterday that Gabriel was a man of strong appetites. She would hardly expect him not to have taken his ease where he could during his years away from England.

Not that his celibacy or lack thereof was any of her business, of course.

"Mary was a game girl. Always willing to work hard and do her part in camp with a cheerful attitude. During the six months or so before Waterloo, she and one of my lieutenants developed a more exclusive arrangement."

They tipped their heads to a shopkeeper who was sweeping his entrance.

"I have no way of knowing what Lieutenant Baker's intentions toward Mary were after the war, nor will I ever. He died at Waterloo."

"I'm sorry," she said, wondering where this was leading. He could have stopped his explanation at "camp follower," but she sensed there was more to the story.

"Did you know that when our armies departed Belgium and France, scores of women and children were left on the bloody battlefields to fend for themselves, without the protection of a man?" he went on.

Penelope felt herself blanch. "Alone?"

"Yes." Gabriel's voice had gone gruff with emotion. "And not just widows and camp followers whose men had fallen. The army only took responsibility for officers' wives and four to six officially sanctioned wives per hundred enlisted men. They were the only women allowed on the transport back to England. The rest of the men's wives and children were stranded with no provisions and no way home. It is one of the uglier realities of war."

"How awful," she whispered, her heart squeezing. She'd felt stranded without Michael. Adrift, without mooring. But even as badly as things had ended, at least she'd been safe in England, with a home and an income and the support of her family. Tears pricked her eyes. Those poor women and children.

And then she just knew. "You found Mary and brought her home with you, didn't you?"

By this time, they had reached the large rectangular gazebo anchored at the rear of the green. Gabriel assisted her up the two steps and through the middle arch of the entrance. He led her to one of the stone benches in the center and released her arm then, stepping back from her.

"I did. And when we arrived in England, I helped her find stable employment and a place to live. That is all."

"That is all? Gabriel, that was"—that was more than even their own country had done; it was kind and noble and—"heroic."

He flinched at the word. What an odd reaction. There were yet more revelations roiling under the surface; she was sure of it.

Then she remembered something else Mary had said, something about *real* widows.

"You helped more than just Mary, didn't you?"

He tipped his head dismissively. "Yes."

After a moment, she realized he meant not to say anything more. Well, she wasn't going to let him get away with that. Whatever he wasn't saying had to be an important clue as to why he suffered so. "Why?" she challenged.

A great heaving breath left his lungs as he scrubbed his hands over his face, and she knew she'd been right to push him. He pivoted away from her, walking a few steps to drop onto one of the ornately carved benches nearby. After a moment's contemplation, he said, "It was the only decent thing I could do, since it was my fault their husbands were dead."

Penelope caught her breath. "I'm sure that's not true," she murmured as she followed him to the bench and sat beside him.

"Oh, it is." He lifted his head just a little, turning his face to her. His eyebrow was raised with a cocksure tilt, and he huffed. "I suppose this is one of those moments when you will say that I must talk it out for my own good." His lips turned up in a half smile that was both boyish and wounded, and that tugged at her heart.

She simply lifted an eyebrow in answer.

"I knew you were going to say that," he grumbled lightly. Gabriel straightened in his seat, leaning back now with his hands clasped over his stomach. He didn't look at her but fixed his gaze out over the green. "It was late in the afternoon and the battle had been raging for nearly seven hours . . ."

Penelope sat in silence, listening as Gabriel told her

a story of messages between Wellington and a Prussian general, of skirmishes that threatened a planned rendezvous point, of a dangerous mission across enemy lines for which he'd handpicked men who had all gone to their deaths. He spoke haltingly, and though she longed to reach over and soothe him, she did not wish to stop the flow of words.

Her heart sped up a bit when he spoke of a week's memory loss. Something significant lay there also. However, that was not the matter at hand, so she tucked that information away without interrupting him.

"I learned that all of my men were lost while in hospital, and naturally, I immediately thought of their widows. One was sanctioned, so I knew she would at least make it home. But I couldn't live with the idea of the others being left alone because of a choice I made."

She thought to argue with him about that, but instead she asked, "How many were stranded?"

"Three, including Mary. One of the women had two children, as well."

Penelope winced at the thought of how terrified they must have been. Even though they had just lived through a war, the prospect of being alone in a strange land must have been even more frightening.

"So you found them and brought them home, too," she said softly.

He nodded. "I could never make up for the loss of their husbands, of course, but I got them home safely and helped them find situations. As I was able, I tracked down each of the dead men's wives here in England, as well . . . seven in all . . . just to make certain they were getting along all right and offering what help I could."

They sat in silence for a moment. Then Penelope remembered something. "That woman in Vickering Place—the widow of your lieutenant. Was she one of these seven?"

Gabriel looked over at her then. "Yes. When I found Mrs. Boyd, she was in the direst of straits. She'd gone mad in the months after the news of her husband's death reached her." He shuddered. "Her sister said it was as if her mind had just broken under the grief and the strain of trying to raise her children alone. Miss Creevey, the sister, had given up her own position in town and was struggling to care for them all herself, but the burden was too much.

"So, I paid for the children to be taken in by a nice family and made sure the sister found a new position. Then I began searching for a sanatorium for Mrs. Boyd. Ironically enough," he said with a twist of his lips, "that is how I first discovered Vickering Place." His hollow laugh rang off of the gazebo's stone ceiling. "Little did I know I'd soon be joining her there."

Penelope blinked. "You have been paying for an impoverished widow to live in Vickering Place all of this time?" Private sanatoriums were not inexpensive by any stretch of the imagination. She couldn't think of another person who would go to such lengths for a stranger, and a mad one at that, no matter how much guilt they felt.

"Of course," he said, as if it had never occurred to him to do otherwise.

"Gabriel . . ." Penelope reached out and placed her hand over his clasped ones. She couldn't help herself. She'd always known he was a good man, but she'd never realized how incredibly kind and decent he was.

She should have guessed it, though. Something she'd noticed while treating battle fatigue was that the majority of men who suffered from it were sensitive souls. She theorized that one of the reasons it plagued them—and not other men who'd lived through the same trauma—had to do with how deeply they *felt* the awful things that had happened to them.

Some people seemed better able to shield themselves from those negative fears and painful experiences than others. It was almost as if they could put them in a box and hide them away, even from themselves. Whereas some harbored them.

"You do realize those men's deaths were not your fault, don't you?" she asked quietly.

Lines bracketed his mouth, and he exhaled a breath through his nose. "Rationally, yes. I understand war is dangerous. I understand that the mission had to be undertaken. I even understand that it was not I who took their lives, but the enemy. What I don't understand"—Penelope watched his throat move as he swallowed—"is why I survived when they did not."

Penelope wondered if Gabriel's illness might be exacerbated by the guilt he carried. The more she tried to unravel what was causing his battle fatigue, the more twisted the knot became. She would have to be patient as she plucked at it and pray it wasn't hopelessly tangled. Because the more she came to know him, the more desperately she wanted him to be well. He had so much to offer the world.

She squeezed his hands tightly. "Some things can't be understood," she said. "We have no control over them. All we *can* control is how we live in the aftermath. How we make our lives count for something."

Gabriel nodded thoughtfully. "I've been thinking much the same. Seeing Mary so well settled today was good for my soul," he said. "And learning all that Stratford is doing for our ex-soldiers has intrigued me. I'd like to do something similar, but for their widows and children."

A curious warmth glowed in Penelope's chest. "I think that is an excellent notion, Gabriel," she said approvingly. "I've long been appalled by Geoffrey's stories of the poverty and living conditions amongst ex-soldiers and how little the government has done for them. I can only imagine military widows have fared much worse. They could do with a champion."

And a whole Gabriel could be a powerful champion indeed. She liked the idea more and more. A man with something to strive for was a man more likely to get well.

"Perhaps," he allowed, determination glinting in his brown eyes. "But I won't be able to help *anyone* if I end up back in Vickering Place."

She piled her other hand atop where theirs were joined, as if making a pact. "Then we'll do everything in our power to make certain that doesn't happen."

Chapter Thirteen

"I know that I said I was willing to do anything you suggested, but how exactly is this supposed to help?" Gabriel asked, eyeing Penelope skeptically.

It was midafternoon the following day and the two of them were alone in Somerton Park's long gallery. The massive high-ceilinged room was dotted with comfortable-looking tufted benches, chaise longues, a walnut pianoforte and the occasional overstuffed chair. A fire crackled in the massive hearth, centered along the interior wall. The other side of the room boasted tall windows separated by scarcely a yard between them, and every available patch of wall space was covered with colorful portraits and landscapes in gilt frames of varying shapes and sizes.

But the only canvas that interested him at the moment was the blank one on the easel in front of him.

Penelope grinned at him as she removed the lid from a cylindrical earthenware container about the size of a large pumpkin.

"When I first started visiting the soldiers at the hospital, I really had no idea how to reach them." Dipping her hand into the pot, she withdrew a walnut-sized pouch and shook droplets of water from it until it stopped dripping. "Oftentimes we would just talk about our lives and interests. When they discovered I was an artist," she said, taking a pin and piercing the pouch, "they asked to see some of my work."

Red paint oozed out of the tiny hole she'd made, and the crisp tang of linseed oil reached his nose. Pen squeezed a dollop onto a wooden palette and then plugged the hole with a tack before placing the bladder of paint back into her container.

"After some great discussions of art, the men wanted a demonstration, so I did some painting for them." She withdrew another bladder and pricked it, this time eliciting a bright green. "Then I encouraged them to try, and over a period of weeks, I discovered some interesting things."

Green was replaced by yellow. "I already knew, you see, that the very act of painting made *me* feel better. I'd been pouring out my emotions onto the canvas since I'd picked up my first paintbrush. Thankfully"—she flashed him an eye-rolling grin—"the melodramatic canvases of my youth have long since been destroyed."

Blue paint now joined the others on the wood. "Anyway, as the men created their own works, I started noticing symbolism in some. Others were able to externalize their emotions through their art, and once they were on the canvas, separate themselves from the feelings enough to talk about them." Purple joined the mix. "And for some, painting simply improved their moods enough to make it through their day."

He crossed his arms and lowered his chin. "You expect me to . . . *paint* my feelings?"

She smiled and added another color to the palette. "I have a theory that the mere act of creating puts us in a place of positive emotion. Sometimes we can gain insight simply by observing what we've created. And I believe that sometimes the artistic process can bring feelings to the forefront for us to see, even when it is not our intention. Once we can view those feelings objectively, we are free to abolish them as we see fit." One last dollop, white this time, and she placed the lid back on her pot.

Setting the palette on the table near the easel, she reached for brushes, fanning the sable hairs with her fingers. "Liliana wants me to prepare a paper on my findings, though if I did, I expect it would be laughed out of the Royal Society before they even read the title. Imagine me, trying to pretend that I'm brilliant."

He looked at her, gathering art supplies and speaking passionately about the ways she'd discovered to relieve others' suffering—men like him. Didn't she see that she *was* brilliant? But even more, she was compassionate and kind. All of the intelligence in the world would be fruitless without those higher qualities that Penelope had in abundance.

But that seemed too deep for the moment, so he just repeated dryly, "You expect me to paint my feelings."

She pursed her lips, but the corners of her mouth tipped up in a smile despite her efforts to look stern. "It might do you good to try, you know."

He snorted, uncrossing his arms and stepping closer to the easel. "I haven't an artistic bone in my body."

Pen slipped a smock over her dress. "Everyone has a spark of creativity within them," she protested.

"Not me. I am utterly unimaginative, I assure you."

She raised a blond brow as she tied her strings. "I'm certain we could find *something* to inspire you."

Gabriel's breath caught in his throat. Pen had already turned her attention to readying her brushes and wasn't looking at him at all. He knew she hadn't meant her words to imply anything, but as he watched her graceful movements, he thought, *You, Pen. You could inspire me to do whatever you wanted.* He'd paint if she desired it. He'd burst into song. Hell, he'd build her a bloody temple with his bare hands if she wished it, chiseling every stone himself. With a spoon.

"However, *I* am going to do the painting today," she said, snapping his attention back to her. "And *you* are going to be my muse."

"What?"

"Well, I've been thinking about your different symptoms. While they may be part of a whole, I'd like to attack them one by one, and the one I'd like to take on today is the vertigo you experience around ballrooms."

"I see," he said, snagging a long-handled brush from the tabletop. "And we're going to defeat it with art supplies," he said, brandishing it in front of him like a sword.

It was easier to tease than to acknowledge the knot already forming in his stomach.

Pen laughed and snatched the brush back from him. "In a way. Remember when I told you that our minds make certain associations—sometimes *unbeknownst* to us—that can then take over our senses?"

He nodded.

"Well, I think that when you entered those ballrooms, your mind may have interpreted something perfectly innocuous as a threat and convinced your body that there was danger—even though you rationally knew that not to be true."

He frowned. As much as he desperately wished that Penelope's strategies would help him, this sounded like so much mumbo jumbo. "How can that be?"

"My *guess* would be that something you saw, heard or smelled recalled to your mind the danger you were once in, and your body reacted accordingly."

"It is an interesting theory." And a frightening one. If this reaction was unbeknownst to him, what could he do about it? "Let us say you are correct. How would we stop my mind from heading down that path?"

"Sometimes, it is as simple as dissecting the situation and figuring out what, exactly, your mind is erroneously associating with danger. Once your rational mind knows what sets it off, you can effectively break that association. So what I want you to do is close your eyes."

Rather than obey, Gabriel lifted a brow.

"Just trust me," Pen encouraged.

"If you say so." He dropped his lids, feeling foolish. "It can't be any worse than blistering, I suppose."

"*Very* funny," she said, but he could hear the smile in her voice. "Now, I want you to think back to that very first ball on the Peninsula and describe everything you see and feel in great detail. I am going to paint what I hear you say. When we are finished, I will stand you directly in front of the painting, and I want you to blurt out the first thing that comes to your mind when you see it. Hopefully, that will give us a clue into exactly what it is that frightens you."

He cracked one eye open and half stared at her dubiously.

She lifted her paintbrush and her eyebrows and stared back.

He sighed and closed his eye again.

"All right, you said your vertigo hit when you approached the dance floor. Was that just a coincidence? Or was there something about the dance floor that reminded you of something else?"

He tried to remember. The air had been humid, the breeze blowing moisture in from the Zadorra River on the warm June night. He'd entered the villa through an ancient stone archway, anticipating a rare night of revelry after a battle hard won.

"I can see you thinking, but you'll have to verbalize everything for me, so I can put it to canvas," she reminded him.

"It was night," he said, "but the room was lit by flame. Candles, torches and fires flickered, casting everything in a golden light reminiscent of late afternoon."

"You certainly talk like an artist," she teased. He heard the first scratchings of her brush against canvas, however, which encouraged him to go on.

"The room was large and rectangular, made up of blocked gray stone. It was laid out much like a cloister, with stone arches side by side by side."

It was the noise he'd noticed first that night. A cacophony of voices. They were raised in celebration, but it made him uneasy, particularly when someone shouted out unexpectedly. "It was crowded . . . very crowded. Not just on the dance floor but throughout the entire room, with people spilling out onto the lawn. I approached the dance floor, looking for a willing partner. But as I got near—"

Gabriel's heart pounded in his chest and sweat broke out on his brow, even though he *knew* he was safe in a manor house in Shropshire. As his head began to spin, he opened his eyes. "I can't, Pen."

"Don't look!" She flashed a hand out, blocking his vision. Linseed and walnut oil flooded his nose as her fingers darkened his sight. "You can do this," she assured him. "Just take me with you. Imagine I'm by your side."

He pictured Pen, not as she was now, in her black dress covered by a smock dotted with smears of color, but as she'd been at her wedding ball, in a flowing dress of the lightest yellow. He nodded.

Her hand fell away from his eyes.

"People were dancing," he said shakily. "A lively

tune. Much swirling and even the occasional leap," he tried to joke.

"Describe the people to me," she said, her voice whistling a bit on the hard consonants, as if she were speaking while holding one of the paintbrushes in her mouth. "Were there equal numbers of women and men? What colors are they wearing?"

In his mind's eye, he walked out onto the dance floor, Penelope by his side. Images swirled around him, but with her near him, they didn't bother him as much. Indeed, his heart had slowed to a clip rather than a gallop, and his breathing was not nearly so choppy.

"Men outnumber the ladies by half. Many of the officers are wearing their uniforms. I see members of the Foot in their waist-length red jackets and gray trousers. There are riflemen in green and the Portuguese officers in blue. Some are wearing black hats. The ladies are in all colors—whites, lighter blues, yellows."

"Good," she said, though it sounded more like *guh* around her brush. "Can you smell anything?"

He frowned. "How can you paint smell?"

"I can't. Just humor me."

"Cigar smoke," he said after a moment. For all intents and purposes, with the multiple arched windows, the ballroom had been open air. It had also been overcrowded. Officers milled about just outside the ballroom with their cheroots and cigars. "There was a slight haze of it wafting over the dance floor, brought in by the breeze."

"Hmmm," she said. The scratching of her brush

against the canvas was a rapid staccato now, as if she made quick, short strokes of varying lengths.

"That is all I can remember," he said after a few moments listening to her paint. "May I look?" he asked, feeling a fool just standing there with his eyes closed.

"Almost . . ." *Scratch, scratch, scratch. Tap, tap, tap, tap.*

Finally, he heard the clicking of wood as she set her palette and brushes on the table. Her small hands curled around his shoulders as she positioned him where she wanted him to be. When she had him just so, she let go. He heard her step off to his side.

"Now, when I tell you to open your eyes, I want you to say the first thing that comes to mind."

He nodded his understanding.

"All right . . . look."

Gabriel did. Before his gaze could even fully focus on the painting, he sucked in a breath. "It's the battlefield," he whispered.

It wasn't, of course, yet . . . "The colors," he said, swallowing against a dry throat. But it was more than that. He marveled at the painting. Penelope had captured the light of the ballroom almost exactly as he remembered it, which now that he saw it, was eerily reminiscent of the evening sky in northern Spain. The haze of cigar smoke floated over the ballroom like cannon smoke, and the crush of bodies seemed to flow around one another as if they were locked in combat.

"You wouldn't think a field of battle could be beautiful," he said, almost seeing the battlefield superimposed upon Penelope's painting. "But it is in its own way. Multiple armies, countless regiments, each following their own drummer, each in their own uniforms and yet each part of the whole . . . circling . . . engaging . . ."

"I think," Penelope said quietly, coming to stand closer to him, "that your mind saw this scene and associated it with the battle you'd just survived. Your body felt as if you were walking into danger even though your mind knew you were not, and the confusion between the physical and the mental is why you reacted the way you did."

He remembered the stark terror of that moment, of thinking he was losing his mind. It had been the first step down the dark road that had led him to Vickering Place. Hadn't it? "So, it *wasn't* the beginnings of madness?"

Penelope's hand slipped into his, and he gripped it tight. "No," she said firmly. "Once your mind associated ballrooms with battlefields, your body no longer wished to go anywhere near one. That is all."

A bit shaken, Gabriel stood staring transfixed at the canvas. "Could it really be that simple?"

"Perhaps," she answered. "Now that you are aware of the association, the hope is that you can break it. If you start to feel panic rising next time you are near a ballroom, you can calm yourself down by remembering this moment, the moment you understood that your fear is unfounded. That it is not real."

He *would* remember this moment, but it would be the woman at his side that he would hold on to, much as he was doing right now. He tore his eyes from the painting and looked at her. Darling, darling Pen. Her hand felt so right in his. He couldn't shake the certainty that if he just never let her go, she would heal him, much as Stratford claimed his wife had done for him.

Was it wrong of him to hope for that? Hope that Penelope would want to stay with him? It had to be, of course, but it was only because of her faith in his chances that he had any hope at all. Even if it was wrong, he couldn't squelch the desire. It burned within him.

It also must have shown in his face because Pen suddenly colored and gently tugged her hand from his.

"Th-this is just a first step toward recovery, of course," she said, stepping away to fiddle with her brushes. "The mind is intricate and complex. It is unlikely this is the only harmful association you've made. Sometimes it is simple to make the connection. For example, one man I worked with experienced vivid daytime terrors anytime he smelled gunpowder or heard a loud booming noise, which are obvious reminders of the battlefields. Needless to say, he no longer goes out on the hunt."

Gabriel nodded. "Neither do I."

"Yes. But it can also be something innocuous and not nearly so clear, like the taste of a certain food. Another man would go into tremors upon taking a bite of mutton. Only after we explored this thoroughly did we realize he'd been eating mutton stew when the Portuguese attacked at Fuentes de Oñoro. He lost his leg in that battle, so you can imagine what his mind associated with a harmless bite of meat."

"Has he gone off the lamb, then?" Gabriel asked curiously.

She looked up from her task of cleaning brushes and

smiled. "No, actually. You see, he quite *liked* lamb and refused to give it up. Once he knew why he reacted the way he did, he fought through it. It took some time, but now it doesn't seem to bother him at all."

"Amazing," he murmured. And it was. To think, if he could reverse the bothersome effects the wars had wrought in him, he might reclaim his life. *Or have it given back to him.* His eyes roamed over Penelope's lovely face. "You're a wonder, Pen. However did you think to even *try* these methods?"

Her nose scrunched, and she shook her head, setting the brushes back on the table. "I'm no wonder," she said. "I haven't a brilliant mind at all. Association theory just seemed to make sense to me when I first heard of it. But honestly, I hardly comprehend half of what I read on the subject, and I disagree with half of what I do understand." She sighed, her mouth opening, then closing, as if she were searching for words. "Perhaps it is the very simplicity of my mind that led me down this path. I just tried to take the logical next steps, combining the theories with what *I* observed and I stumbled into some successes."

He huffed. "You are hardly simpleminded. I've known from the first day we met that you are highly intuitive," he said. "And the ability to turn that intuition into results . . . that *is* brilliant, Pen."

Her brow furrowed. "Well." She took a deep breath and crossed behind him so that he had to turn to follow her movements. She settled into a pace. "We've discovered what could be behind your vertigo in the ballrooms. But we still have much work to do."

He let her change the subject. "As I said," she went on, "we'll look for hidden associations that might explain the more bothersome symptoms first. I'd also like to explore what is behind your fear of tight spaces." She stopped pacing to look at him, tapping the thumb of her closed fist against her bottom lip. "I'm betting that the week you cannot remember after Waterloo has something to do with it. Perhaps if we can unbury those memories, you will no longer suffer that."

"That would be welcome," he agreed. "Very welcome. However . . ." A fist of unease balled just below his sternum as it always did when he thought of the madness looming just out of his periphery, waiting to strike. "I fear we are ignoring the larger problem."

"Your episodes."

He nodded.

"My *hope*," she said as she resumed her pace, "is that they are not caused by madness at all, but rather from the cumulative effect of unhealthy associations. If we can slay the minor demons, perhaps we'll find the larger beast not to be so terrible."

Oh God, let it be. Fear and hope twisted and twined inside of him—hope she was right, fear she was not—in a delicate balance of emotion. "Have you ever found that to be the case?"

Penelope didn't wince, but he sensed her check the gesture. "As I've said, I've not seen episodes like yours before."

The apology was clear in her voice.

For a moment, the balance in his heart shifted to fear, but he refused to let it take root, damn it. Working with

Penelope these past few days, he felt he'd accomplished more than months at Vickering Place and years on his own before then. Even if their time together led to nothing, it felt like he was finally *doing* something tangible toward his own recovery. It gave him back a measure of control, illusionary though it might be.

As Penelope moved to finish cleaning her brushes, Gabriel walked back to stand in front the ballroom scene. It was quite good, he decided. Rather than clean, crisp lines, the strokes gave more of an impression than anything else. He wondered if that was Penelope's preferred style or if it was done because she'd been painting so quickly. Either way, it was clear she was very talented.

He knew she and Michael had met in the park. Each of them had been painting landscapes, and as he'd packed up to go, Michael had stopped to look over Penelope's shoulder.

That painting she'd been working on had hung over the mantel in their London townhome.

But this painting, she'd done for him, Gabriel.

"May I keep this?" he asked.

She turned her head and shot him a quizzical glance.

"As a reminder. That the fear is not real," he explained using her words.

She smiled at him. "Of course. In fact, that is an excellent idea. There is a local assembly in a fortnight's time that I'd like you to attend with me. It is the perfect venue to see whether today's experiment worked."

Gabriel couldn't quell a flare of alarm at the thought,

but the idea of having Penelope in his arms on the dance floor tamped it down significantly.

"Perhaps if you spend a few moments each day till then looking at the painting, it will help." She came to stand beside him as she looked at the canvas herself. Then she reached out to point at it. "See, I've painted you in the center, just there. When you try, I want you to focus your attention on the image of you. Visualize yourself in the middle of the room, dancers swirling around you. If you start to feel panicked, keep staring at the painting and remind yourself that it is not a battlefield. That you are safe. Perhaps it will, for lack of a better word, *train* your mind to the reality."

He looked where she'd directed him, and indeed, there was the impression of a man standing center. But beside him, there was also a blond woman. And it seemed as if their hands were entwined.

"Is this you?" he asked, pointing the woman out.

She blinked at the canvas, then squinted her eyes and pressed her face closer to it. Then her creamy skin flushed pink. "Ah, um." She laughed. "Yes. I suppose it is."

Did she mean it hadn't been intentional?

"Well"—she licked her lips—"it seemed to help you when I told you to imagine me beside you. And—um—I suppose it was only natural to paint myself there."

Gabriel watched her stammered explanation with fascination. What had she said before? That sometimes the painter expressed emotions or symbolism that they would never otherwise voice? He stared back at the image of the woman holding his hand, and heat slid through him. Then he noticed something else, a bit of symbolism if he'd ever seen any.

"You even paint yourself wearing black," he murmured.

"What?" she asked, clearly confused.

He reached out and touched the still-drying painting, his finger coming away from the woman's dress with a smudge of black. He held it up before her. "You do realize Michael's death was not your fault, don't you?" he asked her quietly, in an echo of the very words she'd said to him about his soldiers.

She sucked in a breath, then closed her mouth. Her eyes shone bright with a sudden glistening of moisture, even as they fixed on the tip of his finger. At the visible manifestation of her own guilt.

"You had no control over him."

She shook her head in quick jerks of denial. "I know where you are leading with this, but it is *not* the same," she whispered. "If I would have followed him to Leeds, he might still be alive!"

"If I would have gone on the mission alone, my men might still be alive, too," he countered. "I could have, you know. I reached Blücher and delivered the message. I could have left all of them behind and still succeeded, but I didn't."

She pressed her lips together.

"My point is, Pen, neither one of us knew what would happen. We did what we felt we must at the time. But you didn't kill Michael any more than I killed my men. Other people pulled those triggers, not you and I."

A tear slipped down her cheek. He reached out to wipe it away, remembering the black paint on his finger just in time. He wiped it on the leg of his trousers, but in the time it took him, she'd dashed her own tears away with the back of her hand, to his regret. He longed to have a reason to touch her.

"You told me that all we could control is how we live in the aftermath of trauma—how we make our lives count," he reminded her.

She dropped her head, staring down at the floor. He reached out and curled his fingers beneath her chin, tipping her face up to him. He hated that she trembled. "And in that, I can only strive to follow your lead. Look at what you are doing. Look at the people you've helped. You inspire me, Pen."

She closed her eyes.

"But this," he said, gesturing to her attire. Since she couldn't see him with her eyes shut, he clarified. "You, in black . . . it is an abomination."

Her eyes opened with a startled flutter and focused on him.

"It is antithetical to who you are. You have to let it go. Do you want to know what I thought when I first met you?"

She nodded slowly, almost as if against her own will.

"I remember comparing you to a ray of early-summer sunshine. You made me happy just to look at you. You drew people to you then. You still do, but you've dimmed somehow. And it is not right. This penance, or . . . punishment, or whatever it is that is hiding your light must end."

He dropped his hand from her chin and walked over to the table where her palette still sat. He picked up a clean brush and dipped it in some paint. The he grabbed a rag and walked back to the canvas, using it to dab the excess black paint until the surface was dry. Then he swiped his brush over the woman's dress.

It took several strokes to cover properly, but when he stepped back, a rich yellow had overtaken the black.

"*That* is who you are, Pen," he said gently. "And I think it is time that you find your way back to her."

She said nothing. Just stood staring with wide eyes at that little bit of symbolism he'd put right in front of her.

And then she seemed to crumple in on herself, her shoulders and head curling protectively as her hands came up to cover her face.

His chest clenched at her quiet sob, alarm snaking up his spine. He dropped the rag and brush forgotten to the floor and reached out for her, grasping her shoulders as he stooped to put his face on a level with hers. "Pen, don't cry. Please. Please, look at me," he said as he dropped one hand to gently tug hers away from her face.

The pain he saw swimming in the pale green depths of her eyes pierced him as surely as the lances the French had used at Waterloo with such deadly efficiency. Good Christ, he hadn't meant for this. He'd only been trying to help her in the same way she'd been helping him. "Oh, Pen," he murmured, stroking her face, her tears warm and wet against his palm.

He had to stop her crying. It tore at him to see her in such anguish, even if she'd needed to hear the truth.

So he gave her something else to latch on to, as she'd done for him when he'd needed the distraction in the carriage that night.

He kissed her.

Chapter Fourteen

Penelope stilled with shock as Gabriel's lips touched hers. But then he pressed against her mouth with a fierceness that drove out everything in her mind and everything in her heart.

Everything but him.

She wanted nothing more than to lose herself to the distraction he offered. She grasped at his shoulders, running her hands over their broad, muscled length. But the embrace didn't bring him close enough. Not nearly close enough. So she clutched at his neck and rose up on her toes, trying to pull herself into him.

Gabriel groaned, a raw sound that sent a thrill skittering down her spine. It only intensified when he tightened his arms around her, bringing her tight and flush against his chest—right where she wanted to be.

But she knew the delicious contact wouldn't suffice

for long. Even as her breasts flattened against his hard planes, hot need curled through her. It rose up from her core in twisting tendrils, weaving through her like hungry vines, pulling and stretching within her.

Hands slid into her hair. His large palm gripped her head, tilting it so that their mouths met at a slightly different angle. His tongue slid into her then and she moaned around it, accepting it. *Craving* it—and more.

Still clutching his neck, she rose a little higher . . . just enough to rock her hips against his, tearing a ragged moan from them both. Encouraged, she rolled her hips in a slow circle against his hard arousal as the vines of need stretched tighter. And tighter still when his hands left her hair to grasp her beneath her hips and drag her over him again.

She pulled her mouth away from his. "I need you." And she did. Needed to remember what it was like to lose herself to desire. Needed to forget the ache of guilt that never seemed to leave her. Needed to feel something—*anything* but the pain that pierced her heart. She loosened her grip on his neck and ran her fingers down his arms, over the hands that kneaded her hips so erotically. She tugged his hands into hers and stepped backward, pulling him with her. "Come."

She gave him no time to protest, leading him unerringly to her chamber door. Bless Liliana for putting them on the top floor rather than in the family wing. She'd done so because their adjoining bedrooms opened onto the long gallery, and she knew Penelope would wish to utilize the gallery for exercise should the rains return. But all Penelope could think of at this moment was that it meant her bedroom, and the mindless bliss she was about to find in it, was only steps away.

Keeping one of his hands firmly in hers, she pivoted to fumble with the doorknob with her other. As the door creaked open enough for them to squeeze through, she tugged him inside.

Once the door was safely closed behind them, she turned to face him again. His chest rose and fell in choppy, heaving pants and his golden brown eyes glowed with heat. He leaned back against the door as if he needed it to brace him. He looked dark and delicious and entirely too clothed. He also looked aroused and wild . . . and hesitant.

Her stomach fluttered anxiously. She didn't want him to come to his senses. She couldn't bear it if he did. She stepped into him once more, pressing herself against him from shoulders to toes, sliding her arms around his neck to cup his face. "Please, Gabriel. Don't think," she said, placing light kisses against his jaw, under his chin until she was thwarted by his cravat. Then she trailed her lips back up to whisper against his mouth, "Please. Just take me."

Her plea snapped whatever restraint he was holding on to, and Penelope gloried as he spun with her in his arms and pinned her against the door. His lips took hers in a voracious kiss as he dipped his knees and then rose again, dragging his body against hers in a slow, hot slide. His chest scraped along her breasts, his abdomen bumped her own, and his arousal burned against her mons. Even through both layers of their clothes, the heat between them was enough to make her swoon.

Were she not pinned between his body and the door, she was certain she'd be in a puddle on the floor.

"Gabriel," she gasped, before his name turned into a groan. His mouth had moved to her ear, and his teeth nipped at the delicate lobe before his tongue swiped out to soothe it.

She slid her hands down his chest and pulled at his shirttails. She wanted to tug the garment over his head, but she didn't wish to wait that long to touch his skin, so she slipped her palms under the fabric and ran them over the ridges of his stomach. His muscles leapt beneath her touch, and he sucked in a breath. But then his mouth robbed *her* of breath when it slid down her neck to bite gently where her neck met her shoulder.

She could stand it no longer. She slipped her hand past his waistband and tore at the buttons of his fall. As soon as she got them open wide enough, she shoved his trousers past his hips and down to his knees. Gabriel hissed as he sprang free, a sound Penelope registered with wicked delight even as she used her foot to finish undressing him, pushing his trousers down around his boots.

"Pen," he rasped, his breathing gone ragged. A pleased smile spread across her face at seeing him so undone. So close to taking her.

And then he spun her in the cage of his arms, tearing at her laces. A few tugs and her bodice sagged a little. His knuckles scraped against her back as he wrestled with the spiral lacing. As soon as she was able, she shrugged the gown off of her shoulders, allowing it to slip down to her waist, where she helped it the rest of the way off.

"Good God," Gabriel muttered from behind her. She imagined how she must look, her back cinched tight in her stays, her flared hips and bottom bared to his gaze. She felt amazingly wanton and she wanted him to feel the same. She pressed herself backward into him.

It worked better than she'd hoped. Gabriel made a low growl in his throat and slammed her against the door, bracing his hands on either side of her. His hard body covered hers, his clothed chest to her clothed back, his bare loins to her naked bottom. His hard erection burned between her thighs, tantalizingly close to where she needed him. Her temperature spiked, as did her desire. She laid her cheek against the cool wood, sighing against it. Then she rolled her hips again.

"Ah," he moaned as his mouth opened on the back of her neck. She shuddered violently as he slid his length against her, rubbing along her slickness with firm slides that tantalized but could never satisfy. She burned with her need, but after several sliding thrusts, she feared he would never come inside her.

Just when she thought she could stand it no longer, he turned her to face him again. As she wrapped her arms around his neck once more, he yanked her right leg off of the floor and wrapped it around his hip. She let go of his neck with her left hand and moved it down his body to grasp his swollen shaft. It slid against her palm, thick and heavy and hot. Something clenched within her, knowing she was so close to having him now, to satisfying the gnawing need that no longer lay dormant inside her.

It had been so long since she'd felt this rush of desire. She'd had many offers over the past two years, but none that had even tempted her.

Well, she was more than tempted now. Somehow, Gabriel had broken through the dark shell she'd been hiding in, to the very heart of her. She wasn't certain how or why or even what it meant. She only knew that what she felt for him in this moment was more than just physical need. It was a deep, desperate longing that frightened her—though not enough to stop her from having him. *Now.* She rubbed the head of him against the center of her pleasure, and a shiver of sparks rippled through her before she parted her blond curls and poised him at her entrance. "Come to me, Gabriel," she pleaded.

"Pen," he moaned before his lips captured hers. His fingers dug into her hips as he lifted her, pulling her other foot off of the floor and encouraging her to wrap that thigh around him, too. As her heel dug into his muscled backside, he thrust up into her.

Yes! she wanted to cry, but she hadn't the breath for that. Instead, she thrust her tongue into his mouth, tangling with his as he buried himself in her heat again.

Lord, she needed this. She clutched Gabriel to her and moved her hips frantically, hoping he would grasp what she wanted. It took only a few hard thrusts to know that he understood completely. He filled her with rough, merciless strokes that fed the fire building inside of her. It was everything she'd hoped for—better even. When he jerked his mouth from hers so he could breathe, she simply laid her head back against the door and reveled in the jarring slam of his body into hers as her entire body tightened and stretched, reaching and striving for the explosion she knew was to come.

And then it was there, bursting upon her with a suddenness that made her cry out with the intensity of it. Her orgasm must have triggered his, because Gabriel drove into her one, two, three more times before pulling her hips hard against his and emptying himself within her pulsing heat.

Gradually, their moans gave way to heavy breaths as the sweat on her skin cooled. She was still pinned to the door by his pelvis, and he was still intimately lodged within her, though he'd softened. She had the fleeting thought that she would like to stay here, joined with him forever. But all too soon, her limbs began to tremble with strain.

And her mind began to think again. Oh God . . . what had she done? She loosened her thighs' grip on Gabriel's hips and lowered her legs to the floor. As he slipped from her, she felt an awful pang of loss that alarmed her further still.

She tried to pull back from his embrace but he wouldn't allow it, tightening his arms around her to where she had little choice but to tuck her face against his shirt. She couldn't help but breathe him in, and despite the knowledge that she should never have done any of this, she savored the moment.

"I'm sorry, Pen," he murmured against her hair.

She lifted her cheek from his chest and looked up at him in genuine confusion.

A muscle ticced in his jaw. "That isn't how I imagined making love to you for our first time. You deserve better than a rough tumble against a wall."

"It was a door, actually," she blurted inanely.

She felt, rather than heard, his grunt.

Her eyes roved his strong brow, his defined cheekbones and tapered jaw, which was clenched tight with concerned regret. He had nothing to feel bad about. Whereas she . . .

Shame filled her. He'd said "first time," as if he hoped—or even expected—there would be more. And why wouldn't he? He'd as much as told her he harbored deep feelings for her that first day at Vickering Place, even though he hadn't known it was really her he was confessing them to. That made her selfish lapse of good sense all the worse. She had no business—none—crossing the lines of intimacy as she had.

Penelope tucked her head back against his chest, unable even to look at him as she said, "No, *I'm* sorry, Gabriel."

He huffed beneath her cheek. "Why?"

Why? So many things were wrong with what she'd just done. "I never should have kissed you. *Again*," she added, given she'd kissed him in the carriage the other day as well. Goodness. Perhaps Mr. Allen had been right about her after all.

Gabriel laughed softly, the sound a quiet rumble beneath her ear. "I kissed you this time, if you remember."

She did. Her toes curled with the memory, in fact. "Yes, but I should have pulled away. Don't you see?" She lifted her head to look up into his face. "In our time together, you have made yourself vulnerable to me, for your treatment's sake. It is unconscionable that I took advantage of you and—"

His soft rumble turned to true laughter then. "Took advantage of me? Pen . . ." He shook his head and his eyes crinkled as he looked at her as if she'd lost her mind. "Making love to you is the *best* thing that has happened to me in—well, perhaps ever."

Her heart tripped even as a new guilt joined her shame. "You may think that now, but I've violated a trust between us. Feelings can easily be confused during the type of treatment we've been attempting and—" Her stomach lurched at her next thought. "God," she croaked. "I will never forgive myself if my mistake undoes any of the progress you've made."

Gabriel's hands moved up to frame her face. "Shhh," he said, stroking her gently. "This—what happened between us just now—is not a mistake. Nor are my feelings confused. Madness aside, I know my own mind."

She shook her head in denial.

He just smiled tenderly at her. "I think I can understand where your worry might be justified if I were just some stranger you'd taken on for treatment. But, Pen . . ." His brow furrowed and his lips twisted, as if he struggled with how to phrase what he wanted to say. Then his face smoothed. "You asked me once why I was able to dance at your wedding and why I was able to attend other balls throughout our acquaintance without you sensing my struggles." His thumb stroked her cheek. "Haven't you figured it out yet? It was because of *you*.

"You kept my darkness at bay. When my anxiety

would threaten, you always seemed to sense when I could do with a diversion—be it a witty remark or an irreverent observation. And whenever I would get near a dance floor and my head would swim and my breath would tighten and my heart would pound, all I had to do was look at you and everything would ease. You were my talisman long before you ever agreed to treat me, Pen. You *always* have been."

She stopped breathing as her heart squeezed. *His talisman?*

"What happened between us just now only strengthens that for me, so don't waste another moment fretting it. Besides . . ." His tender smile turned decidedly wicked, which sent a fresh lick of heat through her middle. "After being in your arms, I feel as if I could take on the world. I think you should kiss me again. Perhaps I will then associate this feeling with your lips so that whenever I need to"—he dipped his head and pressed a quick kiss upon her mouth—"all I have to do is steal a kiss to remember exactly how powerful I feel right now. *That* will do more to heal me than all of the talk in the world, and I daresay it might be good for you, too."

And he took her lips again. She let him. Because despite her lingering worries, right now she felt *alive*. And powerful, too. And hopeful, not only for him but for herself. She didn't want that feeling to end until it absolutely had to.

She broke from the kiss to turn once again in his arms, her decision made. "Help me out of my stays," she commanded, her voice gone husky.

He hesitated for a moment, as if not believing she

meant to let him touch her again, but then his fingers flew over her lacings, pulling them free of their holes. When he'd finished, she turned ever so slowly, allowing him to peel the stays from her body. When she pulled her chemise over her head, it left her standing only in her stockings and slippers.

Gabriel's eyes roamed over her hungrily, seeming to singe her skin wherever his gaze lingered. She reached out to untie his cravat, which while decidedly askew, was still knotted. For that matter, his trousers were still puddled around his ankles because the man still wore his boots. Penelope couldn't stifle a laugh.

Gabriel glanced down at himself, then back at her, the wry half grin she was beginning to adore lifting his lips. "A ridiculous pair we make," he said. "You in only your stockings and garters and me mostly dressed."

"I would say we made a perfectly pleasurable pairing," she teased, enjoying the flash of heat in his eyes. "But I do think, for comparison's sake, we should both be naked, don't you?"

With that, she tugged at his cravat again. Together they managed to rid each other of their remaining attire, issuing small kisses or touches as they went about the pleasurable task. Hovering over each small caress were questions and doubts, almost as if they hung in the air between them: Was she making a terrible mistake becoming Gabriel's lover? Would she end up harming him? Or was he correct, that strengthening their bond in this way might benefit them both?

She couldn't know. She only knew that this felt more right than anything she'd done in years.

When they were both completely bare, Penelope stretched up to kiss Gabriel once again. Dear Lord, it was ever so much better to flatten her body against his when nothing lay between them. His body was well developed. Taut skin, covered with a light dusting of hair, stretched over lean muscle. When he moved against her, gooseflesh prickled her skin—not in a cold way, but in warm, pleasurable shivers as his body brushed hers.

He let her take his lips once . . . twice . . . as he sent his hands skimming over her back, stroking lower over her bottom and then back up again. But just as she was about to deepen her kiss, he moved to tuck his face into her neck as his arms tightened around her.

"Wait, Pen," he said, though at least his breathing was as labored as hers. "Damn me for a fool for saying this, but . . ." He pulled back so that he could see her face. His body vibrated with leashed tension. "Are you certain this is what you want?"

He could be asking so many things with that seemingly innocent question—things about them, things about the future. Whatever he meant, his concern for her feelings filled her heart with warmth. Well, she was certain of only one thing: that she wanted this—*him*—right now. And that was all that mattered. She framed his face, lightly running her fingers over his austere features as she pulled his face down to whisper, "Yes," against his lips before she captured his mouth with her own.

Gabriel felt the dizzying rush of desire flood him, Penelope having broken through the floodgates he'd erected with that one breathy word—*yes*.

Some small distant part of him was still slightly troubled, but it was drowned by the sea of undiluted pleasure coursing through him. Whatever providence had conspired to make Penelope his, if even for a moment, he would not tempt it with worries.

But he would, by God, take her properly in a bed. He ran his hand down her arm and caught her wrist, tugging her gently toward it. She came willingly, even allowing him to lift her body and place her seated on the edge of the bed, although she'd gripped his head and refused to relinquish his tongue in the process.

Not that he wished to take it back from her. Ever.

His hands slid to her knees, and he spread them just enough to step between them. Her warm, silky thighs closed around his hips as they held each other there for a moment, mouths blending and merging, her seated on the tall bed and he standing. Her arms were thrown around his neck, her hands moving in his hair in strokes that were both relaxing and arousing. His own arms were wrapped around her waist, leaving his fingers free to caress her back and hips at will.

But her delving kisses were too much, too erotic. Already lust poured through him, and he'd be damned if he would lose his control and take her quickly once again. He disengaged from her questing lips and slid one hand up to her nape, dropping his mouth to her neck and finding her rapid pulse with his tongue.

It fluttered frantically beneath her skin, a tempo matched by his own. He had to find a way to slow them both down. He was determined to savor her this time, as she'd be a fool to ever let him into her bed again.

Sweet Penelope, his at last. He leaned back to simply take in the sight of her, burning it to his memory. Her form leaned more to the fit than the voluptuous, though while her breasts were not ample, he thought them perfect. Their tips were pale and soft and pink, and he imagined they tasted like heaven. He decided to find out.

He slipped a hand beneath one of her bare breasts, enjoying the weight of it in his palm. He lifted it just enough to meet his descending mouth and opened to suckle her gently.

A small gasp reached his ear even as her nipple beaded against his tongue. Fire shot through him at this tangible taste of her desire. She was sensitive there, he realized, and so he pressed his tongue more roughly over the tight little bud. Penelope quivered in his arms, encouraging him all the more. He brought his other hand to her neglected breast, kneading and teasing it to let it know it was next on his list of pleasurable experiences.

As he continued to tease her breasts, her hands moved upon him. At first they clenched in his hair, pressing his mouth tighter to her chest as his tongue traced circles on her heated skin. But then he felt a hand sliding down his side, slipping between them. Slender fingers curled around his straining erection, and he froze with pleasure, his groan muffled by her breast.

A ragged sound escaped him as she pressed a firm stroke down his length, the skin of her palm dragging along his shaft with a friction that threatened his best intentions. He pulled himself back from her and stepped away, out of reach of her eager hands. "Christ,

Pen." He laughed. "If you keep touching me like that, it will all be over too soon."

Her head tilted as her unfocused gaze settled on him with . . . confusion? "Isn't that . . . ?" Her brow furrowed as she struggled to verbalize her thoughts. "Don't you want . . . ?" she tried again, unsuccessfully.

Understanding washed over him, cooling his ardor just enough for him to be able to think properly.

He'd been a little shocked, he had to admit, by her uninhibited response to him, first in the carriage and then a few moments ago. No, that wasn't true. It wasn't so much her unconstrained sensuality that had surprised him. She'd been married before and obviously enjoyed the act of love. It was the speed with which she gained it.

And he realized something he should have seen before. She didn't realize that lovemaking could be slow and sensual. It made perfect sense. Her husband had possessed a manic energy in everything that he did. That had to have spilled over into their bedchamber, resulting in quick, vigorous couplings. Penelope was like a Thoroughbred, trained to race for her pleasure the moment the gates opened.

God, he should have seen it before. But she'd driven him so very wild with lust that he'd missed the signs.

He watched her now, her lithe body breathing heavily, her nipples hard and straining, her body humming with an energy he sensed with an answering part of himself—one he ruthlessly tamped as the tantalizing possibilities unfolded before him.

Who knew what lay ahead of them . . . him, her.

Who knew if he would ever be whole enough to go after what he wanted—a life with her. But he did know one thing. In this, at least, he had something to offer. He could teach her what pleasure truly was and open her mind to everything she could have in that realm.

"I very much *do* want," he assured her. "However, all I want *you* to do is to relax and let me touch you."

A delicate vee appeared between her brows, and the cloud of passion cleared a bit in her gaze. "I'm sorry?"

"Just trust me," he said as he stepped back into the cradle of her thighs. He grasped her wrist when she reached for his manhood once again and moved her hand gently behind her. "I get to touch *you*," he reminded her. "Not the other way around."

Darling Pen tugged her lower lip between her teeth, but she nodded slowly in understanding.

Lust rocketed through him. If she only understood what he meant to do . . . He was going to take this slowly, draw out every bit of pleasure in her body until she was writhing with it. All of this before he took her. If this were the only time he got this chance, he intended for her to remember it. He raised his hand to stroke her face.

Penelope trembled at Gabriel's light touch. There was a determined heat in his eyes that warmed her whole center. She had to clench her hands into fists to obey his dictate not to touch. Lord, how she wanted to pull him into her so he could fulfill her rising need.

But it was clear he had something else in mind entirely. He stroked the curve of her cheek with a single fingertip. Her every nerve was so sensitized with desire that she felt even that tiny stroke deep in her middle. Her breath sped as he lifted her chin, tilting her head back for his kiss.

Yes, she thought, opening for him even as she tried to press her own tongue into his. He gently pinched her chin between his thumb and forefinger, and she understood she wasn't even to touch him with her mouth. Penelope wanted to growl with frustration, but she ceased her foray.

Gabriel's tongue slowed, coaxed. The tip brushed her teeth, clipped in to explore the soft lining of her cheek, the underside of her tongue, the sensitive roof of her mouth. Slow, languorous kisses that made her light-headed while at the same time ratcheted up the desire within her.

She couldn't resist pulling his hands to her breasts in a bid to get him to touch her again. He complied but with such infuriating slowness that she arched against him with frustrated longing.

"Shhh, my love," he crooned against her. "Be patient. I promise you it will be worth it in the end."

Penelope groaned. Now, what did he mean by that? At this rate, she'd never last until the end.

He continued to take her mouth in long kisses that drew a strange pleasure up from her mons straight through to her mouth . . . drugging, it was. Sensuously wicked. His hands slid into her hair, massaging and caressing in a way that both soothed and set her further on edge. A harsh breath escaped him, and she knew that despite his restraint, he was closer to that same edge than he let on.

She could push him over it, she knew. She'd proven that. He might be angry with her after, but at least it would quench this burning inside. She could beg forgiveness later.

And yet . . . the slow boiling that built within her intrigued her. A part of her yearned to know exactly *what* would be worth the wait. So she kept her hands clenched by her sides.

His hands moved to her breasts again, and Penelope almost cried out with the sharp pleasure of it. Who knew those small mounds could bring her such delight? And then the devil bit down lightly on her hardened nipple, sending a bolt of electricity shooting straight to her core. She couldn't resist clutching at him then, holding his head to her breast as he alternated suckling, nipping and tonguing her. She whimpered with pleasure, writhing in his arms.

"Lie back, love," he whispered.

Oh, thank goodness. He would come to her now, fill her with the powerful thrusts that would drive her to completion. She dropped back to the coverlet with profound relief.

He didn't join her on the bed, but rather tugged at her hips and slid her to the very edge of the mattress. Odd positioning, but she didn't care if he wanted to stand, as long as he took her now.

But instead of stepping between her thighs, he spread them wider and dropped to his knees on the floor. She raised her head, but he shushed her as his fingers found her wetness and stroked the plump, silken flesh.

Her body jerked and sizzled with longing, arching off of the bed as he found the tender peak of her sex with his questing fingers. He rubbed gently, circling, tugging. "Oh!" she gasped as sensation pulled in from the rest of her body to center there.

Then he brushed the swollen bud with his thumb as he deftly slid two fingers inside of her. The sensation was so close . . . so close to what she wanted but not nearly enough. She tossed her head from side to side as her breath shortened further.

"You're torturing me," she accused on a groan.

"Not yet," he breathed, and the very sound sent gooseflesh prickling over her flushed skin.

His fingers found a rhythm counterpoint to his circling thumb, and all Penelope could do was twist and writhe as the tension within her mounted. Despite his pressing digits, she felt empty inside. Why would he not just take her?

And then a shocking jolt of desire speared her as his tongue took the place of his thumb. "*Gabriel,*" she cried out as his mouth took her in a way she'd never before experienced. Her hands clenched and unclenched, twisting the counterpane mercilessly as he lashed her with his tongue—flat, hard strokes against her clitoris— and then replaced his fingers to delve inside her.

Penelope trembled as pleasure spiraled upward from her middle, pulling her into an arching tightness like an invisible string that threatened to snap and send her spinning. Gabriel was no longer touching her gently, but driving her toward release with relentless licks and strokes.

She screamed when she came, the sound wrenching from her as indeed she spun with the dizzying pleasure. It was like nothing she'd felt before. His mouth stayed on her, drawing every bit of it from her before he finally released her.

As her breathing subsided enough to speak, she admitted, "You were right. It was worth it."

Gabriel's husky chuckle vibrated against her skin as he placed a kiss against her inner thigh. "Oh, Pen, that was just the beginning."

Her breath caught in her chest as he rose, wondering how anything could possibly be better than that. But Gabriel spent the next hours answering that question decisively. By the time he took his own pleasure within her, there wasn't a place on her body that he hadn't worshipped with his hands and mouth. She'd peaked twice more by the time he entered her, and even then, it was with slow, steady thrusts that wrung even more pleasure from her exhausted flesh.

Who knew it could be like this? she wondered more than once during their lovemaking. Part of her whispered that it was more than just technique, but she didn't want to think about that. All she knew was that after making love to Gabriel, she would never be the same again.

And she didn't want to think about that, either.

Chapter Fifteen

Two hours before they were due to depart for the coming evening's assembly, Penelope made her way along the long gallery to her room to dress. She'd instructed the maid to lay out the only ball gown she owned that would be appropriate for the small country affair: a simple dress of fine gray muslin woven with stripes of black and trimmed with black satin. Additional angled bands of satin decorated the front and back, too, as well as created an attractive vee along the bodice.

The empire waist was slightly out of date. She'd had the gown made when she'd gone into half-mourning eighteen months ago, but she'd never worn it. No matter. She doubted anyone here would judge her for wearing a dress that was no longer in the height of fashion.

If anyone would be let down by her attire, it would be Gabriel. He'd known she'd sent for part of her wardrobe after their discussion two weeks ago, and every morning that she emerged from her chamber still wearing black, she saw the disappointment in his face. He hadn't mentioned her choice, however, for which she was grateful.

Because she was frustrated with herself, too. But for whatever reason, she couldn't bring herself to don one of the colored dresses that had arrived last week. She'd tried for an hour to put on a lovely lavender day dress the morning after her trunks showed up, but the effort had left her physically ill. After some reflection she realized that she'd been wearing a lavender gown the afternoon that Michael had exploded at her in his studio—the morning her perfectly happy life had begun to unravel. She didn't think she'd ever be able to wear the color again.

Even the other pretty gowns now hanging in her wardrobe seemed to mock her. She'd stare at them every morning, an array of yellows, blues, creams and pinks— remnants of her old life. She'd run her hands over the rich fabrics and imagine herself wearing them—would even select one for the day. But in the end, she'd arrive in the breakfast room in one of the black gowns that had been both her penance and her protection during the past two years.

She couldn't believe she hadn't seen what she'd been doing all this time, especially given how she'd helped so many others discover their unconscious associations. Perhaps she'd just not looked at herself closely enough, so focused as she'd been on others to drown out her own pain. Or perhaps she'd been unknowingly eschewing the frivolous life she'd led before. But now that she was aware of what she was doing, she still clung to her blacks, even though Gabriel insisted they were antithetical to who she was. How could he know that? Even she wasn't sure who she was anymore.

Penelope entered her rooms to find the maid already there, pouring hot water into a ewer and setting out combs, brushes and other such accoutrements in preparation to ready her for the evening. She started to loosen her bodice when her eyes were drawn to the gown hanging over the dressing screen.

Her breath caught in her throat even as her feet stilled, for rather than the gray gown she'd expected, there hung a flowing creation of jonquil silk satin. Though very simple, the dress featured a lowered waist and wider skirt, as was the current style, and was trimmed with silk bobbin lace in the same cheerful shade of yellow.

"Where did this come from?" she asked, but she already knew. Gabriel was somehow responsible for it.

"I dunno, m'lady," the maid answered, frowning. "I laid out the gray, like you told me. But when I came back from fetching the hot water, this is what I found in its place. I thought you must have changed your mind," she said, eyeing her uncertainly.

Penelope flicked her eyes to the inner door that joined her chamber to Gabriel's via a shared private sitting room, then returned her gaze to the maid and tried to cover. "It must have just arrived, then. I'd ordered it earlier," she lied, "but hadn't hoped it would be ready in time for tonight's ball. I am pleased to be wrong."

The maid nodded at her explanation and went back to her task. "It's lovely, m'lady. And much better suited to your coloring, I'd say. You are going to look very beautiful tonight."

Penelope had to concur as she stared at the dress. She couldn't believe Gabriel had purchased her a ball gown, nor did she know how he'd managed it. Her adherence to black must have bothered him more than she'd thought. Since he'd gone to such effort, she had to wear it, didn't she?

She hurried through her ablutions, wondering at his motivations. She remembered him covering the painted black dress with yellow that afternoon in the long gallery. *That is who you are, Pen,* he'd said. *And I think it's time that you find your way back to her.* Was this gown his way of pushing her in that direction? Or had he purchased the dress for himself? Maybe he was afraid of how he'd react in the ballroom tonight and wished for his "talisman" to look as he remembered her, keeping his darkness at bay in her dress of sunny yellow.

Her mind was still reeling at his revelation. She wasn't certain how she felt about it, either. But if Gabriel needed her to wear yellow to feel safer or stronger, she could manage it for one evening.

However, as she gazed at her reflection in the mirror once she was fully dressed, Penelope wondered if he would be getting what he'd hoped for. She didn't *feel* like a ray of early-summer sunshine. Oh, the gown was lovely, the color warm and perfect. It was *she* who was different. She had dark places inside now that weren't there before, and she was certain they showed.

But if they did, Gabriel didn't seem to notice.

"Pen," he breathed when she entered the parlor where Liliana and Geoffrey were waiting to see them off.

She colored under his hot gaze. Since they'd become lovers, she was quickly getting used to that particular look in his eyes, but this time there was more to it. There was passion, yes, but also tenderness. Endearment. And immense pleasure and pride. The look upon his face made her doubly glad she'd worn the yellow.

They opted for an open gig to the neighboring estate where the ball was being held, in deference to Gabriel's dislike of closed spaces. The night was cold and crisp but clear. Penelope didn't mind wrapping up in a heavier cloak if it meant Gabriel would have an easier time of it. Taking the gig rather than the carriage also afforded them privacy, as they were able to drive themselves.

"Thank you for the dress," she murmured as they started down the lane leading away from Somerton Park.

"Thank *you* for wearing it," he answered, his voice low and suspiciously rough. She barely heard it over the clopping of hooves.

"It fits me exactly," she said. "However did you manage it?"

His wry grin flashed in the cool moonlight and was

illuminated further by the warm flicker of the lantern that hung from the pole near his face. "I filched a gown from your wardrobe, of course. I took it to the draper I'd noticed in the mining village and inquired whether he could do what I wanted. He was able to get the fabric and lace from a shop in town and he and his wife worked night and day to get it done for me. I know it's far from the elaborate gowns you used to wear to such soirees—"

"No. It's perfect, Gabriel." And it was, she realized. The simple, modern style was very different than she'd ever worn, which she found she liked, because it didn't feel to her as if she were trying to step back into who she'd been before. Maybe that's why it hadn't bothered her so much to put it on, as her old clothes seemed to.

His grin turned to a genuine smile before he turned his attention to driving them.

The trip to the home of Mr. and Mrs. James Bell took only a few minutes given the brightness of the moon and the well-maintained roads in this part of Shropshire.

"I've been thinking about tonight," Gabriel said as they made the turn onto the drive of the early Georgian manor. "If our main purpose for attending is truly to see whether our work together has helped me conquer my aversion to crowded ballrooms—and therefore that this association theory of yours is making me better— then I think I should try it alone."

She turned toward him and frowned.

"The thing is," he went on, "I was able to manage it

before when you were by my side, and not so much when you were not. For me to trust that I'm improving, I need to face it on my own."

"Without your talisman," she said.

"Precisely," he said, though his voice didn't sound quite as confident as his words. "I'd like to go in together, but after we've greeted our hosts, I'd ask you to retreat to a retiring room or such and let me go into the ballroom without you." He gave her a smile. "If I've not run screaming from the place within a quarter hour, we can assume I've met with success."

"All right." She nodded slowly, understanding his reasons but not necessarily liking the idea.

The gig swayed to a halt in front of the well-lit manor house. Penelope was taken aback by the amount of activity going on around them. Carriages were backed up, letting passengers out, while others were parked wherever there was room on the drive. A harried-looking servant stepped forward to take the reins. Penelope didn't miss the odd look at their choice of conveyance. Gabriel leapt down first and offered his hand to Penelope to assist her, placing her gloved hand upon his arm as they made their way to the house.

Music and conversation spilled from the open door of the manor as they neared. Bell Hall was not nearly as large as Somerton Park, but it was still a grand country home. Having been to a couple of affairs here two years past, Penelope remembered that the ballroom wasn't far from the entrance. The Bells' soirees were generally very well attended, packing nearly most of the area's residents into the small space. Judging from how many revelers lingered in the foyer and parlor, tonight's to-do was even more so.

Gabriel's arm was tight beneath her hand, but he gave no outward show of nerves. Penelope resisted offering any words of reassurance, letting him do this his way.

After their cloaks were taken by a servant, they moved into line to greet their hosts in the parlor just off of the ballroom.

"Lady Manton," Mrs. Bell said warmly when they reached her and her husband. "How fortunate we are that you are visiting your cousin at the same time as our little fete."

"The good fortune is mine," she returned with a smile. "Lady Stratford sends her regrets, but as her lie-in is fast approaching . . ."

The older woman laughed. "Ah, yes. I well remember those days, having borne five of my own—all daughters, mind you," she said, her assessing gaze shifting to Gabriel.

Penelope smiled as Gabriel's eyes widened slightly. "May I introduce Lord Bromwich? Gabriel, Mr. and Mrs. Bell." Not that an unmarried marquess needed any introduction. She was certain word of his stay in Shropshire, and his expected attendance here tonight, had reached the ears of every matchmaking mother in a twenty-mile radius. It might even be the reason the Hall seemed filled to overflowing. It looked to be a crush to rival any London ball she'd ever attended. She glanced over worriedly at Gabriel. Perhaps it wasn't such a good idea to let him face this alone.

But after greeting his hosts and spending a few moments in masculine conversation with Mr. Bell, Gabriel made his excuses, leaving her to answer Mrs. Bell's questions about him as he forged on to the ballroom. As Gabriel departed so did Mr. Bell, while several matrons found their way to where Penelope and her hostess chatted, wanting to appease their own curiosity about the very eligible marquess.

Penelope, however, had a difficult time keeping up with the conversation. *Yes, he was the Marquess of Bromwich. No, she didn't know if he was in the market for a wife nor what kind of female he preferred. Yes, he was very rich, owning three estates, plus a palatial townhome off Grosvenor Square. No, she wasn't aware of any mistresses or by-blows.* Instead her eyes kept straying to the ballroom door. She'd heard Gabriel being announced a few minutes ago, then nothing. Her insides twisted as time crawled by. How was he faring? Was he fighting off the urge to flee or had breaking his association of ballrooms to battlefields worked? She gritted her teeth harder with every tick of the nearby ormolu mantel clock. This waiting was awful!

Less than seven minutes in, she could no longer stand it. She extracted herself as politely as she could and quick-stepped her way into the ballroom. She had to shoulder her way past the clapping masses, who were clearly enjoying a rousing quadrille, but she finally broke through the crowd enough to scan the throngs of faces for his.

She saw him almost immediately and her breath caught in her throat. Gabriel wasn't just in the room, he was *dancing*. More than that, he was smiling—grinning from ear to ear, to be more precise. Her hand came to her chest, which ached as she watched him. His was the smile of a man who'd been freed from a terrible burden. Her eyes pricked with tears. How happy—how grateful—she was to have played even a small part in making that happen.

His eyes found hers then, almost as if he'd sensed her presence even from across the crowded room. They flared with some intense emotion she felt all the way to her toes before glancing away to focus on his partner—the eldest Miss Bell, if she wasn't mistaken.

Having seen that he was well, Penelope felt a strange urge to fade back into the crowd. He would find her if he had need of her. She found a spot very near a large potted plant and tucked herself against the wall where others would be discouraged from approaching her, but where she could still see Gabriel.

He was getting better. Even though she knew they had a long way to go, they were making significant progress. Relief welled up in her, causing the tears that had only been prickling threaten to fall and her hands to begin to tremble. She'd done the right thing, stealing him away from Vickering Place. Only now could she admit how terrified she'd been of making a mistake. Of making things worse. As she had with Michael.

But look at Gabriel now. As he laughed at something his partner must have said, Penelope marveled at how at home he seemed, where only weeks ago even the thought of being here had shaken him so badly he couldn't breathe. Now *she* was the one hiding at the back of the ballroom like the wallflower she never was, shaking like a leaf.

The quadrille came to a close. Penelope watched as Gabriel escorted Miss Bell back to a group of young ladies who were probably not that much younger than she. And yet, as they twittered and laughed gaily, she felt so far removed from that kind of innocence, she might as well have never been so.

A swift, sudden anger overwhelmed her, burning through her heart. A blanket of confusion and guilt doused it quickly, however. Who was she mad at? Michael? Miss Bell and her friends? She had no right to be angry at anyone but herself for the turn her life had taken. She never would have thought she'd be uneasy in a ballroom, however. When had she become so? She wouldn't know, she supposed. She'd avoided them since Michael's death herself, a part of her past she hadn't felt comfortable returning to. But just like her penchant for black, she'd never analyzed the change. She'd just gone on.

"Is everything all right?"

She started at Gabriel's question. She'd been so lost in her thoughts, she hadn't seen him bid Miss Bell and her friends good-bye and cross the room.

No. No, it wasn't all right. But she didn't wish to talk about it, especially not there. She wanted to go back to Somerton Park. Penelope pasted on a smile. "Of course. More important, is everything well with *you*?"

The concern on his face didn't precisely disappear, but it *was* pushed aside by an expression of triumph. "I've never been better. Truly." He breathed in, as if experiencing the world in an entirely new way. "Thank you, Pen. It's really working."

She nodded, her smile turning real. "I think so, too."

The strains of a waltz met their ears then, and Gabriel held his hand out to her. "A celebratory waltz, m'lady?"

She stared at his fingers for a long moment. She used to love to waltz, but that was another thing she hadn't done since Michael had died. Another part of her that had apparently been spoiled, because right then, with the unpredictable way she was feeling, she didn't think she could bring herself to dance it, even with Gabriel. Anger spiked again and flitted away just as quickly, leaving her feeling even more off kilter.

She shook her head. "A-another time, perhaps?"

His gaze became troubled again, but he merely withdrew his hand. "Of course."

"Actually," she said, touching her fingers to her forehead, "I think I would like to return to Somerton Park. If you don't mind."

A frown turned his lips. "Certainly," he said, taking her elbow gently. "Let us go." He steered her through the crush, tension vibrating off of him, but somehow Penelope knew it had nothing to do with him and everything to do with her. She accepted her cloak gratefully when they reached the front door, wrapping the heavy garment around herself and pulling the oversized hood up around her face. A few minutes later, Gabriel handed her into the gig and they were on their way back to Geoffrey and Liliana's.

He didn't press her on the short ride home, though

from the worried looks he sent her, he'd dearly wanted to. Penelope pulled her cloak more tightly around herself and stared out at the passing scenery. The night had chilled, leaving a sheen of moisture over the foliage that glistened in the moonlight. The landscape looked as cold as she felt, and nearly as bleak.

When they arrived at Somerton Park, Penelope slipped down from the seat on her own and hurried to the entrance. She didn't wait for anyone to meet her but rather went straight to her room and shut the door behind her. For the first time in a fortnight, she went to bed alone.

Gabriel stood at the interior sitting room door that joined his room to Penelope's, his hand poised to knock—much as he had been these past few minutes. He lowered his fist to his side. Did it matter if he knocked? If she told him to go away, he wouldn't listen. He'd go in anyway.

So that's what he did.

Thankfully she hadn't locked the door. He'd have hated to be forced to explain to Stratford why he'd kicked in the man's door.

Gabriel had to search to find her. Her room was dark, the only light coming from a weak fire in the grate. His eyes looked for her on the bed, but her silhouette was not there. Nor was she at the vanity, on the chaise near the foot of her four-poster, or pacing anywhere in the room.

Finally he spotted her, or what had to be her, curled up into an impossibly small ball in a wingback chair in the far corner. Her arms were wrapped around her knees and her head rested atop them, her blond ringlets pulled back into a simple knot, making her look very much like a vulnerable child. His stomach clenched into an aching fist.

He moved quickly into the room, dropping to his knees on the carpet before her chair. "Pen? What is it?"

His chest clenched, too, when she lifted her head and he saw her tear-ravaged face. Actually, the tears had dried away, but they'd left their tracks behind, and her eyes were swollen and rimmed red. She sniffed in a rush of air. "I can't waltz anymore," she said, as if that explained her pitiful state.

"All right," he said carefully, shaken to see Pen thus.

"A-apparently I detest ballrooms and I can't wear colors anymore, either," she said, nodding to an open trunk piled high with haphazardly tossed dresses. Fresh tears sprung to her eyes and spilled over, which seemed to appall her. Her lips pressed hard together even as she trembled. "And every few minutes or so, I'm angry as *hell* about it!"

"All right," he repeated softly in an attempt to soothe her. He wasn't certain exactly what she meant, but he recognized her fragile state. He'd witnessed men on the battlefield in various stages of emotions, ranging from despair to rage to terror—and everything in between— and he saw that it wouldn't take much to push Penelope over the edge of something or another. "You're angry," he agreed. "At me?"

She blinked several times. "No."

Even though he hadn't thought he'd done anything

to upset her, he still breathed a sigh of relief. He *never* wanted to be responsible for her tears. "At yourself?"

Her nod was more circular than anything, as if it couldn't decide what to be.

So she was angry with herself, but that wasn't quite it. He glanced again at her messy trunk, and the dresses draped over it or stuffed within. If she *couldn't* wear colors, as she'd said, it meant she felt she had to stay in black, an obvious reference to her guilt and widow-hood. "You're angry with Michael," he said, under-standing.

"Yes!" Her face crumpled. "What kind of person does that make me? I can't be angry with him. He was *sick*."

He reached and covered her clasped hands with one of his. They felt like ice beneath his skin. "Of course you can, Pen. Hell, I'm angry with him myself."

Her eyes widened and she stared intently at him. "You are?"

"Yes. When I realized he'd taken his own life—" He stopped, unable to voice the whole of his feelings. Be-cause along with having to accept that Michael's death had been a pointless tragedy—and his anger at his cousin for that thoughtless, foolish act—he also had to cope with the knowledge that had Michael lived, Penel-ope would never have been driven to treat soldiers, and therefore never would have been able to help *him*. She certainly wouldn't be in his bed, and God help him, he didn't know if he would give her up even to bring Mi-chael back. What kind of person did that make *him*? "I would think it perfectly normal. He may have been sick, but Michael's choices changed *your* life forever. Through no fault of your own, everything you'd hoped and expected for yourself was taken away from you."

"No, you don't understand." Her lip quivered violently, letting him know all was not well beneath the surface. "Michael's death *was* my fault. Even *he* said so, in the letter he left for me near his body."

"*What?*" The word shot out of him with the shock of it all, but his stunned confusion swiftly turned to rage. That bastard! How could Michael have left such a thing for her to find?

"Not in those exact words, of course. He said he was"—the first sob escaped, a broken sound that cracked him as well—"that he was s-sorry he'd been such a disappointment to me." She sniffed as tears poured in earnest. "That he'd never thought there was anything wrong with how he was until he m-met me."

"Oh Christ, Pen." He reached for her, but she pressed her shoulders back into the chair in a bid to escape his embrace.

"He lived his whole life happy," she said, "until I came along. He would still be alive if I hadn't badgered him constantly, if I hadn't pressed him so hard, if I had just been the society wife I was *raised* to be and let him live his own life when he asked it of me. I even failed him in *that*."

"That's—" *Bollocks*, he almost said. "Rubbish. Pure tripe. You *loved* him. You wanted him to be well. There is nothing wrong with that. I don't care if you turned into the veriest fishwife. Michael made his own choices. The responsibility lies with him."

She shook her head, and he could stand it no more.

He leaned forward and tugged her into his arms, crushing her to him as he rose to a standing position that pulled her upright as well. He didn't relent as she struggled. Instead he stroked her hair, whispering nonsense until she settled against his chest, her poor body shaking with silent sobs.

They stayed that way for a long time, Gabriel alternately wishing to take her pain for her and fantasizing about digging up his cousin and shooting him himself. Five, ten, fifty times over.

"Pen, you have to see . . . You were a *baby*, for God's sake," he murmured against her hair. "You weren't equipped to handle an illness like Michael's. And from what you've told me, he did nothing to help himself. He could have reached out—if not to you, then to *me*. Hell, to a complete stranger. But he didn't. It sounds to me that he thought of no one but himself, even to the end. I *pray* he was sick. I *pray* he didn't think about the damage he'd inflict on those he left behind—on you—because if he had, that would only make him cruel."

She shuddered in his arms, once, twice. He continued to just hold her and eventually her crying ceased. When Pen pushed against his chest again, he let her go. She stepped back, but didn't look at him. Instead she stared off over his shoulder, her mind having gone somewhere else. Her eyes looked haunted. Haunted in a way he recognized. He'd seen those same eyes in his own mirror many times.

"Have you—" he began, realization dawning. "Have you ever considered that *you* are suffering from battle fatigue yourself?"

Her pale eyes turned to his then.

"Not from the wars, of course, but the same principle. Trauma fatigue, maybe?"

Her brow furrowed and she said weakly, "No, of course not."

But he was right. He knew it. "I can think of nothing more traumatic than what you've been through, Pen. It must be why you've had so much success helping soldiers when you've had no formal studies in mental philosophy," he said. "Because intrinsically *you understand* what we are going through."

Several emotions played on her face as she took in his words, staring at him as if she'd never seen him before. After several long minutes, her expression smoothed. "You may be right," she said, a touch of wonder in her voice.

"Yes. And that makes you a *survivor*. Like all of the men you've helped." He reached out a hand to touch her cheek. "Like me. *You* decide how you go on from here, as we all do. If you want to wear colors again, you can. If you want to haunt the ballrooms, you should. And if you want to waltz . . ."

He dropped a hand to her waist and ran the fingers of his other hand down her arm to lift her hand into his. A lone, remaining tear slipped down her cheek as she looked up at him, but then she placed her hand on his shoulder, light and fragile as a butterfly. "Then we waltz," he said, and pulled her into a slow twirl.

He hummed in three-quarters time, and god-awful humming it was, as he had no sense of pitch. But they waltzed around that darkened bedchamber until he was nearly hoarse.

And then Penelope let him hold her while she slept. As he lay awake, stroking her skin, he prayed he'd gotten through to her. Pen was too beautiful a soul to suffer a moment longer over things that were not her fault. He also gave thanks that he'd been given the chance to help her even the tiniest bit as much as she had him.

Chapter Sixteen

Later that week, Penelope sat in the parlor with Liliana, poring over the bolts of fabric that had just arrived from London. The two women were sorting them
by color and style, matching them to the patterns Penelope had selected. Tomorrow she would take it all to
the village and leave the lot with the draper. The man's
wife had done such a lovely job creating the yellow ball
gown for Penelope on such short notice that Liliana
had decided to employ them to create a new wardrobe
for two-year-old Charlotte, as well as layettes and other
items for the coming baby, rather than taking her business to Town.

"No, Lily," Penelope clucked as her cousin held up
a striped muslin next to a patterned silk that clashed
terribly. "You would never put the two of those together in the same dress."

"*You* wouldn't," Liliana said wryly. "I, on the other hand, have the fashion sense of a chemist. Oh, wait . . ." She scrunched up her nose in a face that made Penelope laugh. Liliana put down the fabric she'd been holding and looked woefully over the array of materials before them, shaking her head. "Charlotte, no doubt, will be ecstatic. Even at two, she has a better sense of style than me. You should see the mutinous pouts she gives me some days, and usually on the days when I think I've dressed her quite well." Liliana sighed. "I am so grateful to have you here with me."

"Me, too," Penelope answered warmly, even as a twinge of sadness settled in her heart. Her niece, Charlotte, had been born barely a fortnight after Michael had taken his own life. Penelope had been in no state to be of any help at all with the new baby, and she always felt a bit of guilt for what she'd missed out on. She knew Liliana also felt guilt of her own, as she had been unable to support Penelope as she would have liked to, so caught up was she in the demands of her newborn.

Nor had Penelope been able to turn to her society friends. It had been quite some time before she'd felt able to reengage, and by then, she'd lost any interest in the parties and fashion that had once been so important to her, which left her nothing in common with the young ladies and matrons who'd been her friends. Her life had quite literally entered a black phase that she was only just coming out of.

"Oh, not just because you are saving poor Charlotte from fashion mortification," Liliana said. "Did I tell you that you were right about the nurse Miss Eden?

Penelope looked up from her task with a start. "No. What do you mean?"

"Upon your recommendation, I asked Geoffrey to have his man of business look more closely into Miss Eden's background. It turns out that the references she'd provided were forged. Eden wasn't even her real name. It was Haley, and she'd been turned out from her previous employer's home for drunkenness that resulted in neglecting her charge."

"Oh my," Penelope said, shocked.

"Yes. Thankfully, the babe wasn't hurt, but I am so grateful you listened to your instincts and said something to me."

"So am I," Penelope agreed. Maybe she had been too hard on herself these past years. Maybe she did need to forgive herself. Maybe she needed to trust herself more, too.

The women worked quietly for a few moments, each lost in her own thoughts.

"I am glad to see that you've put away the blacks," Liliana said as she held up two more clashing color swatches. "It wasn't right, seeing you in them."

Penelope looked at Liliana in surprise, but her cousin had turned her eyes back to the layette patterns on the table. It seemed everyone had noticed what she was doing except her. But no longer. Since the day of the assembly, she hadn't worn black once.

Gabriel's eyes had lit up that following morning when she'd entered the breakfast room in a morning dress of light blue muslin. The smile that had wreathed his face had filled her with a quiet happiness. Oddly enough, however, while it didn't bother her to wear her old dresses anymore, they no longer seemed to suit her. Even Gabriel had remarked after a few days that pastels didn't seem to fit her anymore. He suggested she might order a new wardrobe, selecting rich fabrics in jewel tones. Better suited for the deeper, more mature woman she'd become. *You've been through fire, Pen*, he'd said, even as he was removing a lovely pink frock from her body. *It's only right that you come through it swathed in a more vibrant shade*. And then he'd taken her through an entirely different sort of fire, the kind that scorched her nerves to cinders before leaving her sated and sleepy and immensely pleased.

"Did you decide to put away your mourning because you are ready to move on with someone else?" Liliana asked then with characteristic bluntness and a pointed look that brought heat to Penelope's cheeks. Had her cousin just read her mind?

Was she hoping to move forward with Gabriel? Emotion clogged her throat, a combination of excitement and hope and longing all mixed with a very real fear that it would be an awful mistake. *You'll get hurt,* her heart warned.

And yet the past three weeks had been some of the best she'd ever known. She and Gabriel had spent their days together, out-of-doors when the weather permitted, or pacing the long gallery when the rain or sleet dictated. Most of that time was spent in deep conversation, digging to uncover hidden associations that contributed to his battle fatigue. Some they discovered quite by accident, such as when they'd been walking by the stables when one of the horses was being shoed. The clanging sound and the whinny of the protesting horse had thrown him back into a terrible memory of his own stallion being lanced by a French cavalryman, right from beneath him. Others came from the hard work of taking those memories out and examining them. Many moments had not been easy, not for him—and not for her, either. When he spoke of the deep terrors and hardships he'd experienced over the years in battle, she'd often been unable to check her own tears.

She'd heard many horrors of war, of course, from many a soldier. But never had she experienced them as deeply as she had when they came from someone she love—

Oh, God. Someone she loved.

"Would it be so bad, Pen?" Liliana asked gently.

Penelope's gaze snapped to her cousin, who was looking at her with understanding. Goodness, her love must be written clearly on her face for Liliana to have picked up on it. Matters of the heart had never been Liliana's strong suit.

"I don't know," Penelope whispered. And she didn't. She pictured Gabriel in her mind as he'd been these past few weeks, every day growing stronger and more confident in his future. He and Geoffrey had developed a friendship of their own, and Gabriel often rode out with him and assisted with projects on the estate. While he still couldn't bring himself to venture into the mine, he'd spent many afternoons helping to build a schoolhouse in the small mining village.

Luncheons and dinners with the four of them were lively and terribly interesting, with much of the conversation centered around ways Gabriel could support the plight of war widows and their children. Much talk was made of how to attack the problem with both policy—which Geoffrey vowed not only to support but to help Gabriel present in the House of Lords—and practicality. Discussion of opening a mill on Gabriel's estate in Birminghamshire, along with a small village similar to what Geoffrey had done here at Somerton Park, was well under way, the men putting numbers to paper to explore the feasibility of it.

Early evenings were spent playing cards and games with Liliana and Geoffrey. Penelope learned that Gabriel was *not* horrible at whist. When she asked him later that night why he'd lost so often when she'd partnered him in London, he'd retorted that he hadn't been able to concentrate on his cards in those days, as his mind was so focused on wanting her.

When she'd held up their winnings and tartly demanded if his superior play that night meant he no *longer* wanted her, he'd scooped her into his arms and growled, "It's different now, because I have you." She'd happily let him have her again and again throughout the long night.

All in all, her time spent with him was the perfect blend of quiet domesticity and scorching sensuality. Everything that she wanted.

Unless . . .

"Are you still worried he might be mad?" Liliana asked. "I must say, I've seen no evidence."

"Neither have I," Penelope admitted. "Not really. Not since we left Vickering Place."

"Do you think it had something to do with his environment there, then?"

Penelope shook her head. "It can't be that, since he was having the episodes at his home long before he went to the sanatorium. No, it must have been the accumulative effect of his battle fatigue that brought on the attacks." And he was getting better every day. How well he'd handled the assembly the other night showed that. "I believe he will continue to improve." But was she willing to stake her future on that?

The future of any children they might produce?

At the idea of a baby of her own, sheer longing settled into her middle. She clutched the pattern of a tiny nightdress to her, imagining that it was for her baby. Hers and Gabriel's. Was that what she wanted?

She could already be with child, she knew. She and Gabriel had spent every night of the past three weeks in each other's arms. After that first passionate encounter against her chamber door, however, Gabriel had insisted on spilling his seed outside of her—so she knew the prospect of passing on any madness worried him, too.

And yet there had been that once . . . Just because she'd been married for a half year without conceiving didn't mean it wasn't possible.

"Then is it the fact that he's Michael's cousin?" Liliana probed. "Do you feel like you'd be betraying your husband's memory with a member of his own family?"

"No," she said firmly. She might not be proud of the

wife she'd been while he was alive, but she did not feel that finding love again would be a betrayal.

"Well," Liliana said, "I can hardly answer whether or not Lord Bromwich is the right person for you, but I can say I'm glad he is in your life for however long he remains there. You've been more yourself in the past month than in the two years before it. I was afraid that Michael's death had damaged you beyond repair—that you might never let someone else into your heart."

Penelope stared at her cousin, the moment seemingly eerily familiar. She'd said much the same words to Liliana once, long ago, in this very house. But where Liliana had been mourning a father's unconditional love, Penelope was only now coming to terms with the love she and Michael had shared.

Gabriel had helped her to realize that Michael had loved only Michael. Oh, he'd cared about her in his own way, but it was more that he saw her as an extension of himself rather than loving who she was. She didn't know if Michael would ever have done what it would have taken to get well. He'd been too addicted to the elation when he was feeling high. Not that anyone could get well for another person, of course. But Penelope wondered if he *could have* given it up for her, for their marriage, would he have made the sacrifice if it would have meant her happiness over his?

Gabriel, on the other hand, was a man accustomed to sacrifice. She had a feeling he would give everything for someone he loved.

The question was, did he love her? And if so, was that love worth taking a risk of her own?

*   *   *

Rain chased Gabriel into the stable, just behind Stratford. The sudden deluge had cut short their afternoon of laboring with the men in the village, but nothing could dampen his spirits.

He couldn't remember having ever felt so alive! Not even as a young man, before the ravages of war had marked him. He still couldn't sleep at night, but it was no longer horrid dreams that kept him awake into the wee hours. It was plans. Plans for his future. They tumbled about in his mind—even when, by all rights, he should be exhausted from days of hard work and nights of sweet passion in Penelope's arms.

Penelope.

It had been so long since he'd dared to dream about what lay ahead for him. Contemplating a lonely descent into madness had taught him to live moment to moment. But now . . . it seemed that a whole world of possibilities was open to him once again, that everything he'd ever wanted was within his grasp.

Even her?

She was another thing he'd never allowed himself to hope for—first because she'd been the wife of another and then, later, because he'd been fit for no one.

But now?

Could he allow himself to hope? Because it was one thing to share a bed—two grown people enjoying pleasure and comfort in each other's arms. But would she even consider a life with him after what she'd suffered with Michael? Yes, as days slipped into weeks without experiencing any bouts of madness, even he'd begun to believe that perhaps battle fatigue was all that was behind his episodes. But was that belief enough to ask Penelope to risk a future with him?

Or would the specter of madness always be in the corner of both of their minds, keeping them from being truly happy?

Thunder rumbled loudly across the sky, followed by a crack of lightning as he and Stratford dismounted. The stable was alive with noise and activity, as stable hands tried to settle the spooked horses.

"Would you mind if we rubbed our mounts down ourselves?" Stratford asked. "It appears the grooms have their hands full."

"Of course not," Gabriel said, tying his horse off next to the earl's. He followed Stratford to collect towels and a curry brush and then started the circular strokes, working from head to tail, enjoying the task. He had to admit, the storm and the whinnies of frightened horses made him a bit edgy, too, but keeping his hands busy stroking the horse seemed to calm him.

Coping. That's what Penelope had called it. Every day he got better at it. Perhaps in a few months he'd trust himself enough to ask for Penelope's hand. And perhaps she'd feel confident enough to accept.

"It's a shame about the rain," Stratford commented as he rubbed down his own horse. "But I suppose you'll be wanting to see plenty of it now that you are planning to build a mill on your land. You'll need full streams to power your machinery, even if you decide to use the newer steam engines as your main source."

Gabriel moved his towel over the horse's back. "Yes.

I think I know just where I'll situate it. There's a small waterfall that has a goodly portion of land around it. I may still decide to build with the steam engine in mind, as it does seem to be the way of the future. But the falls will give me options.

"Much depends on the cost, however, what with the need to build housing right away. I'm planning to start with cottages straight off, rather than barracks, as you did. Since I'll be employing mainly women, many of whom will have children, I'd like to get families settled into real homes as quickly as I can. I'll need to get a schoolhouse up, as well."

"Do you think you'll be able to manage that much expense up front?" Stratford asked over the back of his own horse.

"Possibly," Gabriel answered. "The estate can support the initial phases. I've written to my solicitor, as well as to my man of business, to inquire about taking out loans for the rest."

"Good." Stratford nodded. "I think you have a solid strategy in place. When do you hope to break ground?"

Gabriel's hand stilled midstroke, causing the horse to flick his tail irritably. That was the question, wasn't it? It had been invigorating to make plans and explore possibilities, but the reality was that in order to bring them to fruition, he would have to leave the earl's home and return to his own.

Without Penelope.

Just the thought made his heart clench. This time at Somerton Park with her had been sanctuary. *She* was the reason that he was on the road to recovery, he had no doubt. But once he stepped back into his life, he would be stepping back into it alone. He could not ask her to accompany him and live with him as an unmarried woman. Even for a widow, that would be beyond the pale.

But he had to have the courage to move forward and reclaim his life. "I'd like to get started this spring," he said.

How was he going to manage without her?

Why should you have to? a voice whispered in his head. After all, Stratford had told him more than once that he would have accomplished nothing without the love and support of his wife. He'd spoken honestly and frankly about his need for her to help him be the best man he could.

Gabriel needed Penelope, too.

But his needs were of a different sort than the earl's. It would be unfair of him to ask Penelope to make them her own, even if she were the only woman he knew who could meet them.

Thunder crashed overhead.

Then came the loud splintering of wood and the scream of a horse. Gabriel dropped his towel and rushed out of the stall with Stratford on his heels.

A terrified stallion had kicked through his stall gate and reared up. Hooves flailed dangerously as grooms ducked and dodged to avoid being kicked.

Without thinking, Gabriel pushed one of the younger lads aside and stepped to the horse, grabbing the reins firmly. He'd had plenty of experience calming frightened animals on the battlefield. This was no trained war horse, but the stallion should respond to similar tactics. Gabriel pulled the horse's head down to his own, talking softly as he soothed the animal.

When the stallion once again had all four hooves on the ground, he handed him off to the stable master.

"Well done, m'lord," said a shaken groom.

"Indeed," Stratford added, slapping Gabriel on the shoulder. "You moved so quickly, you were out of the stall before I'd even recovered from my start."

Only then did Gabriel realize that the sudden crash of sound hadn't bothered him. Only weeks ago, an unexpected noise like that might have thrown him into a fit of panicked breathing, trying to fight off the living memories of a battle fought long ago.

But aside from the normal acceleration of his heart from wrestling the powerful animal, he was unaffected.

He really was getting well.

Perhaps a marriage to him would not be such a burden to Penelope after all. He'd been able to help her in his own way—to slowly let go of her guilt, to discover the heights of her passion. Would it be enough to balance all he needed from her?

Only she could answer that question.

He was suddenly anxious to pose it to her.

He turned to Stratford. "Well, at least this storm gives us the afternoon to spend with the ladies, guilt free. Shall we?"

Stratford agreed with an eagerness that spoke of exactly how he planned to spend the afternoon with *his* wife.

As Gabriel dashed out into the rain to sprint for the

back of the house, he decided that was exactly how he wanted to spend his afternoon with Penelope, as well. But first he'd ask her to marry him. Or even better, perhaps he would make love to her first and *then* ask her, while she was caught up in postlovemaking euphoria. Underhanded to ask her a question of such magnitude while she was in a moment of sated weakness, but he needed every advantage he could get.

Because despite the many hours they'd spent together, sharing intimacies both of body and soul, he still wasn't sure how she felt for him. Not that he expected Penelope to love him as he did her, but what *did* he mean to her?

His darkest fear reared its ugly head. Was he just her penance—her way of making up for where she felt she'd failed Michael? Not that she would intentionally view him that way. He knew Pen cared for him.

But did she love him?

He took a deep breath. He supposed he'd find out soon enough.

Partway across the stable yard, he was forced to stop as a carriage came around the corner, headed for the carriage house at the end of the stable block.

Unease crept up his neck as he recognized the equipage as one of his own. As soon as the carriage rolled past him, he sped for the house, knowing the passengers would have debarked at the front of the manor and would already be inside.

It seemed his family had finally run him to ground. But who had come looking for him, and what was it that they wanted?

Chapter Seventeen

"——Out with my husband, I'm afraid."

Gabriel heard Liliana's voice as he neared the formal parlor where guests of Somerton Park were received.

"May I offer you a spot of tea whilst we wait for their return?" the countess offered graciously.

"That will not be necessary. We will be staying only long enough to retrieve my brother."

Edward, then, Gabriel thought, still half a room away from the parlor's entrance, but the openness of the rooms allowed voices to carry easily.

"And just where are you planning to take him?" Penelope's question came next in that clipped, formal tone that brooked no nonsense. He'd heard her use it on Allen several times, and he imagined his brother was being subjected to the haughty stare that usually accompanied it. Edward would shrink beneath it. His brother didn't typically fare well with strong women, and Penelope could be every bit the marquess's daughter when she wanted to be. He smiled. She'd make an excellent marquess's wife, as well.

"Why, back to the sanatorium, of course." This from Amelia. Christ, what the hell was she doing here? "Where he belongs."

Gabriel's smile fell, turning to irritation in a flash.

Penelope sounded equally outraged. "I hardly think—"

"Good afternoon," he interrupted as he stepped through the doorway. Four sets of eyes turned toward him at once: Edward's, Gabriel was surprised to see, were not swollen and reddened with drink—as he'd become accustomed to seeing him—and oddly resolute. Amelia's were shrewd and calculating. Liliana's were merely curious. And Pen's were both worried and clouded with anger.

It was Amelia who recovered first. "Gabriel," she said sweetly. "Don't you look . . . well." Her eyes scanned him up and down as her tone and the purse of her lips said otherwise. A touch of heat reached his cheeks. He was dressed more like a laborer than a gentleman today—he and Stratford both, actually—since they'd been helping men in the village to erect the schoolhouse. Being caught in the deluge hadn't helped his appearance any, he was sure. From the way Amelia stared at him, he'd wager he looked a bit wild.

Stratford entered the parlor behind him and went

straight to his wife. After awkward introductions, Lord and Lady Stratford excused themselves.

Edward and Amelia looked pointedly at Penelope, but she held her ground, refusing to leave him. Gabriel was glad of it. He needed her near him as the outside world unexpectedly intruded upon his sanctuary.

"Edward." He finally nodded. "Amelia. What brings you all the way to Shropshire?"

No one said anything for a moment; then Amelia cleared her throat in Edward's direction.

His brother straightened his shoulders. "We were quite distressed when we received Allen's missive that you'd been *taken* from Vickering Place." Edward shot Penelope a hard glance, again surprising Gabriel. It seemed his brother showed more backbone when sober. Edward's eyes returned to him, and Gabriel glimpsed the worry in them.

"I am sorry to have concerned you, Edward, but surely my own correspondence on the heels of his relieved your mind."

His brother's lips pressed into a hard line. "We were, of course, glad to know that you were safe. However, Vickering Place is where you belong. You know that. And we've come to deliver you back there."

Penelope bristled beside him, but Gabriel put a stilling hand on her arm. "I have no wish to return. In fact, I intend to—"

"Whether you wish it or not," Amelia interrupted, "that is where you are going."

Gabriel sucked in a breath as Edward flushed at his wife's rudeness. "What Amelia is trying to say is that we feel it is in your best interests to return. Allen says—"

"Mr. Allen doesn't know the first thing about what is best for Gabriel," Pen argued from beside him.

Edward lowered his chin and looked down his nose at her. "Allen is the respected director of one of England's finest sanatoriums—one I might remind you, brother," he said, cutting his eyes to Gabriel, "that you picked out yourself.

"Whereas *you*"—he turned his stare on Penelope again—"are not qualified in the least. I don't know why my mother ever asked you to get involved."

"Because I help soldiers suffering from battle fatigue—"

"Yes," Amelia chimed in nastily. "Allen has told us exactly how you go about helping them."

Penelope gasped as Gabriel saw red.

"That is quite enough!" he roared, startling them all. "I will *not* allow you to insult Penelope." Edward and Amelia looked at him with wide eyes, and he sighed. "And I will not be returning to Vickering Place."

"But, Gabriel, your episodes . . . ," his brother protested with a frown, but the concern in his eyes seemed genuine.

"I haven't had one in nearly six weeks," he said. "The longest I've *ever* gone between bouts since they started was a fortnight. The treatment I've been receiving from Penelope is helping, Edward."

His brother's eyes widened and his mouth eased slightly, but then his frown resurfaced. "But Allen informs me that lucid moments are perfectly normal.

That doesn't mean the madness won't come back unexpectedly."

"Your brother is not mad," Penelope said. "He's simply suffering from battle fatigue. The horrors many of our soldiers experienced manifest themselves as wounds of the mind as well as the body. I'll admit, Gabriel's episodes were frightening. *Were*. But as he said, he's gone weeks without one, and in that time, we've treated his other symptoms and will continue to. I have no reason to believe that he'll ever have another."

"He's not mad, you say?" Edward asked.

"He is not," Penelope said firmly.

"*I* would say that is up for the Court of Chancery to decide," Amelia interjected. She snapped her fingers. Edward winced, but dutifully pulled a sealed parchment from his waistcoat and handed it to Gabriel.

What was this? From the triumphant gleam in Amelia's cold eyes, it could not be good. With numb fingers, he snapped the wafer, opened the missive and started to read.

> *By virtue of a commission, in nature of a writ de luni-cato inquirendo, under the great seal of Great Britain, we require you to produce before us the said, Gabriel Devereaux, to inquire whether he be a lunatic or not before twenty-four honest and lawful men of the city of London on the 27th day of March next, by ten of the clock in the forenoon, at the public house situated on the street of Piccadilly, commonly called or known by the name or sign of the Gun Tavern. Fail not at your peril.*

Gabriel couldn't seem to draw a breath. That was less than a fortnight from now. "When did you file this?" he asked, hating the scratchy whisper that passed for his voice.

"Nearly six weeks ago," his brother answered.

"But your mother told me she would make sure no writ was filed until I'd had the opportunity to try my treatment," Penelope cried.

Edward's face went carefully blank. "My mother does not rule me, Lady Manton."

Gabriel's eyes went from his brother to Amelia, whose lips had turned up in a satisfied smirk. *No, your wife does,* he thought grimly. Amelia hoped to wrest control of the marquessate's coffers. Once Edward had full power over the estate, she could spend indiscriminately. Edward wouldn't stop her. Maybe he even thought his wife would remain faithful if she had enough incentive.

Oh, Christ.

"Edward, this was filed before you knew that I had recovered," he said. God, he sounded like he was pleading, but he couldn't help it. The very real possibility of being locked away in Vickering Place again after having just tasted his freedom—he'd rather die. "You must rescind your affidavit."

But his brother shook his head sadly. "No. While I *am* glad that your episodes plague you less often these days, I do not think you are in your right mind. I was willing to let you rusticate here in hopes that you were recovering. But our solicitor now informs me that you have inquired about taking out *loans* against the estate.

He says you intend to plow over fertile farmland and build some sort of *mill*. On Devereaux land?" He snorted in disbelief. "No, I must protect the family from your crazy schemes."

A cold rage swirled through him. "It is not a crazy scheme," he said, his voice low and deliberate, but he could see that his explanations would be for naught. Nor would any argument. Because regardless of what Edward or Amelia believed of him, it would make no difference. Amelia saw an opportunity. While she would not actually be able to call herself marchioness while Gabriel lived, she could certainly live and spend like one once he was declared *non compos*. And Edward . . . while his brother might have his doubts, he could justify his actions behind "protecting the family" and, at the same time, make his wife happy.

And even though his plans for the mill were perfectly sound, none of it would matter. Once the lunacy commission heard from Allen and the staff of Vickering Place, they would find him insane.

He clenched his jaw tight, fear and betrayal snaking over his skin, leaving him even colder. But he would not beg, particularly not when he knew it would do no good. "Very well. Until the twenty-seventh, then."

He waited to move until his family departed the room. Then he headed straight for the sideboard to pour a drink. He sloshed two fingers of brandy into the snifter, then added a third for good measure. Yes, it was barely past noon, but if there had ever been a cause for imbibing before dinner, this was it.

He closed his eyes as the warm liquor burned its

way down his throat, savoring it. Once he was locked away in Vickering Place again, he would never taste fine liquor again.

Just as he would never again taste Penelope.

Gabriel's knees began to shake. He moved three steps and slumped upon a settee.

Without making a sound, Penelope appeared before him. She dropped to her knees between his spread legs and gently took the half-finished glass from his hands. She set it off to the side, then fitted herself against his chest, wrapping her arms around his waist in a bid to comfort him.

He squeezed her around her shoulders, dropping his head into her hair, breathing her in. He wouldn't forget her smell—this blend of mandarin and vanilla and something wholly Penelope—for as long as he lived.

"'Twill be all right," she murmured against his chest, just as she had their first dance, just as she had in Vickering Place. God, he wanted to believe her now as he had then, but he knew it would not.

"You have to know that isn't true, Pen." He knew what was to come.

She pulled back and fixed him with a fierce glare. "It will. I will testify that—"

"You will *not*," he growled, taking in her beautiful face. She looked so young, so fresh and lovely today in a plum gown. Strangely, the color made her eyes appear greener than ever. They shone bright in her face. He let the vision burn into his memory, knowing he would gaze upon her often in his dreams. Hell, even in his waking hours, when he closed his eyes. She would always be his talisman, but she would now also be the way he coped with a life locked away without her.

"I don't want you on that stand, Pen. If you testify, you know Allen will make the same insinuations that Amelia did today. You would be opening yourself to that line of questioning. And then what? Are you going to lie under oath that we are not lovers?"

A troubled frown kissed her brow, there and gone again, but he saw it. Reputation was important to a woman in good society, and she knew it. And yet her lips took on that stubborn tilt he'd come to love. Damn it.

"You know these trials are held in a public tavern," he added. "It will be packed to the gills with strangers off the street, all trying to get a look at the lunatic, just for the spectacle of it. It will be even more a circus when they learn I'm a member of the peerage. Every bit of testimony will be twisted and turned as salaciously as it can be, all in the name of good entertainment. Printed up in the *Times* for all of your friends to read. Do you really want them calling you the Mad Marquess's Widow Whore?"

Penelope flinched at his harsh words, but her eyes narrowed and her shoulders straightened. "I don't care, Gabriel. I refuse to let this stand. Not when we can mount a very credible defense. I have detailed records of men I've treated. Dozens of success stories. I can get a few of them to testify, I am certain.

"And Geoffrey is an influential and respected peer. He will stand character witness. After all, you've been in his home for six weeks, with his *pregnant* wife in residence. No one will believe he would allow that if he thought you truly mad. He can also refute that your plans for the mill are a crazy scheme."

Her earnest words broke through some of the chill that had settled in his chest.

"I have sat in on some of these commissions," she said, "and yes, all of what you say is true. However, *you* get to take the stand in your own defense. If you come across completely sane and rational . . . well, that along with my and Geoffrey's testimony should give us at least even odds. Don't forget, the commission is made up of men like you. Men of the peerage—along with a few lawyers and respected members of the church. None of them truly want to declare one of their own insane if there is reasonable doubt. It would set a precedent that would make it easier to lock one of them away someday."

He cupped her face in his hands, brushing his thumb over her soft, soft cheek. "And if I refuse to let you testify?" he asked, knowing from the determined glint in her eye how she would answer.

"I'll do it anyway. I do not need your permission."

"I could refuse to take the stand in my own defense and negate the need altogether," he threatened.

She blanched. "You wouldn't," she said, but she didn't sound sure. "Please say you wouldn't."

He pulled her lips to his, desperate to taste her. Beautiful, stubborn girl. She was willing to have herself branded a whore on the chance that they might succeed. For him. He kept up the kiss until they were both panting for breath, then eased back from her. This isn't how he'd meant to ask her, but it was how it would have to be.

"All right, Pen, I will agree on one condition."

She tilted her head, her eyes still unfocused a bit from the passion of their kiss.

"If we are successful and I am found competent, you will marry me *that day*. Your reputation would be blemished but not blackened. We both know all manners of sins are forgiven by society as long as there is a wedding in the end."

She blinked several times, rapid flutters of her eyelids, then simply stared at him without speaking.

Gabriel held his breath. Without his lungs moving, there was nothing to distract him from the hard pounding of his heart in his chest. She might be willing to put her reputation at stake for him, but her entire future? Tie herself to a man who at the very least would suffer from battle fatigue his whole life through, but who might also go mad if they were wrong about that?

"Is—" Her tongue came out to wet her lip, and then she swallowed and tried again. "Is my reputation the only reason you want to marry me?"

"*Christ*, Pen," he muttered, and dragged her face back to his. He poured everything he felt for her into the strokes of his tongue, into the movement of his lips on hers, into the way he caressed her face as he kissed her. She was so many things to him—the woman he'd loved from afar for so long, his savior from the darkness, his angel of mercy, his sunlight, his very soul.

Just when they were at risk of tearing at each other's clothes and making love in the middle of the main parlor—damn the servants, damn her cousin, damn them all—she pulled back from the kiss and tucked her face into the crook of his neck.

"All right, Gabriel," she said against his neck, her voice breathy and aroused. "If we win, I will marry you that day."

Elation sang in his veins as he squeezed her closer to him, dropping kisses along the top of her head.

"But what happens if we lose?" she asked quietly.

The euphoria from her agreement to marry him didn't precisely die, but it did take on a sickening pallor. Not succeeding was unthinkable. He would be branded a lunatic, she a whore, and he wouldn't be able to marry her anyway, were he found unable to govern his own affairs. It wouldn't be legal.

He dropped another kiss on the top of her head and struggled with what to say. There was no acceptable answer. There never would be.

Chapter Eighteen

The next several days were spent in intense preparation. Penelope had her records sent up and spent several hours poring through them, pulling copious notes from her most successful cases. She wrote letters to several of the men she'd worked with as well and was thrilled when three of them replied that they were willing and would be available to speak at Gabriel's hearing.

She also interviewed Gabriel extensively again. She already knew most of what he told her, but she wanted to get it fresh in her mind. Then she, Gabriel, Liliana and Geoffrey sat down with everything she'd compiled and laid out their defense.

Penelope had never been so grateful for her cousins as she was now. Logic had never been her strong suit, and that was before her emotions were all tied up in knots over this. But logic was practically Liliana's middle name, and Geoffrey was a gifted strategist. All Penelope had to do was write down their points and put her evidence in order—which she did twenty times if she did it once, hoping that if she did it enough, it would be automatic to her when she was in front of the commission. Otherwise, she feared she'd lose her place and not only make a fool of herself, but harm Gabriel.

She tried not to think of what it would be like when Mr. Allen made his accusations about her. She prayed it would not turn into a horrid ordeal, but consoled herself with the knowledge that even if it did, in a few days' time she would be Gabriel's wife and it would all be worth it.

Then she would get back to work to ensure that that's what happened.

Where the days were focused on readiness, the nights were spent on passion. In the weeks since she'd taken Gabriel into her bed, he'd striven to drive her slowly, madly insane with need. He'd drawn out her pleasure past the point of bearing and then pushed her even further before letting her find release. He delighted in showing her places on her body she'd never have thought to put tongue, hand or sex to, much less imagined finding bliss there.

But as she closed the bedchamber door the night before they were to depart for London, she sensed tonight would be different. She could taste the tension in the air, like metallic honey on her tongue—sweet and heady but with a sharpness that raised the tiny hairs on her arms.

As the door clicked shut, Gabriel whirled on her so quickly she actually yelped. He swept her into his arms in one fluid motion that carried them both to the bed and dropped her in the middle of it even as he climbed up with her.

"Pen," he said hoarsely, tearing at the buttons of his trousers. "I need you now. Can you forgive me?" he asked as he pulled her dress up past her waist and kneed her legs apart.

She understood his violent need to be inside her. She felt it, too, as if despite all that they'd done to prepare for what was to come, they both knew they might fail. They each feared this would be the last time they would lie together.

"Come to me," she urged him.

He pushed into her, his shaft hard, hot steel. She moaned, the friction a raw pain/pleasure, as she wasn't as wet as she normally was by the time they reached this particular intimacy. When he was lodged deep, Gabriel hung over her, his arms braced on either side of her shoulders, taking in great gulps of air.

She felt herself softening around him, adjusting to his invasion in small, pleasurable degrees.

Gabriel's muscles strained with the effort not to plunge into her. Instead, he dropped to one elbow and took her mouth with his, sending his other hand between them to find the bud of her center. He stroked her in little circles that sent pleasure rushing through her like a drug. Circles he mimicked with his tongue in her mouth. His ministrations combined with the pulsing flesh that invaded her soon had her flooding with sweet moisture.

The very second he felt her wetness surround him, Gabriel rose back up and took her in unrelenting thrusts that rocked the bed with their ferocity.

Penelope simply held on, taking, wanting, *needing* everything he had to give her. Neither of them could last long at this pace, nor did they, exploding into a maelstrom of sensation that wrung hoarse cries from their throats.

After, Gabriel stripped them both and cleansed them with warm water that had been left in the ewer. As she floated in sleepy exhaustion, from not only the intensity of their lovemaking but from the days of frantic work, he curled his body around hers and they both succumbed to sleep.

It was only at her very last moment of consciousness that she realized he hadn't pulled out before spilling his seed. She fell asleep with a smile on her face, dreaming of golden-eyed, brown-haired babies.

A crash of lightning awoke Penelope just after dawn. Well, what should have been dawn, as any sun that was meant to greet the earth in morning's glory was buried behind angry clouds. She watched out of the bedroom window as they rolled through the sky in a unbreaking wall of gray, casting a pall over everything below.

Gabriel eased up behind her, wrapping his naked body around hers, and settled his chin upon her shoulder as he, too, scanned the sky.

"Are you still going to try to ride in this?" she asked anxiously, staring outside with dismay.

It had been decided that they would all go to Town together. Geoffrey had tried to convince Liliana to stay in Shropshire, as their baby was expected in a matter of weeks now, but she wouldn't hear of it. Penelope knew that Liliana worried that the hearing would not go well and refused for Penelope to be all alone in her grief if that happened, as she'd been when Michael had died. But Penelope knew nothing and no one would be able to console her if she lost Gabriel. Not ever.

They planned four days for the travel to London, allowing that Liliana would not be able to push as quickly as they might without her. The intention was for the women to share a carriage while Gabriel and Geoffrey rode alongside, Geoffrey because he didn't relish being cooped up for four days with two worried women, and Gabriel because he didn't relish being cooped up at all.

But he wouldn't be able to ride outside in a cold rain.

She turned in his arms just enough to see his face, which had gone dark as the storm clouds outside.

"That is my intention, yes," he said. "If the rain holds off."

The skies opened up before they'd even broken their fast. They waited a few hours longer than they should have, to see if it would let up, but it did not. Knowing they already risked slower travel times due to mud or potential flooding, Gabriel finally ordered Penelope's carriage to be brought around. He said it was so that Liliana would not be overly cramped and uncomfortable with four in a carriage, but Penelope understood that he neither wished her cousins to know of his weakness, nor for them to be subjected to the surliness the trip was bound to bring out in him.

As Penelope settled herself against the plush green velvet squab, Gabriel pulled himself into the carriage behind her. Unlike the cramped conveyance that had spirited them to Somerton Park, Penelope's carriage was a traveling coach with wide seats made for four and multiple carriage lamps that lit up the interior almost as well as a room. It also boasted large windows. She'd pulled back the shades in order to give Gabriel as much sense that he was not trapped in the dark as she could.

Still, she could see that tension gripped him. He settled across from her with a stiffness unlike him, and she noted his chest fell very shallowly. As the coach swayed into motion, she said gently, "Remember, Gabriel. All that you are feeling is *not* real. It is simply your body reacting to an association we've yet to discover."

He nodded tightly and closed his eyes, but she could see that he suffered.

For the next half hour, she kept up murmured conversation in an effort to calm and soothe him. The cursed weather did nothing to help her cause, thunder rumbling in booms and lightning flashing with cracks that startled even her.

After a particularly harsh streak, a small groan reached her ears. Gabriel's knuckles were white where they gripped his knees. Penelope bit her lip with despair. Nothing she was doing was helping him.

Then she stripped off her gloves and slipped out of her heavy cloak. She spread it on the floor of the carriage before slipping to her knees in front of him.

Her hands slid over his and his eyes flew open. "Shhh," she said at the question in his golden brown depths. His gaze was fixed on hers with a mixture of desperation and blossoming awareness. "That's right," she said, running her hands over his thighs, letting her thumbs drag along the sensitive inner parts before stopping just shy of his manhood. "Keep watching me," she purred. "Keep all of your attention focused on what I'm doing."

Without breaking eye contact, she slipped her hands into the fall of his trousers, loosening buttons until the flap parted. His flesh had yet to harden, probably because so much of his energy was occupied just holding himself together. But she didn't mind.

She took him into her hand, stroking gently, then harder. Squeezing on a stroke, then running her fingers lightly to the tip and circling it with the pad of her thumb.

Soon Gabriel was stiff and groaning for an entirely different reason.

By the time she took him into her mouth, she knew he was thinking of nothing but the hot flick of her tongue and the suction of her cheeks as she pleasured him. His hand fisted and relaxed in her hair, again and again until finally, he spilled himself with a hoarse shout.

He returned the favor, of course, with an intensity that left the inner carriage walls ringing with throaty cries of her own, and afterward, they dozed in each other's arms. He was at peace for a time, but it wasn't long after they woke that the tension gripped him again. All Penelope could do was hold him and whisper that all would be well.

They met Liliana and Geoffrey for dinner at a coaching inn that night. The rain had not let up enough for Gabriel to ride outside even for a short period. He asked Penelope if she would mind forgoing stops and pushing through to London—the idea of having freedom from the carriage for a few hours' respite only to face the prospect of having to get back in was too much for him to bear. She agreed, of course, and they made plans to rendezvous with her cousins after the latter reached Town a couple of days behind them.

They rode at a relentless pace, stopping only to change teams every three hours or so. And each mile they traveled, Gabriel's hold over himself seemed to fray. Penelope bit her lip as she watched him, sweat beading on his forehead. She hated seeing him suffer so, but a part of her also wondered if this forced confinement could actually be a good thing.

She reasoned that this was the longest time he'd ever allowed himself to suffer thus. Were it not storming, he'd be out of the carriage in a shot. But what if the prolonged time he had to remain here was, in effect, pushing his deeply buried memory to the surface like a sunken splinter? If she could just see the end of it, perhaps she could help him pull it out.

So when he cried out a few hours later, waking himself from a fitful sleep, she placed her mouth next to his ear.

"Tell me what you dreamt of," she coaxed, her voice as low and hypnotic as she could pitch it. "Don't let it fade away, Gabriel. Tell me what you see."

He moaned, his head turning away from her. "Where are you?" she pressed. "What can you smell? What do you hear?"

"Blood," he rasped. "Death. Cloyingly sweet. Rotten."

Her heart squeezed in her chest, then accelerated to a rapid beat. What on earth? "Do you hear anything?"

He shook his head, his eyes squeezed shut. "No, it's quiet. Too quiet. Still and . . . and dark. So much pressure, pinning me down. I can't breathe," he cried. "I can't breathe!"

His chest was rocketing beneath her hand. He *was* breathing, but too fast. Too hard. She knew panic was setting in. Everything in her told her she must keep pushing. If she didn't get this out of him now, he might never be free of it.

But what if you push him too hard, like you did Michael?

A cold fear shivered through her. No, she'd only been trying to help Michael.

You're only trying to help Gabriel, too.

For the briefest of moments, doubt crippled her. So much that she trembled with it. But then she shoved it away. She'd learned much and she'd helped many since Michael had died. Gabriel insisted he trusted her instincts. She would have to, too. Because he needed her to.

"Where are you, Gabriel? Answer me," she commanded harshly.

"Buried," he groaned. "Buried alive."

What? Penelope's breath caught in her chest. Surely he couldn't be—

"Buried," he said again. "Under my dead horse. Under the bodies of my men. Help me!"

His eyes flew open, rolling wildly around the carriage as he tried to place himself. His breathing had sped up to a dangerous level, and his hands shook like an apoplectic. He banged his fist against the wall frantically, signaling for the driver to stop. A relentless, unceasing banging that she knew would leave his hand bruised.

Her heart beat desperately in her chest as she watched helplessly. Had she pushed him too far? "I'm here, Gabriel," she said, trying to reach him, but the moment the carriage rolled to a stop, he flung open the door and leapt out into the rain.

She followed, pelting cold drops smacking her face as she hopped down into the mud. She searched for his figure through the driving rain. In a flash of lightning, she spotted his silhouette several yards ahead. He was bent over with his head near his knees. She rushed to him, heedless of the sucking mud that ruined her boots and threatened to send her sliding to her bottom beside the road.

"Gabriel?" she called out as she drew near.

He looked over at her. She could tell that much in the darkness, but unless another flash of lightning hit, she would not be able to see his features. Was he all right?

When she reached him, she bent at the same angle as he, trying to get close enough to read his face. Rain drenched them both, though truthfully, she didn't notice her own shiver until she registered his.

"Gabriel?" she asked tentatively. "Do you remember what just happened?"

He straightened wearily. "I remember more than that." Her heart broke at the pain in his voice. He scrubbed his hands over his face, whether to sluice the water from it or hide from her, she didn't know. "I know what my mind refused to let me see."

"What?" she asked, half terrified to know.

"It was on the final charge of the battle," he said. "I was pulled from my horse." His breaths came harsh as he struggled to tell the story. "A French infantryman caught me by surprise as I was fighting the lancer in front of me, and I hit the ground so hard it knocked the breath from me."

As he spoke, she could see it all happening in her mind's eye. Her Gabriel, battling for his life. Her own breath strangled in her chest as she listened, even though he was standing here safe in front of her now. Thank God. Thank God he'd survived.

"As I was scrambling to rise, cannon shot exploded not feet in front of me. I was spared, but—" He shuddered, and she felt an answering shiver snake through her, even though she did not yet know what he would say. "The spray of blood and flesh knocked me back to my arse, and before I could scramble out of the way, I—I was pinned by the body of my dying horse."

She gasped, clapping her hand over her mouth.

"He screamed for what seemed like hours before he died," he said, his eyes squeezed tightly closed now. "The battle raged on around me, but no one could hear my cries for help. Bodies fell and piled left and right— horses, men."

He opened his eyes to look at her then, just as a streak of lightning flashed. The bleakness on his face knifed through her.

"I remember a woman falling next to me," he said, his voice gone flat. "She may have been a camp follower, or perhaps an officer's wife, but her face was so lovely and so *peaceful*, I thought for a moment that she might be an angel come to save me. Before I realized she was dead."

"Oh, Gabriel," she whispered, tears coursing down her face. She felt them hot on her cheeks before she even registered she was crying. The terror he must have felt was unimaginable. She had no words, could only whisper again, "Oh, Gabriel."

"When it was all over, I lay there still. Trapped beneath the rotting corpses of friends and enemies alike. The air was heavy with death and the sun so hot. It had rained the night before the battle, so everything was moist and steamy. I thought I would die of thirst, and then . . . then I prayed for death as the days went by, until finally, I lost consciousness."

"You were there three days," she whispered, remembering what he'd said the nurse at the hospital had told him.

"Yes."

She wanted to hold him. To pull him to her bosom

and assure him that nothing so horrible would ever happen to him again. That he would never be trapped and helpless, ever. But if they lost at his lunacy commission, he would be. No, not beneath bodies on a battlefield, but trapped just the same, helpless in the decisions made for his own welfare. For his very life.

They simply had to succeed. And to do that, they needed to reach London without having caught an ague.

"Come. Let's get out of this rain," she said, tugging him back toward the carriage. He got in with hardly a hesitation, though he still tensed like steel. But he let her hold him as he dropped off into an exhausted sleep, and they remained that way until they reached the next coaching inn.

Penelope made the decision that they would stay the night. They both needed dry clothes and time to recover from that ordeal. She hadn't been able to stop crying for the past hour. *No wonder*, she thought. No wonder his battle fatigue had manifested itself in mania, what with horrid, *horrid* memories like that bottled up in his mind.

As she watched him sleep, she prayed they had reached the bottom of the well now, and that from this day forward, the only things that would bubble up inside of him would be clean and fresh.

She prayed he was finally healed.

It was dusk on the third day when they rolled into London. It was still raining, just a light mist now, but even the moist air couldn't mask the distinctive smell of the city.

After three days' hard travel, not to mention the emotional wringer they had both been through, when the carriage approached his columned town house just off Grosvenor Square, neither of them was at their best. Yes, they were in fresh clothes—travel worn, but clean. That wasn't what she meant, however.

Penelope watched Gabriel with concern. He'd been quiet most of the day. He'd made it into the carriage this morning with barely a hitch, at which point she had breathed a sigh of relief. And while he was still on edge, the day's ride hadn't seemed nearly as awful for him.

He'd been kind when she engaged him, even smiled at some story she'd told. But he also seemed . . . fragile. More vulnerable to her. Was it the wounded quality around his eyes when he stared out of the window? Was he worried, as she was, about the trial just two days hence? Or was she simply making up excuses for his withdrawn silence?

She wished she knew.

The carriage was met by servants in the blue and silver livery of the Devereaux family. Gabriel stepped out of the carriage first, handing her down himself. He placed her hand upon his arm and started up the front stairs. Before they were greeted by the rather dour-looking butler who'd just opened the door, Gabriel leaned down and whispered, "In two nights' time, you will be entering this house as its mistress, you know. It will be the happiest day of my life, and not because we've prevailed. Simply because you will be my wife."

A melting warmth drizzled down her middle, coating her sudden case of nerves with pleasantness.

A woman appeared behind the butler, her dark skirts limned in the light spilling from the doorway, giving the oddest illusion that the butler was wearing a dress. When the servant stepped aside to grant them entry, Penelope saw it was the marchioness. Soon to be the dowager marchioness, though the woman did not know it yet. She allowed herself a small smile.

"Lady Bromwich," she said with a curtsy. Seeing Gabriel's mother gave her a surreal jolt. She hadn't given any thought to the strange reality that her future mother-in-law was the identical twin of her former. In truth, she hadn't given her upcoming marriage to Gabriel much thought at all.

It wasn't how she'd intended to pursue love again. She'd intended to take her time, to select a nice, quiet man. One with no drama in his life.

But then he wouldn't have been Gabriel.

Her soon-to-be husband was dutifully kissing his mother's cheek. "It is good to have you home, Gabriel," the marchioness said, her voice suspiciously gruff.

"Thank you, madame," he said, straightening. "I expect it shall become the norm shortly."

He led Penelope into the foyer as he conversed with his mother, not relinquishing her hand.

"—sister is here," the marchioness was saying as they pressed farther into the house.

A smile lit Gabriel's face at that news, but it dimmed

a bit when she added, "And, of course, your brother and Amelia. There is something else you should know—"

Gabriel stopped short just at the base of the grand staircase, his arm tightening beneath her hands. Penelope glanced up and saw immediately why. Her stomach knotted. Mr. Allen.

"Good evening, my lord. Lady Bromwich, Lady Manton." The director's overly solicitous tone oozed like oil paint over her skin. "I am happy to have the chance to thank you for your hospitality on behalf of myself and my staff."

Penelope turned her head to the parlor, where indeed, Carter and Dunnings stood conversing with another man she did not know. The two attendants were dressed not in the linen uniforms of their profession, but dark suits, making their presence seem even stranger to her.

"What the devil are they doing here?" Gabriel demanded. Penelope frowned. It wasn't like him to be so sharp, but she could understand why he was. He'd just been through three days of hell, was facing the terrifying prospect of losing everything in his life and then, when he arrives home, the very people who wished to take it all from him were drinking brandy in his parlor.

He was likely furious. At the very least, his nerves had to be on edge.

Only to be made worse when his sister-in-law came forward and said, "They are guests, of course. They've graciously come to Town to testify on behalf of the *family*. Surely you didn't expect them to stay in rented lodgings." Lady Devereaux turned her gaze to Penelope with a disdainful flick. "What is *she* doing here?"

"She is testifying on the behalf of the *head* of this family," Gabriel growled.

"Enough!" Lady Bromwich's voice cut in.

The unease that had settled in Penelope's middle since seeing Mr. Allen and his attendants grew. After all that Gabriel had been through during the carriage ride to London, he needed to recuperate in a place of peace and quiet, to prepare himself for the ordeal to come.

"Please, Gabriel," she said low enough that only he could hear. "Let us decamp to Stratford House."

He squeezed her arm and said sotto voce, "I will not be driven from my own home, Pen. And neither will you."

She pursed her lips, worry mixing with irritation. Stubborn man. And rotten, rotten in-laws.

"Now," he said, taking her hand from his arm and brushing it lightly with his lips, "I should like a quick word with my brother and then I will show you to your room."

She wished he would show her to her room now, and stay with her, but he'd already headed for where his brother stood in the far corner of the parlor.

"Edward tells me that Gabriel has not had an episode in nearly two months now." Penelope turned her head to see the marchioness standing near, her eyes on Gabriel much the same way Penelope's own were. The older woman watched her elder son with the same worry and hope she did.

"Yes," Penelope said quietly. "None since the first day I arrived at Vickering Place."

Penelope looked at Gabriel now. How far he'd come. She could tell he was angry with his brother, not because he gave it away by expression but because of the large gulp he took from the brandy he'd just accepted from a passing maid. She'd seen him drink only when he was upset. But he was keeping everything together.

"Hmmm," the marchioness replied. "So you really think he's cured, then, do you?"

"I do," she said, looking back at Gabriel's mother. She spent a few minutes detailing what she thought had caused Gabriel's problems and the progress they'd made—not sharing any of his most personal things, but enough so that the marchioness might understand. "So you see, while he will always carry the mental scars, I do believe the worst is over."

She glanced at him then—more and more, her eyes automatically sought him in a room. At this rate, she'd be staring at him several hours a day in a year or two. She perused his handsome face and froze upon it. Something was amiss.

He was holding his lips in a way that he never did. She frowned at the odd expression. When he brought a hand up to scratch at his shoulder, alarm screamed through her.

"I am glad to hear that," the marchioness was saying beside her. "It is a terrible thing to see one son trying to wrest power from another. Almost as terrible as thinking one has lost his mind."

But Penelope was hardly listening. Instead she started moving toward Gabriel as if in a daze. *Oh no,* she thought wildly as he started tugging at his cravat. *No. No. No. No.*

When he started shedding his jacket, his brother frowned. "I say, Gabriel. Are you well?"

At that, Mr. Allen's head perked up and his eyes narrowed on Gabriel. Carter and Dunnings started paying attention, too, particularly when Allen discreetly waved them toward the corner where Gabriel was now tipping back the empty brandy glass as if it offered more to quench his thirst.

He growled with frustration and smashed the snifter on the floor.

Behind her, the marchioness gasped.

This couldn't be happening. It couldn't. She had to get to him. If she could just get to him, perhaps she could stop this before it got out of hand.

But Mr. Allen's men reached him first. Carter tried to grasp Gabriel's arm, but the move seemed to enrage him. "Get off of me!" he roared, shoving the attendant away. Dunnings tried next, grabbing for Gabriel's feet, but he kicked the man's hands away.

"Don't!" Penelope yelled.

Somewhere, Lady Amelia shrieked. "I knew it! I told you he was a lunatic!" Penelope wanted to slap her.

In the corner, Carter had managed to get behind Gabriel and was about to grasp him around the shoulders when Gabriel saw him and turned to defend himself— which put his own back to Penelope.

She'd reached him at last. She touched his shoulder. "Gabriel—"

"I said get *off*!" His arm shot out behind him, catching her with a force that knocked her at least a yard and slammed her into a small table. She caught her forehead on the corner as bursts of white exploded behind her eyes and hot liquid started to run down her face.

"He's gone mad!" she heard Gabriel's brother shout. "He's just hit a lady."

"No," Penelope said, wincing against the pain. She pressed her palm hard against her aching brow, hopefully stanching the blood in the process. She struggled to rise even as her head spun, making it only to her knees. "No, he thought I was one of the attendants. He didn't mean to hurt me. It was my own fault. I shouldn't have touched him."

But no one paid her any mind. Through the one eye she could partially see through, she watched Mr. Allen join his men and the three of them subdue Gabriel. His howls of protest ripped through her, joining with the anguish already tearing her apart. What had happened? And how had it happened so fast?

"Are you all right, m'lady?" A young maid knelt in front of her and pressed a square of linen against Penelope's bleeding head.

"I'm fine," she answered, trying to look around the girl to see what they were doing to Gabriel. "I just need to—"

"Take him upstairs and lock him in his room," Edward Devereaux ordered. "Post guards outside of both exits."

"No!" Penelope shouted, trying now to use the kneeling maid as leverage to get to her feet as the attendants dragged a fighting Gabriel from the room. "Gabriel!"

His face jerked around when he heard his name, but the eyes that looked at her were not golden brown. Nor did the round, black irises flicker with any recognition at all.

Her Gabriel was gone, replaced by a madman.

Chapter Nineteen

Gabriel sat with his head in his hands, squeezing against the throbbing pressure at his temples.

He sat upon the bed in the marquess chambers, where he'd been confined for two nights and a day now—most of which he had no memory of. A blessing, he was told. The last episode had come on faster and was more intense than any he'd ever had, they'd said. And he believed it. The pounding in his head, the nausea and the jittery feeling in his limbs that usually came after was so much worse than before.

I hurt Penelope.

A swift ache sliced through his chest, laying him open.

He'd never once imagined he would be saying this, but *thank God* he'd had the episode when he had. Had it happened tomorrow or the next day or next week or next year, for that matter, Penelope would have been bound to him, trapped in a marriage with a madman.

If there was anything good that would come out of this mess, it was that she had escaped that fate.

His heart ached again, a fierce, sharp pain, one he knew would never truly go away. It would forever hover over his heart, threatening like an executioner's blade—waiting to slice him open whenever he thought of her . . . whenever he missed her, as he would every day of his life.

The weight that had settled over him when he'd awoken yesterday grew heavier. *His life.* It was over as he knew it. All of the hopes and plans he'd made gone along with his freedom. Now all that was left was to wait for the madness to eventually overtake him, locked away. Alone. Perhaps he could have borne it better a few weeks ago, before he'd allowed himself to dream so high. Before . . .

His chest squeezed and twisted like a bathing cloth being wrung, flinging moisture to the back of his eyes and clogging his throat.

If a lonely descent into madness was what awaited him, did he even wish to go on at all?

The dark question circled him, whispering that he didn't have to feel this pain if he didn't want to. Murmuring that he had control over himself in this moment, that he had a choice. That he could end it all before the choice was taken from him.

Voices rose in the hallway, drawing his head up. He listened, but didn't recognize the speaker. Nor could he hear the man's muffled words. Then he heard Edward. "—might as well be. The hearing is tomorrow."

"Tomorrow is not today," said another voice that sounded very like the Earl of Stratford. "Now, open the bloody door."

Gabriel came to his feet, wincing as blood rushed to his aching head. Why had Stratford come here? Surely Penelope had explained all that had happened.

The lock gave way with a rusty click, and the door swung open.

His heart leapt as Penelope swept into the room. She slowed only when she reached him and then just long enough to slip her arms under his to wrap around him. "Gabriel," she said against his chest, and her voice was the sweetest sound he'd ever heard.

He couldn't help himself from returning her embrace, from dropping his face to her hair and breathing her in. He closed his eyes and breathed again, trying to store up enough of her sweet scent to last him a lifetime.

Too soon, she pulled back and looked up at him.

He felt gut punched when he saw her face. An angry gash, more than an inch long, streaked red across her forehead. It was thin and shallow, but it would leave a mark. Christ, he'd marred her precious face.

"I was so afraid I wouldn't see you again," she said, her face lined with both worry and relief. "I tried all day yesterday, but your rotten brother refused to allow me into the house."

Bile had risen into his throat at the thought that he

had done that to her. How could she be here, talking to him as if she cared for him, when he was responsible for injuring her so?

"But I'm here now," she went on, reaching out to take his hand. "And I am taking you away with me."

"What?" He pulled his hand from hers and eyed her warily. She had the same intent look on her face now that she'd had when she'd demanded he get into that damned black carriage on the road behind Vickering Place so many weeks ago.

His throat closed with emotion. He was glad he'd gone with her. He wouldn't give up the past two months with Penelope for even his sanity. But he would not go with her again, no matter how much his heart cried out for him to. "Pen, you can't just kidnap me out of this," he said gently.

Her chin jutted forward. "It is not kidnapping this time. I've gone to rather a lot of trouble to get you out of here, *legally*," she said. "I convinced Geoffrey to persuade a solicitor of the Court of the Chancery that it was unlawful for your family to hold you against your will until you were proven *non compos*. We then had to bring the man here and force our way inside. Now, *come along*. We must hurry. There is much to be done before tomorrow's hearing, and we haven't much time."

A small part of him exalted. Pen *must* care for him to have gone to such lengths. He would lock that truth in his heart, taking it out when he needed a kindness.

But the rest of him stayed rooted in reality. "You

don't seriously think we stand a chance of proving me competent now, do you?"

Her brows dipped, shading her eyes. But she didn't lie to him. "No. No, after what happened in the parlor, I think it is safe to say the commission will find against you for certain."

Even though he'd known that would be her answer, hearing the words aloud hurt worse that he'd have thought. "As they should. I am mad."

"I don't believe that."

Anger flushed his cheeks at her stubbornness. "Damn it all, Pen. When are you going to face facts?" His gaze found the mark on her forehead. The cut had already started to heal, but the surrounding skin bloomed purple, and the sight lashed him with guilt.

"When they make sense!" she countered, eyes flashing. "Yesterday was a setback. That is all."

"A setback?" he roared, his eyes fixed on the ugly bruise. "I could have *killed* you. What if I'd shoved you harder than I did? What if you'd hit that corner table with your temple instead of your forehead? Or what if I'd punched you? Or snapped your neck?" An image of Penelope limp and broken at his feet flashed through his mind, and his knees weakened. *"A setback?"* He snorted in disbelief.

Pen's eyes had gone wide during his tirade, but besides that she didn't seem daunted by it.

"A setback," she repeated slowly. "It happens even in the most successful cases. And this one—" Her voice broke as sudden tears glassed her eyes.

His anger deflated in the face of her distress.

"—is my fault, Gabriel," she went on, as a lone tear slipped down her face. "I never should have pushed you so hard to remember the horrors of your past, not when you were already strained by the carriage ride and the upcoming hearing. I should have pulled back. And now look at what I've done to you." Her lip quivered violently.

Damn it all. He'd known she would blame herself if all didn't go well. His heart squeezed at the sight of her pain. He took back what he'd thought before about being glad he'd gone with her. He would give anything to go back and make her leave him at Vickering Place— to save her from this.

He stepped toward her and cupped her face in his hands. "This is *not* your fault, Pen. You've done nothing but heal me, in every way imaginable."

"Then come with me," she insisted.

"To what purpose?" he said, letting go of her. "The hearing is scheduled for tomorrow. It is over." And even if it wasn't, he would never trust that another "setback" might not strike him at any moment.

"There are options, Gabriel," Pen said earnestly. "We could try to negotiate with your brother to call off the hearing, or postpone it at least. You could agree to temporarily sign over power of attorney in return for a trust—enough to buy a small cottage somewhere tranquil where we can continue working on getting you well. That would buy us time—"

"Edward, or rather *Amelia*," he amended darkly, "would never accept such a proposition, not when they are so close to having it all free and clear anyway."

Pen released a disgusted huff. "You're probably right." She closed her eyes for a long moment, just long enough for him to wonder what was going on in that mind of hers.

But then she opened them and pinned him with a fiercely determined gaze. "There *is* another option," she said steadily. "We can marry."

He sucked in a breath so quickly that he choked. "*No*, Pen."

"*Yes*. You've already procured a special license," she argued. "If we wed today, before your hearing, the marriage will be legal. Or at least it would be more of a challenge to set aside. If you are declared *non compos*, your brother still gets what he wants, which is control of the marquessate, so he would have no reason to try to force an annulment.

"And I would get what I want—control of your person. As next of kin, *I* would dictate your care. There would be no Vickering Place, no blistering or cold baths. Just all of the time in the world to make you whole."

He stood gaping at her, stunned. Not even Pen would be self-sacrificing enough to do such a fool thing if she didn't love him, would she?

"Why would you do that?" he whispered, needing to know. "Why would you tie yourself to another madman?"

She pressed her lips together in irritation. "I've told you, I do not think you're mad."

"But if I am—"

"Then you are mad!" she cried, shocking him to his

toes. "I will marry you anyway. At least I would know where you are—*how* you are. Do you know what it has been like for me the past day and a half? Watching people I don't trust drag you away from me? Being utterly helpless to stop them? To not even have a say?"

Some strong emotion flared in Pen's eyes, strangling the breath in his chest.

"I lay awake, agonizing over the unknown," she said, her voice cracking. "Were you recovered from your episode or were you still in the throes of it, lashed to the bed and hiding your eyes from the light? Had you awoken surrounded by the enemy, wallowing in despair because you thought your madness had returned?" Her eyes had gone bright and glassy. "Did you lie there all alone, wondering if I had abandoned you?" she asked, her chin trembling.

"No, Pen," he whispered. "Never."

Her features firmed and her eyes gleamed with resolution. "Good. Because I never will. I don't *care* if you are mad, Gabriel. If that is the case, then we will live with it. We will learn to fight it together."

At her words, his heart filled with a searing, bittersweet joy. *She loved him.* She had to, to be willing to enter into another marriage like her first. To risk living every day wondering when the madness would next strike.

He couldn't *not* take her hands in his. He had to touch her one last time. "I am humbled," he whispered. "Deeply. Truly. But I won't let you sacrifice yourself for me."

Her eyes closed. "Gabriel—"

"Look at you, Pen. Bruised. Exhausted. Emotionally spent, and this just in two days. You are a nurturer, love. You will kill yourself trying to make me whole."

She blinked up at him, unable to deny that truth.

"And it would kill me to watch you do so," he said.

He brought her hands to his lips and brushed a kiss across each. "You taught me so much in our time together. How to forgive myself for the things I cannot control. How to take control of the things I can. Well, I can control this. Staying here is *my* choice."

The tears that had been brimming in her eyes spilled over. "You're *not* just going to give up. You can't."

His memory flashed back to that night at Vickering Place, when he'd tried to send her away the first time. She'd been so stubborn about seeing him well, right from the start. He heard her fervent vow as if she'd spoken it yesterday:

I cannot know if we'll meet success. But I do know that as long as you are still fighting, I won't give up either. I swear it.

They'd been holding hands just like this then, too. And now they'd come full circle.

He knew what he needed to say to set her free.

"Yes, I can. I'm through fighting my madness, Pen. I accept my fate."

He pulled his hands from hers, even as it killed him to do it. Christ, he loved her. That was the only thing that gave him the strength to say the rest.

"And you must, too."

Penelope curled her fingers over her palms, desperate to hold on to the warmth from Gabriel's touch, which was fast slipping away from her, just as he was.

He wasn't coming with her.

He wasn't coming with her and there was nothing she could do about it. He would stay here, and she would be forced to leave. Tomorrow his family would present him for his hearing, and by nightfall he'd be locked away in Vickering Place once more.

Fresh tears spilled beneath her lashes as she closed her eyes. God help her, she'd never felt so helpless in her life.

And she couldn't even be angry with him. He was convinced he was broken and that he needed to protect her from himself. As misguided as he was, she couldn't help but love him a little more for it.

But she still didn't think he was mad. Even in the face of his relapse, everything in her remained convinced it was not lunacy behind his episodes. But she also meant what she'd said. Even if Gabriel *was* mad, she still wanted to be with him.

Because she wasn't afraid anymore. Gabriel wasn't like Michael. Michael had embraced his madness. He'd found it necessary to his happiness. He'd craved the highs, no matter what it had cost him—and her.

And she didn't care what Gabriel said right now. The man she knew would not be able to lie down and accept this forever. Eventually, he'd be ready to fight again.

She had to make him see that no matter what was causing his illness, they were *both* better off fighting it together. She opened her eyes even as she prayed for the right words to come. "Gabriel, I—"

A light scratching was the only warning before the

door opened a few inches. A maid entered, pushing the door open wider with her hip since she carried a large tea tray in her hands.

Penelope turned her body half away and dashed her tears with her hands as discreetly as she could. As she was busy righting her appearance, she heard the click of the metal tray meeting wood as the maid set it down on the table just inside the door.

Penelope tamped down her irritation with the girl. The poor maid was just doing her job. She had no way of knowing that she was interrupting a discussion on which Penelope's future happiness precariously hung.

With her back to the room, the maid said, "Here you are, m'lord. Just the way you like it."

It wasn't until she turned with the steaming cup that she seemed to notice Penelope's presence. "Oh!" She hastily dipped her head into a bow, snatching the cup she'd been offering to Gabriel close to her chest. "I'm sorry, sir. I didn't know you had a visitor. Should I fetch another cup from the kitchen?"

Gabriel shook his head. "No, thank you, Janey. Lady Manton will be leaving shortly."

Penelope's heart squeezed. No, she wouldn't. She couldn't. Not until she'd convinced him to come with her.

The maid glanced awkwardly between her and Gabriel, still clutching the tea. She started to back out of the room, cup in hand. Penelope wondered that she didn't just give it to Gabriel as she'd intended. "I'll—I'll just come back later, then."

Tiny hairs rose on the back of Penelope's neck. Why

had the girl stammered? She could be the nervous sort, or embarrassed to have come upon her master with a crying stranger. And yet . . . She narrowed her eyes on the maid, trying to see her face as the girl turned away.

"Wait," Penelope said impulsively. Both Gabriel and the maid looked up at her in surprise, and she flushed. She was probably making a fool of herself, but something seemed wrong here.

She looked more closely at the maid. There was something familiar . . .

"You were in the parlor the other night," Penelope recalled. "You held the compress on my wound after I fell," she said, remembering where she'd seen the girl.

The maid's cheeks pinkened, and she dropped her eyes to the floor as if embarrassed to be singled out. The girl gripped the teacup nervously. "Yes, m'lady."

"Thank you for your aid," Penelope said, and she swore a flicker of guilt flashed over the woman's face. Odd.

This was the same maid who'd given Gabriel the brandy he'd drunk just before his episode, too, wasn't it?

Her mouth went dry. Gabriel hadn't had an episode for weeks until he'd come back here . . .

Her eyes dropped to the teacup that the maid still held close to her, the one the woman seemed to think better of giving to Gabriel in front of Penelope. Could it be?

No. No. Liliana had said it was *possible* for Gabriel to ingest something that accounted for his mania, but she'd never unearthed what that substance might be. And besides, he'd had episodes both at his home and Vickering Place. Who would be able to slip him something in both places . . . ?

Penelope gasped, her eyes flying back to the maid. Of course she'd seemed familiar. Penelope had thought it was because of the other night, but now she remembered where else she'd seen her. "Miss Creevey?"

The maid flushed.

"Forgive me for not recognizing you before," Penelope said, trying to mask her astonishment for social embarrassment, so as not to alert Miss Creevey of her suspicions. "I didn't recognize you in your uniform." Or outside of the hooded cloak she'd been wearing in the garden of Vickering Place.

"I wouldn't expect you to, m'lady," Miss Creevey mumbled.

A million thoughts flew through Penelope's mind at once as she scrambled to put them together. Gabriel had said he'd found the mad widow's sister a position sometime last year. He just hadn't mentioned it had been in his own household. He must have installed her in his country house in Birminghamshire, so that she could be near her sister.

His episodes had started nine months ago . . . *at home in Birminghamshire* . . . episodes that, she'd said from the beginning, seemed strange and unlike any madness she'd ever seen.

But then what was Miss Creevey doing here in London? Maids didn't typically travel between households unless specifically assigned to one of the ladies of the house. Could she be lady's maid to Gabriel's mother, then? Or . . . *Amelia?*

How she came to be here wasn't what was important right now, however. Penelope's gaze fixed on that teacup as Miss Creevey glanced back at the door, clearly wishing to leave.

Dash it all. Everything in her screamed that there was something in addition to tea in that cup. But how could she prove it?

"Well, if that is all, m'lord, m'lady," Miss Creevey said, preparing to escape.

If she left with that cup, Penelope would never know if what her instincts were screaming was true. And Gabriel would forever think he was mad.

She raced to the maid and snatched the cup from her, spilling a bit on both of their wrists.

Miss Creevey gasped as Gabriel gave a startled, "Pen!"

But she paid neither of them any mind. She tipped the teacup to her lips and gulped, quite noisily. The warm, sweet milky taste splashed over her tongue, flavored with a healthy dose of brandy. To mask the taste of whatever else was in the drink?

When she'd finished it all, she looked up. "Sorry." She gave a fake smile and a shrug. "Thirsty."

Both Gabriel and Miss Creevey were looking at her as if *she* were mad. Well, with any luck, she soon would be. It had come upon Gabriel very quickly the other night in the parlor.

Miss Creevey, she noted, looked more than stunned.

She looked nervous as she backed the rest of the way to the door and slipped away.

No matter. If what she thought was about to happen did, they'd have plenty of time to catch Miss Creevey and figure out who she was working for. Gabriel's rotten brother and his wife, no doubt. Maybe even in collusion with Allen.

Gabriel whirled on her as the door closed. "What's gotten into you, Pen?" he asked, half appalled, half bemused, if his expression were to be believed.

"I just wanted some tea," she said lightly.

"Obviously," he said, his lips twitching.

"Did Miss Creevey often prepare your tea when she visited you at Vickering Place?" she asked. Lord, it was getting hot in here. Penelope tugged at her bodice, wishing she'd worn something easier to get out of.

"Yes. No one pours a cup like Janey. She even smuggles in a bit of brandy to top it off with, now and again. At least I'll have her visits to look forward to when I'm sent back," Gabriel was saying, but he sounded very far away.

Oh. My. Her skin prickled mercilessly. Penelope scratched at her arms. When she looked down at them, she cried out. Hundreds of ants scurried all over her, engulfing her bare flesh in a wriggling mass of black.

Gabriel blanched and ran to her. "Pen?"

No. No. *It is just some sort of drug*, she tried to remind herself, but panic was quickly overtaking her senses. *I'm not really seeing ants*. But her throat closed and her heart rocketed. They certainly looked real, and her skin was crawling. And, Lord, she was thirsty. So thirsty. And the light brightened unbearably, causing her to squint against its harshness.

Gabriel's hands cupped her face, and he tipped it up to his. "Pen, what is it? Oh Christ!" he cried. "What is wrong with your eyes?"

"Your madness," she whispered. And that was the last thing she remembered.

Chapter Twenty

"You knew it was drugged, didn't you?"
    Gabriel's voice floated and echoed, reverberating and washing over her. Penelope struggled to open her eyes. When at last she got them slitted just a bit, she let out a cry and slammed them shut again. Dear Lord, she hurt everywhere.

"I suspected strongly," she said, pushing the "S" sounds around a tongue that felt two sizes too big and dry as dust.

"Christ, Pen," he muttered. "You do realize there was more than enough poison in that cup to send a grown man into a fit?"

Drugged. Poison. Even through all of the aching pain, her heart soared as she realized she'd been right. Gabriel wasn't mad. And more important, *he* realized it, too.

"You're lucky to be alive," came Liliana's worried voice somewhere off to her left. She cracked her eyes open again, very, very carefully—and only enough to make out her cousin's profile.

Penelope groaned. Her stomach rolled and her head pounded mercilessly. She let her eyes slip closed again. "Yes, well, I don't feel so lucky right now."

She heard the dripping sounds of water, like a rag being dipped and squeezed out, and then coolness touched her forehead. Penelope sighed with relief. Liliana must be wielding the rag, because Gabriel had both of her hands in his, squeezing so tightly she wondered if he meant to ever let go.

She hoped not.

"What time is it?" she asked, trying to get her bearings. She opened her eyes again to help with that. As they began to adjust, it got easier.

"Nearly noon," Liliana answered her. But that didn't make sense unless— "You were gone from us for more than a full day."

Which meant— "The hearing?" It was scheduled for ten thirty tomorrow—er, today. How strange, to have lost hours she would never get back.

"Once presented with the evidence," Gabriel said, "Edward withdrew his affidavit. And before you ask, no, Miss Creevey was not poisoning me at the behest of my brother, or even Amelia."

Penelope's muzzy brain tried to work that out. "Then why?"

She felt, more than heard, Gabriel's sigh. "She blamed me for her sister's madness."

What? The lingering effects of the drug must be affecting her hearing, too. "But that makes no sense."

"To a sane person, no. But after spending an afternoon interviewing Janey, Allen assures me she is not well."

Penelope frowned. "'Not well' is slightly easier to accept than 'pure evil,' I suppose. But how could she blame *you* for her sister losing her mind?"

"Allen thinks that in Janey's mind, I'd all but admitted my fault. I blamed myself for Lieutenant Boyd's death, as you know, and told her and her sister as much when I found them in their desperate straits.

"It was my trying to make amends that damned me the most in her eyes. She decided that I wasn't telling the entire truth, that I must have done something horrible to her brother-in-law to make me feel guilty enough to pay for his widow to be placed in an expensive sanatorium and to have provided for his children. Apparently she didn't think I should get away unpunished."

Anger, swift and true, sang through her veins. "And the best punishment for your good deed was to suffer the same fate as her sister?"

"That seems to be the right of it." Gabriel's lips twisted wryly. "A cruel sort of irony, that."

When she thought of what that woman had cost Gabriel. What she'd almost cost *her* . . . "What's to become of her?"

"I've arranged for Janey to have a room at Vickering Place, with her sister," Gabriel said. "*With* the caveat that Allen stop the more barbaric remedies and be open to new ideas for treatment."

Of course he had. Gabriel's heart for those who'd suffered because of wars was one of the reasons she loved him so. Still. "It's better than she deserves," she grumbled, her anger slow to die. Perhaps she'd feel more charitable when she wasn't still suffering the aftereffects of the woman's madness. Which brought to mind— "How did she do it?"

"*Datura stramonium*," Liliana answered.

Penelope shot her cousin a glance. Ever the scientist, Liliana practically *thought* in Latin. "In English, please."

Her cousin had the grace to blush. "It's an herb," she explained. "Otherwise known as Jamestown weed, so named because of an incident in the seventeenth century when a company of British soldiers accidentally got its leaves mixed into their salads.

"It is said those poor souls got enough of a dose that their mania lasted almost eleven days before they came to their senses, after which none of them remembered a thing. She got it at the Apothecaries' Garden here in London when she would go pick up medicines for the household."

Penelope grimaced, still jittery and weak because of this noxious weed. "There is medicinal value in this?"

"Apparently. I am told it is used in very mild doses to treat asthma, as well as an analgesic during surgery and bone setting." Liliana made a moue of distaste. "However, given its hallucinogenic properties and high toxicity, I myself wouldn't attempt to use it on anyone. Which is probably why I'd never studied it in any depth and was therefore unfamiliar with all of its effects. I *am* sorry I missed it."

Penelope shook her head. "Don't be. As you say, you can't know everything," she said with a weak smile that Liliana returned.

Her cousin stood carefully then, levering herself out of the armchair beside the bed.

Gabriel let go of Penelope's hands, rising to stand as well.

Liliana reached down and stroked Penelope's cheek. "Yes, well, you are through the worst of it now. Therefore, I shall leave you two to talk, but I will be by this afternoon to monitor your recovery."

Penelope nodded her thanks, closing her eyes as Gabriel escorted Liliana out of the suite.

She may have dozed for a moment, because his voice startled her.

"What made you try the tea?"

Gabriel hadn't returned to her bedside, but rather stood a few feet away. And unless she was mistaken, he sounded angry.

She blinked. "A feeling. At first. But it made me take a closer look at Miss Creevey." *Thank God* she'd listened to her instincts this time, even though she'd been plagued with doubts and guilt when she'd thought she'd been to blame for Gabriel's supposed relapse. If she'd given in to her fears . . . if she hadn't trusted her gut feeling— She shuddered, unable to even think about that. "I knew if I didn't do something drastic, we might never know the truth."

"Pen," Gabriel said then, his voice low and scratchy.

She peered across the distance at him. Since her pupils were still so dilated, Gabriel appeared sort of smoky and washed with light, but she could not miss the stricken look on his face.

And she understood. He wasn't angry. He'd witnessed her in the throes of an episode, as she once had him. And it had terrified him.

"You knew what would happen if you drank that tea. You'd seen me—" His voice broke. "But you did it anyway. *For me.*"

"Gabriel—"

"No one else would have done what you did. Nor could they have. You *saved* me, Pen. You and your intuition and your faith and your damnable stubbornness . . ." His eyes drifted closed for a long moment before opening again to pierce her with an intense stare. "I can't thank you enough. I—" Gabriel's throat worked violently, but he seemed unable to say anything more. He didn't have to.

"I'd do it again," she whispered.

He came to her then and took her hand in his. "So would I," he said fiercely. "I would suffer *all* of it again, *and more*, if it meant that in the end, you would be mine." He pulled her hand to his lips and pressed a kiss to her skin. Fervent. Reverent. *Eloquent.*

For that one precious kiss told her more than a thousand words.

"I love you, Pen."

Well, it *was* still nice to hear the words, she decided as joy infused every part of her.

In this moment, she could feel nothing but happiness and a deep, deep gratitude. They'd both been given another chance at life, and they'd both been brave enough to take it.

"Thank you, Gabriel," she said, unable to govern the smile that spread across her face. "Now, will you please get in this bed and hold me so that I can tell you how very much *I* love *you*?"

He did. And she kept good to her word, proclaiming her love for him with whispered words and gentle kisses. It was all she could manage in her present exhausted state. But it was perfect.

Sometime later, she lay against him with her head cradled in the crook of his arm, listening to the steady thump of his heart.

"You do know what today is, don't you, love?" Gabriel murmured.

She looked up at him sleepily and shook her head.

"The twenty-seventh," he said with a grin. "Thankfully, we did not have to endure a hearing, but I do believe proving that I am *not* mad qualifies as success. Which means . . . you promised to marry me today."

Penelope groaned, dropping her head back to his chest. She didn't think she could manage to get out of bed right now, much less—

Gabriel laughed, a low rumble beneath her cheek. "You're lucky I understand what you are going through right now, or my feelings would be very hurt." He dropped a kiss against her hair to let her know he was teasing. "I *suppose* I shall have to give you a reprieve, at least long enough to have a proper wedding dress made."

"Let me guess," she said with a yawn. "A yellow one?" As much as she felt the color no longer suited her, she would wear it for Gabriel gladly, because it seemed to mean so much to him to see her in it.

"I don't think so," he said thoughtfully.

"What?" She tipped her head back to look at him once more, curious as to what he was thinking.

"I always loved you in yellow, in life and in my imagination. It is the color you wore in my mind's eye whenever I thought of you. A color of sunshine and optimism, of enlightenment and happiness—and I will always see you that way."

She'd known that, which was why his answer surprised her so.

"But it is also the color of unrequited love," he said quietly. "It felt safe, imagining you in yellow, because it reminded me that you could never be mine. First, because you were the wife of my cousin. But later, because despite how very much I wanted you in my life, I could never tell you so. Not when I had nothing to offer but a life of madness."

Tears pricked her eyes. She'd never realized the depth of his feelings for her. It humbled her to know that he'd loved her for so long and that he'd kept his feelings locked away inside of himself to protect her.

"What *would* you have me wear to our wedding, then?" she asked tenderly.

"I should like to see you in red," he decided, his gaze roaming her face. "That is the color of passionate, courageous, all-encompassing love. And *that* is how I see you now."

He cupped her face in his hands and took her lips in a kiss.

"Courageous, am I? And passionate, you say?" she teased when she could speak again. She rather liked the vision of herself that he painted for her. She'd never really thought of herself as either. But looking back at the past months—truly the past *years*, at least since Michael had died—she had to admit she'd been both. And she couldn't see herself ever going back to the woman she'd been before.

A thought struck her then—an irreverent one, to be sure, but also one she couldn't resist saying aloud. "You know, some people say that the equilibrium of the mind can be dislodged by a surplus of passion." She mimicked Mr. Allen's pompous nasally tone. "'It is a *well*-documented cause of insanity.'" She smiled at Gabriel as she cocked a brow. "Are you certain *you* want to take the risk of a life of madness with *me*?"

Gabriel stole her breath with another kiss before whispering in her ear, "Oh yes, Pen. For it would be a life of sweet, sweet madness, indeed."

Author's Note

I hope that you enjoyed *Sweet Madness*. Penelope was an interesting heroine for me to write, particularly as she was so different from Liliana, the chemist heroine of *Sweet Enemy*, and Emma, the criminologist and mathematics genius of *Sweet Deception*. You see, those heroines were born with brilliant minds and fought against what society expected of them. Penelope, on the other hand, was happy to be a debutante and content to live the life she was born to. Unfortunately for her, life (or in Penelope's case, the author!) had other plans for her.

What made her a challenge for me was that I needed her to do something extraordinary, even though she wasn't brilliant—at least not in the classical sense. Where Liliana and Emma strove to discover things and purposefully pushed their boundaries, Penelope didn't.

Nor did she want to or even believe that she could. But to be able to save Gabriel, she had to. Therefore, I had to give her a terribly difficult reason—the suicide of her husband—to dig within herself and discover her inner gifts.

Since Penelope was not necessarily the scholarly sort, I had to be true to her nature and really resist making her hit the books and attack her problems with confidence, as my other two heroines would have done. Not that she necessarily could have. Psychology was a much different science than it is today. The study of mental maladies was a very muddy field in the nineteenth century. Many irreconcilable theories and misunderstandings abounded. Some thought madness to be evidence of moral failing on the part of the patient. Others thought it was due to an imbalance of bodily humors, which itself was faulty medicine (blame it all on that pesky spleen!). Some still suspected the devil had a hand in lunacy. Others argued that madness was a "lesion of understanding" and that lunacy was simply a self-contained defect of reason or a misuse of will. The mental philosophers of the day expounded on their variant theories with lengthy treatises that would have made Penelope's head spin (as they did mine just reading them!).

So I gave Penelope good instincts and common sense. She took bits and pieces of what made sense to her and experimented practically until she found things that worked. She wasn't trying to prove anything. She simply wanted to help people. She was an intuitive soul, even in *Sweet Enemy*, and that is the strength (and weakness) I tried to give her in her own story.

The theories I had her work with came out of the British associationist school of thinking. Association-ism had its roots in Aristotle, but really started to take shape in the seventeenth century with the philosopher John Locke. He believed that our ideas formed from our experiences and sensations, and that madness could result from the wrong joining together of ideas rather than simply uncontrolled or disturbed "animal passions." In the eighteenth and early nineteenth cen-turies, many others ran with that idea, working on theories of how those ideas/associations were made and could be broken (such as David Hume's Law of Causality), which would later lead to such treatments as cognitive behavioral therapy. Penelope simply ap-plied those theories to otherwise sane soldiers to try to explain where their harmful associations might be coming from in relation to their war service.

While "art therapy" didn't become its own distinct profession until the twentieth century, visual and cre-ative expression has been used in healing throughout history, according to the American Art Therapy Asso-ciation. Penelope's art therapy experiments came from who she was as a person and artist. Painting made her feel better, so she gave it a try with the soldiers she worked with and noticed positive results.

As for other parts of the story, lunacy hearings were the public spectacles that I described and were printed up as entertainment in newspapers. Nearly two hundred such cases were featured in the London *Times* alone between 1820 and 1860, and about a dozen of them were considered the top news of their day, depending on how salacious the hearing was, how depraved the testimony, or how well-known the lunatic. One of the most sordid was the 1823 hearing of the 3rd Earl of Portsmouth, which shocked the reading public with claims of abuse, adultery and threesomes, and which resulted in the earl's marriage being set aside and his wife's children being declared bastards.

Finally, the inspiration for Gabriel being trapped beneath his dead horse actually came from the life of the real Prussian general who also plays a small part in this story. During a serious defeat at the Battle of Ligny, the then seventy-two-year-old Blücher was repeatedly run over by cavalry as he lay beneath the body of his dead horse for several hours. He was rescued by his loyal aide-de-camp, and after bathing his wounds in brandy (and drinking some, I'm sure!), he was able to rejoin his army and later lead them to victory at Waterloo two days later. Color me quite impressed.

Shropshire, April 1817

He'd never wanted to be the earl, but the one thing Geoffrey Wentworth had learned since becoming such was that an earl could get away with practically anything.

He sincerely hoped that included matricide.

"Let me understand you plainly, Mother," he growled, resisting the urge to brush the road dust from his coat onto the pristine drawing room floor. "You called me away from Parliament claiming dire emergency . . ." He swallowed, his throat aching with the need to shout. By God, he'd nearly run his horse into the ground to get here, aggravating an old war injury in his haste. His lower back burned almost as badly as it had when he'd been run through. He breathed in, striving to keep the irritation from his voice. "Because you would like to host a house party?"

Genevieve Wentworth, Lady Stratford, sat serenely on a floral chaise near the fireplace, as if he'd politely dropped in for tea instead of racing at breakneck speed to answer her urgent summons. Geoffrey eyed her suspiciously. His mother was typically a calm woman, but he'd been known to send seasoned soldiers scurrying with no more than his glare. She hadn't so much as flinched in the face of his anger. No, in fact, she looked strangely triumphant. His stomach clenched. Mother was up to something, which rarely boded well for the men in her life.

"Geoffrey, darling, do sit down," she began, indicating the antique caramel settee across from her. "It strains my neck to look up at you so."

"I should like to do more than strain your meddlesome neck," he muttered, choosing to remain standing despite the ache that now screamed down his leg. He turned his gaze to the older gentleman standing behind her. *"Et tu, Brute?"*

His uncle, at least, had the grace to look chagrined. Geoffrey shook his head. Uncle Joss always had been easily led. Geoffrey knew his mother played Cassius. This conspiracy had been instigated by her.

Joss squared his shoulders. "Now, m'boy, I must agree with your mother. It's high time you accepted your responsibilities to this family and provided an heir."

Hell. So that was what this was about. Well, he wasn't going to fall in with their scheme. He'd nip this and, after a hot meal and a night's rest, be on his way back to London. The Poor Employment Act wasn't going to finish writing itself, and Liverpool wanted it ready to present next month. What was more, Geoffrey had received a disturbing letter that needed to be dealt with. He itched to return to Town to investigate whether the blackmailer's claims held any credence. The note implied that his late brother had been paying the scoundrel for his silence to protect the family, but Geoffrey couldn't believe a Wentworth had done anything treasonous. Still, the threat needed to be neutralized.

"Host all of the parties you want, Mother. I've never tied your purse strings." He pivoted toward the door, determined to escape yet another lengthy discussion about duty. Pain flared through his back and leg. Christ, he'd very nearly given his life for duty. Yet his mother didn't understand that. No, in her mind, duty was defined by one word—*heirs*. "I shall be quite tied up in Parliament for the foreseeable future, so you needn't worry about inconveniencing me with your entertainments."

He'd barely stepped one booted toe into the rose-marbled hallway when her words stopped him cold.

"It is not I, dearest, who is hosting our guests, but you."

Me? He scoffed for a moment before the rest hit him. *Is?* As in right this moment?

The fist in his stomach tightened. The ride to Somerton Park had quite jarred his teeth loose. He'd blamed it on spring rains, but it could have been . . . Hell, it would have taken a *legion* of carriages to rut the road so deeply. He scanned the hallway.

Where were the servants? He'd yet to see one, not even Barnes. Sure, Geoffrey had bounded up the front steps straightaway, but there were always a few maids milling about in the entryway or the main rooms, unless . . .

Unless they were all busy seeing to the settlement of guests.

He turned slowly, his only family rotating back into view. Uncle Joss' easy smile faltered at whatever he saw in Geoffrey's expression, but Mother's widened with a familiar gleam that struck fear into every wealthy titled bachelor in Christendom.

Geoffrey advanced, his boots clicking an irregular rhythm against the drawing room's walnut floors. He prayed his suspicions were incorrect. "What have you done?"

"Taken matters into my own hands," his mother confirmed in a satisfied clip. She stood, her skirts swishing smartly as she retrieved a handwritten list from atop her escritoire. "I have been observing ladies of suitable age, station and character for quite some time now." She waved the list for emphasis. "Since before you returned, even. In fact, wartime is an excellent time to judge one's integrity, at home as well as on the battlefields. It is imperative that the future Countess of Stratford be above reproach." She sniffed, probably expecting him to argue, as his older brother would have done were he still alive. Since Geoffrey wholeheartedly agreed with his mother on that one point, he remained silent.

"Though I'm sad to say we've lost some wonderful candidates to marriage recently, there remains an excellent list from which to choose," she finished, tapping the vellum she held with one perfectly manicured finger.

"Absolutely." Uncle Joss nodded, his head bobbing

several times in quick succession. "I've even added a few names m'self. And they are all here on display, just for you." He winked.

Winked! As if they fully expected that Geoffrey would just fall into line, peruse their list of names and pick a wife at their whim. He imagined they intended him to court said wife during their little house party and propose by the end of the week.

Bloody well not.

Geoffrey straightened his shoulders and raised his chin, slipping into the stance that had become so natural during his military life. "I hope you have better entertainments planned for your guests than Catch an Earl by His Nose or I fear they will be sorely disappointed." He again turned to the door, lamenting for only a moment the hot meal and good night's rest he would have to forgo. "As *I* shan't be here."

He strode toward the hallway, contemplating the wisdom of pushing his horse another two hours back to the nearest coaching inn. It couldn't be helped. A man had to stand on principle, after all. He would not have a bride foisted upon him. The earldom, yes. The responsibility of bringing his family back from the brink of financial ruin after more than a decade of his brother's negligence and reckless spending, certainly. But a bride?

Never. Whom he married would be his choice alone. And he had very specific requirements that his mother wouldn't possibly understand.

"Before you leave," his mother called out, her voice still too smug for his liking, "you should know that when I sent the invitations—marked with *your* seal, of course—I made sure to include the Earls of Northumb and Manchester. Oh, and Viscount Holbrooke, I believe, as well as Lord Goddard. They were thrilled to accept."

For the second time in as many minutes, Geoffrey halted with one foot out the door. *She sent invitations using my name, my seal.* By God. Were she anyone else, he'd have her thrown in Newgate. Hell, the idea sounded rather appealing at the moment. How she'd gotten her hands upon the seal when it was kept under lock and key in his study, he didn't know. He'd have to see it moved. But now he had a more pressing problem. She'd invited powerful political allies he couldn't afford to offend. Had she known he was actively courting the support of these particular men?

She must have.

He closed his eyes—embarrassed, really, at having been so outmaneuvered. His mother had managed to arrange this entire farce without even a whisper reaching him. Had he underestimated the French this badly, he'd never have survived twelve long years of war.

As he faced her once again, Geoffrey eyed his mother with grudging respect. Her smile held, but her knuckles whitened as she gripped her list. At least she wasn't completely sure of his capitulation. Geoffrey took some small satisfaction in that.

Still, she'd left him no immediate choice. He knew when to admit defeat.

"It seems, Mother, that you have won the day," he conceded with as much grace as he could muster. He gave his relatives a curt nod and, on his third attempt, quit the room.

Geoffrey slapped his leather gloves against his aching thigh as he climbed the grand staircase to his rooms, one thought reverberating through his mind in time with his echoing footfalls.

But I am going to win the war.

Miss Liliana Claremont fixed what she hoped was an appreciative smile on her face as she viewed Somerton Park for the first time. She found the Earl of Stratford's country home rather attractive, for a lion's den. But then, so was the Colosseum, she imagined.

As her aunt and cousin bustled out of the carriage, Liliana studied the imposing redbrick home. A columned templelike portico dominated the front, forceful and proud. Like the rest of the house, it annunciated the wealth and power of the Wentworth family.

Liliana swallowed. Had she really considered what she was up against?

"Do hurry, girls!" Her aunt Eliza's anxious voice interrupted Liliana's contemplations. "That infernal carriage wheel has made us terribly late. We'll be fortunate if we have time to make you presentable before dinner." She eyed Liliana and her own daughter, Penelope, shrewdly. "The competition for Stratford shall be fierce. It's not often young ladies have a chance to engage him in a social setting, and you can bet those other chits have spent all afternoon turning themselves out just so." She clucked her tongue, reminding Liliana even more than usual of a fretful hen. "We are so far behind already. First impressions, my dears, can be the difference between becoming a Lady or settling for just plain *Mrs.*"

Penelope turned and gave Liliana a conspiratorial smile. Liliana tried not to squirm. Contrary to what she'd led her aunt to believe, she had only one objective in mind here at Somerton Park, and it *wasn't* to lure the Earl of Stratford into marriage.

No. She wanted to uncover the truth about her father's murder.

Liliana reached into the pocket of her pelisse, fingering the red wax seal of the letter that had led her here. An unfamiliar chill slithered down her spine, causing her to scan the many windows of the facade. She had the oddest feeling, as if the house itself knew why she had come and was keeping its eye on her. She gave her head a quick shake at the ridiculous thought.

Liliana hardly noticed the elegant front hall with its Roman pillars and prominent dentil moldings, or the grand staircase, as she rushed to follow her aunt and cousin. Their excited chatter rang off the gleaming marble, but she barely heard. Instead, she struggled for breath as the band around her chest tightened with every step she took into the lair of her enemy.

Still, a surge of excited determination shot through her. This was where she would finally unlock the mystery of her father's death. It hadn't taken her long to realize that those letters she'd found had been in code, but none of them had been in her father's handwriting. She could only assume his side of the conversation was hidden somewhere else.

An unexpected jolt of anguish stole her breath. For a moment she missed her father fiercely, pain slicing through her heart as if he'd been taken from her only yesterday. She remembered his gentle smile, his infinite patience as she'd asked him hundreds of questions about his work, about the world . . . about her mother. How she'd loved to listen to him talk.

Find them at summer. His last confusing words had often plagued her thoughts. But when she'd learned the seal belonged to the house of Stratford, she'd understood what her father had been trying to tell her. *Find them at summer.* He hadn't said *summer*, as she'd thought, but *Somer*. Yes, the letters she needed to crack his code were here at Somerton Park, and she had just less than two short weeks in the Wentworth house to find them.

Maids fluttered about the airy guest room she'd share with Penelope, unpacking dresses and accoutrements to be aired and pressed. Penelope got right to work on her main contribution to the scheme. Sifting through various evening gowns of muted silk, satin and sheer muslin, she began making selections.

Useless in matters of fashion, Liliana instead unpacked the sketch pad and pencils she planned to use to map out the house. Hers would be an organized search, one she would begin as soon as she could feasibly slip away.

"It wasn't easy creating the perfect ensemble for you on such short notice. Thank goodness Madame Trompeur values our business." Pen let out an exaggerated sigh. "Mother was so excited at the prospect of your being willing to consider marriage, she didn't bat an eye at the added cost for such quick work. It really is a shame to get her hopes up so." She contradicted her words of censure with a grin.

Liliana winced as her eyes traveled over the array of lustrous fabrics and winking jewels. "She really should have known better, given how vehemently I've eschewed every suitor she's presented over the years. I do feel guilty about the expense, however. I intend to pay it back." *Somehow.* The inheritance from her father was enough to allow her to live independently, but only if she scrimped.

Penelope, whose back had been turned while digging through a trunk for matching slippers and gloves, straightened and looked over her shoulder. "Bah, we're rich enough. The entertainment value Mother will get from trying to tempt you to marry will be ample repayment, I'm sure. I don't think I'll ever forget the rapturous look on her face when you begged her to secure you an invitation to Somerton Park. She views this as her last chance to see you properly settled. You know it galls her that your father's will didn't stipulate you finding a husband. I don't think you comprehend what you've let yourself in for."

Liliana groaned.

Pen held a gown away from herself and eyed Liliana as though she were one of the paper dolls they'd played with as young girls, waiting to be dressed and accessorized at Penelope's whim. "Pastels just don't do you justice. A deep blue or a lovely aubergine would suit your darker coloring so much better." Penelope *tsk*ed, her blond curls bouncing as she shook her head. "However, as delicate colors are all the rage this season, at least the lavender will bring out the violet in your eyes."

Liliana waited until the maids moved out of earshot. "I have no desire to be all the rage. I leave that to you. I just want to appear as if I'm here to catch an earl, like everyone else. I'm counting on the machinations of the other women to keep Lord Stratford adequately distracted, leaving me free to investigate."

Penelope laid the ensemble out upon the counterpane and turned to Liliana. "And I will do my part, as I promised, out of love for you—even though I'm not entirely convinced the Wentworths are complicit in Uncle Charles' death."

"It's the most reasonable explanation, Pen. It was a letter from someone in *this* family that lured him to his death. It had to have been a Wentworth who betrayed him." Liliana swallowed her frustration. She couldn't blame Penelope for her doubts, since she'd been unable to bring herself to tell Pen the rest of her suspicions.

Once Liliana had realized that the letters had been in some sort of code, a hypothesis naturally formed. Though she had been only ten at the time, Liliana remembered her father acting oddly in the weeks before his death. Hurried. Distant. Secretive. The timing was suspect, also. The Treaty of Amiens had broken down by the time the first letter was written, and hostilities between Britain and France had recommenced in May of that year. So why would her father have coded letters in French *and* from the late Earl of Stratford, dated well after war was declared? Given her father's claims of betrayal and his violent death, the most logical conclusion was that he and a member of the Wentworth family had been involved in some sort of espionage gone wrong.

But she would never voice such an accusation. Not without proof. Proof she intended to find before she left Somerton Park.

"Well, if that truly is the case," Pen said, her voice softening in a rare moment of gravity, "the Wentworths will surely not want their involvement known, so please . . . be careful." Penelope turned to select her own wardrobe for the evening.

Liliana clutched a sketch pad to her chest, mulling over her cousin's warning.

"La!" Aunt Eliza sailed into the room, dressed for the evening in a turquoise organza gown, a matching turban covering her hair—a concession to the rush to get her charges downstairs, no doubt. "Why are you trifling with that now?" She snatched the pad from Liliana's hands and tossed it aside, shaking her head as if she'd never understood her niece and never would. Catching Liliana by the elbow, Aunt pulled her to the dressing screen. "You both must get washed and dressed at once."

A maid came around the screen bearing the lavender evening gown Pen had selected. Liliana gave herself over to the hurried ablutions, turning her mind to the meeting ahead.

Penelope had reason to worry. With the current earl's connections to Wellington, he was fast becoming a powerful political figure. He would not want any complicity in her father's death made public. She'd have to school her features well, not betray any emotion or thought. If he suspected what she was about, he'd banish her from Somerton Park without delay.

Or worse. She mustn't forget that. Not for one moment.

"It is as I feared. We've missed the reception line," Aunt Eliza grumbled as the trio pushed their way into the crowded salon. Guests milled about in stylish clusters. The assembly, more female than male in number, certainly seemed energized. Bright faces and even wider smiles abounded. And why not? One of London's most eligible bachelors stood on the marriage block.

Aunt raised her voice over the din. "Some other girl has probably already caught the earl's eye," she groused, stopping just inside the door. She craned her neck in a frustrated half circle. "I can't see Stratford, but judging by the collection of women near the back corner, I'd say he's holding court somewhere in that vicinity." She nodded her head in the direction where, indeed, a small crowd had gathered. "Come."

Liliana followed her aunt and cousin, turning this way and that as they squeezed between rustling skirts of taffeta and silk. Cloying perfumes—a hodgepodge of orange blossom, tuberose, jasmine and plumeria to name but a few—assaulted her nose. The diverse scents proved quite unappetizing when mingled in the same room. The overly sweet haze wafting from dozens of husband hunters only increased the churning in Liliana's stomach, and she quickened her step, anxious to get her first meeting with the Wentworth family over with.

Though taller than most, Liliana struggled to see over elaborate coiffures and plumed headwear. The slow trudge reminded her of one of her earliest experiments. When she was seven, she'd decided to find out how quickly snails could move. She'd meticulously observed and recorded the progress of six different specimens. They'd averaged four inches every seven minutes. Liliana shook her head as her party inched forward. Those snails would have reached the Earl of Stratford before she would.

She strained to get a glimpse of her adversary amongst the glittering masses.

"—more handsome than his brother, don't you think?" an older woman in the crush was saying to her daughter. Liliana turned her head, drawn to any snippet of information she could collect.

"Wellington himself has said Stratford exemplifies the best of English courage—"

"—almost died saving another man's life," came a whisper.

"How heroic," said another woman with a dramatic sigh.

Heroic. Liliana frowned. The word contradicted her expectations of the man—though she had, of course, heard tales of his bravery.

"Sure, he ruffled a few feathers with that poverty-relief bill he championed last season, but all great men have their crusades. He'll step in line, with the right woman's influen—"

Aunt Eliza tugged Liliana forward before she could hear any more.

These women talked about Stratford like he was some sort of paragon.

Liliana firmed her jaw. Well, maybe he was. But hero, saint or crusader for the masses—it mattered not. She would discover what had really happened to her father, even if she had to ruin Stratford to do it.

"At last," Aunt Eliza said as they came to the pastel-clad barricade surrounding the earl. Not to be denied, she dug a discreet elbow in here and there until she broke through, Penelope and Liliana in tow. Liliana drew in a lungful of air and braced herself.

"Lady Belsham, you've arrived." A woman, presumably the countess, stepped forward to greet them. Her smile was that of an accomplished hostess, though not a particularly warm one. The countess was flanked by two men of remarkably similar appearance. As one of the men looked obviously older, Liliana assumed the gentleman to be an uncle.

Her eyes fixed upon Stratford. He stood mere feet away, tall, rigid and oddly detached, as if his mind were elsewhere. Black hair complemented winged brows of the same hue. An aquiline nose lay above long, full lips that Lothario himself would envy.

Stratford devastated her senses—she, who was normally very much inured to the physicality of men. The realization shook Liliana. Air expanded in her lungs, relieving the tightness but doing little to calm the unusual tension that thrummed through her limbs.

She lowered her lashes. It wouldn't do to be caught

staring, though the desire to observe the Wentworths' faces nearly overwhelmed her. Could you see guilt in someone's eyes? And if so, how did you quantify it?

Liliana kept her head politely bowed through the tale of their broken carriage wheel. But her breath shortened and her nerves tingled. Gooseflesh prickled her arms as an urge to flee swept over her like a frigid breeze. She curled her toes to keep them firmly planted.

When she looked up again, Stratford's attention was on Penelope's introduction, giving Liliana an opportunity to settle herself. She couldn't say what she'd expected upon finally meeting the earl, but certainly not this riot of indefinable awareness. She drew another deep breath. All she had to do was get through the moment and she'd feel normal again.

"And may I present my niece, Miss Claremont?" Aunt Eliza said, touching Liliana's elbow.

Stratford's gaze moved to her, and he stiffened. She'd never seen eyes so sharp, so blue. His eyes narrowed and focused intently upon her.

Liliana's heart thumped—hard—then skipped a beat. Claremont was a common enough name. So why was he looking at her so? Unless her arrival alarmed him because he knew whose daughter she was and guessed why she'd come . . . Unease rolled like waves through her.

She affected a small curtsy, as much to compose herself as because his rank dictated. But as her eyes dipped, she noticed the signet ring on Stratford's pinkie and her resolve solidified. The Stratford seal was emblazoned on the ring, only inches from her. She was this close to learning the truth. She straightened, snapping her gaze back to the earl.

The man's expression smoothed to one she could not fathom. "Miss Claremont," he acknowledged with a slight bow, his voice deeper, rougher than it had been when he'd conversed with Aunt or Penelope.

Lady Stratford's mouth creased into a frown. And didn't the uncle's eyes widen, just slightly?

A hot flush spread over Liliana's face and neck. Stratford and his family had reacted to her name. . . . She was sure of it.

The dinner gong sounded, the reverberating clang startling Liliana. She automatically looked toward the noise. When she turned back, all three Wentworths wore polite, benign smiles. And then they were gone, leading the assembly into the dining room.

Liliana stood still, immobilized by a surreal uncertainty quite unlike her. Had she imagined their responses because she'd expected to see something?

She stared after their retreating forms. Lady Stratford whispered something to her son. Liliana noticed his frown in profile, and her suspicion deepened.

No. If her hosts had nothing to hide, then she would find nothing. If they were guilty, however, she owed it to her father to bring the truth to light.

The question was, if she discovered something of an incriminating nature, to what lengths would the powerful Earl of Stratford go to silence her?